Cion

A NOVEL

Cion

Zakes Mda

Picador   Farrar, Straus and Giroux   New York

www.picadorusa.com

Picador® is a U.S. registered trademark and is used by Farrar, Straus and Giroux under license from Pan Books Limited.

For information on Picador Reading Group Guides,
please contact Picador.
Phone: 646-307-5259
Fax: 212-253-9627
E-mail: readinggroupguides@picadorusa.com

Design by Gregory P. Collins

Images are copyright © Mayang Murni Adnin, 2001–2006.

ISBN-13: 978-0-312-42706-1
ISBN-10: 0-312-42706-9

Originally published by Penguin Books (South Africa) (Pty) Ltd 2007

First Picador Edition: September 2007

10 9 8 7 6 5 4 3 2 1

My gratitude to my friends: Jim Shirey, Spree MacDonald, Nakedi Ribane, Letsatsi Ribane, Elly Williams and my wife, Gugu Nkosi. Their invaluable feedback enriched my story. I am also grateful to my dearest friends and fellow writers Sello K. Duiker, Phaswane Mpe and Yvonne Vera, who continue to transmit to me buckets of inspiration from the world of the ancestors. More inspiration comes from all my children, old and new: Nduku, Thandi, Dini, Zukile, Zenzile, Luthando, Gcinile, Simphiwe and Nonkululeko.

Thanks also to Barbara Parsons and Irene Flowers of the Kilvert Community Center for the oral history; to Jean Cunningham for introducing me to these formidable women; to Terry Gilkey, who meticulously keeps cemetery records in Athens, Ohio; to the ghost hunter John Kachuba who took me to the Court Street Halloween block party in his ghostmobile; and to writers and historians: Keith P. Griffler (*Front Line of Freedom: African Americans and the Forging of the Underground Railroad in the Ohio Valley,* University Press of Kentucky, Lexington: 2004), Jacqueline I. Tobin and Raymond G. Dobard (*Hidden in Plain View: A Secret Story of Quilts and the Underground Railroad,* Anchor Books, New York: 2001) and J. A. Rogers (*Sex and Race: A History of White, Negro, and Indian Miscegenation in the Two Americas,* J. A. Rogers Historical Researches, New York: 1942).

Cion

Of Saints and Pagans

*T*he sciolist has delusions of Godness. At his whim I find my- self walking among colorful creatures that are hiding in stolen identities. I am wandering on Court Street in Athens, Ohio, trying to find my way among the milling crowds.

Every year at this time, I am told, the natives go wild and invoke their pagan gods who descend upon the earth in the guise of these Court Street creatures. Some take possession of the bodies and souls of decent men and women and turn them into raving lunatics who run up and down the street breathing fire. It is a celebration of blood, as evidenced by many of the creatures who are bleeding. The best of the bloody lot are bandaged all over their bodies like Egyptian mummies and are walking on crutches. Blood oozes through the bandages at strategic places.

It was the bloody ones that I followed to this street from the cemetery at The Ridges where I was abandoned by the sciolist. Perhaps he did not know what to do with me after dragging me halfway around the world.

First he had abandoned me in Durham in the United Kingdom. This, I later learned, had been at the suggestion of one Sam Crowl, a Shakespeare professor at Ohio University. The sciolist had been giv- ing a public lecture to an august audience of scholars when the pro- fessor had asked, "Have you ever thought of taking Toloki the Professional Mourner to another culture, say to Durham in the United Kingdom?"

The sciolist had jumped at the idea.

I suppose Durham was mentioned because it was at that cathe- dral city that the sciolist in his Godly madness had conjured me into existence a decade or so before. It was at the time when he was resident at St. Chad's College, just across from the cathedral that gloriously looms above all the buildings in the vicinity, where he was commissioned to write a play that would be performed in that imposing Norman cathedral as part of its nine-hundredth anniversary celebration. Instead of focusing on the play his mind had wandered to other matters—hence my conception.

I must admit that I found the idea of mourning in the Durham Cathedral quite attractive when it was first mooted to me. It elevated me to sainthood even before my death. Or at the very least it placed me in the ranks of the monks who had trodden on those grounds for centuries before me. Here was the opportunity to recapture my austere and ascetic ways that I first cultivated years ago after being influenced by the aghori sadhu of India, but that I lost in my travels with the love of my life, Noria, who did her best to reinitiate me into the ways of normal men. Here was a chance to commune with the saints at their own sanctuary.

As a votary of my own Order of Professional Mourners nothing could be as inspiring as walking in the Chapel of the Nine Altars on the eastern side of the cathedral where the tomb of St. Cuthbert—the Wonder-Worker on whose open hands birds used to build their nests—is located. Nothing could be as fulfilling as holding erudite conversations with the Venerable Bede whose bones lie buried in a splendid tomb in the Galilee Chapel on the opposite end of the cathedral.

In any event my professional mourning practice in South Africa was in a rut. Death continued every day, for death will never let you down. But the thrill of mourning was taken away by the sameness of the deaths I had to mourn on a daily basis. Death was plentiful—certainly more than before—but it lacked the drama of the violent deaths that I used to mourn during the upheavals of the political transition in that country. Now the bulk of the deaths were boringly similar. They were deaths of lies. We heard there was the feared AIDS pandemic stalking the homesteads. Yet no one died of it. Or of anything related to it. Instead young men and women in their prime died of diseases that never used to kill anyone before—diseases such as TB and pneumonia that used to be cured with ease not so long ago. At the funerals I mourned, the dreaded four letters were never mentioned, only TB and pneumonia and diarrhea. People died of silence. Of shame. Of denial. And this conspiracy resulted in a stigma that stuck like pubic lice on both the living and the dead.

I continued to attend the funerals, to sit on the mounds and to mourn in my designer wails and groans, but there was no longer any fulfillment. My once revered howls and whines lacked sincerity. I felt contaminated by the lies, for my mere presence even as a paid mourner made me part of the conspiracy.

To break the monotony I decided to take up a new hobby, that of studying headstones and imagining the occupants' deaths and then mourning them. At least such deaths were as exciting as I could make them. Gradually it became more interesting to mourn the deaths that I had created than to mourn the deaths of lies.

Another factor that influenced my decision to take up Crowl's challenge was the disillusionment I suffered after discovering I had not invented the art of mourning for remuneration after all. In ancient Rome there were professional mourners. I learned this when people who saw me in action at funerals asked me questions about my trade. Where did it come from? Did I learn it from the ancient Greeks? Or from the Romans? People from other contemporary cultures who got to know of my activities in the cemeteries of South Africa (and later of Lesotho, where I lost Noria, the love of my life—but that is a story for another time) began to tell me about professional mourning in Spain or in Italy or in India or in Ireland or in Zambia. This discovery left me depressed for a long time.

When the sciolist sold me Crowl's idea I grabbed it with both hands for at least it introduced a new concept in the art of mourning—that of an itinerant mourner. If I could not invent the profession of mourning for remuneration then I could surely invent itinerant mourning. Perhaps in my wanderings I would meet other professional mourners, learn their methods and incorporate them into my mourning routine. That would spice it a bit and would imbue it with a new vigor. Yes, I would travel the world in search of mourning.

A combination of these factors—the lack of interesting deaths in a South Africa that had become a stable society, the hope of creating more exciting deaths from the tombstones of the world and the chance to be an itinerant mourner and to learn new tricks from other mourners—contributed to my allowing the sciolist to drag me all the way to Durham, and when that did not work for him since he could not find a story that would go with my wanderings there, to his dumping me at the famous cemetery at The Ridges in Athens, Ohio.

As soon as I was placed there I set out to choose a headstone at random, to read the information inscribed on it and to mourn in my usual style. Creating the deaths of the occupants of these graves would be especially interesting for they were all inmates of a mental asylum in years gone by. From 1874 until about twenty years or so ago the grand High Victorian Italianate building near the cemetery was the Athens Mental Health Center, its wings housing men on one side and women on the other. Those were the days when women were committed as lunatics for disobeying their husbands or their fathers, or for suffering from what was then called "a change of life": menopause. Andropause had not yet been discovered, though I doubt if men would have been punished for it. Instead they were admitted for "self-abuse"—otherwise known to us as masturbation. And for melancholia. Even the truly physically sick found their home here: the epileptic, the alcoholic, the tubercular. This also became the place for removing the unwanted people from society: the indigent, the homeless, the lovelorn. They were all signed in never to leave again, except for the clever hobos who sought shelter and food when the situation was bad, and slipped away when they thought good times had returned in the outside world. The rest left only in coffins.

I envisioned all sorts of dramatic deaths: a woman strangling herself to death after being overwhelmed by hot flashes in one of the kerosene lamp–lit tunnels of the asylum; another one drowning in her night sweat; a man standing for hours on end against the wall in another tunnel masturbating himself to death; men and women writhing on the sprawling lawns dying from melancholia; an Ohio University student who had previously been admitted for "excessive study" committing suicide by chewing all his books and swallowing them. The richness of re-creating deaths lies in the fact that you first have to re-create the lives of the deceased before they died. I looked forward to the joys of examining those events in their lives that led to these wretched souls' perceived madness. What troubled these poor men and women, to the extent that they were forced to spend their days in this asylum? How different was their madness from the madness that possessed the sciolist? And why was the sciolist not confined to a mental facility where he deserved to be?

After admiring the gravestones that stood in rows as if they had grown from the ground I picked a prime one. Only then did I realize that they did not have names. Only faint numbers eroding in the sandstone. I could not create the deaths of nameless people. I could not mourn in a cemetery of numbers. Yes, there were about four or five bigger tombstones hewn of more expensive rock— perhaps limestone or granite—with names and dates on them. These stood out incongruously among the hundreds of small flat stones in rows, some almost buried by the lawn. The tombstones were placed by descendants in loving memory of, say, a great-great-grandmother who died a hundred years ago. Then of course there would be the name of the deceased, the dates of birth and death and the date of the dedication of the stone on the hundredth anniversary. But these did not inspire any mourning on my part for they were not the original headstones.

Darkness had fallen.

Crowds began to invade the cemetery, perhaps votaries of some necromantic order. I was caught in a frenzy of flashlights from different directions. The light bounced against the headstones and flashed across the branches of the trees that encompassed the cemetery in a half-circle. I would have thought they were ghosts if I believed in ghosts. I don't. I have mourned in cemeteries for a decade at all hours of the day and night and I have yet to see a ghost. I could make out the silhouettes of the creatures against the light of the full moon, gamboling among the trees and making shrieking noises and then laughing at the horror movie they were creating for themselves in which they were the actors.

When they got tired of prancing around, hiding behind the trees and booing each other, they left the cemetery in a procession. I decided to follow. We walked down the road cobbled with red bricks, passed two blocks of townhouses (formerly the asylum doctors' residences), one of which was the sciolist's home when he first came here, into Richland Avenue. The creatures did not seem to mind my following them. They continued with their boisterous prancing. When we crossed the Hocking River on Richland Avenue Bridge we joined a throng of other creatures, all going in the same direction. Among them were Roman sentries and their ladies in white and gold togas. They walked silently, some pairs holding hands. They did not seem to mind a bloody gang of Visigoths, Vikings and Vandals in horned helmets led by Hagar the Horrible, which was bent on confounding and conflating history, and on disturbing the peace for everyone. Some of these savages were as young as six, while Hagar himself was a doddering old man. Possibly a retired professor with too much time on his hands. I kept my distance. Just in front of me was a very cute Little Red Riding Hood walking hand in hand with a big shaggy wolf.

I followed the crowds until we got to brown brick–paved Court Street.

❧

No one pays any particular attention to me here. My stocky figure, broad face and thick eyebrows are less foreboding than the ghoulish faces of some of these creatures. My small eyes that have always been praised for having a permanently sorrowful look, my yellowish complexion and my small oval mouth do not invite stares as they have always done elsewhere, even in my own country. My funereal costume of tall shiny black top hat, tight-fitting black pants, sharp pointed black shoes and a velvety black cape buckled with a big gold-colored brooch with tassels of red, yellow and green, is not out of place here. A small suitcase of my worldly possessions, including clean underwear, is obviously looked upon by the rest of the celebrants as an accessory to the outfit.

The mention of fresh underwear may alert you to the fact that many things have changed in my life since we last met. For instance, I used to stink like death. It was a sign of respect for the dead. Or you may say it was a badge of honor—my trademark, so to speak—as a professional mourner. Noria changed all that. She taught me that there were other ways of honoring the dead without necessarily smelling like the corpse of a dog left to rot by the roadside. She brought cleanliness into my life. One will do anything for the woman one loves, even take a regular bath.

People stop and look and smile and move on. Friendly smiles, not the derision that I had become used to back home. They are a jolly lot, these creatures, and don't hesitate to admire one another. They admire me because they think I am one of them. But fortunately they do not crowd around me as they do to those they deem more interesting . . . those who are not only parading but are also performing. Not far from where I am standing under a lamp post a group of them are applauding a creature with the face of a mandrill and the body of a well-shaped woman in a pink tutu. It is prancing about and preening itself with the aid of a mirror that hangs on Vice-President Dick Cheney's chest. At the same time the creature is clearing the path for him. He sports a stupid grin that stays on his face without changing. He does not even blink despite the flurry of activity around him.

"Ladies and gentlemen," the mandrill-girl announces, "Mr. Dick Cheney and the Halliburtons!"

The crowd cheers and applauds as he takes three bows; each time the mirror swings and hits his knees. His white suit is rather tight for his bulk.

The Halliburtons are three little people in green suits and white fedoras. Glowing smokeless cigars hang carelessly on their lips. They carry violin cases like old-style movie gangsters. They follow Mr. Cheney closely and will not let anybody touch him. My eyes follow this gang until it disappears in the crowd.

You don't stand still in the parade of creatures. You walk from one end of the street to the other, sometimes elbowing your way through yet thicker crowds. Where Court Street crosses West Union a band is playing on a makeshift stage. But the creatures don't dance. They just stand in front of the stage, eyes agog. Others soon get bored and start drifting to the concession stands on West Union. The pagans must be fed: they purchase gyros and French fries from food vendors whose vehicles are lining the street. A patriotic entrepreneur has crossed out the word *French* on the French fries sign and has replaced it with *Liberty*. A demonstrator stands across from the patriot's trailer with a sign that reads: *We need an enemy. Even if it's the French. We won't survive without an enemy. Otherwise we'll start eating each other.*

Another enterprising creature is selling kisses instead of food. He walks inside his mobile kissing booth inviting female prospective customers to swing by and sample his wares. There are no takers even though his price has gone down tremendously: the sign above his booth shows that he started at ten dollars, then crossed it out and went down to five, then to two, and now the kisses are free. Only queer creatures in drag are prepared to take the offer, but he tries to ward them off as they attack with pursed lips and purring sounds. They are persistent and he turns his tail and runs for dear life. The queer creatures laugh at him as he disappears in the crowds, and then they go their way.

I buy a slice of pizza and a can of soda from a bloody girl at the window of a trailer and walk back to Court Street to watch and be watched.

And there is the sciolist strutting about in a brown hooded robe. He looks like a friar. If it were not for his complexion, which is decidedly brown like the earth, he could easily pass for one of the Durham saints. His belly hangs out like an apron. Like the belly of a saint. He resembles the holy men who gloried in rich food cooked by aging cloistered virgins and in the good wine that the monks produced from their own vineyards.

At this point I am not keen to have anything to do with the sciolist, so I stand against the wall next to the door of a noisy bar until he has melted into the crowds. I may be avoiding him now, but I know that one of these days I will need him. Sooner or later I'll be grappling with the problems of shaping my life in a meaningful way in this strange culture. He brought me here; he will have to provide the answers.

I do not have the time to think about the sciolist for long since my eyes are drawn to a number of devils with red tails, red horns and red forks. The rest of their bodies are of different colors, all of which are glowing as if fires of hell are raging in the fiends' bowels. They are nevertheless not menacing at all. They manage to maintain the cuteness of Hot Stuff, the Harvey Comics lovable devil, though they obviously are not patterned on him. I follow them back to Court Street, negotiating my way among nurses in white miniskirts, fishnet stockings and heels; yodeling cowboys galloping alongside "Indian" chiefs with feather headdresses; a giant SpongeBob SquarePants looming above superheroes Superman, Spiderman, Batman and Robin; more devils and witches; more Supermen and Spidermen; penitentiary inmates in orange coveralls or in black and white horizontal stripes; a number of bleached Paris Hiltons (if you are reading this five years from now you may not know who I am talking about here, but at this moment she is America's intriguing cultural icon) in all shapes and sizes; sizzling Playboy Bunnies and fairies with purple hair; a doctor and a patient in a bloody nightshirt; Hasidic Jews in black suits and black hats and hair braided into long ropes that hang on each side of the face; more glowing ghouls and ghosts; and another Dick Cheney with an oversize plastic face—a creation of a vengeful god. This one wears a gray suit. His heart is hanging out of his chest and is furiously pumping green fluorescent blood. Unlike the first Mr. Cheney, this one cuts a lonely figure without an entourage.

There are other politicians too. There is the Jimmy Carter of old with a self-satisfied Plains, Georgia, peanut farmer grin. He holds a placard that reads: *Without an independent electoral commission elections wouldn't pass as free and fair anywhere else in the world.* No one pays much attention to him though. The board he is holding is not easy to read since it is not big enough and the letters are all crowded together. And there is President Bush's Defense Secretary, Donald Rumsfeld. Bloody plastic dolls of different sizes hang all over his body in all sorts of grotesque positions, so that only his oversize black boots can be seen. Some of the dolls are limbless while others are without heads. He is flanked by two men in Hawaiian shirts and hula skirts holding a banner with bold letters in front: *Stuff Happens,* and at the back: *Collateral Damage.* Mr. Rumsfeld walks lifelessly under the banner despite the many admirers who crowd around him with breathless exclamations of "Ooooh!" and "Aaaah!"

One can't see every creature in this parade, and I have tried very hard to look for President George W. Bush, to no avail. Even John Kerry and his running mate, John Edwards, don't seem to be here and I wonder why. After all, it is October 30, 2004, only three days before the presidential election. One would have expected the three gentlemen to be all over the place canvasing for votes or just playing the fool as presidential candidates are wont to do. Instead,

Mr. Bush has sent his surrogates in the form of the two Cheneys and one Rumsfeld, and Mr. Kerry is seen only on the *Kerry/Edwards: A Stronger America* buttons that some of the pagans are wearing. Not even Bill Clinton, an immediate past president, can be seen. Has he lost currency so soon?

The respectable citizens of Athens do not show any signs of missing these politicians. A few of them are sitting on the courthouse steps watching the creatures and their performances on the street below and on the sidewalks. They are stone-faced and do not seem to enjoy the spectacle, which makes me wonder why they came here in the first place. They do not seem amused even when a group of heavily bejeweled women wearing fur coats and elaborate hats stand in front of them and, inviting them to participate by looking directly into their eyes, chant in unison: "Stimulate the economy, start a new war! Stimulate the economy, bomb a third world country!" Those respectable citizens who are with their young children reach for them, giving them reassuring hugs. The children are all eyes agog, obviously envying the freedom of the creatures and hoping that one day when they are able to make decisions about their own lives they will initiate themselves into this cult and will prance about in all sorts of glorious identities.

I notice that the woman who leads the chants wears a sash with *Billionaires for Bush* embroidered on it. The respectable citizens are obviously scandalized by this group and look quite relieved when it moves on to torment other innocent souls. It leaves a stench in its wake, perhaps from a stink bomb. It smells like death.

I find it quite fascinating that death hangs so heavily in the air. Remember that as a professional mourner I am an angel of death—or at least that's what I have been called by others. But I must admit I have never seen death glorified to the heights that I see here. This is definitely a celebration of a culture of death among the young: those who must die so that old men and women should live. Yet one does not see women celebrate the belligerent culture in this parade of creatures. Yes, some of them—quite a small number of them compared to the male of the species—are bloody, but none of these display any militaristic arrogance in their attire, performance and demeanor. They limp, one may surmise, from car accidents rather than from acts of war.

Even I who exult in death find the abundance of blood and bloody situations overwhelming. A bloody Yoko Ono passionately kissing a bloody John Lennon under mistletoe gingerly held by a bloody kaftan-robed Maharishi Mahesh Yogi. The only throwback to another era that I have seen this evening. Well, besides Mr. Carter—although one can't really call Mr. Carter a character of the past since his placard carries a contemporary message. A bloody marine in camouflage dragging with a rope around his neck a bloody boxer in the Rocky boxing shorts of stars and stripes. His boxing gloves are huge and heavy and on his head he wears an Arafatesque kaffiyeh. At the back of his off-white silk robe *Enemy Combatant* is printed in bold red letters.

Blood once more. This time it flows from the wounds of Jesus Christ of Nazareth. A group of men and women who are obviously in their own everyday identities are crowding around a tall thin wooden cross and singing hymns. A bulky preacherman—wearing a T-shirt with the words *Live your life so that the Preacher won't have to lie at your funeral*—holds the cross with one hand and waves a Bible with the other. He is hollering something about the fires of hell that are waiting for those who observe pagan rites. His assistants are handing out business-card-size cards to passers-by. I reach for one. *There is power in the blood,* it declares in bold red letters. And then in tiny blue letters: *In whom we have redemption through his blood, even the forgiveness of sins. Colossians 1:14.* Some of the creatures boo the preacherman and mock him and his group, which responds with a loud hymn. The preacherman says, "They mocked Jesus Christ too. They went further than that and crucified him."

I move on, weaving my way in the crowd, drawn by music at the corner of Court and Washington Streets. Another band is playing a very upbeat bluegrass tune. Three blonde bees are hovering about in black miniskirts with yellow horizontal stripes, black fishnet stockings and stilettos, flapping their silvery wings to the rhythm of the music. The band here seems to be more popular than the one I saw earlier on West Union.

It is beginning to be too crowded here so I elbow my way across the street, past a man who is holding a life-size inflated rubber doll upside down and is giving it a blow job between its legs; and a few Arabs in white robes and black kaffiyehs being hustled at gunpoint by marines in camouflage.

"Great costume," says a voice behind me, while a hand taps me on the shoulder. I turn to face a tall young man, perhaps in his late twenties or early thirties, with a dusky complexion and long black hair tied in a ponytail. He would have been classified a colored in my country. He is barefoot and is wearing a bloody tattered shirt and knee-length pants that are also bloody and frayed. He has red weals on his bare arms, face and legs, some of which have caked blood. He is inspecting me closely from toe to head and then back to toe. I do the same to him.

"Who're you supposed to be?" he asks.

"I am Toloki the Professional Mourner," I say, mustering as much dignity as I can and placing the necessary solemnity on the job title.

"A professional mourner? Never heard of that. From what story?"

"Ways of Dying."

"A manual on how to die?"

"No. The story of my life."

"Can't say I know it. Can you guess who I am?"

"You are from a story too?"

"Ain't we all from stories?"

"We are indeed all from stories. Every one of us. All humanity."

"Guess?"

"I have no idea. I have never seen anyone like you before."

"I'm a fugitive . . . from the slave breeding farms of Virginia. My name is Nicodemus. I escaped on the Underground Railroad to freedom. That's who I'm; Nicodemus."

"Nicodemus . . . Underground Railroad?"

"I was beaten to death. I was murdered."

"You do look like death. Well, not you . . . you are a fine young man, I'm sure . . . your clothes, I mean."

"You ain't from these parts then? You got one heck of an accent."

"I am from South Africa."

"They have this sort of thing in Africa, or did you learn it here?"

"In South Africa, you mean? Africa is not a country. It is not a village. It is a continent with many countries and hundreds of cities and villages and cultures."

"They have this kind of thing?" he insists.

"What kind of thing?"

"This . . . ," he says, sweeping his arm at the multitudes.

"No, they don't have it. I see it for the first time here. And I find it quite amazing."

"Then how come you're all dressed up for it?"

"I am dressed like this every time I mourn the dead."

"You a minister or something?"

I tell him of my life in South Africa, of how I invented the profession of mourning, or thought I had until I learned of its existence in other cultures, both ancient and living. I tell him about Noria, how she taught me to take an active interest in the affairs of the living so as to mourn their deaths more effectively . . . with greater passion. That is part of the reason I am at this ritual, which actually turns out to be a celebration of death. I add that my aim is to travel the world in search of mourning. This is only the first leg of a long journey. Or the second leg if you count Durham.

"There's mourning everywhere," he says. "You don't have to search for it. Ain't you satisfied with all the mourning you can still do where you came from?"

He has a point. No mourner can finish all the mourning that can be done at any one place. However I do not want to bore him with a long story about my disillusionment. Instead I tell him of my feeling that the deaths I will mourn here are different kinds of deaths from the deaths I used to mourn back home. Variety will add another dimension to my routine. But most importantly I am keen to discover new ways of mourning. He is enthralled by all this, and says he wants to learn more about it. His own people, he adds, may find some of my "powers" useful. He sees a shaman in me, even though I assure him that I do not have any powers nor am I a priest of any kind. He says his people would love to meet me, and he invites me to his home. I gently turn the invitation down because I do not want to impose. He insists until I finally agree. He is so excited that he wants us to leave right away. After all, he says, nothing of great interest will be happening here tonight.

At this point the parties at the apartments two or three stories above the street are beginning to rock. Revelers are looking down at the parades and the parades are looking up at the revelers. Revelers are sipping beer from their Styrofoam cups quite ostentatiously, driving the creatures down below—forbidden from drinking in the streets by open container laws—mad with envy. Nicodemus is salivating, not because of the beer, although he does express a desire for a few sips before we leave, but because of the girls who are lining the balconies, flashing and mooning the milling crowds on the street. He joins the rest of the spectators to cheer the inspiring sight.

"It's the full moon," he explains to me. "People go crazy."

"What's with the full moon?" I ask.

"There's more stuff going on when there's a full moon. Ask any nurse or cop or ER worker . . . more stabbings . . . more shootings . . . more car accidents . . . more DUIs . . . more arrests."

"All the more reason we should leave," I suggest. "I have had my fill of the parade of creatures."

"Sure thing," he says. "But let's have a beer first. One for the road."

"You can have a beer. I'll wait."

Before we can slip into a Court Street bar we are stopped by two cops. One is a local Athenian officer and the other is from Belpre. Athens often seeks assistance from the police departments of neighboring towns when there are such rituals. Between the officers is a frightened girl in a nightgown and slippers. She points at Nicodemus and says: "That's him, officer."

The cops pounce on Nicodemus. He is struggling and proclaiming his innocence as they handcuff him.

"Bail me out," he says to me as they drag him away with the girl in tow.

I stand there for a few seconds, watching them disappear in the crowd. All the while he is screaming that he "didn't do nothing" and that this is a matter of mistaken identity and that he is going to sue their pants off for wrongful arrest and that for centuries his people have suffered indignities. I rush in the direction they are taking. I do not know why I am following them, or what I can do to help poor Nicodemus. I lose them when I stop to give way to a giant mouse chasing a giant cat. The musophobic cat hits me very hard in the stomach in its frantic attempt to escape. I am reeling a little bit and the mouse apologizes very quickly on behalf of the cat and then resumes the chase.

The natives are gradually dispersing and I gather they are going to parties all over the town. But diehards are still out there when mounted police decide to clear the streets at about 2 A.M. Even the ambulances and emergency vehicles at the corner of Court and Washington Streets drive away.

I have to go somewhere too. I have no idea where. Damn that sciolist!

∾

I open my eyes just before sunrise. Fall leaves of golden brown and yellow have piled up on me under the tree at the West State Street ball fields where I spent the night. I am debating with myself as to whether I should look for Nicodemus or not. For all I know he may be a scoundrel who deserves to be in jail. But what if an injustice has been done? He mentioned something about his people, whoever they are, who have suffered indignities and he asked me to pay bail for him. There may just as well be an injustice here; but who am I to right American wrongs? I have left quite a few where I come from.

I pick up my little suitcase and slowly walk back to the uptown area. I find my way to the police station. After waiting for almost five hours—many pagans were arrested last night for unruly behavior or for carrying open containers of beer in the street or even one or two for stabbing fellow pagans—my turn finally comes to be assisted. At first the police do not take me seriously because they think I am one of the pagans. I tell them about Nicodemus and they say there was never anyone of that name in their custody. They do not seem to have much patience even after I have given them a detailed description of the young man. Did I perhaps dream Nicodemus under the ball fields tree?

Fortunately on my way out I see the cop who arrested him and I confront him about Nicodemus. He arrested quite a few offenders last night, but none of them was named Nicodemus. I must be talking about someone else. Recognition dawns on his face after looking me over and he asks me to follow him back into the office where he punches a computer.

"His name is Obed Quigley," he tells me.

As soon as he mentions the name the other officers laugh.

~

Obed Quigley, I later learn, is in jail for impersonating the ghost of Nicodemus, a slave who was murdered in the basement of a house on Washington Street about a hundred and sixty years ago. He had escaped from the plantations of Virginia across the Ohio River through the Underground Railroad. He found refuge in a house that served as one of the Underground Railroad stations in Athens. But pursuers got wind of his whereabouts and invaded the house in the deep of the night. He fought back valiantly, but was shot dead.

Today the house belongs to a sorority. The ghost of Nicodemus continues to take permanent residence in the basement. For long periods, sometimes months, it rests silently and everyone forgets its presence. And then out of the blue there'll be strange noises on an otherwise calm night. Invariably when there are such scratching and moaning sounds a sleeping sorority girl will feel her breasts being fondled. In the morning the girl will have a strange giddy feeling and her sisters will say she has been "touched." All the females who have had contact with Nicodemus feel touched.

Some girls are known to go to the basement alone just to challenge Nicodemus. A girl may be by herself in the house and she would hear whining sounds and footsteps coming from the basement. She would tiptoe to the basement hoping to be touched. Often she would come back disappointed because Nicodemus ignored her. But sometimes Nicodemus fondles the girl's breasts with his long thin fingers, and she runs up the steps giggling and breathing quite heavily in what she professes to be fear. No one has ever admitted to the others that she has gone to the basement to be touched. And yet everyone knows that everyone else does just that when no one is around. A girl really feels like the chosen one when Nicodemus touches her in her sleep without any provocation from her.

Apparently last night when everyone was busy appropriating identities from American icons—living or dead or fictional— Obed Quigley decided to steal Nicodemus's identity. He did not only end there; he stole his pastime as well. He slipped into the sorority house and hid himself in the basement. In the evening when all the girls had left for Court Street, Beth Eddy went down to the basement hoping to be touched before she joined the others. And she was touched. She giggled as Nicodemus's fingers dug deep into her firm mammary glands. But soon she realized that there was something different about the fingers today. She had been touched before and Nicodemus's fingers never felt solid at all. The fingers she knew so well were like mild electric currents that ran through her veins. But these seemed to be crude and fumbling. And the breath that came from the ghost stank of a combination of beer and garlic. She screamed and reached for the switch that dangled in the middle of the room. And there was Obed cowering in the corner, bloody tattered clothes and all. He dashed out and disappeared in the night. Beth Eddy told the cops that she was just grateful that she had not been raped by the bloody imposter. Of course in the police report she omitted the little fact that she had remained alone specifically to be touched by the real McCoy. And that lately she had developed an addiction to the touch.

I get most of this story from Obed himself after I had paid the bond for him. It is late in the afternoon by now because I had to wait for a long time at the police station. Then the police sent me to the sheriff's office to pay the bond. Again there I had to wait for three hours before the papers could be processed and Obed released from jail.

"I slept in the pokey," he complains. "I thought you was gonna bail me out last night."

"I slept under a tree . . . you were better off," I tell him as we walk to a bagel place for a very late breakfast.

Here we find one of those rare commodities in the city of Athens—a public telephone. Obed calls his mama to come and pick us up, but she says she is too busy making relish so he'll have to see how he gets home without her assistance.

"We can take a cab," I suggest to him. "I'll pay for it. How far is it?"

"It's a village called Kilvert . . . about eighteen miles from here."

"Maybe you should have told her you are coming home with a visitor."

"She won't mind. She likes folks from Africa."

As the cab drives on East State past the sign that marks the

Athens corporation limits into Route 50 East Obed pleads with me
not to say anything about his arrest to his mother. "She's gonna kill
me," he says.

We are racing on the freeway. The Hocking River follows us a
few feet from the road, winding with it. Its muddy water flows
quite lazily in small ripples that belie the volumes of water, some of
which overflows on patches of cultivated land on the banks. Sometimes the river disappears among the trees whose summer greens
remain only in fading whispers and a fall cacophony of brown, purple, yellow, orange, red and yellow now dominates. Some are already naked while others are ready to shed their final leaves. And
then the river appears again, meandering its way close to the road.

It is important that I observe the landmarks very carefully in
case I have to return this way on my own. I cannot put my total
trust in this man who is now dozing next to me.

After about eleven miles or so we turn left at a Marathon gas
station onto 329 North. We drive into the village of Guysville, with
its houses that line both sides of the road quite closely. They are all
residential houses—except for the community church and a mini-
storage place. Some are very old but well maintained. Where I come
from houses are built by bricklayers and stonemasons, whereas here
they are built by carpenters.

The Hocking River flows in a deceptively slow drift only a few
yards from us; I didn't quite see at what point it abandoned Route
50 to follow this narrower country road. We are driving above the
river, and once again it twists and turns with the road. Despite the
sharp bends the cabdriver speeds on without paying attention to
signs that warn of school bus stops ahead. But then every other mo-
torist seems to relish turning the road into a NASCAR track. Cars
going in the opposite direction swoosh past us like bullets. Our
cabbie does not make even a feeble attempt to avoid a squirrel that
is crossing the road. It becomes part of the roadkill that I have seen
splotched on the road; vultures feasting on it and only flying away
when the cars get too close.

A mile or so out of Guysville we are stopped by an expanse of water in front of us. The river has spewed onto the road and the surrounding fields and the whole place has become a lake. Cars on both sides are waiting patiently for the flood to subside. The cab-driver says he cannot wait because no one knows when the road will open up. He has many passengers who are waiting for him in Athens. Despite Obed's pleas he insists that we either go back to Athens and pay double fare or he leaves us here for the one-way fare up to that point. I pay him his fare and he drives back. I am wondering if we'll ever get a ride, with Obed looking all bloody and tattered. People may think he is an escaped convict or even a mental patient. But none of the waiting motorists seem to think there is anything wrong with him. Or with me. Instead, from what I can tell, they are ogling us.

While we wait on the side of the road Obed tells me about the floods. They happen quite often and villages like Stewart, Kilvert and Cutler are cut off from the rest of the world. Sometimes for days on end. Especially at this particular spot where the bridge on the runlet that joins the Hocking is very low. Like now: though we haven't seen any sign of rain in the past few days it has obviously rained elsewhere and the rivers and creeks have brought the floods to this innocent area. When the road is flooded like this, one can take the New England Road just after Guysville, which is mostly gravel. But sometimes it is flooded too. It is most likely flooded to-day; that's why all these cars are here. Waiting.

"Floods here are very unpredictable," he adds.

"Why can't the people move to better places?" I ask. "What keeps them here?"

"It's the pull of the ancestors."

It is my first time to hear an American talk of ancestors. I thought ancestor veneration was our sole preserve. Granted, I only know Americans from soap operas and situation comedies, and they never talk of ancestors there. I do not ask him to elaborate though.

After about two hours the water is beginning to recede, but not enough for any of the cars to risk being swept away by the current that still looks strong. A heavy but unloaded truck approaches and it seems the driver is prepared to brave the water. He stops when he spots Obed and hollers at him to swim across if he "ain't no pansy." Obed tells him that he is not suicidal yet. The driver offers us a ride to our destination if we don't mind getting swept away, since there is no guarantee that he'll make it to the other side. He is going to die trying though, because he has to spend the night with his children "who ain't got no mama or nothin'." Obed says if he is willing to risk it, so are we. When he notices my reluctance he assures me that his friend is an excellent driver. His truck, he adds when he notices I am still reluctant, is safe in this sort of situation because it has a diesel engine. "When the water splashes up on the engine it ain't gonna short out the ignition because there ain't no ignition to short out," he says.

We jump in and the engine roars. He introduces me to the driver as his friend from Africa. The driver's name is Nathan, he tells me, and he works for a water hauling service in Athens, delivering steel tanks and cisterns to construction sites all over the county. He lives in Cutler, about five miles beyond Kilvert.

After the two men have exchanged a few cuss words about the flood, Obed turns to me and picks up the conversation where it had been interrupted by Nathan's arrival.

"We don't move from here," he says. "Even those who leave to work in Columbus or Chicago, they come back all the time because the darn place pulls them back. You know why? It's where our race of people was molded."

He stops when he realizes that I am no longer paying any attention to him. I am holding my breath because the truck is sinking in the water as Nathan slowly forces it forward. It moves on in jerks. He seems to find his way on a road that is completely under water by instinct. We sink deeper when we reach the vicinity of the low and narrow bridge. "The current is strong," says Nathan. "If the water gets a few inches up on the door we are screwed." Apparently the vehicle will become too buoyant to maintain traction and the additional force against the door will make it float off the roadway.

Fortunately the monster machine is quite high and Nathan is able to maneuver it very slowly until it reaches the other side. Both Obed and Nathan break into loud laughter when Nathan steps on the accelerator as soon as the vehicle hits the solid black road. I am not laughing at all because I am trying to bring my lungs back to settle at their appointed place in my body after they almost jumped out of my mouth.

In no time we are in Stewart, a pretty little village of white houses and well-trimmed lawns and gigantic trees. We begin a series of sharp bends as the road snakes its way in a forest of elms and sycamores.

"My people call them ghost trees . . . the sycamores," says Obed to me. "They're carriers of memories."

"Come on," says Nathan. "It's just because they're very light in color and stand out among other trees, especially when the moon is shining."

"They are carriers of memories still," insists Obed. "You wouldn't know nothing about it."

They argue. I am more concerned with finding the Hocking River. I think we lost it somewhere at Stewart. I ask them where the river went, if only to stop their loud boyish banter about someone called Orpah who is playing hard to get, which is beginning to irritate me. Nathan explains that it took another direction on the outskirts of Stewart toward West Virginia to join the mighty Ohio River.

The monster truck is devouring sharp curves down the hill and then up the slopes and down again. The road is quite bumpy, although thankfully there are no potholes. Very much unlike the roads in the city of Athens, which have more potholes than I have ever seen on any road in all my life. That is one thing that has made an impression on me about roads in this country: potholes. And it is not only in small cities like Athens. On my arrival I was struck by the potholes on the road between the airports in New York and in Newark, New Jersey. Where I come from such potholes would have been the subject of a national news story or even of a commission of inquiry and somebody would have to pay the price for them. Thankfully this county road, though its surface is uneven, is better maintained. And so are the sprawling lawns on the side of the road. They are always so well trimmed in front of the farmhouses and log cabins and corrugated iron structures of different shapes and sizes that are hiding among the trees. And sturdy barns that pay homage to a German heritage. I am able to see them only because of their bright colors. Those that are red or brown manage to blend with the trees in perfect camouflage. Judging by the barns these are farming communities, although I don't see much farmland on the side of the road. Mostly trees and gullies and lawns. There is, however, tall light brown corn on sporadic patches of land.

About four miles from Stewart we cross the Federal Creek, and there is Kilvert, nestled in the middle of one of the three units of Wayne National Forest. Nathan drops us on the side of the road.

"Tell Orpah Northwest Territory is playing at the Stuart's Opera House in Nelsonville on Saturday," he hollers after us as we walk on a narrower blacktop road that leads into the village.

"She knows that," Obed hollers back without stopping.

"I'd like for us to go."

"Ask her yourself."

Nathan laughs and breaks into the band's all-time favorite, "The Veteran's Song": *If they didn't sacrifice for us, we would be eating rice and drinking German beer.* Then the engine roars and swallows the rest of the song as he tears away.

I follow Obed as we walk deeper into the village among mostly run-down houses strewn with scrap metal, muddy gardens, broken-down vehicles and rusty trailers. There are however a few buildings that are beautifully painted white and have neat gardens.

Outside most of the houses, near the doors or in the porches, big yellow pumpkins are exhibited, and some of these are jack-o'-

lanterns with crudely carved eyes and mouths. Children are trick-or-treating in small groups. Toddlers are accompanied by their mothers, all of whom carry their robust bodies with grace.

"I have never seen so many fat people in my life," I say with a chuckle. Obed ignores the comment.

We walk past a little church with a red roof. It looks like a toy. Or like a confectionary creation of dark brown and light brown chocolate bricks arranged in symmetric patterns. I can see, to my great relief, a beautiful graveyard between the church and a wooded area, the few headstones peeping on a sprawling green lawn. It looks very inviting. Whereas the grass grows high on the side of the road, the lawn in the graveyard is trimmed. All the graves have fresh flowers on them. The people here obviously care for their dead.

❧

The house has a wrap-around porch. Like all the houses here it is built of timber, painted white. Peeling in places. But from the ground to the porch it is built of brown bricks. The porch is quite high, which makes it look more like an Iberian balcony; you climb a number of steps to get to the front door. Under the porch is the brick part of the building with a door and small basement-type windows. A rusty brown GMC pickup is parked in the shade under the balcony.

A man is sitting on a white swing in the porch. He is looking fixedly at some spot in the garden. His lips are smiling. But none of that smile has crept to his eyes. They are deep-set and sorrowful. He is quite big, with a gigantic handlebar mustache that is gray with streaks of black. His skin is golden brown and his thinning silver hair is tied in a humble ponytail. He is in faded blue jeans and a T-shirt that used to be white. It has a number of small holes and smudges of what looks like mud and ketchup. The jeans are kept in place by a slim belt and a pair of broad suspenders.

When he does not return my greeting my eyes follow his to the garden. Nothing grows here but a solitary shrub decorated with foil strips of different colors. Next to it are a birdfeeder and a spinning wheel with small golden bells hanging on it. And then all over the garden there are gnomes and other figures of varying sizes and colors made of cast plaster. There is a cupid with his bow and arrow aimed to the sky, there are birds and angels in frozen flight on the ground and there are swans and flamingos. The dogs and deer are made of water-stained stone. There is a Jesus in red and white robes, his hand raised in benediction. From the cracks on his flowing garments I can see that he is made of painted wood. There are a number of miniature American flags planted among these figures.

"Mr. Quigley used to be a flower man," says Obed. "As you can see he don't care for flowers no more. He grows gnomes."

Mr. Quigley does not even blink. It is as if he is not there. The wind chimes that are hanging in line on the ceiling of the porch fill the air with notes of different tones and pitches. They blend with a haunting music that leaks out of one of the windows. It would be bluegrass if it were not for the strange-sounding instrument that I cannot place.

We walk through a living room cluttered with motley furniture, including vinyl car seats and a metal table on which there is a sewing machine and bits of fabric and pairs of scissors, into the kitchen. The air is suffused with a delicious aroma of spices and simmering beans. A gloriously obese woman with fluffy three-tone hair—silver, brown and black streaks that frizzle from her round head down to her nape—is slicing tomatoes with an old Ginsu knife.

"Still making relish, Mama," moans Obed in a voice that has become that of a spoiled little boy. "You've been doing it for hours now, haven't you? Couldn't pick me up because of the darn relish."

She turns around to glare at Obed. She moves with difficulty and is out of breath. Her faded navy blue tracksuit is very tight on her body emphasizing tiers of fat on her waist and the stomach that hangs like an apron. It is even bigger than the sciolist's. Now I am really ashamed of my offhand remark about Kilvert's fat mothers.

She is not particularly beautiful. Her face is round and bronze and smooth, except for a few expression lines on the brow and at the corners of the mouth. She is obviously going to lash out at her son. But before she can do so she lays her eyes on me, and her face breaks into a puzzled smile.

"I like your costume," she says. "Who might you be?"

"I am Toloki the Professional Mourner, ma'am."

"A professional mourner. That's an original."

"I thought so too, but now I know better."

"And what's with the funny accent?"

"He's from Africa, Mama," says Obed helpfully.

"From South Africa," I correct him. "Remember?"

"From Africa? I'll be damned!" she says. "You got into the spirit of things well and good for a stranger."

"She's Ruth," says Obed. "She's my mama. The mama who don't bring me home because of relish."

"Grow up, boy," says Ruth sharply. "If you get yourself drunk out there in Athens all night long you don't expect your mama to come to your rescue all the darn time. And with them floods, too!"

"That's another thing, Mama, you didn't tell me nothing 'bout them floods."

She decides he is not worth the effort and returns to her tomatoes, and to me.

"How come you don't look like Africans?" she asks. "You're yella."

"Africans come in all colors of humanity, ma'am."

"I'll be damned," she says.

Perhaps it is necessary to account for myself for having what she considers an unusual complexion for an African. I try to explain to her that there are strong possibilities that my ancestry is a Khoikhoi one, which is the case for many Southern Sotho and

Nguni people in South Africa. I am aware that I may well be speaking gibberish; this will not make sense at all to either mother or son. At least I have offered an explanation. "I'll be damned," is Ruth's only response.

After running her eyes up and down Obed's height she declares that he smells and looks like a dead cat and orders him to take a bath and change into clean clothes immediately. He protests, claiming that he is famished and will clean up after he has had a bite to eat. Ruth only has to glare at him and he scurries out. She says I can wait for my friend right there in the kitchen if I like and watch her make the relish.

"Or you wanna sit with Mr. Quigley on the porch?"

"I'll be fine here, ma'am," I say as I pull a tall bar stool next to her table.

She is very fast with her fingers. She chops the vegetables, mixing green tomatoes with red bell peppers and jalapeños and mangoes and pickles and brown sugar and vinegar and Hungarian wax peppers. "Them honky peppers," she says, and goes on to tell me about the art of making great relish. Her tone is conspiratorial, as if she is revealing a secret recipe that will make her millions one day.

"I'm gonna mix that stuff by the ton," she says. "I'm gonna make something so hot them men gonna say, 'man, this is hot!'"

Her voice is thick and mellow. She is clearly having a great time making the relish. She promises to lace a few hot dogs with her sauce especially for me and my eyes will water when I eat "them dogs." After the relish she is going to make green tomato pickle. "Ain't nothing like green tomato pickle," she adds.

The music becomes louder. Without the wind chimes, whose sounds do not penetrate the walls unless there are stronger winds, the lone instrument whines in a manner that causes nostalgia in me. Nostalgia for something I do not know. Some place I have never known.

"Don't you worry your pretty little head about it," Ruth assures me. "It's only Orpah and her darn sitar."

↪

A clean Obed looks quite impressive in his black denim shorts, white and blue sneakers and blue shirt. It is obvious to me that he likes to look good and is particular about what he wears and how it matches with the rest of the outfit. He moans that he is hungry. Ruth sends him out to get some Swiss chard from the garden while she lays the table. I offer to go with him.

The back garden is quite different from the front one. Here we have a vegetable patch: one row each of onions, kale, cabbages, carrots and Swiss chard. Under a plastic sheet that protects them from frost there are tomatoes and peppers. This is Ruth's garden, Obed says. There was zucchini and lettuce as well, but they are all dead now after the late October frost. Whereas his father, Mr. Quigley that is, cultivates gnomes, Ruth likes to grow vegetables and flowers. Well, they no longer have flowers now because Mr. Quigley has taken all the space, but Ruth still has fond memories of the flowers she used to grow in the front and sometimes talks about them as if they were her dead children. And yet she's never lost a child to death. Both he and Orpah are still alive, as I can very well see. But Mr. Quigley will never give up his garden. He is attached to it. He spends most of his time tending to it.

"Tending to it? All day long? How do you tend to something like that all day long?" I ask.

"He sits on the porch and looks at it. That's how he tends to it. Sometimes he rearranges two or three of the figures. Or he straightens a flag that's been disturbed by the wind."

I am beginning to hold Mr. Quigley in great awe though no word has passed between us.

Obed says that on some days his father visits the Kilvert Community Center and sits with other brooding elders on the porch or watches the women quilt inside. Among donated items he may pick up a figure to add to his garden collection. A plastic dog or a porcelain pink flamingo. Ruth, on the other hand, spends her time tending to her vegetable garden or quilting in her own living room, not at the Kilvert Community Center, since her falling-out with the women there.

In the house dinner is served and Mr. Quigley is already seated at the table. After giving Ruth the Swiss chard we take our places and she mumbles a few words of grace. Obed says to his father: "Mr. Quigley, this is my friend from Africa."

Mr. Quigley stretches his arm across the table and gives me a firm handshake.

"My name is Toloki, sir," I tell him.

"Mahlon Quigley at your service," he says. And that's the last I hear his voice for the evening. Throughout dinner he ignores me as he does the rest of the table, as if I have always been part of his family.

The home-cooked food is good, after living on fast foods for the past few days. The corn bread that Ruth breaks with her hands and places on the bare table in front of everyone is particularly tasty. And so is the cannellini bean soup in which lie chunks of meat. I do not want to waste time with the Swiss chard and tomato salad even though Ruth praises the dressing which she made herself.

The meat is pork, Ruth says, expressing her hope that I do eat pork. Mr. Quigley slaughtered the pig a few days earlier. This, she warns me in her conspiratorial tone once more, is illegal because it is against health regulations to kill animals in your own backyard. It is a sore point because it has changed the people's way of life.

"We used to slaughter lotsa hogs," Ruth says. "I used to pickle them legs. I still do though we don't slaughter that much no more because we don't wanna end up in the pokey. Mr. Quigley likes the liver . . . the way I do it."

"It's against the law, Ma," Obed cuts in. "You can always buy liver from Wal-Mart. We gotta stop this slaughtering of hogs."

"Todoloo!" says Ruth, turning her forefinger on her forehead as if to say her son has lost it. "We ain't doing no harm to nobody.

Our people have always grown their own food. We ain't gonna stop now."

I have been hearing this refrain about "our people" since last night and I wonder aloud who these people are. But all Ruth can say is: "We don't belong to nobody. Our race of people is different from any race of people that ever lived on earth."

Obed adds helpfully: "Yeah, we don't belong nowhere. White people hate us because we ain't white enough. Black people hate us too. They call us high-yella-niggers. They are jealous of our complexion."

This does not help me at all. But I let it go. We eat quietly for some time. Obed wolfs his food while Mr. Quigley chews with a slow deliberate unchanging rhythm, his smiling face savoring every morsel. Ruth looks very pleased with herself that her menfolk are enjoying her cooking. Obed breaks the silence by telling them about my job: I mourn for the dead. Neither parent shows any astonishment at all. Instead Ruth wants to know how I do it. My respect for this family is further enhanced: most people, when told I am a professional mourner, want to know why I do it . . . not how.

"I came in search of mourning," I tell Ruth when she inquires what my mission is in these parts. I do not think they will understand if I tell them about the sciolist and Sam Crowl's challenge. So I leave that bit out.

"Have you found any yet in our good ol' U.S. of A.?" Ruth wants to know.

"I was at The Ridges last night . . . at the cemetery there . . . just before I went to join the Court Street parades. I was disappointed."

Ruth says the family is disappointed about that cemetery too. Mahlon Quigley's mother lies buried there and the family has been struggling to locate her grave. They need to lay a memorial stone, which will make him a very happy man and will change his fortunes. He will never really know peace until a proper stone is laid there with her name and her dates of birth and death and words to the effect that she is remembered with love. But no one knows how to go about finding her grave since the graves have no names.

Obed's face shows that this is not his favorite topic. He suddenly remembers that Orpah also needs to eat. There is silence while he goes to call her from her room. The music of the sitar stops. Obed comes back and announces: "She says she ain't hungry. Maybe she wanna lose some weight."

"If that girl loses any more weight she'll blow away!" shouts Ruth, clearly for Orpah's benefit in her bedroom.

The sitar resumes with a vengeance.

🐾

It is still dark outside. I had a restful night in Obed's bed while he took refuge on a sponge mattress in the attic. But I must wake up. Force of habit. I find it difficult to sleep beyond 5 A.M. Perhaps I will take a walk in the garden, as long as I make sure that I don't step on Mahlon Quigley's crops. I may even venture further into the village; maybe walk to the cemetery while the village is still asleep. Why, I may even mourn a bit. Just for a few minutes. Surely there'll be names on all the headstones and even epitaphs on some of them. I may be able to engage in my old pastime of re-creating the lives and the deaths of the dead for the pleasure of mourning them. My body cries for mourning. It has been quite some time.

In the living room Ruth is already sitting at the metal table sewing a quilt. She is in a bathrobe and I am wondering if she slept at all. She looks at me tiredly and smiles.

"No rest for the wicked," she says.

"It's just that my body is used to waking up early."

"I'm talking about me," she says, and offers me coffee.

"I am fine, ma'am; I am not really one for coffee."

"You know something about quilts?" she asks.

I confess my ignorance. Her eyes brighten as she tells me how her people are a quilting people. For generations and generations before her. Old quilts embody the life of the family. Not only was the batting of some of them made from the clothes that people had worn; but people were made on them—"If you know what I mean," she adds in that conspiratorial tone—people were born on them, people got sick on them, people died on them. Cycles of loves and losses were enacted on the quilts. The souls of those who are gone rest in the very threads of the quilts.

Then she walks with the aid of a cane to her bedroom and returns with two very old and dirty-looking quilts.

"Smell these," she says.

It is a peculiar smell. Musty, yes, but also aromatic.

The two quilts, she says, were made by her great-great-grandmother before the Civil War. One is an Irish Chain—that's the name of the design. The other one is an African quilt. That also is a design. Or a series of designs. And then she gives me her beaming smile and asks: "Do you know why it's called an African quilt, you being from Africa and all?" Without waiting for my answer, which would not have been forthcoming in any case because I do not know and none of the patterns look African to my untrained eye, she explains that her African ancestors used these quilts to escape from slavery. She does not elaborate on how quilts could be used to escape from slavery, except to vaguely mention something about following slave trails on the designs.

The peculiar smell is the smell of history. Like Obed's sycamores, this pile of worn fabric on Ruth's metal table is a carrier of memories.

The story is told by the earthy scent of the quilts.

Quiltales

*T*he story is told that the wizened old woman taught mothers never to love their children. She walked from cabin to cabin dispensing her wisdom. Because her message must be infused through the veins of the earth, the sciolist even makes her walk from plantation to plantation, silent as the air we breathe, without attracting the attention of the owners. Mothers eagerly lapped up her words, for they knew the dire consequences of loving. Those who were weak enough to love in spite of themselves received special lessons on how to cease confusing love with ownership. Invariably they failed to appreciate the fine distinction and ended up regretting that they loved at all. Some women imbibed the lessons so well that they went beyond just not loving their children; they developed a deep hatred for them. They hated them for being the children who could not be loved. If they had had the power they would have strangled them in the womb.

Sometimes lessons failed and the wizened one resorted to concoctions that she brewed in her cabin. Concoctions that she had learned from those who learned them from the shamans of the old continent, generations before. She gave them to pregnant mothers to harden their hearts so that they would be immune from loving what was growing in their bodies.

Men could be loved, but with caution. It was that kind of an age. They too could not be possessed by those who were weak enough to love them. *Once more, don't mix things up: love and ownership are two separate notions.* They would be here today and gone tomorrow. But there would be others. The auction block would provide. Or a woman may be fortunate enough to find one from the domestic stock. From those who had been bred to procreate and feed the insatiable markets. Men and women did not abjure what came naturally even though they knew that the unions they formed would be fragile. They continued to manufacture babies despite the ever-threatening dangers of loving them.

David Fairfield was The Owner. He had a better remedy for love . . . much more effective than the wizened one's. He was a compassionate man, so he devised a strategy of saving the women from the pain of loving their children. The midwives were given strict instructions that the birthing mothers should never be allowed to see their newborns, let alone touch them. As soon as the babies came out of the passage of life they were whisked away to a communal nursery. At feeding time mothers were not given their own babies to breastfeed. Mothers therefore never got to know which babies were theirs, in the same way that they never got to know who the fathers were. The Owner made certain that there was a rotation of studs— the well-bred young men whose most important function was to impregnate the women to populate the plantation with the future generations that would meet the demands of the auction block.

Nicodemus and Abednego were children who could not be loved.

First came Abednego. They called his mother the Abyssinian Queen, even though none of her forebears ever set foot in Abyssinia. The first of them in the new world had been captured from the mouth of the Kongo more than a century before. She did not know that. The Kongo man's family tree was chopped down successfully after a generation or two and no one knew anything anymore.

She was the Abyssinian Queen—black like a moonless night with dark clouds hiding the stars. Yet her big white teeth beamed sunrays into people's hearts, leaving them melting.

Her face was round and smooth. So was her belly. It radiated life: there is nothing as beautiful as a pregnant stomach. The fullness of the moon. Gleaming stretch marks like moonscape rivers. In the folk tales that were told when work was done and fires were

roaring the sun was king and the moon was queen. Perhaps that is
why they called the woman a queen, for the sobriquet started only
when she was sashaying in voluminous dresses, with Abednego
kicking in her body.

In her case the father of the child was known, for he never allowed any rotation to take place on top of the Abyssinian Queen.
She was his and his alone. Of course he never acknowledged the
child. It was an age when some children were destined never to be
acknowledged by those fathers who prided themselves on being
pillars of the community.

The Abyssinian Queen cleaned the big house and took care of the
acknowledged children. She provided friendship and companionship to the lady of the house. When work was done she took care of
the needs of The Owner, providing him with alternative warmth
during those long winter nights. To facilitate this last task of the day
she was allocated a comfortable room adjoining the big house, and
did not consort with those who lived in the cabins and toiled in the
fields. Her duties were to the family and the hawk-eyed Owner.

The Owner had to be vigilant because he knew the kind of
shenanigans property was capable of getting up to behind the master's back. He had seen it all when he was growing up at his father's plantation in Fredericksburg, Virginia, decades before.

Charles Fairfield, David's father, had determined quite early
on that slave children were a more profitable crop than tobacco
or cotton or corn, especially after the 1808 abolition of the for-
eign slave trade. Since the Fairfields—then famous in all the South
as slave traders of repute—could no longer import slaves from
Africa and the West Indies, they decided to start their own slave
breeding farm to meet the growing needs of labor in the thriving
plantations of the South.

The Fairfield operation in Fredericksburg was quite rudimentary. The breeding process was not formalized or planned in any
scientific manner. Children happened when they did and were sold
just before they reached their teens. Shenanigans were not discour-

aged for it was from them that new stock would come. Rather than discourage them, Charles participated in them with gusto.

There was a lot of inbreeding. But the senior Fairfield never gave any thought to its implications, nor was he bothered by the possibility that he was sire to some of the mulatto teenagers he bedded.

Mulattos were highly priced, as long as they were not so light in complexion as to be mistaken for whites. So, the senior Fairfield was eager to have more of them at his plantation. He used to organize binge parties to which students from a nearby college were invited and let loose among the females, which helped in the production of more mulatto children.

David Fairfield started his own adventures with slave girls in his early teens. By the time he got married in his mid-twenties to a beautiful debutante from a neighboring plantation he had become so addicted to black pussy that his daddy feared it would jeopardize the marriage. And it did. After only two years the wife decided that she could not share him with property anymore and divorced him.

He was an enterprising sort. Whereas his siblings were content with inheriting the plantation and continuing with business as usual, he trekked to the west across the Allegheny Mountains and settled in the Putnam County of his home state of Virginia where he bought a small plantation with his portion of the inheritance. It was more of a farm, really, although its occupants ambitiously called it a plantation. He had observed as his train of wagons and oxen and horses and slaves crossed the Appalachians that in this region there were no real plantations. There was therefore a new type of slavery where slaves worked for families as farmhands— quite different from the grand plantation slavery he had been used to in the eastern part of Virginia from which he had emigrated.

It occurred to him that on this new farm the only viable crop would be slave children. But unlike his father, who cultivated other cash crops and only dabbled in slave breeding as a sideline, he would go all out to devise new ways of improving production. Slave breeding would be the sole business of the farm, and all arable land would be utilized for cultivating vegetables and cereals only for subsistence. The husbandry of hogs and chickens and cows would only serve to provide meat, eggs and dairy for the family and the slave population. It was important to have strong well-fed slaves who would fetch a good price at the market.

In a few years the place became a prosperous breeding farm. David Fairfield married a literate Appalachian woman who blessed him with acknowledged children and with management skills that benefited the business. He bought more land from neighboring farmers and established an efficient plantation, with rows of cabins for studs, black females, selected mulattos, white slaves and nurseries for the children. The whole machinery was geared for the smooth and fast production of children, who were then sold when they reached fifteen. Only those boys who had the potential of becoming excellent studs and those girls who looked sapid enough to spur the most tired of studs to action were spared the auction block.

The Abyssinian Queen had been one such woman. The Owner first noticed her when she was sent to deliver some vegetables from the gardens to the big house. He immediately harnessed her for duty as a house slave, which was regarded as a promotion. Even though the household was well served by a team of white female indentured workers, who were in practice slaves, she became Mrs. Fairfield's daytime companion. She won this position because of her storytelling abilities and her great humor. She also became Mr. Fairfield's nighttime companion. She was their own special pet and was therefore never in any danger of being sold.

Mrs. Fairfield was not unaware that on the nights he was not in the master bedroom he was with the Abyssinian Queen. She totally accepted his infidelity for breeding purposes. It was merely a commercial arrangement as far as she was concerned. In any event it was fashionable to have an African concubine, and many of his friends had one or two and boasted about them in good company.

Pregnancy gave the Abyssinian Queen some respite from his

attentions. She was able to spend restful nights without his flabby body heaving on top of hers. Much as he found her particularly toothsome, he knew better than to bother her in her present state and jeopardize the well-being of the baby. It was important that children were born healthy and grew up strong. He survived the nine months of her pregnancy and the months allocated for breast-feeding without much problem. He was spoiled for choice. Not only did he sample mature women of her caliber, he also had a field day with teenagers, many of them mulattos, and some of them undoubtedly the fruit of his own loins. Like his father before him, he never gave incest a second thought.

Abednego was born and, as was customary, he was not ac-knowledged by the father. The mother was not supposed to ac-knowledge him either, for like all the other babies who could not be loved he had been whisked away at birth before the mother could even have a good look at him. The baby was taken to the nursery to be brought up by nursemaids. But the Abyssinian Queen commanded respect and influence. The midwives conspired to keep track of her baby. When nursing mothers gathered at the feeding bay four times a day the nursemaids gave the Abyssinian Queen her own baby to breastfeed. She and Abednego got to know each other very well and bonded.

Other mothers suspected that she was receiving preferential treatment—otherwise why was she given the same baby all the time to breastfeed? Yet they did not say anything about it. She was, after all, the Abyssinian Queen. They would know in later years that the midwives did devise ways of keeping track of their babies too, and when it was safe to do so without being betrayed to The Owner, found a way to secretly introduce toddlers to their mothers—thus pissing on The Owner's compassion.

Abednego was brought up at the nursery with the other chil-dren. As The Owner had decreed that all breastfeeding should stop after six months, the Abyssinian Queen saw less of her son after that period. She was not supposed to see the boy at all or to recognize him if she chanced upon him, but once again with the connivance of the nursemaids she was able to creep into the nursery, cuddle the baby quickly, make a few cooing sounds, kiss him once or twice, remove a tear from her eye with the back of her hand, and then sneak back to the big house.

Abednego was about a year old when The Owner renewed his carnal interest in the Abyssinian Queen. In fact, he was seized by a raging desire for her that could not be slaked. To the extent that there were no longer any conjugal visits to the chamber of the lady of the house. Nights were spent with the Abyssinian Queen. All nights. Silly games were played with the Abyssinian Queen. Laughter was shared with the Abyssinian Queen. So was news of business highlights and lowlights. Even Sunday afternoons, previously reserved for visiting neighbors and entertaining friends, were spent with the Abyssinian Queen. To the lady of the house, who previously did not have a jealous bone in her slim body, this was no longer commerce. The black woman must have used some voodoo potions—or whatever black women use—to ensnare the poor man and render him powerless. He became a blithering fool at the whiff of the Abyssinian Queen's scent.

He took to following her everywhere she went. This was most inconvenient for her, for it meant she could not steal away to see Abednego at the cabins where he was being brought up by those women who had been assigned the task, or to the gardens where children his age were already being acclimatized to the smell of the soil. But the man's lack of control was an embarrassment to the lady of the house, especially when it became a source of mirth for the house slaves and white maids.

Sometimes a mischievous little devil possessed the Abyssinian Queen and made her play unkind tricks on the poor man. For example, she took to hanging her most intimate garments up in a hickory tree—hidden among the leaves. She was a great tree climber. He surely caught the scent and came sniffing about with his tongue hanging out. He circled the tree, jumping about like a puppy and caressing the trunk. The shred of dignity left in him did not allow him to climb it, though he was clearly tempted to do so. Then in a fit of passion he stripped the scaly bark with his fingers. All the while she was watching him through the window, while darning socks or crocheting a hat for the coming winter.

There were snide whispers in the slave community about all these goings-on. The Abyssinian Queen's stature was enhanced among her peers: no one ever thought they would see the day when The Owner was reduced to a raving lunatic by his craving for a mere slave.

The lady of the house got wind of her cruel games and reprimanded her strongly. The Abyssinian Queen, of course, was adamant that she had nothing to do with his behavior. She was merely performing the duties that were expected of her.

"I'll talk to him," said the lady of the house. "From now I want you to lock your door at all times. I don't want him spending his nights with you ever again."

He came at night and tried the door. It was locked. He knew at once it was his wife's doing. The doors to his concubines' rooms were never locked, allowing him free access at all hours of the day or night. He knocked and when she refused to open he threatened her with a flogging that she would remember for the rest of her life. She was not swayed by his threats; she was, after all, carrying out the lady's instructions. He was banging on the door and threatening to break it down when the lady arrived and ordered him to stop making a fool of himself and to go back into the house and get some decent sleep. He submissively followed his wife, but repeated the ruckus for the next three nights. Again and again Mrs. Fairfield came out to drag him back into the main house.

Until he finally gave up.

After a few weeks he was back to his normal self again, working his slaves hard in the fields and driving them in yokes and chains to auctions throughout the west of Virginia and the whole of Kentucky, and spending his randy moments with the mulatto concubines, some of whom were a more beautiful and graceful version of his image.

Everyone believed The Owner was finally cured of the Abyssinian Queen.

Everyone but the lady of the house. She suspected that sooner or later the power of the woman's voodoo would return and her husband would fall victim to madness again. She therefore planned to marry the Abyssinian Queen off to a house slave from a plantation owned by a family friend in Kentucky, who paid a good price for her since as the wife of his principal house slave she would now be his property as well. Although the prospective bride and groom would only set eyes on each other for the first time on their wedding day, they resigned themselves to their fate and braced themselves for a lifetime of mutual bondage. There could be worse fates.

There was great excitement at the big house as wedding preparations were being made. The lady of the house, her children, her servants and her house slaves were taking the wedding quite seriously. It was as though a Fairfield daughter was getting married. The meticulous planning took months. The wedding gown was purchased in Charleston: an elaborate construction in silk dupion with gold and silver thread embroidery and layers of lace in places, a long beaded boned bodice with corset, and a velvet train with appliquéd detail. No expense was spared, although everyone knew that she would not be taking the gown with her to Kentucky. It belonged to the big house and would be used for future weddings of house slaves. Marriages that would only be recognized as valid by The Owner and his family, and would subsist at his pleasure.

As the day drew near everyone at the big house was getting the wedding jitters. The lady of the house did not want anything to go wrong.

And yet it did. One morning the Abyssinian Queen came with a bombshell: she could not marry the man chosen for her, because she was pregnant. No, not by The Owner. The Owner had not touched her for months. But by a nondescript field slave she met when she went to see Abednego at the mulatto cabins.

It was a slap in everyone's face. She had disgraced the family by sleeping with a field slave. She had scandalized generations of house slaves who had been groomed to know and cherish their superior place. Obviously the tastelessness of her original breeding had not abandoned her despite her living in the big house all those years: you could take a slave out of the field but you couldn't take the field out of a slave. Refined house slaves were those born of house slaves.

The marriage must go on, insisted the lady of the house. A lot of planning had gone into it, and a lot of money spent. The multi-tiered cake had been baked by a slave borrowed from a neighboring plantation. It was waiting to be unveiled in the hall. It did not escape The Owner that her main motive was to get rid of the Abyssinian Queen once and for all. The Kentucky man supported the lady of the house: the marriage could not be canceled at this late stage. Again it did not escape The Owner that his real reason was not that he had already paid for her, for the money could always be refunded, but she had become more valuable since she was with child. The Kentucky man would be getting two slaves for the price of one. The Owner put his foot down: the woman was impregnated by a Fairfield slave, and therefore the child belonged to Fairfield Farms.

"But I had already bought her when she got pregnant," moaned the Kentucky man.

"From my calculations she conceived even before we engaged in negotiations to marry her over to your property," said The Owner.

"How would you know that?" asked the Kentucky man. "You weren't there when she conceived, were you? Unless it's your little bugger."

"That's preposterous, old coot, and you know it!"

The Abyssinian Queen was summoned to answer some questions to determine at what stage she conceived. She was rather vague about it, especially because she wanted to protect the identity of the father. She knew exactly what would happen to him for engaging in copulation outside the sanctioned boundaries: castration. The man would be reduced to an ox fit only for labor. No one personally knew anyone who had ever received such punishment at Fairfield Farms, but it was common knowledge in the slave community that it was meted out to those who were foolish enough to sleep with The Owner's special concubines.

The Kentucky man, still adamant that the conception must have happened after the transaction and therefore the child belonged to him, suggested that the woman be whipped until she came out with the truth. And she was whipped. Not by The Owner, but by the Kentucky man. The Owner was a compassionate man and never undertook the often necessary but unpleasant task of whipping his slaves himself. He delegated it to others—particularly the burly male mulatto house slaves.

This was the Abyssinian Queen's first experience of the whip and she found it very humiliating since it was done in public under the very hickory tree she had previously used to play her cruel games on The Owner. As the whip cut deep into her flesh, spectators could not help noticing that not only the wielder of the whip was breathing heavily, but The Owner as well. A sudden bulge had developed in the general area of his crotch, just as it had developed on the Kentucky man. In no time the wielder of the whip was screaming and cussing and foaming at the mouth. There was a wet spot on his pants. He thrashed even harder as the pants got wetter. Yet she was determined to maintain her dignity and only winced inwardly as the whip slashed her bare back. She maintained a stoic face; she wanted to deflate the flogger. And this made him even madder. He lashed out indiscriminately, no longer taking particular care to create symmetric patterns of oozing blood on her back. He even lashed at her dangling breasts. This did not sit well with the Fairfields.

"She messed up my wedding," said the lady of the house. "But it ain't no reason to kill her!"

"It's enough," said The Owner. "You stop now."

His pants were wet too, and he was finding it difficult to stay steady on his feet.

"That's why they are so stubborn," said the Kentucky man, struggling to regain his composure. "You spoil them."

Once more the Abyssinian Queen was interrogated about the conception. The Owner looked at her appealingly, and his eyes were clearly pleading: *Please give us the answers we want. It kills me to see you going through such pain and humiliation.*

She was now aware that her answer would determine whether she remained with the Fairfields or was taken over by the Kentucky man and an unknown groom. Although she did not know when negotiations for her marriage were first made and the transaction was finalized, she came up with a date that was a few months back.

"She lies," said the Kentucky man.

"The child rightly belongs to Fairfield Farms," said The Owner.

"We can work out a compromise," said the lady of the house. "We'll send the woman over to Kentucky soon after the birth. After all, our children here are brought up by nursemaids and not by their birth mothers."

But the Kentucky man demanded his money back and left in a huff.

The Abyssinian Queen's status in the household was reduced. She had to vacate her comfortable room for the cabins. She also had to say goodbye to the luxury of having other slaves clean her chamber and wash and iron her clothes. Although her demotion from her aristocratic position as a house slave was supposed to be serious punishment she was much happier in the surroundings she had known so well as a young girl, and enjoyed the communal spirit that existed among the hoi polloi. The place was brimming with life. Family units were formed, even though everyone knew how tenuous they were. Mothers established new connections with those they believed to be their children, even though most of them did not sleep under the same roof. She discovered that she had gained an even greater stature among her peers. People remembered how she made The Owner run around in circles like a mad dog. She was admired even more for standing up to the masters, foiling their evil plans and depriving the Kentucky man of the pleasure of her screams.

The child was born and was named Nicodemus.

As with Abednego, the father was known in the slave community. When he and the Abyssinian Queen started behaving like a family he was exposed as the culprit to the occupants of the big house, particularly to The Owner, who had been smarting for a long time because his favorite concubine had been impregnated by a field slave. It was more that his ego was hurt, because in any event the concubine's fate had already been determined through the botched marriage, and he was never going to see her again.

Contrary to every gossip's expectation, Nicodemus's father was not castrated but was immediately sold to a different plantation in Kentucky. As he marched in the hot sun chained and yoked to other young men destined for the auction houses of Lexington he hollered to the women working in the fields: "Y'all tell my queen that I'm gonna find my freedom. I am gonna come back for her and Nicodemus. We all gonna be free."

Slave drivers didn't take kindly to this type of wild talk. They gave him a few lashes on his naked back.

Like all the slave children of Fairfield Farms Nicodemus was brought up by nursemaids at the nursery, and then transferred to the African cabins at the age of about five or so. The Abyssinian Queen made it a point that Abednego, who lived at the mulatto cabins, got to know Nicodemus as his brother. This was achieved with the active assistance of those who were assigned to look after the children as they grew older and to oversee their labor. Right from the beginning the boys hit it off, and with a great deal of connivance at various levels it became possible for them to spend some evenings together.

The Owner was becoming even more compassionate and more liberal with age. The Abyssinian Queen took advantage of this weakness and asked him if she could have the boys stay with her at the cabin she shared with two aging matriarchs.

"How do you know they're your boys?" asked The Owner.

"It don't matter whose boys they are," said the Abyssinian Queen. "I just like them to stay with me."

"Those boys are marked already," The Owner warned her. "The black one is gonna be a good stud. The mulatto will be ready for sale soon. In the meantime it makes no never mind to me if they stay with you."

The lady of the house was dead set against this arrangement. But The Owner, who obviously still had a soft spot for the Abyssinian Queen, prevailed, and the woman lived with her sons in her small cabin. The matriarchs were happy to have young ones under their roof to spoil with treats as grandmothers are wont to do.

The Abyssinian Queen's main occupation was to sew and mend clothes for the whole slave community. She was one of three women assigned this task. Two of them were the aging matriarchs, who had been saved from the auction block decades before because of their skill as seamstresses. It was from one of them that the Abyssinian Queen learned not only how to sew the most wonderful shirts and dresses from feed sacks, but how to create quilts from scraps of fabric gathered from all odd places, including old clothes from the big house and leftovers from the muslin that the lady of the house occasionally purchased for the Sunday dresses of house slaves' children.

She spent her nights sewing the quilts. When the matriarchs discovered her interest in and flair for needlecraft they took upon themselves all the sewing and mending tasks, and let the Abyssinian Queen focus on her quilts. She became better by the day, and was voracious in learning new patterns. Soon the matriarchs taught her that the quilts her people made carried secret messages. Beauty that spoke a silent language, they called it. Openly it was there for all to admire, yet its meaning rested only with those who knew the code hidden in the colors and the designs.

Before learning the language of the quilts she used to specialize in crazy patchwork, at least four decades before these constructions of odd pieces of randomly arranged fabric became a fad in that part of Virginia—which had, of course, become West Virginia by the time the crazy quilt flourished. It was in the 1830s, and she did not know she was founding a tradition. Even if she had been conscious of the fact it would not have mattered to her that she would get no recognition for it.

Abednego and Nicodemus learned that there was some rhythm in the madness of her compositions. These were not crazy designs in the true sense of the later tradition. In the seemingly haphazard arrangements, she taught them to identify some landmarks. A hill here. A forest there. A creek. A river. The Kanawha River, the boys later learned. She had painstakingly stitched and knotted the map of the plantation and beyond, using information she had gathered from those who had seen those places. Patches of different colors represented actual landmarks.

She herself had never been outside the borders of Fairfield Farms, yet here she was teaching the boys directions to places that existed only in stories that adventurers and foiled escapees told. It was a rudimentary map, but to the boys it represented a world of dreams out there. It was an attainable world; the mother drummed that into their heads. Dreams could be lived.

"One day you gonna see all them places," she told them. "One day you gonna cross the River Jordan."

The boys loved her beautiful voice as she sang to them about the River Jordan and about the Promised Land and about wading in the water. She taught them that there were two promised lands: "One happens after we is dead and gone. But before you get to that one you better reach the Promised Land across the big river."

This was rather confusing to the boys, but they imbibed the songs and the stories until they were utterly intoxicated by their beauty and promise. It was like the happiness that the preacherman spoke about in the makeshift church on Sundays. But the difference was that the Abyssinian Queen's promised happiness did not happen after death like the preacherman's. It happened in this life, in a real Canaan that existed beyond the river.

In the evenings the boys sat under a quilting frame and listened to stories of escape. Though the mother, it seemed to them, had resigned herself to a life of slavery, she had high hopes that her sons would grow up to carry on the great tradition of plotting escapes established by their forebears from the first day they were shackled into slave castles on the old continent. She relentlessly brought them up on a daily diet of stories of great flights and heroic attempts— often repeated with variations and embellishments to make them sink deeper into the boys' minds.

Soon word of her wonderful stories spread and children from neighboring cabins came to listen. Even white children from the big house came some evenings. They gathered around bonfires of fall leaves to hear of Ananse the wily spider who came with the ancestors from the old continent and whose bag was always full of tricks. She developed a performance where she played all the parts, and incorporated the shadows and the flames and the smoke as characters in the elaborate tales that she seemed to improvise on the spot. To the frenzied drumming of Abednego, who had developed into a keen and nimble drummer, she draped herself in layers of quilts and donned masks of feathers and leaves and woven grass and frayed feed sacks. She pranced around and walked on air; becoming a demonic monster in one story, the wily Ananse spinning a web of deceit in another, and a kindly spirit that guided the children from the world of the unborn through the maze of birth in yet another one.

She climbed the sycamore tree in front of the cabin, stood on the highest branch and flapped her wings like a hawk. Then she swooped down in a spinning flight and landed in the midst of the open-mouthed children. Her gleaming black face reflected the flames and became purple as a result. They danced on her smooth skin until they jutted out of her eyes like red-hot blades. She became the sun as she narrated the story of The Sun. *The Sun was very lonely because she was the only living thing in the whole wide world. She sat there brooding and feeling sorry for herself.* The sharper children noted that the sun was now female whereas it was usually the moon that gloried in that gender. *Yes, she sat there brooding and feeling sorry for herself. A big tear rolled out of her eye and dropped on the ground. It rolled on and on down the hill, gathering dust until it hit a boulder and divided into many tears that became children as they continued to roll. They were Children of the Tear. They lived in peace in a dust bowl and did not have any need for food, clothing or labor. Then one day The Sun farted. Instead of the bad wind coming out, a giraffe and Divided came out. A giraffe is a long-necked animal from the old continent, whereas Divided was a creature with the head and torso of a man and the body of a lion.* She paused. She stared into the eyes that were almost popping out with expectation.

The children screamed in unison: "And then what happened?"

She pretended she had forgotten what happened after the giraffe and Divided came onto the scene and challenged the children to complete the story themselves. They came with their various versions of how the giraffe and Divided conspired to spoil the peace of the Children of the Tear, and how later the giraffe and Divided fell out between themselves and then fell into a crevice that The Sun had opened on the earth to save the Children of the Tear.

But one of The Owner's sons would not buy the very beginning of the story.

"You say there was nothing in the world . . . only The Sun?" he asked.

And when all the children shouted that it was indeed so, the world was empty except for The Sun, the boy asked: "What about Jesus? Where was Jesus when all this was happening?"

"It was before there was nobody," the Abyssinian Queen explained. "Not even Jesus. Not even trees and rivers."

"Not even chickpeas," his little sister piped. He loved chickpeas and at lunchtime they had fought over some that she had spilled on the floor by mistake.

The next day the Abyssinian Queen was surprised to see the shadow of the lady of the house looming at the cabin door. She immediately put her sewing on a bench and rushed to welcome her. The lady of the house was, however, not in any mood for pleasantries. She told the Abyssinian Queen that she was greatly offended that she was teaching her children voodoo stories, telling them that there was a time when there was no Jesus. Jesus has always been there.

"It's only a story, ma'am," the Abyssinian Queen said. "Maybe you gotta stop them kids from coming. It will break their li'l hearts though."

"I ain't gonna stop them from nothing," said the lady of the house with finality. "This is their plantation, you know, so they gonna go where they wanna go. All you gotta do is stop the voodoo stories and tell Bible stories instead."

Of course the Abyssinian Queen continued unabated with her "voodoo" stories and the children, including The Owner's, continued to gather in the evenings. They even learned to sing along and to join in the choruses and in call-and-response chants.

The Owner never suspected anything subversive about the storytelling sessions, even when the lady of the house complained that they accorded too much mixing of the children, who would normally be segregated and quartered according to their breed and pedigree. The Owner was indeed becoming too soft with age. For instance, the white children who came for the stories were not only the freeborn from the big house—the lady's own kids, that is. There were also the white girls who had been sold to Fairfield

Farms by their indigent parents, and those who were said to be illegitimate and were then given to African women to bring up. All these would be reduced to slavery when they grew up, and would be used for the breeding of the much valued mulatto slaves. In the meantime The Owner turned a blind eye as these children mixed and filled their lives with the magic of foxes and buzzards and rabbits and wolves and scallywags of all types that all tried to outdo one another in knavery.

But stories of how Nat Turner, a preacherman, led more than fifty fellow slaves to take the armory in Southampton County, Virginia, and was hanged after being captured, were told in whispers, when the white children had gone back to the big house and to their various quarters. The pain of this particular story was still very fresh in the community because it happened only three or four years before. Stories of how Denmark Vesey, a respected carpenter and minister of religion, himself a former house slave, led a rebellion against slave owners in Charleston—not their Charleston, but another Charleston in South Carolina—and was executed a decade or so before, waited for the time when only the two boys remained.

At first the boys took these stories passively, but as they grew older the stories acquired new meaning. So did the quilts that their mother gave them one Christmas. Abednego's was the crazy quilt with the map. For Nicodemus she created a wonderful sampler with the well-known designs: the Drunkard's Path, the Log Cabin, the North Star, the Monkey Wrench, Crossroads, and the Flying Geese. Those who saw the quilt admired its beauty—the way she had arranged each of those designs and the color combinations that made each pattern stand out and yet blend in with the rest.

This was not beauty for its own sake; the Abyssinian Queen stressed that to the boys. Each design carried a message. The idea of making quilts talk a secret language first came with the forebears from the old continent, she went on. In the old continent works of art, including garments that people wore and lids that covered pots, talked secret languages that could be understood only by those who had been initiated into the circle.

In the same way that she taught them how to read the map on Abednego's crazy quilt, she taught them how to interpret the sampler. They enjoyed it most when she told them what the Drunkard's Path meant, for she acted out with silly exaggerations the staggering walk of a drunkard. The pattern, she said, told them never to take a straight route when they escape. They should always take a zigzag path. That way the evil spirits would not catch them, for evil spirits always traveled in a straight line. Like the evil spirits, slave chasers would be confused and lose track of them. The boys were not only fascinated by the meaning of the pattern but by the actual sewing of the Drunkard's Path . . . how their mother cut one-quarter circles and then rearranged them to form the zigzags. It looked so simple when she did it yet so complicated when one looked at the finished product.

The other patterns on Nicodemus's sampler transmitted messages to escapees along similar lines: the North Star advising them always to follow the North Star for that was the correct direction to Canaan, which existed on official maps as Canada; the Monkey Wrench warning them of the necessity of thorough preparation and of acquiring appropriate tools and provisions for an escape; the Flying Geese and Crossroads once more identifying the directions to be taken; and the Log Cabin denoting Underground Railroad stations. There were many other patterns that they would learn all in good time, most of which she herself had yet to learn from the matriarchs.

What registered in the boys' minds throughout all these lessons was that rather than identify a specific direction for escape as her map on Abednego's crazy quilt attempted to do, the designs on Nicodemus's sampler were general warnings and advice. Although they did not give specific instructions on what to do at a specific time and point, they inspired the boys to aspire to escape. But most of all, as the Abyssinian Queen indicated through her performances, they

celebrated acts of escape, hence encouraging others to do the same.
She taught the boys the code every night, until they mastered it. It did
not matter at all if it would ever serve any practical purpose in their
escape. It was enough that it served them spiritually and nourished
their hopes of freedom.

The closer Abednego got to the age when he would have to be
sold, the more frantic the Abyssinian Queen became. Her stories of
escape were filled with more urgency. Songs of escape permeated
the very air that the occupants of Fairfield Farms breathed. The
mother taught the boys to have sharp ears for every sound spoken
of escape. The warbling of the birds in the morning. The croaking
of the frogs in the evening. The chirping of the crickets. The
hymns that the worshippers sang on Sunday. All these spoke the
language of flight.

The boys learned that the biblical chariots that were coming to
carry them home referred to the wagons with secret compartments
that would take them to freedom. In the fields as men and women
toiled they delivered the message about the presence of the Underground Railroad people in the vicinity by singing "Steal Away" or
"Let My People Go," passing the songs from person to person and
from group to group, until the excitement permeated Fairfield
Farms, and those who were ready indeed stole away. Why, even the
rhythms of the blacksmiths talked. The hammer that repeatedly
hit the anvil encoded messages of successful escapes or of the presence of abolitionists—both whites and free blacks—who were
hiding in the gullies, biding their time, waiting to steal slaves away
from their masters across the Ohio River.

The boys' resolve to escape was strengthened by the flogging
they received in the same week for different transgressions. Abednego was caught drumming. A month before, The Owner had decreed that drums and all percussive instruments were prohibited at
Fairfield Farms. He had been told by his spies that wily slaves used
drums to send messages and to broadcast news of escapes. There
were murmurs of disgruntlement in the community, for drums

were essential in church services. Abednego particularly found it difficult to give up his pastime. Although his dream of one day playing the drums in church was now smashed, he woke up some nights when he believed the whole plantation was asleep and practiced on his drum, beating it softly under the sycamore tree outside the cabin. He was caught by an insomniac overseer who, after failing to extract a bribe from the Abyssinian Queen in exchange for his silence, reported the boy to The Owner. Abednego was seriously flogged.

Nicodemus, on the other hand, was punished for learning to read and write, which was a very serious crime for a slave. It turned out that when one of The Owner's daughters came to the storytelling sessions at the slave quarters she struck up a close friendship with Nicodemus. One thing led to another and they ended up teaching each other what they knew best: she teaching him how to read and write, he teaching her how to fashion a reed flute, how to tongue and slur it to produce full-bodied notes, and also how to play the commies—the unglazed earthenware marbles that the white kids bought from the plantation store. She was so excited that she blurted out these activities to everyone at the big house, including her mother. Nicodemus received the whipping of his life.

The Owner was becoming increasingly restless, and there were good reasons for that. Lately untoward things were happening at the plantation. A trusted white servant escaped with her African lover, crossing the Ohio River at Gallipolis and melting into the Underground Railroad, possibly to Canada. The Owner felt that he was losing his grip because it was the second time there had been such a scandal on his plantation—although on the first occasion the escape was foiled and the woman—who had disguised herself as a man to facilitate the escape—was now languishing in the county jail charged with the theft of Mr. Fairfield's property. The property, of course, was the man with whom she was escaping with a view to settling in Ohio where they could live as husband and wife since they had heard that there was no slavery in that state. The man was severely flogged and then chained outside like a dog for weeks on end. The Owner hoped this would serve as an example to all those who planned to take such daring but fool-hardy action. But now here again he was faced with a similar situ-ation, and to add to his frustration the escape had been carried out successfully. Slave chasers with their vicious dogs and trusty steeds had returned empty-handed.

Random escapes had happened at Fairfield Farms before, but this caused a buzz of excitement in the slave community because it involved a white woman. Whites rarely escaped from the planta-tion because they had better privileges than black slaves.

The Owner had devised various ways of keeping white women as slaves. Even though white slavery was thought to have come to an end soon after the Revolutionary War, at Fairfield Farms the practice continued right into the 1840s because white women were essential for the breeding of mulatto children. Gone were the days when The Owner could obtain mulatto children from mating white men with black women. With the large-scale breeding that was happening at the plantation, there were just not enough white men to service the black women. White men were free to seek their fortunes elsewhere. And they did. They worked their way up and bought their own farms and their own slaves. Or sold their la-bor in the cities. Mating white women with black studs was the an-swer. In an age where women were considered inferior to men in any case, and wives were the property of their husbands, it was eas-ier and more cost-effective to hold white women in bondage than to employ white studs.

The Owner got away with keeping white slaves by marrying white women in reduced circumstances to blacks, which enabled him to hold the women legally as slaves. If any curious official asked questions, especially those self-righteous church people who cringed at the very notion of white slavery and condemned it as un-christian, The Owner took refuge in the one-drop rule, claiming that the women were rightly "colored"; concocting some distant non-white ancestry for the wenches. Often he randomly designated some of the women octoroons or quintroons, using manufactured evidence. Their mulatto children were therefore born into slavery.

At Fairfield Farms there were mulattos who had been bred so white it was impossible to tell them apart from the rest of the whites, and they were all slaves. As they were too white to sell easily on the open market, they served The Owner by being overseers and slave catchers.

The breeding of mulatto children who looked mulatto rather than white had become the core business of Fairfield Farms; hence the indispensability of the white female who had to mate with pitch-black studs. On many occasions the boys saw young white women receiving a good whipping for refusing to sleep with black studs. Nicodemus knew that one day he would be one of those studs and would be having a field day among specially selected females of all colors. Abednego, on the other hand, knew that sooner rather than later his head would be on the auction block.

The very thought made the Abyssinian Queen frantic and she intensified her performances. Taking her cue from the Monkey Wrench she packed provisions of extra clothes, dried fruit, ropes and knives for the boys, and had two bundles ready in case they had to take off without warning. Abednego's bundle was wrapped in the crazy quilt and Nicodemus's in the sampler.

But now her stories and songs included celebration, for the plantation grapevine had brought it to her that Nicodemus's father had been manumitted in Kentucky, and had settled across the Ohio River in a community of free blacks on the outskirts of Cincinnati.

"Y'all gonna be free, my boys," she told them. "One day y'all gonna cross the River Jordan to be with Nicodemus's papa."

~ *3* ~

Mediation

The ghost of Nicodemus takes me back to the city of Athens. I am sitting next to Obed, who is driving Ruth's rusty GMC and is enthusing about his famous Native American forebear, Harry Corbett, who distinguished himself in this or that theater of the Civil War. He compares him to the strong and ancient sycamores, hickories and walnuts among which the truck is burping its way. I listen without comment, my squinting eyes fixed on a perfectly round sun floating like a big silver balloon above the black trees that are wading in fog. Its rays cannot penetrate the denseness. I wonder how Obed's eyes are able to see through it since he is driving like a stuntman in a cheap movie chase scene even though only a few feet of the road in front of him are visible. To add to my discomfort the window on his side is half-opened—it is stuck and can't roll up, he explains—and a crisp wind hits against my face. The smell is clean and fresh, but the chill pierces my skull with needles that leave me with a headache.

He is crunching on tortilla chips as he expresses his disappointment that the man's name was Harry Corbett and not Singing Ankle or Coughing Horse or something "Indian" like that. He blames the white man for proselytizing among his forebears until they lost their names that were full of poetry and music so that today he is saddled with an "Indian" ancestor with a name like Harry Corbett. I remember that it was with great pride that Ruth told me when the two of us sat on the porch yesterday afternoon that Harry Corbett was a good Christian man who had done away with "them funny Indian names." I also remember that when I sought assistance from the sciolist on how to deal with the ghosts of the past in rural America, he told me always to bear in mind one thing: *memory thrives on transforming the past to palliate the present.*

It strikes me that as he negotiates the sharp bends on this road to Athens: Obed is desperately negotiating his way along the paths of a foggy past to validate his present. He cannot let go, for the past is all he has. They can't let go; he and his mother. Two sides of the same coin. Even as these thoughts run through my mind I am well aware that I am being judgmental. But I cannot help making these observations even though I have only spent four days with this family because the past is all they ever talk about with joy and pride in their eyes. Ruth told me yesterday as we sipped her homemade root beer: "There's one darn thing they ain't gonna take from us . . . our heritage." Generations of mothers teach their children to be proud of their origins because, and she stressed this: "We're everybody. One day the whole world will look like us."

Perhaps that is why when others were posing as leprechauns, politicians and superheroes, Obed resurrected a ghost from the dramatis personae of his ancestry. And this, unfortunately, landed him in the trouble we are trying to resolve today. He doesn't seem to be worried a bit about it, though, and would rather boast about Harry Corbett than focus on the plan I have been trying to outline for him to avoid a court case that will surely land him in jail. I wish I could wipe the bravado off his face and force him to face his situation, especially because it took me a lot of patience and persuasion to get the victim of his silly actions to agree to meet us today.

Yesterday I phoned the sorority on Washington Street and talked to Beth Eddy for a long time, begging her to withdraw the charges against Obed. It was in the spirit of the day, I pleaded. He had gone to the house with the sole intention of scaring the girls rather than for any sinister motive. It was an innocent prank that went awry.

After consulting with her sorority sisters she finally agreed to meet us, provided members of the Athens County Mediation Council were invited. Even if we were to convince her to withdraw the charges she would not do so without proper mediation, she said, for there should be some form of restitution for the indignity she suffered. She agreed to contact the mediation people when I explained that I could not do so since I am a stranger in these parts. I would not know how to go about arranging such a meeting. Then I had to persuade Obed to come with me this morning. He was not quite convinced, especially because I could not explain exactly what mediation entailed. I have no experience of it. It was only after I told him the chances of Ruth finding out about his arrest were very slim if we tried to resolve the case before it reached the courts of law that he agreed to borrow his mommy's truck under the pretext that we were going to fix my papers—whatever that meant—in Athens.

"Much as I'd like to hear more about Harry Corbett I think we should talk about what you're going to say to the girl," I finally tell him, seizing an opportunity availed by a pause while he stuffs more tortilla chips into his mouth.

"Don't you worry yourself, homeboy," he says. "I'm gonna walk. And you know why I'm gonna walk? 'Cause I ain't done nothing."

"We are not going there to walk, Obed. We are going there to show remorse and to ask for forgiveness."

"I'm damned if I ask for nobody's pardon. It's like saying I'm guilty. You don't know these guys, man, they gonna nail my ass!" he screams.

"We don't want a trial because they're surely going to nail your ass if there's a trial. We are going to beg Beth Eddy to withdraw the case, so you better humble yourself starting now."

He throws a glance at me and smiles cynically, shaking his head as if he pities me for my ignorance. Obviously he has no faith in my strategy. I imagine what he is thinking: what does a stranger from Africa know about the workings of justice in America, which, judging from what he was hollering to the police when they dragged him away that night of the parade of creatures, has always been unfair to his people? He brushes his jet-black hair with his fingers, adjusts the rubber band on his ponytail and then, with the same fingers, reaches for the tortilla chips in a packet next to the gear shift. He shoves them into his mouth and then goes back to fiddling with his mane.

"Harry Corbett was an old Shawnee chief," he says. "This is Shawnee hair."

Shawnee? The Harry Corbett that Ruth told me about yesterday was Cherokee. She was gushing about her being a Cherokee princess since she was a descendant of Cherokee blue blood in the form of the same Mr. Corbett. Her eyes were shining with pride and her ample body was gently rocking Mahlon Quigley's swing on which we were both relaxing. Although I don't know if I can accurately call it relaxing on her part since her hands were quite busy. She was crocheting what she called a Navajo blanket, the bulk of which was resting on her knees in its deep blue, light blue, white and cream colors.

Obed had remarked before he left for Stewart that I had done wonders for his mama because he had never seen her so relaxed. She was always working herself to death and yelling at everybody and didn't have time for anybody. Yet there she was . . . sitting with me on the porch sipping root beer and occasionally forgetting about the heavy blanket to focus on giving me an education about her world and its politics.

From time to time she reached for red pieces of some delicacy from the pocket of her sweat shirt and threw them into her mouth. She closed her eyes as the pieces melted in her mouth. Her teeth were red as a result. She told me she wouldn't share the delicacy with me because I would not like it. It was an acquired taste, I presumed. It was fired shale—she referred to it as red slate rock—that they used to eat as kids and pretended that they were bleeding because their tongues were red. She had been addicted to it from childhood. It was her only vice. It was a habit her people learned from slavery. Slaves ate mud to keep the hunger pangs away. They fired or baked it.

"It's a tradition now of some folks. When I came from Alabama in a bus a woman and her little daughter were chewing on little pieces of baked mud."

Down the narrow blacktop a number of men and women were all walking in the same direction. Big mothers in sweat suits and lean willowy fathers in faded jeans and colorful check shirts. Young men and women who were fast approaching the heaviness of the mothers. They walked unhurriedly, some in couples and others singly.

"This is a neighborhood of color," said Ruth, her arms making a grand sweep in the direction of her passing neighbors. I marveled at the fact that people here all had similar features, as if they belonged to one family.

"They're all related, that's why," she said. "There's very few people who ain't my relations."

"And you all have strong Native American features," I observed.

"Ain't no pure Indians no more. Them pure Indians was all bred out. Like whites will all be bred out. That's what scares them most. They gonna be bred out and everyone in the world will look like us."

The people of Kilvert were going to vote at the firehouse in Stewart, she told me. Democratic Party sympathizers had organized a bus to ferry those who did not have cars to the polling station because they were scraping around for every little vote they could get for John Kerry, their presidential candidate. She herself had voted quite early in the morning, which was why she could now relax with me and enjoy a well-earned drink. It was Election Day and she was not going to desecrate it by working, except of course cooking dinner for her family. Just like Sunday. Although on Sundays she did sneak in some quilting in the afternoons when she thought God was not looking. Even as she was saying all this she continued with her crocheting. Perhaps she does not consider it work.

Unlike her neighbors, who were surely going to vote for the

Democrats, she voted for George W. Bush. And did I know why she voted for George W. Bush? Because George W. Bush was a man of God. He got his messages direct from God. God's truth was revealed only through him. And did I know again why she voted for George W. Bush?

"Because the GOP freed them slaves!" she said with a triumphant flourish.

And none of the people of Kilvert knew that. They had all bought into the lies propagated every day by the liberal media. That was why they were out in droves voting for the Democratic Party candidate. The "old-timers" knew the truth, which was why the Republican Party was the party of "them colored folks." The phrase jolted me a bit because I had only seen it in old books and didn't know that it was still in use . . . like the old-time "high-yella-nigger" that was dropped at the dinner table that first evening. The "old-timers" knew what the Kilvert folks didn't know, that the Democrats fought a whole Civil War in order to keep "them colored folks" as slaves and then committed lots of atrocities during that war. They captured and tortured and slew the revered Harry Corbett to boot. They raped and pillaged and killed indiscriminately. The Civil War hero certainly did not sacrifice his life so that today his descendants should vote for people who were responsible for his murder.

"I tell them every day, if it was not for the GOP you'd all be slaves today," she said, looking at them pityingly as their numbers increased toward the three-way stop where they would catch the bus.

Ruth looked at me as if she expected me to say something, or perhaps ask a question. She saw my befuddled look and decided to ask the question herself: did I know why "them colored folks" turned their backs on the GOP even though it had freed them from slavery?

"Franklin D. Roosevelt!" she provided the instant answer. "He was a cripple in a wheelchair. He gave them poor people programs.

Colored folks got lotsa programs 'cause they was poor. Roosevelt bought them colored folks with food from them Republicans."

She was fuming as if she was talking of some treachery that happened only yesterday against her own children.

Ruth was a lone voice because everyone else in the village, including members of her own family, was on the opposite side. She saw a political virgin in me, someone who could be groomed and won over to the side of sanity. A prospective ally in the political battlefields of her dinner table and living room.

"You being from Africa and all," she said, "you gotta love George W. Bush. He give lotsa money to Africa. You know why he give lotsa money to Africa? 'Cause America owes Africa plenty for slavery."

It was interesting to see how animated she got when she talked about these matters. I was affording her a captive audience, a luxury she never has because no one in her family seems to share her obsession with politics, let alone her political perspective. I was also a receptive audience and did not disagree on any issue as Obed often did—if only to annoy her. Of course, even if I disagreed on any point I would not have the heart to say so. I would not want to hurt her feelings by being a disagreeable guest. She certainly has welcomed me with open arms into her family. Hers is the generosity of the poor. Nowhere in the well-to-do sectors of society would a stranger be welcomed so warmly . . . without even knowing anything about him.

On my second day here she allocated me the root cellar under the wrap-around porch to sleep in—a big room with the door opening to the outside on the brick portion of the building. This is where she keeps her preserved food. My single bed is surrounded by walls of shelves laden with bottles of sauces and relishes that she has made herself. A salted and smoked side of a hog hangs from sharp hooks on the ceiling. She actually prepared the room herself, sweeping and dusting everything in sight, including the carcass. At the same time she kept on apologizing for putting me up in a cellar: it was not the most comfortable room in the world because of its generous ventilation so that her meat would not spoil. People did not normally keep meat in their cellars, she explained—cured or not cured it would spoil because of the heat and humidity. But her cellar was different. It stayed cool because of the gaps between some rows of bricks which allowed free circulation of air. It was all due to Mr. Quigley's inventive mind, she beamed proudly. It was a brilliant feat to have a dry cellar in Kilvert, which is low-lying and wet. Of course in winter no one can sleep here. If the smell of smoke from the meat was too overpowering at night I must not hesitate to tell her in the morning. She would transfer either me or the meat to the attic. She could be preparing the attic for me right away but it would take a lot of work and time since it was crammed with Obed's and Mahlon's junk and there was hardly room to breathe there.

Out of embarrassment that she should be doing all this work for me I offered to help, but she would have none of that. Instead she ordered Obed to take me shopping for clothes at the Kilvert Community Center.

"You gonna scare people in that getup," she said.

I discovered what it meant to "shop for clothes." Men's, women's and children's clothes of all types and styles were displayed on rails and on a number of rickety tables on the porch of the smaller of the two buildings that comprise the Kilvert Community Center. Other garments were in piles on the concrete floor. There were also shoes and handbags and old suitcases and cushions and books—all second-hand items donated by philanthropists for distribution to the poor citizens of Kilvert. People are free to come any time of the day or night to select the clothes they want at no charge. I chose the pair of jeans and the black and red check shirt I am wearing today. Obed suggested I take more and assured me that the stuff was free. Those who know me from way back will remember how impossible it was for me to take alms even at the worst of times. People change. Corrupted by the learning that initially happened as a by-product of a foolish quest to find meaning in my mourning, I have changed too. I have had a brush with the world, and therefore am no longer the simple professional mourner of yesteryear. But there is one aspect of me that has not changed: the guilt that eats me for a long time after partaking of the charity of my fellows. I told him that it was not necessary to take more than I really needed. After all, I still had a set of some of my civilian clothes in my suitcase.

On the porch of the main building I could see seven or so brooding elders in a row of seats lining the wall. Among them was Mahlon Quigley. I wondered what occupied their thoughts as they stared vacantly at the blue sky. I would not be surprised if they were lamenting a disappeared utopia as every generation before them has done and every generation after them will do. It is the way of brooding elders the world over, this longing for the "good ol' days" that never really were.

"You know why they call us WIN people?" asks Obed, bringing me back to the present.

"Oh, is that what you call yourselves?"

"We don't call ourselves that. Other folks do. Know why? 'Cause we got three bloods in all of us, homeboy. We got the White blood and the Indian blood and the Negro blood. Get it? WIN people. My Indian side is Shawnee. That's why I tell you this is Shawnee hair. If you look at them pictures you gonna see Harry Corbett had hair like this."

"But Ruth told me Mr. Corbett was Cherokee," I say.

Suddenly the man is angry.

"She don't know nothing, man. She just wanna screw up things for me."

I am mystified how being Cherokee instead of Shawnee will inconvenience him. In any event there is no difference between Shawnee and Cherokee hair, is there?

"I seen you, man," he says, still angry. "I seen you conversate with my mama. My mama . . . she don't like nobody but you."

What's all this sudden bitterness? Can it be that mama's little big boy is getting jealous? For the rest of the way to Athens he is quiet. Perhaps fuming inside but not showing it outwardly. Mercifully the noisy tortilla chips are finished. Only the burping muffler continues unabated.

The rayless sun now looks like a giant moon in a silver-gray sky.

🐌

The meeting takes place in the tiny office of the Athens County Mediation Council on the third floor of a Court Street building. Beth Eddy sits on a sofa directly facing me and Obed. We are sitting in easy chairs. A coffee table separates our territories. She looks quite different from the slip of a girl in sleepwear that I saw on the night of the parade of creatures. This time she decided to respect the occasion with a black pants suit that has a long jacket, possibly reaching her mid-thigh when she is standing. The blouse is white and maybe silk or some synthetic material that pretends to be silk. Her feet are shod in black closed-toe pumps. This office outfit tells me that she takes her appearance before the mediation council seriously. She is petite, yes, but she looks fearless and confident in her thick spiky brown locks. When we enter the room her clear oval face and big brown eyes return my greetings with a smile. That gives me some hope.

There are two mediators on chairs facing each other: a man and a woman. Both quite mature and gray. Both friendly and informal in their attire of jeans and T-shirts. Each has a number of loose sheets on a clipboard. Occasionally they jot down notes. They smile a lot, even at Obed. Hopefully that will make him feel at ease. He is a bit uncomfortable when he first sees Beth. He becomes even more fidgety when he sees the grinning face of the male mediator. It is before the woman's arrival. I wonder why the man seems to give him the jitters and I pat his back, asking him to relax. He whispers his problem to me when the man goes out to get pop from a vending machine on the first floor: he had a terrible encounter with the man some years back. More than twenty years ago, in fact. The man used to work at Kroger. Obed had previously learned from his father that he—Mahlon, that is—used to steal bottles at the back of the store where they were kept and then sell them at the front. Those were the days when pop came in real bottles, not plastic, and one was paid two cents for every bottle returned to the store. Little Obed, hoping that history would repeat itself and in the process enrich him, gathered bottles from the Dumpster behind the store and attempted to sell them at the front, as his daddy had done before him. It didn't register in his little greedy mind that pop bottlers had long since gone for non-returnable bottles. The man shooed him away. Angry at being denied his God-given right to participate in the capitalist system, Obed dumped a garbage bag full of pop bottles on the floor of the store and dashed away for his life. But he could not outrun the man. Soon he caught up with him. "Yeah, he beat the shit out of me," whispered Obed. "You could beat the crap out of kids back in them days and nobody would say nothing."

Now his fear is that the man will be prejudiced against him. But the man does not seem to remember him. He is all smiles as we all introduce ourselves to one another. After realizing that I really did not have a direct role in the events in question he says that only the parties involved in the dispute should be in the room. I cannot sit in to support Obed since Beth has no one to support her. It would not be true mediation with supporters and advocates in attendance. I am about to leave and wait for Obed outside when Beth tells the mediators that she does not mind my presence. She, in fact, pleads that I stay. I know. It is the result of the talk we had yesterday. She sees me more as her support system than Obed's.

The man explains the mediation process. It is not a trial. Mediators are not judges. They merely serve as neutral and impartial guides to enable the conflicting parties to reach a solution that is acceptable to both parties. Theirs is not to establish guilt or innocence.

Theirs is to help the disputing parties reach some kind of reconciliation. This will not be forced on the parties; the parties themselves must work toward finding an acceptable solution. All decisions reached through this process will be the disputing parties' and not the mediators'. Everything said in this room will remain in this room. We therefore must share our ideas freely and respect confidentiality.

"We all hope that by the end of the process Obed and Beth will reach an agreement," says the man. "But even before we start the process we need to reach our first agreement: we are going to listen to one another, aren't we?"

Both Obed and Beth agree that indeed they are going to listen to each other.

The mediators display great excitement at this, but I suspect they are faking it. The woman says, "You see, it shows that we are capable of agreeing on something."

This gives me hope that Obed will cooperate and forget all ideas of "walking." But I am wrong. After the mediators ask the parties to tell their stories, and when Beth gets to the point where she switches on the light and spots the cowering flesh-and-blood Nicodemus, Obed shouts that it was not him. He was never anywhere near the sorority house that day. In fact, he does not even know where the sorority house in question is located. In any case, he goes on with his rant, how does Beth know it was not the real Nicodemus who fondled her breasts? Where does she get off blaming a poor man just because he is poor and is not white and is not from the university?

Beth is astounded. She starts to weep and the female mediator hands her a box of tissues. I spring to my feet and, begging the mediators' pardon, drag Obed out. In the passageway I tell him how disappointed I am in him: "Do you think you can just piss on all the trouble I took to get this girl to agree to withdraw the case if we have mediation? I tell you, if you continue this way I will not be in your corner anymore and for sure you will find yourself in jail."

We return to the room and Beth is able to complete her story without further interruption. The woman mediator is curious to know why she wants mediation in what should rightly be a criminal case . . . why she doesn't let the police and the courts handle the matter. Beth tells her that she could feel the sincerity in my voice when I begged her to withdraw the case and believed me when I said the young man had no evil intentions. Now that she has heard Obed's denial she will not withdraw the case and doesn't see the point of the mediation. The man suggests that perhaps Beth and I should have a private talk to decide whether the mediation should be salvaged or not. He gives us thirty minutes. The woman is not pleased with these repeated attempts to save Obed's ass, as she delicately puts it. She is obviously disgusted with him and would like to see him rot in the county jail where he rightly belongs. I must admit that I share her disgust, though I think I must not give up on him just yet. Otherwise what am I going to tell Ruth?

I suggest to Beth that we go to a coffee house downstairs and see if we can sort this matter out, without Obed. I ask him to wait in the hallway and not dare go anywhere until we come back.

Over steaming mocha I once more plead with her to withdraw the case and continue with the mediation. She admits that she is more inclined to withdraw the charges because she hates the adverse publicity that will surely follow court appearances. However she will definitely brave the publicity if Obed refuses to show remorse. Already she is taking a lot of flak from some of her sisters for even considering withdrawing the charges. If the breast fondler gets off free, they argue, that will help perpetuate sexual assaults on women, which have increased in the city lately.

I feel very sorry for Beth Eddy. She looks fragile and all the confidence I'd seen earlier has disappeared. She confesses that she feels partly responsible for what happened. She went down to the basement to provoke the ghost. I can see her anguish and this makes me mad at Obed. I am no longer interested in persuading her to withdraw the case, and I tell her so. She must not be scared of publicity,

I now argue, because she is the victim here. The press will be sympathetic to her and will expose Obed for the scoundrel he is. Yes, Ruth will find out about it and will be unhappy with me for not letting her know in the first place. But really Obed does need to learn a lesson. I am sick of his attitude: his lack of appreciation for the trouble I took to set this up and for Beth's readiness to forgive.

It is Beth's turn to talk me out of the case. There was a rape in Athens a few weeks ago, she tells me. It was in the papers every day and the case dragged on and on, with lawyers questioning the reputation of the victim. She doesn't want to go through that. She fears that her reputation will be tainted by the revelation that the girls enjoy playing naughty games with the real Nicodemus. Lawyers always manage to dig up such scandals. She can do without the publicity. After all, she was not actually raped. The scoundrel merely touched her breasts in the manner that Nicodemus had touched them before . . . to her pleasure. Yes, the mediation should continue.

"Okay, but if that boy continues with his silly stunts I'll insist that you do not withdraw the charges," I tell Beth. And I mean it. "I think it's high time our breast fondler learned a lesson."

After this the mediation continues without further incident. I notice that the mediators listen very attentively. After each side has given its story they summarize the key points, all the while complimenting both parties for trying to work out their differences. Obed's story is a very simple one. Yes, indeed, he went to the sorority in the spirit of the day. He had heard of the ghost of Nicodemus, who had died at the sorority house more than a hundred and fifty years ago, when it was one of the stations of the Underground Railroad. He decided to appropriate Nicodemus's identity because there were rumours circulating that he haunted the sorority house and the girls enjoyed his company. He thought he would share in the ghost's good fortune because in any event Nicodemus was his relative who was mercilessly murdered by slave catchers. He really did not have any intention of committing a crime. All he wanted was to scare the girls, and then proceed to the Court Street parades to enjoy the evening.

After Beth Eddy has expressed her own feelings about the incident—how she felt soiled and violated by it and how she thought her life was in danger—the mediators ask the parties what they think the solution should be. To my surprise Obed expresses his remorse and asks to be forgiven for his foolish and thoughtless behavior. He vows that never again will he play such dirty tricks on anyone as long as he lives, and he is willing to put that in writing, provided Beth puts it in writing that she will withdraw all the charges she has laid against him at the police station. Beth is ready to forgive him unconditionally when I butt in. Surely the young man must not get off so lightly. I remind Beth: "When I spoke with you yesterday you said there should be some restitution before you withdraw the case."

"He has shown remorse," says Beth.

"Obed and I think that is not enough," I insist, looking at Obed for confirmation. "We think there should be some kind of restitution."

"We don't think no such thing," says an indignant Obed.

"Oh, yes, we do!" I stand my ground.

"Hey, you ain't even supposed to be here," he screams at me.

"Perhaps he can paint your sorority house," I suggest. "Why don't you discuss it with your sisters? I'll help him if he needs an assistant."

The woman mediator does not think it's a good idea to let Obed loose anywhere near the sorority house. Who will guarantee the girls' safety?

Once again Beth surprises me.

"I think it is a good idea," she says. "I'll call you after talking with my housemates."

The mediators incorporate that in the agreement and both parties sign. The mediators are happy. Especially the man. The mediation has been a great success. We all shake hands. Beth and the female mediator are the first to leave while the man asks me about my origins and what I think of their beautiful city and the fine weather that was quite foggy in the morning. As we walk out of the office Obed glares at me and mutters: "I thought you was my friend, man. I thought you was my freakin' friend."

"I think I *am* your freaking friend, Obed," I say, chuckling to myself.

The man stands at the door and calls after Obed: "Hope you've learned your lesson, Mr. Quigley."

"I sure have. No more playing with them girls' breasts."

"And no more dumping bottles at Kroger," says the man, wagging his finger at him.

Obed is slightly taken aback. He didn't think the man had recognized him. He didn't imagine he remembered after all these years.

"Come on, man," he says. "I was only a kid."

Out on Court Street it is after midday and the sun has become the sun again. Yet its rays do not reflect any joy on the people's faces. Men and women are walking in a daze, shoulders drooping and faces crestfallen. Their gait is that of mourners. Ohio has once again given America to George W. Bush and Athens's world has come crashing down. Athens, the only county in the state to give John Kerry a landslide vote. And now, on this beautiful November 3, Kerry has conceded defeat and gloom has fallen on the Athenians' lives. Ruth must be celebrating back in Kilvert.

Crowds have gathered on the steps of the courthouse, spilling to the sidewalks. Some are milling across the street in front of the bank. There are those who cannot contain their emotions and are weeping openly, while others are resorting to group hugs as some form of consolation.

It beats me how a rally has been organized so fast. The elections were only yesterday. The Democratic Party candidate conceded only a few hours ago. Yet here we have multitudes gathered and equipped so well for the mourning of their hero's defeat. This has turned into an anti-war demonstration judging from the slogans on the posters and banners, none of which even mention Kerry's name. Some read in red: *Vengeance Is Not Justice*; while others are printed in bold black: *A Call for Humane Treatment of All Detainees*. I can see the group of young women I first spotted at the parade of creatures, the Billionaires for Bush. They are the only people who are all dressed up in fur coats and extravagant-looking—but obviously fake—jewelery. They are not chanting slogans as they did at the parade, but are quietly listening to a speaker who is leaning against the pillar on the topmost step making a speech. Only the banner they are holding above their heads speaks for them: *How did our oil get under their sand?*

One agitated person after another climbs the podium, grabs the megaphone and makes a speech. They all berate Bush in measured tones and pained voices. It is like we are on the set of a tragic play, which is completed by a big backdrop with photographs of American soldiers who perished in the war and bold black letters that read: *1,110 Soldiers Dead, 8,030 Wounded, 100,000 Civilian Iraqis Dead—Support Our Troops, Bring Them Back Home*.

As we walk away to the city parking garage behind the bank I can hear the demonstrators sing Holly Near's "We Are a Gentle Angry People" in sad and subdued voices.

🐾

If I thought I would find Ruth celebrating I was deluding myself. She has taken Mr. Bush's victory in her stride, in a matter-of-fact manner, for she knew all along that he would win. God told her so right from the beginning, even as she was casting her vote.

So, today she is spring-cleaning. That is what she calls it, even though it is not spring but fall. She does it once every few weeks, especially in fall when homes are invaded by Asian lady beetles—so called because they were first imported to these parts from China to eat aphids that destroyed trees and other agricultural crops. Now the tan little buggers with faint black spots have become a nuisance at this time of the year. A silent menace that leaves the feeding sites with the end of summer and swarms into buildings to hibernate for the winter.

They multiply at alarming rates annually because they have no natural enemies in these parts, except for Ruth and her fellow humans who are not keen to share their abodes with the pests. She seeks them out in crevices and cracks around window and door frames with a broom and sweeps them on to an old copy of the *Athens News*. After covering them with the newspaper she stamps on them with her heavy feet shod in worn-out sneakers. They emit an acrid odor and stain the paper with a yellowish secretion.

"I wouldn't be killing them that way if I was you, Mama," says Obed.

"You ain't me, so shush and get working on the spring cleaning," she says and continues to search for the enemy. She is leaning on the cane with the left hand as the right hand operates the broom, reaching for the remotest nooks in the furniture.

"They always think they are smarter than God," she complains to no one in particular as she discovers more lady bugs hiding behind the portrait of Jesus the Shepherd on the wall. "Them crazy scientist people, I mean. They brought them bugs to our good ol' U. S. of A. 'cause they think God didn't know what he was doing when he created them in China."

"Better spray them with House Defense Insect Killer, Mama," says Obed, watching his mother with amusement, his hands in his pockets. "That way they won't stink to heaven."

"If the spray killed them dead the last time I used it why do I still see them here?"

"You didn't spray the insect killer before the first freeze, Mama, that's why. You gotta do it before the first freeze for it to work."

Ruth turns to me and says that all Obed can do is give orders on how things should be done. That's what he knows best. He never does anything with his own hands. He always finds the slightest excuse to shirk work. He thinks things will just fall into his lap. Like manna from heaven. He has no ambition. Just like his sister, Orpah, has no ambition. She was brilliant at school, but had no interest in furthering her education even when her classmates from the high school in Stewart went to Hocking College and at least one to the university in Athens. She had the potential to be the first university graduate in the family. Ruth nagged her no end about her lack of ambition but Mr. Quigley said she must be left alone. Mr. Quigley has always been soft with the children. Only God knows what she has done to be cursed with lazy children like this.

From the first day I landed in this country I have admired the American work ethic. Americans take pride in their work. To them service is not servitude. And they don't "class" work. I think that's how they got to where they are today. I wonder why Obed is so different. And Orpah. If, of course, their mother is right about them. And so far there is nothing that has shown me she could be wrong. At their age, both of them are still living with their parents. And neither of them seems to be engaged in any gainful employment.

"And to think after Orpah I prayed to the Lord to give me a boy," she says. "I want a boy, Lord, I said; give us a cion who'll carry our name to the future. Now see what I got?"

"You can't complain, Mama," says Obed. "I'm trying to find myself but you don't let me." He turns to me to explain himself and perhaps solicit my support: "My mama, she thinks I don't do nothing. But every time I do something she say it's a rotten scheme."

"He's tall like a poplar, but he's useless. And with such pretty hair too," says Ruth. She obviously loves her boy despite his shortcomings. She reaches for Obed's head and runs her fingers through his hair. Obed pulls away and moans: "Don't do that, Mama. You know I hate it when you do that."

"Poplars are pretty and tall," says Ruth. "They got flowers but raise no fruit. Just like this boy, they don't raise nothing to eat."

To his embarrassment Ruth does not stop there. She cared for this boy even when he was in her womb. She went out of her way to eat healthily even when things were difficult and there was no food to go around, which is why the boy is so beautiful and strong. Obed feels he must disagree on something if only to spite the woman. He says boastfully: "It has nothing to do with that, Mama. It's because I take after Harry Corbett; that's the only reason I'm big and strong."

"You seen how the children look here? They walk funny with rickets on their knees. Like your Aunt Madge's kids. They talk funny too. It's because their mama didn't have much to eat when she was pregnant."

But, as I can well see, her Obed is not like that. And do I know why her Obed is not like that? It's because she took care of her Obed. Not that the boy was strong and healthy all his life. There was a period when he was a sickly child. But she always managed to nurse him back to health. She remembers when she used to wrap camphor in a piece of cloth which she then tied with a safety pin on the baby's shirt. Obed breathed in the camphor to ward off colds and the deadly spirits of Kilvert. That's how he survived vicious winters. Through camphor.

I follow Ruth to the living room where she continues her relentless war on the bugs. Obed decides he has had enough of her nagging and saunters away. I help her move the chairs and the car seats and the metal table with the sewing machine on it. With a feather duster I dislodge those bugs that thought they had found a safe haven in the cracks between the ceiling and the walls. They would be flying away if it were not so cold. Instead they fall on the floor, she sweeps them on to the newspaper and we both stamp on them. She has a firm grip on my shoulder for support since her cane is on the floor. We stamp with a vengeance, continuing our dance long after the creatures have been pulverized. We find this quite funny and we break into peals of silly laughter.

Orpah appears at the door, hesitates, then walks into the room, all the while glaring at Ruth. She has been crying. Her eyes are red.

She is still sniveling, in fact. In all the four days I have been here it is the first time I am able to take a good look at her. On two occasions, I think, I saw glimpses of her: once through the window as her plaited head fleeted by and again when I saw her disappear into the bathroom and she stayed there for a long time. I don't know when she finally came out because Ruth called me to her bedroom to help her with her old quilt box, which she wanted moved to her living room workstation, and to tell me how she had inherited the wonderful chest from her grandmother who had in turn inherited it from her great-grandmother before the Civil War. I have heard her sitar a lot though, and every time it creates in me those strange feelings of nostalgia that I have already told you about.

And here she is, giving me an angry once-over. She must be in her early forties. She has a well-nourished olive skin. I wonder what mysteries are preserved in that teary moonface. She is slightly overweight, with a great potential for obesity—which surprises me quite a bit because she has skipped the three dinners I have eaten with this family. She certainly doesn't look like someone who will "blow away" any time soon. She is barefoot in her tight blue jeans and white top that hangs loosely on her ample breasts. On her neck hangs a yellow, green and orange gewgaw. On her wrists she wears bangles of gleaming ormolu.

"Orpah, you haven't met the man from Africa," says Ruth by way of introduction.

I take a step toward her with my arm stretched out and I say: "My name is Toloki, miss. It is my pleasure to meet you. I am a fan of your beautiful music."

She recoils, moving backward toward the door, ignoring my hand. She actually pulls her hand away when I try to reach for it. It seems she finds me repulsive and wants to avoid me at all costs. I am wondering what could be the reason for such resentment as she reverses out of the room.

"Don't you worry your pretty little head about our Orpah," says Ruth. "She's got issues. And no one can do nothing about that."

Through the window I can see Orpah out there on the swing. She has her head on Mahlon Quigley's shoulder and is weeping uncontrollably. Mahlon is staring into nothingness and is caressing her arm to the rhythm of the slow-swaying swing.

✍

As usual Orpah is not at the dinner table. And I have not heard her music today. Somehow I miss it. The silence leaves a hole in me. Don't ask me why. I am sitting with Ruth, Obed and Mahlon Quigley, yet all of a sudden I feel lonely, as if someone very important in my life has suddenly taken leave of me.

Today's speciality is hot dogs with carrot and cilantro relish. The carrots and the cilantro are from Ruth's backyard garden. She leaves the carrots in the garden, waiting for the ground to get cold, because the colder the ground the sweeter the carrot. In the morning when we were leaving for Athens I saw her digging them out and now she has made the sweetest of relishes from them. The cilantro, on the other hand, went to seed in the summer and she says she picked it quite early in the fall in order to keep it fresh. She laments that she had to buy tomatoes because she no longer has them in her garden. It is against her principles to buy tomatoes or any kind of vegetable because her people have always raised their own food. Did I know that her people—"them Indian people," that is—gave the world tomatoes? And corn? And potatoes? I congratulate her on it, and she turns to Obed and orders: "Take some hot dogs to your sister."

"It won't help, Ma," says Obed gleefully, as he takes two buns and puts hot dogs in each of them. "Maybe you should tell her you're sorry."

"I ain't sorry for nothing," says Ruth adamantly.

Obed takes the hot dogs, ketchup, mustard and relish to Orpah's room. I don't know why today Ruth is concerned that Orpah should eat. Usually when she has not turned up for dinner she only exclaims that "the girl will blow away" and then we continue with our meal as if nothing has happened. For some reason today she sends Obed to take her food to her room, as if it is some peace offering.

Ruth wants to hear about my day in Athens. Did I manage to fix my papers? I avoid answering that particular question because I don't want to lie to her. As it is I am burdened enough already trying to keep Obed's secret from her—both his misadventure at the sorority house and the mediation. I find the load too heavy to bear and I am unhappy with myself for promising him, after he begged me again and again on our way back from the mediation, that I would keep the secret.

Instead I tell her about the sad demonstration we saw on Court Street.

"Uh-uh, now you gonna get her started, man," says Obed, dreading another one of his mother's political lectures.

But there is no stopping Ruth when she is provoked into analyzing the ills of politicians. She believes that you cannot totally trust politicians because politicians crucified Jesus Christ. George W. Bush is an exception. He talks to God. And God talks to him. Very much like the prophets of the Old Testament.

As for Kerry, God would never have allowed him to ruin America because America is a chosen nation. Did we know that Kerry asked the United Nations to rule America? She heard him with her own ears saying so on television.

"How can he ask other nations to rule America when America is a super-nation?" she asks in dismay.

There is no end to Kerry's wickedness. He supports abortion, which is against the laws of God. He supports marriage between man and man; and between woman and woman. Again, she heard Kerry with her own ears saying this. When Obed argues that Kerry never said such a thing but has insisted that issues pertaining to marriage should be addressed by the states rather than through a constitutional amendment, and that Kerry himself believes in

marriage between man and woman, Ruth dismisses him as an ignoramus who never watches the news. It will be a disaster if anyone
changes God's laws of marriage. Some men—and they are already
doing it here in Kilvert—will have harems of women, make them
all pregnant and collect welfare. The taxpayer will be paying for all
this, all because of the likes of Kerry.

She pages through the Bible, which she keeps handy on a side-
board next to the dining room table. She reads from Leviticus
18:22: *You shall not lie with a man as with a woman.* And to corrob-
orate that point she goes to a letter that the Apostle Paul wrote to
the Romans 1:26–27: *For this reason God gave them up to vile pas-
sions. For even their women exchanged the natural use for what is
against nature. Likewise also men, leaving the natural use of the
woman, burned in their lust for one another, men with men committing what is shameful, and receiving in themselves the penalty of their
error which was due.* She is about to read from another letter that
the same Paul wrote to the Corinthians I 6:9–10, but Obed has had
enough. He declares that Paul was obsessed with homosexuality.
He must have been a closet homosexual as is the case with many
homophobes. Ruth is scandalized by this blasphemy, especially because it is uttered in the presence of a visitor. Obed needs to pray to
save his soul from eternal damnation.

She feels very sorry for me after I make the mistake of telling
her that in South Africa gay rights are no longer an issue since they
are protected by the constitution. In that country the courts have
pronounced that the common law stipulation that marriage is between man and woman is unconstitutional, and have given the
government two years for parliament to amend the law to allow for
gay marriages.

"Todoloo! Your country is Sodom and Gomorrah," she pro-
claims. "I'm glad you came to the good ol' U. S. of A. to escape the
death and pestilence that the Lord is surely gonna visit on Africa."

"On South Africa, to be exact," I correct her, hoping that nar-
rowing God's wrath to only one country will comfort her a bit.

"The rest of Africa doesn't have such laws. I think the rest of Africa would rather agree with you."

But Ruth hasn't finished with John Kerry yet. He is a traitor, she says. He even speaks French, a fact he tried to hide but that was exposed by the vigilant Fox News. He is so wishy-washy he is likely to be a drinker of French wine and an eater of French toast when all good people the world over are boycotting everything French. Didn't we all see him on television? He looked ridiculous creeping around in the wilderness shooting geese in order to prove that he was not a liberal.

She breaks out laughing at the strange image of a camouflaged and gun-toting Mr. Kerry bumbling in the woods, which obviously is still quite vivid in her mind. I can see what Ruth is talking about. The man tried to play to a jingoistic gallery but it did not applaud. It knew he was a fake. He only wanted to win their favor and as soon as he got it he would surely lead the country down a ruinous path of personal freedoms.

No one interrupts Ruth when she is on her political platform, except an occasional snide remark from Obed, who obviously does not share his mama's politics but would rather not prolong the agony of sitting through another harangue by debating with her. Mahlon Quigley, on the other hand, just sits there and smiles. I have caught Ruth stealing a glance at him and breaking into a soft smile of her own, even in the middle of her fulminations against Kerry. He returns a sly look and the smile on his lips creeps to his eyes. It is obvious to me that the two are still very much in love.

At first I found Mahlon Quigley's silence unnerving. I am getting used to it now although I still find it uncomfortable that no one attempts to draw him into any conversation. I wonder what thoughts are brewing in his head. What memories. Ruth told me the other day that there are things her Mr. Quigley remembers and there are things he has chosen to forget. One of the things he has tried to forget but that stubbornly continues to haunt his memory is the fact that his mother was unjustly confined to the mental hospital at The

Ridges and no one in the family saw her again. She is one of the
numbers on the headstones in the cemetery. Could that smile be
hiding a quietly seething anger? Of course this is mere speculation
on my part. Perhaps I am desperately searching for a motive for his
aloofness. Those unsmiling but soft and compassionate eyes do not
seem to be capable of any anger.

"It must be fun spending some time at the Center with your
mates, Mr. Quigley, talking about the good old days," I say, trying
my best to draw him out of his private world into the communion
of his family.

"As you can see," he says without looking at me, "I'm old and
decrepit. That's a crime in this country."

Ruth jumps to his defense: "Mr. Quigley is just feeling sorry for
himself. He ain't old at all." And she smiles reassuringly at him.

The phone rings and Obed reaches for it. It is for me.

"You getting calls already?" Ruth wonders.

It is Beth Eddy. She withdrew the complaint, but with great
difficulty. The police were at first adamant that they would not go
along with her messing up an open-and-shut case that they had
built against the perpetrator. They said they were still going to
charge Obed with breaking and entering. She had to claim that she
was drunk and didn't quite remember what exactly happened: she
must have opened for him, so he didn't break into the building. I
am amazed that she should go so far as to lie to the police to protect
Obed. When it became clear to the police that she, the only witness
to Obed's crime, would not be a reliable witness they reluctantly
withdrew the case.

It was more difficult to convince her sisters at the sorority because they were making a very good point. We live in a society with
high rates of violence against women. Rapists are lurking in every
corner and a new sexual assault is reported at least every month.
Many incidents of sexual abuse and rape go unreported because of
the intimate nature of the crime. It is part of the program of
women's organizations in Athens to encourage victims to come

forward. After a long debate the sisters agreed to give Obed a chance. Again I am surprised that she went out of her way to give such a spirited defense of the scoundrel. But I keep that observation to myself.

She is the sorority's judicial board head and sisterhood co-chair, she adds, and was therefore well placed to convince them to let Obed paint the building, which does need a coat or two.

"So, your friend can paint the house if he wants to," she says.

"Not if he wants to, Beth. He has to, whether he likes it or not."

As soon as I return to the table Obed asks anxiously: "What's up, man?"

"Don't worry, everything is fine," I assure him.

"What have you two been up to?" Ruth wants to know.

"Never mind, Mama, it's man's talk," says Obed. He is obviously gloating over the fact that there is something that is only between us men, to which his mother is not privy. He displays a self-satisfied grin. But Ruth is not impressed.

"You know how to work magic, man," says an excited Obed. "I wanna be a professional mourner like you one day."

He may be joking, but this is not the first time he has indicated that he is attracted to my vocation and to my austere ways. He has told me that I was chosen and placed on his path that night of the parade of creatures by the spirits of his ancestors . . . which, of course, is ridiculous. It was when he was happy with me. He regrets why he ever brought me here when he thinks I side with Ruth against him. Which I never do. I only tell the truth the way I see it, and most times it is against him because he is in the wrong.

"That's a silly ambition, boy," says Ruth, and then in a lowered voice she asks: "How's Orpah? Did she eat?"

"You want me to say she's fine, Mama, don't you? So she's fine."

"She'll get over it soon enough," says Ruth, as if to convince herself.

She must have done something to Orpah, but I am afraid to ask what. I do not want to seem to be prying into the family's affairs, though I must admit I am intrigued by this Orpah. I have gathered already that she enjoys indulging herself in solitude. She imposes it on herself for she identifies closely with the tales of female confinement of classic Gothic narratives that she devours relentlessly when she is not playing the sitar or drawing quilt designs that never get translated into quilts. She is not exactly the "mad woman of the attic" though. She is very brilliant and her hands know how to create beautiful things. She sees herself as a tortured soul that will one day be released by the return of a stranger mentioned in some Native American tales.

"Maybe it's because of the mark of the Irishman," said Obed the other day, in a vain attempt to make sense of Orpah's behavior. Ruth shushed him immediately. Whatever this mark of the Irishman is, it is not something that should be mentioned in the company of strangers. Certainly there is a lot of secretiveness about it.

Ruth, on the other hand, curses the sitar. Before the sitar the "girl" was outgoing, even though she still made her "fancy drawings" and read her "ghost stories." She taught herself the instrument and started playing bluegrass on it. At first to everyone's annoyance. But ultimately they all learned to live with it. Ruth remembers the first day she came with the sitar.

"I got it from an Indian family that runs the motel," Orpah said.

"Real Indians from India," Obed interjected.

"Which motel?" Ruth asked. "All motels are run by Indians."

"Does it matter which motel?" asked Orpah.

"It does. I want you to take it back. What was you doing in a motel anyways?"

She was not in a motel for any hanky-panky though. She was caught in a flood and couldn't come back home for three days and everyone was worried. She had to find a cheap motel and sleep there. Ruth had assumed she stayed with friends all that time because when she phoned she had not specified that she was staying at a motel. But anyway, Orpah was worried to death staying at that motel and the floods continued as if they were fulfilling some biblical prophecy.

She was driving Ruth's GMC and made an attempt to take the gravel New England Road just after Guysville, which is the alternative route when there is a flood. But it was flooded too. She did not even try the road via Amesville for it is always the first to be flooded. So, she was marooned in Athens. She cried most of that time, and an Indian girl, the daughter of the motel owner, played her the sitar. She thought it was the most beautiful instrument ever, and begged and cajoled, until the girl sold it to her on credit. Her father could bring her another one since he would be going to India soon.

That was the beginning of her life as a loner. She gave up her daytime soap operas to spend time with her sitar. She gave up *Oprah* in the afternoons. She does not even come out in the evenings when everyone watches prime time sitcoms and reality shows or in the night when Obed spends his time flipping channels and giggling between Jay Leno and David Letterman—incidentally his main source of news about the world.

Orpah hasn't come out this evening as we sit in front of the television watching a beautiful war lighting up the screen, depicted like a series of video games. Live night bombings hitting the targets with startling fire in the black background of the night. Targets hit as they sleep. Obed and Ruth cheering. It is fine, for no one sees any death. There is no human element. Just the sound effects and the flare of the fireworks. Mahlon Quigley dozing off. Smiling still. Embedded journalists emerging in their neat camouflage jackets, analyzing every move in the game, and condemning surreptitious attacks on the homeland forces by the enemy as cowardice. If they were man enough they would come out and face our firepower, and not attack us when we are not looking. Big titles on the screen: *Operation Thunderbolt!* Just like in the movies. Just like in the superhero comic books. Court Street parade superheroes. Kapow! Boom! There are the good guys and the bad guys. The bad guys are ugly and evil and envious. The good guys are beautiful and altruistic and have God on their side. The good guys are sure to triumph. Just like in the movies. Only here real people die.

Mothers and their children. Young beautiful soldiers who are only children themselves. Although we never see them. We shall never see them. We are therefore able to sleep in peace at night and dream beautiful dreams.

Bombs rain some more and light the sky. Ruth and Obed cheer. Mahlon smiles. Still no one dies. Only the depersonalized collateral damage. Superheroes rise unscathed from the rubble and fly to the sky to save the world elsewhere.

Bombs plough the lands of ancient civilizations cultivating new crops of terrorists. Again and again we cheer.

A knock at the door interrupts our beautiful war. It is Nathan and he has brought Ruth coupons from a fast food restaurant in Athens. When I first saw him in that big truck he was an imposing figure. Perhaps it is just the memory of his booming voice. He is a tiny man with the features and the hairstyle of the Jesus on the wall. He is developing a roundish paunch though, and it is beginning to strain the buttons of his shirt. Unlike Obed, he does not seem to pay much attention to his appearance. I am not sure if Nathan is one of the WIN people or not. He looks Caucasian—although Ruth did tell me that her people come in all colors.

Ruth spreads the coupons on her lap, and Nathan points at the choice dishes with his dirty fingernails. There are special offers for fish and shrimps and other seafood delicacies, all pictured in mouthwatering color. Ruth and Nathan admire the pictures and he says he knows that fish is Ruth's favorite food and when he saw these special offers the first person he thought of was her. She thanks him and says that indeed next time she visits Athens she will go to the fast food place, provided the offers have not expired.

"I know you wanna see Orpah," says Ruth with a naughty twinkle in her eye.

Yes, he does want to see Orpah because he wants to invite her to a concert in Nelsonville. After calling her name twice without any response, Ruth sends Obed to call her, and then introduces me as the man from Africa. Nathan tells her that we met before and wonders how I like it so far in Kilvert. I tell him how beautiful it is and how hospitable Ruth and her family have been.

"Yeah," he says, "our people are like that. It don't matter that we are poor."

"Todoloo," says Ruth, tapping her forehead. "Today they call it poverty; back in them days we called it our way of life. We didn't know we was poor until they came and told us we was poor."

Outsiders instilled it in the minds of her people that they were poor and gave them food and clothes. That changed their way of looking at the world. Now they cannot do without the charity of strangers.

Nathan explains, for my benefit, that despite Ruth's misgivings about the dependency mentality that has been created among her people by well-meaning donors, poverty is a fact of life in southeast Ohio, not just in Kilvert. Even the CBS television program *60 Minutes* featured a whole segment on the subject. People were shocked to see on their screens Americans waiting in food lines, and to hear of the increasing numbers that now have to depend on food banks and pantries for their meals; of retired veterans and workers going hungry because they have lost their jobs to plant closings; of children forced to rely entirely on the school lunch program for daily meals; of families going to bed without supper. And this situation continues year after year. It is more than a year since the program was aired. Yet nothing has changed. People are still hungry.

"Oh, yeah, them kids are hungry," says Ruth, "but their parents don't have no trouble buying beer and cigarettes and lottery tickets."

Appalachian poverty is news to me. You do not see it from the landscape: from the hills and the forests and the valleys and the creeks and the fields whose beauty inspires awe and effectively hides the suffering that Nathan is outlining for me to Ruth's consternation.

"We always raised our own food," she insists. "It was our way of life. Things only got bad when we stopped raising our own food . . . when they brought free food from them food banks."

Obed returns without Orpah.

"What took you so long?" asks Ruth.

"Orpah . . . she won't come. She won't see nobody 'cause mama messed her stuff bad."

Ruth is furious. There must be something terribly wrong with that girl. Where does she get off treating a gentleman such as Nathan like this? The very Nathan with whom she went to school at Amesville. The Nathan who was her after-school playmate. The Nathan with whom she used to ice skate on the Federal Creek and on the pool next to the river when it was frozen in winter. Most importantly, the Nathan who has a regular job, unlike some people she knows—and she looks at Obed. Orpah missed her chance to marry the man the first time he asked her. She turned him down until he married someone else. Unfortunately that someone else died, leaving him with two lovely kids. Orpah should be grateful that the man once again is showing some interest in her. Nathan is a good man and Orpah will surely die an old maid. She is already an old maid as it is.

Of course this diatribe embarrasses Nathan. He keeps on assuring Ruth that it is okay; Orpah will come around one of these days. He is a patient man. He will wait.

Ruth is too cross to enjoy the war on television. She takes her cane and waddles to her room.

As if on cue Orpah strums her sitar. The sound cuts through my insides and reverberates on the timber walls.

"She is a very sad woman," says Nathan sadly.

He takes leave of us and Obed offers to walk him to his truck.

Before I saw Orpah in person her sitar caused a feeling of nostalgia in me. Now that I am able to associate the sound with the person it no longer does. Instead it arouses me. It arouses me so terribly that I think my veins are going to burst. My heart is pumping blood in such a crazy rhythm that I have to walk away from here. I have got to be as far away from Orpah's sitar as possible. As I walk out in agony I can see the wicked glint in the sciolist's eye. Whatever did I

do to him to be punished like this? Does he perhaps resent the independence and the freedom to determine the course of my life that I
seem to have gained since joining these wonderful people? Is he
taking vengeance on me for having lost myself in the lives of the
living and momentarily forgetting my mission in life: to mourn the
dead and to search for ways of mourning?

Obed and Nathan are standing next to the truck gossiping.
They cannot see me as I attempt to flee from my own erection. I
can hear Obed boasting: "I told you I was gonna walk, man."

"So you did?"

"Do I look like I'm in the clink now? I nailed the bitch, man. I
nailed her ass good."

The scoundrel!

I stop under a gigantic sycamore near the road to the churchyard.
Here I cannot hear the sitar and hopefully there will be some relief.
I can see why they call this a ghost tree. Its trunk and branches are
shimmering in the thin light of the stars and the diminishing last-
quarter moon as if they have been splashed with fluorescent white
paint. As soon as the trunk leaves the ground it opens into a gaping
grotto, with dried-up veins and arteries running amok in it. I can
see something whitish in the grotto. I retrieve it. Even in the faint
light I can see that these are some of the most wonderful drawings I
have seen in my life. They are designs of sorts and at the bottom of
each one the artist has signed: *Orpah Q* and then a date. All of them
were created late last month, except two that are dated the second
and the third day of November. Today. One of these wonderful creations was painted on this very day.

The ghost tree. It is a keeper of secrets. It has many stories to tell.

4

*T*he story is told by ghost trees; that's why most of it does not
unfold before your eyes but is reported in the manner of fire-
side or bedtime storytelling. The ghost trees: the one in front of the
Abyssinian Queen's cabin with its wide span of white branches and
others that witnessed the whole journey of her two boys, right up
to the demise of Nicodemus and the exile of Abednego in Tabler
Town. People remember fondly that she, the queen of stories, used
to flap her wings while perching on the highest branch almost one
hundred and twenty feet above the ground. But the tree was more
than just a place for launching her swooping tales. Its white bark,
mottled with green and brown, provided her with enchanting
characters when the moon shone on the trunk like a spotlight,
shaping out figures in deep contrasts of dark and light. She spoke
with these characters and made them do things that none of the audience ever imagined a bark could do. She made them speak words
never heard from any tree on earth. Although the tree was at its
best at night, during the day it kept itself useful still. Its hollow
trunk served as Nicodemus's hiding place when he wanted to be
alone and practice his writing or play his reed flute. Everybody
pretended that the ghost tree produced the music. Yet they all
knew it was Nicodemus inside the tree. It made them feel good to
play along and call it a singing sycamore.

The singing sycamore was haunted. Not because it was a ghost
tree but for the well-known fact that it harbored in its soul the
spirits of little children who once sat under it listening to stories
and telling their own eons before the world was killed. These were
spirits waiting to be reunited with all the children from the tribes

of the universe on a regenerated earth that would be free of sickness and death; an earth where man, woman and child would roam free, owned by no one. When the trills from Nicodemus's flute became multiplied as if many flutes were playing, people knew that the voices of the little children had merged with the slurs and staccatos of his flute. So, the singing sycamore was a singing sycamore after all.

This hollowed sycamore hid another important secret in its heart. Provisions for the road. Dried fruit. Knives. Ropes. Tinder. Lots of tinder. Flint. Pairs of old socks. Rags. Odds and ends of tools and mementos. Just as the Monkey Wrench design cautioned. And all these were wrapped in two bundles of quilts. One a crazy quilt and the other a sampler. Tied securely with ropes. Waiting for the day when the boys would up and go. No one knew when that day would be. It would not be during that winter though; the Abyssinian Queen was certain of that. She had drummed it into the boys' heads that winter escapes were hard. The boys would therefore be prudent enough to wait for the next round of slave stealers and Underground Railroad conductors who would come in spring or summer transmitting secret messages through spirituals and merging with the worshippers in the run-down barn that the Africans used as a place of worship and subversion. The Queen did not trust they would be safe on their own, and they had solemnly promised that they would wait, although no one knew when the stealers would be back in the region.

In any event escape was not a priority on the boys' minds at that time. Nicodemus had started his duties as a stud and was enjoying it. The older studs were telling him that the self-satisfied smirk on his face would wear off and be replaced by deep lines of pain as soon as the awareness dawned in his head that copulating with unwilling females was not the greatest thing on earth unless one had the mindset of a rapist.

While Nicodemus was romping about the mating bays, Abednego was in love. He had fallen for a spindly legged and heavily freckled Irish girl from the new stock recently imported to Fair-field Farms for the purpose of breeding more mulattos. The young man was having sleepless nights thinking about this girl, and the occasions were very rare when he could steal a few moments with her since there was heavy security around these young women. They were in the process of being "processed," which meant that some of them would be indentured workers while others would be outright slaves, depending on the ancestry that The Owner would be able to manufacture for them. But whatever title they carried, they would all be breeders of future generations that would meet the demands of the market. It was a fate that Abednego did not want to see befall his beloved. He knew, of course, that he had no control over the matter. His mother had warned him about the folly of falling in love and of ever believing that love and possession had the same meaning.

One night . . . deep in the night . . . the moonlight turned snow flurries into spirited flakes of silver. The moment caught the boys fooling around in front of their mother's cabin with their mouths open and tongues hanging out to catch the flakes as they floated in the air before landing on the ground where they instantly melted. The guards and their dogs took shelter in the sheds and barns or sat in front of a log fire in the guardhouse telling tall tales. They would not be bothered with boys prancing about in the moonlight in any case. Unless they were contravening some of the strict rules on which The Owner, compassionate as he was, was not willing to compromise—such as drumming, which was prohibited to the extent that even at church services the Africans had now substituted handclapping. Although the boys were already in their teens, to the inhabitants of the cabins they were children—boys who would always be boys. So, everyone left them in peace to gambol and fool around and play with the flurries and get impatient with them for not piling up into real snow that would make the whole landscape ghostly white.

And then a specter materialized from one of the cabins. It was

not white as specters are wont to be, but was draped in a black cape
that went down to the ankles, and wore heavy black boots and a
black wide-brimmed floppy hat. The specter looked to the left and
to the right and then gingerly walked away from the cabin. When it
saw the boys it seemed to panic, turned back to the cabin, but then
again changed its mind and boldly walked away. The deliberate gait
was familiar. So was the face under the floppy hat. The specter was
none other than the lady of the house—Madame Fairfield, as she
now demanded to be called. The boys knew immediately that their
eyes had no right to see what they had seen. They ran to hide inside
the trunk of the ghost tree. But of course she had seen them and
knew who they were. And she knew that they knew exactly what
had been happening in that cabin at that time of the night. They
were smart enough to deduce that while The Owner was carousing
in Charleston after a successful auction of prime slave stock, the
lady of the house was giving goodies to an African slave. They had
seen the man, newly imported from Louisiana on a trip the Fairfields took to explore prospective business ventures and spend some
time holidaying with their children. Apparently the lady of the
house had spotted the sinewy specimen at an auction of slaves
newly smuggled from the Caribbean in contravention of the prohi-
bition of such importations. She had suggested to The Owner that
they bid for the African since he would infuse new blood into their
mostly inbred stock. An import like this would also silence the jealous neighbors who had been spreading rumors that Fairfield Farms
was selling unhealthy slaves. Through his wife's persistence The
Owner ended up paying a lot of money for the African, even
though he really did not see the need to infuse any new blood into
his stock. Inbreeding had never been an issue before this, and he
had long dismissed the accusation that he was flooding the markets
with syphilitic slaves with the contempt it deserved. He attributed
these newfangled ideas on inbreeding to the new literature that his
wife had taken to reading. But then everyone knew that the lady of
the house always got what she wanted.

The man was allocated a two-room cabin all to himself. At first no one thought much of this because the man was quite exotic. He didn't even speak English but some version of French. And he was mysterious; no one knew where he came from or why he was there. If he was going to be a stud at all why was he never seen at the mating bays? Why did he prefer to keep to himself? Why did house slaves take daily supplies of food to his cabin? Now the boys knew the answers to these questions: he was Madame Fairfield's special plaything. And that knowledge was dangerous to their lives. Unlike the guards who patrolled the grounds, and must have known about the lady's nocturnal naughtiness but knew better than to betray her secret to anyone, she could not trust the boys to respect the virtues of silence. They were too immature and naive to know anything about discretion.

The next day the boys were summoned to the big house. The lady of the house was sitting on the porch drinking tea with cake like some fancy English lady. Despite the heavy fur coat she was wearing the boys didn't understand why anyone would want to have tea and cake outside in cold weather like that. But they put it down to the eccentricities of the rich. Indeed she had developed strange habits ever since she started reading *Godey's Lady's Book* to which she subscribed ostensibly for the stories of Edgar Allan Poe, which were occasionally published in the journal, but in reality for the tips on womanhood and for the elaborate colorful fashion plates that were beginning to influence the way she dressed. Of course, the hoi polloi of Fairfield Farms would not have known what inspired her current refinement, piety and purity.

Even as she sat in the porch she was idly paging through the journal. She raised her head and smiled at the boys as they stood uneasily in front of her. She asked Nicodemus if he enjoyed his newly assigned duties, and he hesitated to answer, thinking that he would be deemed a lascivious little bastard if he openly expressed joy at being a stud. The lady, however, egged him on, and told him that he must not be ashamed of his wonderful job with all the opportunities and perks it provided, including a special diet on mating days. But he must enjoy it while it lasted because if ever he decided to cross her for any reason whatsoever, he would not be a stud anymore but would find himself being the object of furious bidding at some auction in a faraway state where he would never again see his friends, the boy he regarded as his brother and the woman he believed was his mother. It was therefore wise to keep his mouth shut about things that had nothing to do with him.

And then she turned to Abednego and complimented him on his good looks and on the fact that he now had a girlfriend. The young man couldn't imagine how Madame Fairfield knew about the girlfriend and was visibly shaken. The lady of the house giggled naughtily and assured the boys that she knew everything that happened on her plantation. She had eyes everywhere, she said, and no one could hide from her. Another thing that she knew, she said boastfully, was that Abednego was supposed to be auctioned with the last stock that The Owner had taken to Charleston, but she intervened and asked her husband to sell other stock instead. She had that kind of power, she said, to decide on the fate of everyone on the plantation. It was important for Abednego to always bear that in mind in whatever he did or said. If ever he got tempted to talk about things that were none of his business it would do him a load of good first to recall what she was telling him at that time.

"Know where your girl is?" she asked.

"Don't know, ma'am, haven't seen her for a while."

"Know why?"

"Don't know, ma'am."

She had been rented out to a bordello in Charleston. A sudden rage flashed across his eyes, but he was wise enough to contain it. The lady of the house was looking at him very closely, with a playful smile on her thin lips and in her tired eyes. The boys knew that this was not a game at all. The Owner had started a new venture of renting out his white slaves to bordellos in the neighboring cities. It was usually those girls whose wombs were stubborn and defiant despite many attempts at mating them with the best of studs. If they could not produce future stock for the markets they were good only for the bordellos, which was a way of earning more money for the plantation.

Slave breeding was a long-term investment. It required patience before one could reap the benefits. It took many years for the stock to mature and be ready for the market. Unlike cotton or tobacco or even cattle and hogs. The Owner had reached a stage where he now had a steady annual flow of stock and was enjoying good profits. But he could not be expected to absorb the losses caused by white women he had bought so expensively, yet who were proving to be unable to bear children. He even suspected that some of the barrenness was self-inflicted. The women had to earn their keep and the bordellos were a sure-fire way.

After observing the squirming and fidgeting boys for a while she daintily sipped her tea, gave them each a piece of cake and sent them on their way. Although this was the best currant and corn-meal cake they had ever seen, it tasted like dust and Abednego couldn't bring himself to swallow his. He felt angry and powerless when he imagined what was happening at that very moment to his girl in Charleston.

✍

That night it snowed quite seriously and the Abyssinian Queen sat on a stool in her cabin waiting for the boys. The sewing matriarchs, now blind with age, had long gone to bed. But she would not sleep before she allocated the boys dreams for the night. It had been her practice since they were little to give each one a dream to dream every night before she herself sank into a dreamless sleep. So it was that she waited and waited and waited.

About midnight she began to suspect that something was wrong. The boys never stayed out that late. When they had plans to sneak away and visit friends or to play outside in the moonlight they always came to the house first for the evening meal and then for the allocation of dreams because they knew that their mother liked to sleep early.

She worried that something had happened to them, but she never suspected that they had carried out a daring escape. They would have said goodbye to her before the flight, wouldn't they? They would not be so foolish as to escape in the middle of such a viciously cold winter. Dreading what she would find, or perhaps not find, she went out and searched the hollow of the ghost tree. The quilt bundles were gone. The boys would not be coming back. Something must have happened to hasten their escape and they obviously did not confide in her because they knew that she would persuade them to postpone the flight for a better season. She wept softly and prayed for their safety.

It was the season that worried her more than the escape itself. She feared the boys would not get too far. They would be forced back by the weather or by the slave chasers. It was indeed difficult even for the sciolist to come to terms with a winter escape. For instance, what would the boys eat when the dried fruit ran out? If the sciolist had made the boys escape in summer or at least in fall they would trap all sorts of wildlife that was plentiful in the region. They would also eat the cherries and blackberries that grew wild on the mountainside and were ripe in the late summer and early fall. In the late fall deer breed and become stupid. They fall prey to mediocre hunters. The boys would feast on venison. They would survive on the acorns from the red oaks and the pecan-tasting nuts from the giant hickory trees—all of which were good to eat for both squirrels and humans. They would even devour the squirrels themselves.

But in winter, what is there to eat? This was not the boys' immediate concern as they trudged in the deep snow, with the sciolist as the Spirit that must guide them to safety now that he has acquiesced to a winter escape. Their steps were slow and labored because of the bundles they carried; and the oversized boots and three pairs of old stockings each boy wore; and the rags they had wrapped on their hands and around their legs under their britches; and the balaclava-like hats crocheted by their mother the previous summer; and the women's corduroy coats they wore—handed down to their mother by the lady of the house years ago when the Abyssinian Queen was still a much favored occupant of the big house.

At first the boys walked in a southerly direction for they had no knowledge of the world beyond the plantation. The map that their mother had stitched on Abednego's quilt was not helping that much since its cardinal points were rather confusing. Nicodemus had the feeling that they had misread the map and they argued about it. After failing to come to any agreement they decided that the map would not be of any use to them. The quilt would only be good for keeping them warm and also as a keepsake in memory of their mother—not only because it was a gift from her, lovingly made especially for this occasion, but it also retained her peculiar life-affirming scent even though it had spent months in the heart of the ghost tree. The sampler too: it continued to exude her odor, de-spite the fact that not so long ago she had washed it with lye soap after it had become dirty from staying in the heart of the ghost tree for too long. It was like their mother was with them throughout the journey.

They walked in the night with the snow piling to cover their tracks after them.

❧

The snow should not have bothered to cover their tracks. When their escape was discovered—a result of Nicodemus's failure to appear at the mating bays the next morning—slave chasers and their dogs were dispatched to hunt them down and bring them back dead or alive; preferably alive so that a long and excruciating punishment yet to be devised could be meted out to them as an ex-ample to the rest of the slave community. The chasers headed north; for no one imagined that escaping slaves would go south-ward, moving deeper into slaveholding territory. Dogs failed to de-tect their scent. It was covered by the snow. And after a day of scouring the neighborhood and beating up every black person they came across demanding that they tell where the fugitives had gone, the slave chasers returned without the boys.

The Owner took his anger out on the Abyssinian Queen. Everybody knew that this would happen. That was why in the first place the boys had been very reluctant to escape. They knew that vengeance would be taken on her. She had known it too even as she egged them on. She was prepared to sacrifice and be tor-tured for their freedom. When she thought they were getting too comfortable in the world into which they were born she would take out the sampler and use its designs as prompts in her improvi-sation of stories about freedom. Stories about the joy they would know at Berlin Crossroads and the ultimate unlimited freedom they would enjoy in Canada, or Canaan as she fondly called it.

She talked of Berlin Crossroads a lot ever since the plantation grapevine—courtesy of the slave stealers who had come in the night the previous summer—brought it to her attention that a set-tlement by this name had been established somewhere in the mid-dle of Ohio, in Mercer County, by Virginian Africans who had purchased themselves out of slavery. Nicodemus's father was one of the free residents of Berlin Crossroads. After manumission he had settled on the outskirts of Cincinnati for some time, and then joined the Virginians who left Cincinnati in the mid-1830s to es-tablish the thriving community. For a long time the Abyssinian Queen dreamed that one day the man would return and purchase the boys from The Owner. When that did not happen she encour-aged them to escape and find Berlin Crossroads.

When their mother described Berlin Crossroads it was as if she had been there herself. She talked of the gardens that grew all kinds of vegetables and of orchards with the sweetest fruit that no one at Fairfield Farms had ever tasted. The kind of fruit that grew only on the old continent. She had visited the place in her dreams, she told them, and it was beckoning them with utmost urgency. The boys did not really want to hear of this urgency, not only because of the reasons mentioned already—namely, Abednego's new love and Nicodemus's new job—but they wanted to postpone as much as possible the punishment that they knew would be doled out to the Abyssinian Queen. They had heard of people who had been cowhided to death for aiding and abetting fugitives, and did not want that to happen to their beloved mother.

She was, indeed, cowhided. Under the very hickory tree that had witnessed the previous beating. Madame Fairfield personally supervised the cowhiding by the burly mulatto men in the absence of The Owner, who decided to find another urgent business engagement that could not be postponed just at that moment. As the whip cut the Abyssinian Queen's bare back the lady of the house reminded her of how she once messed up her wedding after she had gone to great expense to make her happy. The Abyssinian Queen knew this would be coming, for the lady of the house always reminded her of the botched wedding whenever she was angry with her. Madame Fairfield never forgot that wedding, even though she had organized many others after that—house slaves being married off to other house slaves either from Fairfield Farms or from neighboring plantations.

The Abyssinian Queen's blood drew maps of red on the virgin snow and everyone thought she was going to die. But she was stubborn. She was determined not to die before a blue fly brought her the good news that her children had crossed the River Jordan safely. For days she lay on the mat in the cabin, the blind matriarchs nursing her festering wounds.

🐌

Follow the North Star: the sampler reminded the boys. But they could not locate the guiding star because the sky was devoid of stars that night. The stars were all nestling under a thick gray blanket, hiding away from the cold. The boys turned eastward and walked slowly and with difficulty through the night. Dawn found them on the banks of a big river. The River Jordan, they thought. They had reached the River Jordan. They sat on its snowy banks and wept. They so much wanted to wade in the water, so as to lose whatever evil spirits were following them from Fairfield Farms. Evil spirits never traveled over water. That was part of the wisdom their forebears brought from the old continent. But wading would also lose their scent for the dogs, for they did not know that the chasers had taken the wrong direction and returned to the plantation without any luck. They had no idea that after cowhiding their mother, Madame Fairfield had sent the chasers out again to look for the boys for she did not believe they would get far in that kind of weather, and threatened the chasers that if they came back without the boys it would be their bodies' turn to taste the rawhide. Or she would dispose of them in the most abominable manner possible. The chasers knew that was no idle threat. Although they were an almost-white breed of mulattos, they were slaves nevertheless, and could easily find themselves in deep trouble if they crossed the lady of the house. The fact that it was difficult to sell men who could easily pass for white on the open market would not stop her from getting rid of them to some unscrupulous and cruel master in a private exchange, where they would surely lose the aristocratic status they enjoyed at Fairfield Farms.

The boys were blissfully ignorant of all this as they considered how they would cross to the other side. A sheet of ice covered the river. But it was thin enough for them to see black water sluggishly flowing under it. They threw rocks to break the ice and open a path for them to cross. They took off their boots, pants and stockings and waded in the icy water. With chattering teeth they playfully sang the spiritual: *Wade in the water, wade in the water, children. Wade in the water, God's gonna trouble the water.*

After crossing the river they found a branch with which they removed the snow near an oak tree to uncover the leaves on the ground. After removing the top leaves they took a layer of dry ones and piled them on the tinder of dried punky wood particles that they carried in Nicodemus's bundle. When the sparks from the flint landed on the tinder Abednego blew on it gently until it burst into flames. The pith on the oak leaves made them burn very hot. The boys warmed themselves and dried their clothes.

A large blue fly appeared and hovered above their heads. There was no doubt that this was the fly they had first seen at Fairfield Farms just before they began their journey. That afternoon they had gone to feed their mother's milk cow—a symbol of The Owner's compassion in allowing those who were owned also to have the satisfaction of owning something albeit as custodians, for everything and everyone at Fairfield Farms was truly owned by The Owner. As they caressed the cow, bidding it farewell and asking it to pass the message to their mother that they meant her no disrespect by escaping without her knowledge, it egested a big lump on the ground. A fluorescent blue fly, almost as big as Abednego's pinkie, appeared from nowhere. A fly in the middle of winter was an unusual sight, let alone its size and color. It buzzed around and sat on the steaming cow dung. Then it buzzed over their heads and they tried to swat it off, until it flew out of the stable. Now here it was again. It had obviously followed them. Nicodemus got the bright idea that perhaps the fly was their guardian angel, the Spirit that would lead them to safety. Abednego got the bright idea of naming it Massa Blue Fly. It buzzed around for a while and then flew away.

As soon as blood began to flow in their limbs again they extinguished the fire lest it invite the slave chasers from Fairfield Farms or sundry slave hunters who were always out looking for bounty. They put on their britches, stockings and boots and once again trudged on. They had walked for a few hours when they came across a giant sycamore. They knew at once that it was even older than the one in front of their mother's cabin. Most likely it was over a hundred years old, or even two hundred, for its hollow heart was so big that a whole family could live there. Indeed the ghost tree knew what the boys did not know, that over the years families of runaways had taken refuge inside its trunk, some even staying for days on end. From the dry manure on the floor the boys knew that the tree had been used in the past to house animals.

The boys transferred the contents of the crazy quilt to the sampler. They cuddled up together for body warmth, wrapped themselves in the crazy quilt and slept. They planned to sleep for the whole day, waking up only to nibble at the dried fruit and take a swig of water from their flask. But by midday sleep was gone. Nicodemus decided to while away time by playing his flute, against the advice of his brother who feared that it would call the attention of the enemy. What enemy could there be, since they had already crossed the River Jordan? Nicodemus wondered. Even across the river there was no safety, the brother reminded him, since they had been warned that Ohio would be crawling with slave hunters. But Nicodemus was addicted to his flute. He continued to play, albeit softly.

The flute did call someone's attention: a white boy and his dog on a journey of their own. He immediately identified them as fugitives but assured them that he would not betray them. After all, he himself was a fugitive of some kind, running away from a drunken and abusive father to the succor of aunts who ran a small farm on the western borders of Fairfield Farms. They learned from him that what they had crossed was the Kanawha River and not any River Jordan. They were not in Ohio at all but were still in Virginia. Ohio was in the northerly direction. To figure out the north they would have to look for the moss on the trunks of the trees. It tended to grow on the northern side. The boys were troubled and disappointed by the news that they were still in Virginia, but that taught them to be smarter next time.

The boy did not want to waste time in the ghost tree since he had a long way to walk and wanted to reach his aunts' farm before dusk.

At sunset the boys' longing for their mother became acute. At that time, they knew, she would be singing the sun to sleep. She had a variety of lullabies—one for each day of the week. On sunless days the sun did not set, for it was not there in the first place. Still she sang at the time she estimated the sun would be setting if the clouds had not imprisoned it. They could imagine her sitting under the ghost tree, singing softly as if to herself, and this time adding to the words that were meant to lull the sun to a restful sleep after its long journey across the sky, the plea that it should rally all its heavenly friends and relatives—the stars and the moon and the comets—to look after the boys and to guide them to safety. They imagined her singing until dusk, but failed to imagine that at that very moment she was lying in the throes of death in her room, with the blind matriarchs doing their best to nurse her back to life with a variety of herbs brewed in blindness at their hearth.

Dusk meant the journey should resume. It was difficult to leave the warmth and the relative safety of the ghost tree. If only they could take it with them. Perhaps they would find other ghost trees along the way. Reluctantly they walked on, and the Spirit (or Massa Blue Fly, as Abednego insisted) filled the skies with stars this time. Whiteness flooded the world. Silvery and shimmering. The ground was white. The trees were white. Usually in summer their foliage was green and could not be penetrated by the eye. But now they were naked and ghostly, although only a few of them were ghost trees. If anyone was following the boys, they would have nowhere to hide. They were two little black blobs charting a path on the whiteness.

The sampler nagged them: follow the North Star. Their eyes scoured the skies for the guiding star. Abednego pointed at the brightest star and decided that it was what they were looking for. But that was not the right star according to Nicodemus. The mother's lessons had sunk well into his head, complemented by book reading—rudimentary books stolen for his reading pleasure from the big house by The Owner's children. Books to be returned, of course, before they were missed by the lady of the house.

To find the North Star one had to locate the Big Dipper first. They traced with their eyes the two stars at the end of the cup of the Big Dipper. These were the Pointer Stars, for they pointed the boys to the next bright star, which was the North Star. From there it was easy for them to tell which way was north. They changed direction and trudged northward.

The impression the boys had got from their mother's stories was that throughout their journey they would come across quilts hung out to give them directions. But there were no such quilts. No Jacob's Ladder hanging out of a window or from a fence, empowering them with information that they could use for their survival. Perhaps it was because their whole journey was undertaken at night and people only sunned their quilts in the daytime. In the day they hid in the woods, in deserted barns or among boulders that they roofed with dead leaves retrieved from under the snow. They slept, for they did not want to invite the eyes of the enemy. However, despite the risk of capture, they could not resist building a fire after every few miles to warm themselves lest they be frostbitten.

The sampler reminded them: follow the Drunkard's Path. It was one of the lessons the Abyssinian Queen had drummed into their skulls. *Never take a straight line in all your journeys. Only evil travels in straight lines.* From time to time the boys took a zigzag path instead of walking straight northward. They headed northeasterly. Then northwesterly. Then northward for some time. And then again northeasterly. It was like a game. Occasionally Massa Blue Fly visited and hovered above their heads and then disappeared, only to materialize again when they had forgotten about him. By now they were convinced that it was indeed a familiar spirit: the Spirit that allowed them to escape in winter in the first place and that must now protect them against other spirits that were bent on facilitating their capture. As long as they kept to the Drunkard's Path they would be safe even from trackers.

As the boys followed a combination of the North Star and a Drunkard's Path the Spirit made the snow fall heavily and once more covered their tracks as soon as they had made them. Even the sharpest of bloodhounds would have lost their scent. But, as before, the snow's effort was not needed, for the chasers and their dogs were not anywhere near the area. They were ahead of the boys and were heading toward Gallipolis, reputed to be one of the major crossings of the Underground Railroad. At that time the boys were trudging in Mason County in the direction of Pomeroy.

When it was unbearably cold they prayed for snowstorms. Just minor ones. During snowstorms it was generally not so cold. When snowflakes were thick they knew there would be a blizzard. They sought cover in yet another ghost tree.

The distance between Fairfield Farms and Pomeroy was about fifty miles. But because of the Drunkard's Path it became almost a hundred miles, and it took them a number of days to travel. Delays were caused by lack of food after their dried fruit had run out. A number of times they had to dig in the snow to feed on the soil under it. On two occasions they robbed the scaly bark of the nuts that had been stored by the squirrels for winter survival. Then there were the two nights they had to spend in a cave while Abednego was recovering from fever. Nicodemus had to nurse him back to health by burning twigs and forcing him to inhale the smoke. On the second day Massa Blue Fly visited and Nicodemus knew that his brother would be well again.

But it was the visit of another friendly soul that convinced the boys that the Spirit would always be there to protect them throughout their flight. The soul, in the solid form of a haggard Caucasian male, had been invited by the smoke. He introduced himself as an abolitionist who would save them and lead them safely across the Ohio River. And indeed he saved them from starvation by giving them deer jerky and a swig each from his flask of home-distilled whiskey. There was no time to waste, the man told them. They had to leave immediately and did not have to travel by night since no one would suspect they were fugitives if they were with him. They would pass for his slaves.

Abednego, who was still not strong enough, rode with him on his horse while Nicodemus trotted beside it. But after a few miles it dawned on him that they were no longer moving northward where the great river would surely be, but in a southwesterly direction. The moss on the bark of the trees planted this doubt in his mind, for it was growing almost on the opposite side to the direction they were taking. He voiced his reservations to the abolitionist but he assured the boys that he knew all the shortcuts to Ohio and the route they were following was the correct one. They walked for the whole night and at dawn they reached the river. It seemed the fever had returned to Abednego and he was having the shits all over the abolitionist's horse. The man could not take this affront to his beloved horse. His attitude changed and he was no longer the friendly soul he had been for the past hours on the road. He demanded that the boys clean his horse and bathe themselves in the river before he could proceed on the journey with them. It was a reasonable demand, Nicodemus thought, for who would want to take stinking boys to freedom on a stinking horse?

The facts that they had been constantly moving in a southerly direction and that the river looked just like the one they had crossed previously, although it was now frozen solid—the one they were told by the boy was the Kanawha River since the Ohio was supposed to be much bigger—alerted Nicodemus to the man's chicanery. He was not an abolitionist at all but possibly a bounty hunter who was taking them back to Fairfield Farms for a reward. When Nicodemus voiced his suspicions the man drew his musket and laughed in his face and boasted that yes, indeed, they were back at the Kanawha River. But he was not so foolish as to take them back to their master in Putnam County where he would get a small reward. He was a slave trader in his own right and would forcibly transport them to Kentucky where he would sell them for a much better price. But since no one would purchase a slave that was dying of fever he would have to shoot Abednego dead if he didn't get better soon. In the meantime he would tie both boys with a rope and carry Abednego on his horse like a bundle all the way to Kentucky.

Nicodemus had no choice but to give in to the man while he tried to tie his wrists behind his back with a rope. The road to Kentucky was still very long and surely the Spirit would not desert them. The Spirit knew that there was still the length of Mason County to cross, and then Cabell County and then Wayne County and only then would they reach the Kentucky border. An opportunity would surely avail itself along the way. The slave hunter was reciting these counties while warning them that he would not stand any nonsense and would have to tie them securely as there was still a long way to go.

But the man had not reckoned with Abednego, who was lying flat on the crazy quilt on the snow apparently waiting for his turn to be roped. He reached for the musket and hit the man on the head. The blow was feeble, but good enough to distract the man and give Nicodemus the opportunity to break loose and hit the man hard in the stomach. The man fell to the ground and Nicodemus hit him on the head with the musket. Both boys hit him repeatedly with the musket and with rocks and left him for dead. In the meantime his horse escaped, which was too bad because the boys had hoped to use it for their escape. They headed for the woods knowing very well that they would be dead meat if they were found, and that now every slave hunter in the area would be looking for them.

As they hid in the woods they asked themselves where they had gone wrong. For a while Massa Blue Fly and the Spirit had deserted them. That must have been the only reason they were almost resold as slaves just when they thought they were on the verge of freedom. Abednego felt that even his sickness must be due to some punishment for something they had not done right. They should have received their mother's blessing before leaving Fairfield Farms. The Abyssinian Queen. They needed to feel close to her. The quilts. Their odor would bring her close. The crazy quilt! Where was it? When did they lose it? They must have left it when they fled the scene after beating the slave trader to a paste. They remembered very clearly that when Abednego was riding on the horse he was cosily wrapped in the quilt. When he lunged at the man the quilt was on the snow. He had been lying on it. They must have left it there when they fled. Nicodemus could have strangled himself for remembering only to grab his sampler. It was a selfish act, he told his brother, for he should have known that in his feverish state Abednego would not have thought of rescuing his quilt before fleeing. But Abednego did not think his brother was to blame at all. He, Abednego, should have taken care of his own quilt. He might be sick but he was the big brother, after all, and Nicodemus had better stop babying him.

They could not go back for the crazy quilt. It was much too dangerous for that. Instead they spread the sampler on the snow and examined each design, recalling its meaning. They had obeyed the Monkey Wrench by preparing well and equipping themselves with essential tools and provisions for the flight, they had obeyed the Drunkard's Path by following a zigzag path, and the North Star by taking a northerly direction with the guidance of heavenly bodies. There were other designs whose meaning they did not know how to follow. There was, for instance, the Shoofly, which was made of squares and triangles arranged in such a way that they looked similar to the Monkey Wrench. The uninitiated actually confused the two, the Abyssinian Queen used to tell the boys. Then there were the triangles of the Bow Tie, the squares of the Crossroads, the rectangles of the Log Cabin and the circles of the Wagon Wheel. The boys believed the meaning conveyed by all these would be made clear once they crossed the River Jordan. For instance, they believed that on the way to the Promised Land they would be conveyed in wagons to log cabins of safety where they would dress in suits and bow ties.

One design troubled the boys: the Flying Geese. These were groups of eight triangles arranged like birds in flight in four different directions. Not only did the Abyssinian Queen talk a lot about the Flying Geese, she sang about them: *flee like the geese in spring or summer.* They had not obeyed this commandment. They were too impatient to wait for spring or summer. Instead of listening to the advice of the Flying Geese design they obeyed their anger at the Fairfields for leasing Abednego's girlfriend to a bordello and for unjustly threatening both boys with auction. Now they were paying the price.

After a day and night of intruding on the serenity of white hills, of braving snowstorms and wind-blasted forests and of being overawed by glacial waterfalls, the boys finally beheld the biggest river they had ever imagined. But its majestic waters were not flowing. The whole river was frozen solid. The low clouds absorbed the rays of the midday sun, giving both the heavens and the earth a uniform silvery color. Only the glacial surface of the river distinguished it from its banks and the hills. They walked down to the snow-covered boats anchored under the naked trees and waited for the night, lest they be spotted. But hiding was a futile exercise for they had to do something about the frostbite that was beginning to attack their fingers, toes and ear lobes. Abednego's skin was beginning to get red around the ears, cheeks and nose, and Nicodemus was feeling some numbness in his fingers too. As usual they gathered oak leaves and used the last of their tinder to light a fire. Their stress began to dissipate as the blood in their bodies began to flow. They warmed their hands, feet and faces very slowly, and then wrapped their feet over and over again in dry rags. Then they put on their worn boots.

Abednego, still weak from the fever but feeling much better, expressed his surprise that they had reached the River Jordan but there were no chariots coming to carry them home, no band of angels coming to help them cross the River Jordan. No water flowing either. The river and its surroundings stood still and silent.

"It's a good thing the water is frozen," said the younger brother. "We gonna walk across the River Jordan."

As he spoke Massa Blue Fly hovered above their heads, making irritating buzzing sounds and then flying away. That night the moon shone on the river, giving it a ghostly appearance, and the boys took the first few steps on the river. At first they hesitated, fearing that the ice would break under their weight. But they needn't have feared: that winter of 1838 the Ohio River was frozen solid for two weeks. The ice was thick enough to support the weight of a horse drawing a carriage. Soon they were sliding on the ice; their worn boots performing the work of skates without much resistance. The boys had obviously forgotten about all their fears and were having a great time. Before skating their way to what they believed was freedom they became boys again and played on the ice. Even the weak Abednego was able to follow the bigger and stronger younger brother in tracing the figure eight. They played with the combination of their shadows and reflections cast on the ice by the moon. After drawing the figure eight over and over again in different directions and sizes Nicodemus followed his brother as he unsteadily zigzagged the Drunkard's Path on the ice. Still the ghostly shadows and reflections followed. Making faces at them. Wiggling their way a few feet from them. And then coming close until their feet merged with the boys'. Until the boys were exhausted. Until they finally skated to the Pomeroy, Ohio, side of the river. There they lay on the snow for some time to catch their breath. And then they resumed their walk, climbing the steep hill away from the river.

They had crossed the River Jordan yet the terrain was not much different. They still had to cross gullies and frozen creeks, and had to climb hills and walk on precarious slopes—all undulating in the same rhythm. They still had to walk through naked clusters of woods. It was in the middle of one of these that the Spirit led them to a small log cabin. A skinny mule was roped outside under a thatched shelter. They were welcomed by an old hermit, perhaps over eighty years old, who was so senile he was not aware that the Revolutionary War came to an end sixty years before. He had lived in the woods as a fugitive from himself that long—meeting people once or twice a year to replenish those supplies he could not produce himself and to barter his corn and beans for clothes or the replacement of a dead mule. In all these transactions he stayed away from the communion of other men and women.

The hermit was nevertheless very happy to have his own niggers at last. He felt that he was getting places now that God had given him his own slaves. The fact that he was in Ohio where there was no slavery did not seem to register in his mind. The boys played along to humor him and to get food and protection from the elements while Abednego gathered more strength and recovered fully. Then they would follow the North Star to its conclusion in Canaan—after stopping for a while at Berlin Crossroads to pay their respects to Nicodemus's father and to give him news of the Abyssinian Queen.

The boys spent almost two weeks in the hermit's benign slavery. He helped in nursing Abednego back to robust health by giving him large amounts of blackberry root tea for his diarrhea. He had enough supplies and for the first time after weeks on the road the boys were able to eat cooked meals—mostly grits and boiled beans. Now that Abednego was strong again he was secretly gnawed by the fact that it was his younger brother who had had to look after him when it should have been the other way round. He was determined to prove himself this time, and would be sure to take a leadership role on the road to Canaan.

They bought their freedom from the hermit with the slave trader's musket—in reality they were merely rewarding him for his hospitality—and went on their way. The hermit was sad to see them go, but was at least relieved that his old eardrums would be saved from Nicodemus's nightly flute trills.

The Spirit took charge of their lives once more, as indicated by the occasional presence of Massa Blue Fly, who was nowhere to be seen in the two weeks they had succor at the hermit's cabin. On one occasion the Spirit placed on their path a dead deer covered in snow and nicely preserved, perhaps for months or weeks depending on how long the place had been frozen like that. The boys roasted the meat on an open fire on the spot, had a feast, and then took some of it with them as they trudged the breadth of Meigs County. They had become reckless for they did not only walk in the night but at daytime too. Sometimes the Spirit placed them on top of a hill where they sledded down on pine branches. All the while Nicodemus held very tightly to his sampler and Abednego to the deer meat wrapped in the deerskin. Hills dressed only in snow alternated with white forests devoid of foliage, short-lived valleys of driven snow that suddenly became steep slopes, glorious summits and then sliding down again to deep gorges with frozen creeks. On one particularly steep hill they rolled down the slope, their sleds breaking to pieces and tumbling after them, until they got to a wooded valley. They nevertheless did not let go of their bundles.

They took a rest in the woods and Nicodemus played his flute, which he found relaxing and calming. They were startled by the approach of a huge black man in a double-breasted black frock coat, brownish canvas pants and black calf boots. He wore a woolen hat that protected his ears from the cold and his hands were in thick mittens. The boys were wide-eyed because they had never seen such a well-heeled black person before. Perhaps even snow-covered rolling hills yielded mirages.

Massa Blue Fly buzzed around with much ceremony, mocking the man's attempts at swatting it off, and then flew away never to be seen again.

"What have we here?" the gigantic man asked, looking down at the boys.

He sized them up, and immediately recognized them as fugitives because of their dirty and tattered clothes. "Who said this ain't no season for them runaways?"

They were thinking of dashing away when he grabbed them by the scruff of their necks and said: "Welcome to the Underground Railroad. Calm down. And next time remember it ain't the smartest thing to play music if you trying to hide."

They relaxed a bit when they saw that he meant them no harm.

His name was Birdman, he said, and he was an Underground Railroad conductor. He was always scouting around the woods for runaways, and then transporting them in his wagon to Underground Railroad stations in Athens. He would do the same for them and would place them in a safe house where they would get a thorough bath and fresh clothing. He discouraged them from any notion of trying to reach Berlin Crossroads in Mercer County, for that was far west on the Indiana border. The whole state was crawling with bounty hunters and slave catchers. They would surely be caught and sent back to Virginia for a reward before they got anywhere near Mercer County.

In Birdman the boys saw for the first time an African who was owned by nobody. They knew there were such Africans. They had heard that some of the slave stealers who covertly visited Fairfield Farms on occasion were free blacks, but they had never seen one with their own eyes.

They were surprised to hear that Birdman already knew about the escapees from Fairfield Farms and that Mr. David Fairfield was offering a substantial reward of five hundred dollars—instead of the normal two hundred—especially for his prime stud, Nicodemus. Birdman told them that he knew all this from the Underground Railroad grapevine, which was very effective indeed. Abednego felt insulted and slighted that The Owner did not consider him worthy of any such big reward on his head, even though he was supposed to have sired him. Oh, yes, people gossiped about his pedigree at Fairfield Farms until it reached his ears!

It dawned on the boys as Birdman spoke that the Underground

Railroad was neither a railroad nor was it under the ground. The lines that he talked about were trails, the conductors were people like him, and the stations were safe houses. They were passengers, although they did not understand how they could be called that since they had actually looked for their freedom themselves up to that point and had not been ferried around like passengers.

Birdman was impressed that the boys had made it all the way on their own without any assistance from the Underground Railroad network. "Well, from now on you gonna be my passengers," he said. "I am gonna look after you and hand you over to other conductors until you get to Canada."

When he realized the boys were reluctant to let go of their Berlin Crossroads dream, he stressed once more: "Better you forget about Berlin Crossroads for now. No safe place for fugitives. Besides, it ain't on your way to Canada."

The boys were impressed that Birdman seemed to be so fearless that he operated alone on such dangerous missions. Many conductors, he told them, went around guarded by armed men. But he preferred to work on his own because he attracted less attention that way. Also he was able to escape easily from slave hunters and from the law, using wiles instead of force, unless it was absolutely necessary to use force.

Birdman led them to his wagon hidden in a gully where his two horses were feeding on the hay that was stacked at the back. He unloaded some of the hay to reveal a secret compartment on the wagon. Nicodemus would hide in the compartment. Abednego would dress up as a woman and wear a broad-brimmed bonnet. The gear was all there in the secret compartment. With his complexion he would pass as a white woman. Birdman would be her manservant. But first he would have to discard the deerskin and the meat since they would be well fed from then on. Nicodemus wondered why they had to go through all the subterfuge when they believed that they were now in a free state that did not have any slavery. Birdman explained to the boys that Ohio was not as free as blacks south of the river thought it was. In reality the Ohio River was no River Jordan and Ohio was no Promised Land. In this supposedly free state fugitive slave laws forbade the assisting of escaping slaves and the penalties were high. And of course there was always the danger of slave hunters, who operated with impunity in the southern areas of the state, where sometimes they even captured free blacks to sell in the neighboring slaveholding states.

Birdman rode with his secret cargo and his "white employer" through Meigs County into Athens County without raising any suspicion at all. Lying flat on his stomach in the false bottom of the wagon Nicodemus could hear the rhythm of the shod horses on the cobbled streets of the city of Athens. Abednego sat humped like the old lady he was supposed to be next to Birdman, who kept on reminding him not to stare at the sights and people in the street. In no time they arrived at an Underground Railroad station in East Washington Street, a red-brick building like most buildings in town.

The stationmaster was a middle-aged white man in a black frock coat and top hat and with well-nourished pink cheeks. He was a Quaker, Birdman told the boys as he ushered them into the house, with Nicodemus clutching his quilt bundle.

How come there was no quilt hanging out with the Log Cabin design for runaways to identify the house as a place of refuge? The house was known only to a few conductors, Birdman explained. The stationmaster had a strong suspicion—though he could not be sure of this—that the quilt sign was now known to some of the slave hunters. Sometimes they sent out well-paid black traitors who pretended to be runaways in order to uncover some of the stations. The Quaker man couldn't be too careful who he welcomed at his Underground Railroad station.

"Quilts ain't no use to no one no more," observed Nicodemus.

On the contrary, Birdman corrected him; quilts still served an important function. They bound the individuals into a cohesive

force, and reminded them of their duty to freedom. Abednego reminded his brother that indeed it was the designs that had inspired
them to carry out the escape. The designs, Nicodemus agreed, had
also given them general advice on how to conduct themselves on
the road and what signs to look for in their quest for survival. The
boys had to find their own way. The quilts could not be so specific
as to act as a map to freedom. Quilts were like sayings, Birdman
added, they were like adages and proverbs learned from the elders
and were effective in jolting the people's memory and in recording
the values of the community for present and future generations.
Quilt designs did not map out the actual route to the Promised
Land but helped the seekers to remember those things that were
important in their lives. They did the same work as spirituals. Like
the stories the storytellers and the griots of the old continent told,
whose rhymes and rhythms forced people never to forget them and
the history they contained, the patterns and colors and designs and
ties and stitches of quilts were mnemonic.

The way Birdman talked about quilts made Nicodemus fall
deeply in love with his. He held it close to his chest. He vowed that
he would keep it and treasure it for as long as he lived, and would
of course share it with Abednego since it contained the soul of
their mother. Its batting was made of the Abyssinian Queen's old
dress. As he caressed it he could feel the herbs placed in the batting
to ward off evil spirits and to give it curative powers.

After they had taken a bath the stationmaster gave the boys a
change of clothes and his equally ample wife fed them cheese and
bread.

When Birdman took leave of them, promising to see them the
next day with plans for their escape to the north, the boys were reluctant to remain at the station. It was obvious that they did not trust
the stationmaster because he was white. Birdman assured them that
the man could be trusted as he was a hard-core abolitionist and
many abolitionists were white. Indeed, the term was associated only
with whites whereas in fact blacks were abolitionists too since they

were fighting for the abolishment of slavery. The boys, however, could not forget how they were betrayed by a slave hunter who posed as an abolitionist back in Virginia.

The boys were kept in the basement and were given strict instructions not to venture outside. Nicodemus was addicted to his flute, so before they went to sleep on the mattresses and thick blankets laid out on the floor for them he played it for a while. Abednego could not wait to get into the comfortable bedding after all those days sleeping rough on the road. Soon he was fast asleep and dreaming of the Abyssinian Queen singing a lullaby to the sun.

Deep in the night the boys were awoken by loud banging at the door and angry shouts demanding that it be opened forthwith. The stationmaster rushed to the basement with a lantern. "I know that voice," he said. "William Tobias. Slave catcher from Virginia. Crosses the Ohio with impunity in search of runaways. Works with lackeys in southeast Ohio. His spies must have seen Birdman unloading the passengers . . . you, I mean."

Tobias was known as a dangerous man who would stop at nothing to track down his quarry. He was running a thriving business hunting down fugitives and returning them to their owners for the reward. And it was quite substantial. One hundred dollars for bringing a slave back to Kentucky or Virginia. Two hundred if the slave had already crossed the Ohio. When he couldn't find any runaways the unscrupulous Tobias captured free blacks and sold them to other unscrupulous slaveholders in his home state.

Tobias and two henchmen broke down the main door and the stationmaster ran up the stairs to meet the invaders before they could discover the boys.

"We know they're here," said Tobias.

"Yeah," said another man. "Mr. Tobias can smell a fugitive nigger a mile away. That's why he don't need no dogs. He's a bloodhound hisself."

"There's no one here," said the stationmaster. "Just me and my wife."

"And some parcel that Birdman deposited," said Tobias. "Search the house!"

He knew already that there was a fat reward for the black boy and was eager to lay his paws on him. His men pushed the station-master aside and rushed into the house. "The basement," shouted Tobias. "That's where they gonna be."

Nicodemus was not going to be captured without a fight. As the men rushed down the stairs he lunged at the first henchman and held his neck firmly in his grip. They rolled on the floor while Nicodemus pummeled the man's face. At that time Abed-nego was lashing out with a broomstick, regretting the folly of giving the old hermit their musket. Nicodemus jumped to his feet and saw Tobias and the second henchman ready to pounce on him. He kicked the henchman on the floor very hard and was about to charge at Tobias when a shot rang. Nicodemus fell to the floor. Slowly the first henchman rose from the floor, with a smok-ing gun in his hand.

"You bastard!" screeched William Tobias. "You killed my five hundred big ones!"

Tobias drew his six-shooter and shot the first henchman. He and the second henchman fled and rode away on their horses, leav-ing their dead partner in the basement for the Underground Rail-road people to worry about.

≈

The story is told by the ghost trees that after the death of Nicode-mus, Abednego found refuge in Tabler Town, long before the town changed its name to Kilvert. Nicodemus's dying words were to urge his elder brother not to give up on their dream to follow the North Star to its conclusion, until he reached Canada. Abednego, however, decided not to proceed to Canaan, in order to be near his brother. After Birdman and the Quaker stationmaster left him in Tabler

Town, he found solace in the floods that assumed a life of their own and gave him a feeling of security; in the sycamore trees whose hollow hearts hid beautiful secrets, like the heart of the tree outside his mother's cabin; and in the sampler that constantly reminded him of the Abyssinian Queen singing to the sun.

He never got to know that the blue fly returned and hovered over her, and she died with a broad smile on her face.

And the sampler! Oh, the sampler! He would jealously guard it for it was the only memory of his brother that was left.

For the first time Abednego got to know the meaning of freedom among the tribes—the Shawnee and the Cherokee and the Powhatan—that lived side-by-side in the region. He learned about the God of the Shawnee, the Great Creator known as "Our Grandmother," and paid his respects to Her, and gave his thanks for being brought to this beautiful place. Having been brought up by the graceful Abyssinian Queen, he found it comforting that the Creator was a woman. That was one thing the preachers of his Christian church that met in the Fairfield Farms big barn had failed to teach him.

He was not the only fugitive who found refuge among the tribes. The most famous was the one who gave his name to the town: Michael Tabler.

The ghost trees began Michael Tabler's story at his father's plantation in Ravenswood, Virginia, just across the Ohio River. Young Michael foolishly fell in love with his father's slave, a willowy mulatto beauty called Hannah. The senior Tabler was determined to put to an abrupt stop all this madness, so he sold Hannah to some plantation far away from Ravenswood. But young Michael was just as determined that nothing would come between him and his love for Hannah. He searched for her until he found her, and then purchased her back from the new owner. He dared not take her back to his father's plantation, so like many exiles before him he crossed the Ohio River and settled among the "Indian" tribes in

Rome Township in the southeast of Ohio. He bought a piece of land, founding the village of Tabler Town, which later became known as Kilvert in its incarnation as a coal mining town.

Abednego befriended the Tablers and in later years their eleven sons, many of whom married local Native American women. He was also welcomed with open arms by a community of Africans who had settled there from Virginia over the years, some from as early as the late 1700s and others recent arrivals brought by the likes of Birdman and his fellow conductors of the Underground Railroad. Many of these Africans, all former slaves, intermarried with the Native Americans and with the Irish immigrants who had also received sanctuary in Tabler Town. A new race of people was founded.

Abednego learned that the Ottawa tribe of Ohio had a tradition of helping runaway slaves long before the Underground Railroad. So did the tribes of Rome Township. That was why he found so many black people. This confirmed some of the stories that the Abyssinian Queen used to tell about Africans who were welcomed by Native American tribes, some of them even becoming chiefs.

At first Abednego had great difficulty adapting to a life as a free man. For a long time there was a lot of anger in him at what had been done to his people. As a very light complexioned mulatto he was obsessed with blackening the race in defiance of those who had enslaved him and his mother. An Irish girl fell in love with him, but he was determined to fight against his own feelings for her, because he wanted to marry an African girl—as black as his mother. A woman who would tell stories of the old continent as the Abyssinian Queen used to do.

Love, however, had other plans for him. He fell in love with a Native American woman—the daughter of Harry Corbett, a Powhatan gentleman with vast orchards—and married her.

5

A Taliban in the House

Orpah is obsessed with ghost trees. That's what these designs tell me. The trees feature in them in many forms. Fine detail of the mottled bark in shades of brown and gray and green and red and blue. And in black and white. Cracked branches and hollow trunks twisted in agony. Roots exposed above the earth. Knees bent in prayer. Trees in flight. Trees in dance. Trees caught in a whirlwind. Trees in a trance. White branches spreading on a black background like the web of a demented spider. Ghost trees in all shapes and sizes, often so stylized you wouldn't know they were ghost trees. You wouldn't know they were trees at all. You would just feel their power from the goosebumps that run amok all over your body. At least, that's what they do to me. Damn that Orpah with her sitar! And now these designs; all executed in wax crayons by an adept but naive hand.

It's been weeks since I retrieved them from the ghost tree and I can't help but look at them every day. Before I sleep I take in every detail, and in the morning when I wake up I do the same. I have not told anyone about them. Once I thought I would talk to Orpah about them when I chanced upon her in the kitchen where she was making coffee for herself. But as soon as I entered she abruptly left, abandoning the boiling water on the stove. I went after her as she fled through the kitchen door and around the porch until she disappeared into a door that I later learned was another entrance to her room. They call it the mother-in-law room because of that entrance. I had not been aware it led to her room because there is another door that opens from the passageway into her room. I stood at the door and pleaded: "Please, Orpah, I mean you no harm. I just want to talk to you about something I found."

She ignored me. I went back to the kitchen and removed the kettle from the stove. Perhaps, I thought, I should take the drawings back to the tree. And forget about them and their creator. But I couldn't let myself do it then. I kept on postponing. Just one more time. Let me look at them one more time. I will return them to the tree tomorrow. Just one more time. Until today. This was my last attempt at having some form of communication with Orpah. I am not going to try again.

I believe Ruth: this "girl," she's got issues. Mostly with me, from the way she behaves toward me. I do not know what I ever did to her. Does she perhaps resent the attention that her mother is paying me?

I must say a strong bond has developed between us. Ruth and me. I have become her sounding board. When she is frustrated by her children's inertia she talks to me about it. She calls me to her table as she creates her quilts and asks me earnestly what I think is wrong with her children, after she did so much for them. Why do I think they are repaying her this way? I don't usually have answers for such questions. It is clear to me anyway that she does not expect answers. She never complains about Mahlon Quigley even though he spends his days staring motionlessly at his garden or brooding with the other elders on the porch of the Kilvert Community Center. Instead, she would rather complain about politicians, and would ask me why I think they are all such a scandalous breed, except of course the one politician very dear to her heart. I voice my opinion only in those instances when I agree with her point of view. In all other instances, which are by far in the majority, I keep my opinion to myself. And this has earned me the honor of being referred to as a good listener by her. And of being called "Ruth's African" by the neighborhood.

I learned of this nickname on my first visit to the Kilvert Community Center. I wandered there on my own one day when Ruth was busy with her quilting, Mahlon was tending his garden by shifting the positions of his little American flags, Orpah was buried in her room doing God-knows-what and Obed was whooping it up in Athens. I passed three brooding elders sitting on old car seats on the porch despite the chill. As I opened the door I heard one of them tell the others: "That's him all right . . . Ruth's African." They squinted to take a thorough look at me. One gave me a toothless grin and I smiled back at them.

Inside the hall were many, probably a hundred or more, bales of clothes in black plastic bags. Two middle-aged women—one quite stout and round, the other slim and sinewy—sat on a bale each, sorting out the clothes. A young woman sat at one of the long tables in the room, punching something on the computer.

I greeted and offered to help.

"He's Ruth's African," said the young woman.

"My name is Toloki," I said. "Toloki from South Africa."

"He's a professional mourner," said the young woman, flaunting her knowledge of me to the other women, who didn't seem to grasp the significance of my occupation and to place it in the grand scheme of things.

"We hear so much about you," said the slender one. "Welcome to the Center."

The plastic bags reached almost to the ceiling and it was obvious that the ladies needed a hand to move them about. The young lady at the computer told me her name, and that she was a volunteer from Athens who occasionally helped with the Center's books. The two ladies at the bales introduced themselves as Irene Flowers and Barbara Parsons. Irene was the slender one. "She's almost eighty years, you know?" said Barbara. I could understand why Barbara took such pride in Irene's age that she would announce it unprovoked to a stranger. Irene looked fifty-five at most. That's why I thought she was middle-aged. I expressed my surprise at her youthful looks.

"It's because of onion," she said.

"She eats one raw onion every day," said Barbara.

"Been doin' it since I was a girl," Irene chipped in.

I promised them that from then on I was going to eat raw onion every day, although it might be too late to save me as they could see from my battered looks. They laughed at this and flattered me, saying that I still looked handsome for my age. Of course they knew nothing about my age.

Irene's onion was quite a coincidence. Those of you who know me from *Ways of Dying* will remember that a diet of raw onion and Swiss roll used to be a special treat for me.

"As a matter of fact I had the onion habit too once upon a time," I told the women. "I am tempted to resume it so as to look young and beautiful like Irene."

They laughed once more because they thought I was just joking.

The onion and Swiss roll habit is one of those things I lost when Noria—the late and lamented love of my life—became my habit.

Irene was proud to show me around as Barbara focused on sorting the clothes and pricing them. They were donated by an organization in Lancaster, Irene told me. It was going to take days to price them. Then after that they were going to have a flea market where they would sell the clothes to raise funds for the Center. The clothes that were not bought would be left outside for the poor people to take for free.

"You being from Africa and all you can choose any clothes you want for yourself," offered Barbara. Me being from Africa and all . . . that reminded me of Ruth.

"I'd rather buy to support your Center," I said. "When you've sorted them out and priced them I'll come to the flea market and buy some."

I did not mean to deprive them of the joy of dispensing some charity to an African, and I felt bad at turning down the well-meant act of generosity. However I have always paid my way through life and I was not about to change that by taking alms from my new friends. Besides, I can afford to buy my own clothes.

I have good savings accumulated from the plentiful deaths that I mourned back in my country.

Irene's tour of the Center began at the hall with five long tables for quilting, a glass-panel cupboard with quilts and other odds and ends stored in it and a picture of Martin Luther King Jr. on the wall. Today the tables were all stacked in one corner to make room for the bales of clothes. Then there were the bathrooms for males and females and a big storage area for food donations that were later distributed to the poor. But Irene's pride was the kitchen. Here she practiced her famous culinary skills which, she said, I would experience first hand if I stayed for lunch. I was not about to turn a lunch invitation down.

Irene gave me a brief history of the Center. It was founded by her son James, who died from polio in 1978. She'd kept the Center running for the past forty or so years. She promised James that she would continue to work at the Center after his death. Although she was now a senior citizen—albeit a sprightly one—the community, especially the senior citizens and the indigent of Kilvert, depended on her for the food and clothes distributions, and for the dinners that were held at the Center to celebrate such special days as Halloween, Thanksgiving and Christmas, and for the commemoration and observance of important occasions such as Black History Month and Martin Luther King Jr. Day. In recent years she had the assistance of the formidable Barbara, who was also a fund-raiser and food bank manager.

The women told me that the Center had known some glorious days. At one time it was even the southeast Ohio headquarters of the North American Indian Council, serving people of Native American descent in a ten-county area. Unfortunately a few years back it lost its federal funding, and now it had to struggle to raise funds for its survival. But Irene and Barbara would not let it die without a fight.

I have since become a frequent guest at the Center, and sometimes I assist with minor repairs. Or even with cleaning up and mopping the floors. This does not sit well with Ruth. It had become a source of pride to have an African of her own. Hence her jealousy and injured pride when I befriend others, such as the women of the Kilvert Community Center.

Much as I am Ruth's African to the people of Kilvert, I have earned the ignominy of being "my mama's lackey" to Obed, who feels I owe my loyalty to him and not to anyone else since he was the one who discovered me.

He has obviously not given up on me though, and still hopes I will one day redeem myself as his role model and "African shaman." He still discusses with me some of his hare-brained schemes for the betterment of himself and the rest of mankind. Each day there is a new scheme. I know even as he outlines it that he will not pursue it to its conclusion but will replace it with a new scheme the next day. He dreams these schemes up when he is asleep at night. Some evenings he goes out to have a great time in the bars of Athens with Nathan and comes back in the wee hours of the morning. Even when he is hungover the next morning he will invariably have a new scheme.

Most of these schemes involve some form of dabbling in the occult, which he claims is from his Native American heritage, or on one or two occasions from some African heritage I had never heard of. This does not surprise me one bit because I have observed that people of African descent in America often create African heritages that no one in Africa knows about. There are some who are descendants of kings and queens who existed only in the collective imagination of their oppressed progenitors. I also know that there are many rituals and traditions long dead on the mother continent, that were preserved and transformed and enriched by the slaves to suit their new lives in America. I therefore cannot claim that just because I have no idea of Obed's African mysticisms they are not drawn from practices that once existed in Africa. And of course Africa is very big and there are many things I do not know about the hundreds of cultures on the continent. Perhaps my search for mourning should have started there—from one country to another. But then the sciolist had other plans for me. I will still do it. One day I will do it.

There is always a strong profit motive when Obed dabbles in the mystic. Like when he took up hand trembling, which was one scheme that endured for some time.

I discovered his hand trembling practice by chance when I heard the women at the Center gossiping about it. In the middle of December with all the chill and snow Obed had set up a tent near the pool at the Federal Creek and was telling fortunes. Gullible people were actually paying him money for it.

I decided to go down to the Federal Creek to see for myself. And indeed there was Obed standing over a fire outside a green tent.

"So you heard about it, homey?" he asked with a broad smile. "Am a hand trembler. Didn't tell you about it 'cause I wanted to re-fine my skills first. You ain't the only one who's got powers of them shamans no more, homey."

I didn't know what the heck hand trembling was all about and why it got him so excited. He was going to make a lot of money foretelling people's futures, he said. At that moment a curious el-derly man walked down to the creek, for he had heard in the vil-lage that there was a new shaman camped at the Federal. He was surprised to find that it was none other than the wayward son of Mahlon Quigley. Obed tried to convince him this was serious busi-ness. It was nothing to joke about. He had received a calling in his dreams from his Native American ancestors and he was now a true hand trembler.

"Don't be silly," said the man. "Your ancestors ain't no Navajos. They're Cherokee or Shawnee or Powhatan."

"Shawnee," said Obed. "They ain't no Powhatan or Cherokee."

"Hand trembling is a Navajo thing, man, and ain't no Navajos here," said the stubborn man. "It ain't Shawnee. It ain't Cherokee neither. It ain't nobody's around these parts. And it ain't nothing to play with."

"It don't matter no how," said Obed. "Shawnee . . . Navajo . . . same difference 'cause they all Indians. It's an Indian thing, that's what matters, and I am a freakin' Indian."

He then offered to demonstrate to the skeptic how skillful he was as a hand trembler. He asked the man to blindfold him, which he did with his blue bandanna. He then asked us to hide something and he would tell us exactly where it was. He went inside the tent while I hid my belt in a shrub some distance away from the tent. I actually made sure that the hiding place was behind large boulders out of the tent's view. I took a circuitous direction to return to the tent. Obed came out of the tent with a beaded container, from which he sprinkled some yellowish powdery stuff he claimed was corn pollen on his left hand. As soon as he did this his hand began to tremble. He clapped his hands and both of them vibrated and it seemed as if they were forcing him to go in a certain direction, which was of course a beeline to the shrubs behind the boulders. Still trembling, the hands led him to the belt.

The man burst out laughing. He accused me of being in on the whole scheme. My assurances that I was not were all in vain. It was obvious, the man said, that poor Obed was getting all these funny ideas from me. He had heard that I claimed to be some kind of shaman. You know that I never made any such claim.

But in a way the man was right. Obed did view me as a role model and for quite some time he had taken to following me like a puppy everywhere I went. When my body cried for mourning and I went to the graveyard to mourn the dead he would be there, following at a safe distance, observing every move and listening intently to every moan. After that he would have many questions about the profession of mourning. But his focus was always on the financial aspects of it. I told him how I went to funerals and sat on the mound of fresh soil and punctuated the proceedings with my harrowing moans and wails, how the bereaved placed money in my hat for sharing their sorrow and dignifying the ceremony with my presence, making it exceptional, since professional mourning was never part of any of the people's cultures. I told him how in many instances, especially at the funerals of the higher classes, the bereaved paid me a lot of money to stay away from their funerals, for they had come to view me as an embarrassment. Obed was fascinated by all this, and he told me that one day he would go back to his own past to retrieve from it elements of mysticism. At the time I did not take him seriously, especially because after a few days he seemed to forget about it all and to continue with his wanton life in Athens.

I don't know how Obed found the belt. No one had even told him that I was going to hide a belt. His powers were genuine, he told me. He discovered them in his dreams. His biggest strength as a hand trembler, he added, was in the interpretation of dreams. People could report their dreams to him and he could forestall their consequences.

That day I left Obed at the Federal and went to while away time with the women at the Center.

Obed continued with his hand trembling for a few weeks, and people reported that he was producing results, especially in the interpretation of dreams. They claimed he had forestalled many disasters, including a tornado as big as the one that destroyed every building except the concrete block store in Kilvert in 1937.

But many citizens of Kilvert were skeptical and therefore he could not sustain his business for long. There can only be so many paying believers in a hamlet like Kilvert. Perhaps if he had given word-of-mouth a chance to spread he would have got customers from the neighboring villages as well, but Ruth got on his nerves by preaching daily sermons from Deuteronomy 18:10–11: *Let no one be found among you who sacrifices his son or daughter in fire, who practices divination or sorcery, interprets omens, engages in witchcraft, or casts spells, or who is a medium or spiritualist or who consults the dead.*

"What about Toloki?" asked Obed. "You don't say nothing about him. He's a professional mourner."

"Todoloo!" said Ruth, tapping her forehead. "Toloki ain't no son of mine."

"And I don't consult the dead," I added. "I mourn them."

Obed tried valiantly to defend his practice. "Them Indians gonna take us out of poverty, Mama," he argued. The people of Kilvert must exploit their heritage. What good was it to be people of the future, as Ruth usually boasted, if they continued to live in poverty today? What was the point of depending on food pantries while they were surrounded by all the wealth of their heritage? People who did not have a single drop of Native American blood in them were getting rich from aspects of the Native American heritage. Selling artifacts. Adopting his people's totems as mascots. Looting his people's culture. Why shouldn't he, a true descendant of the great tribes, benefit from what was truly his?

But Ruth was not going to be swayed by any sophistry. She knew what the Bible said, and that was all that mattered.

"Go out there and find a real job like Nathan," she said.

One day Obed packed his tent, and did not return to the creek for hand trembling again.

ᴙ

Orpah's drawings. I come across them again in a trash can in the living room. I have been helping Ruth since early morning with her spring cleaning. There are no Asian bugs this time, so the work only takes us up to midday. When we are done she makes us both cups of steaming Swiss Miss and we sit at her quilting table. We talk about the vicious winter weather, and I know sooner or later she will somehow find a way of linking it with the conspiracies of politicians or the laziness of her children. She is grateful that I am always there to help when her own kids always find an excuse to shirk their obligations.

The radio from Orpah's room is blaring country music. And then the one o'clock news. Something about Lynndie England's court martial next month for her abuse of Iraqi prisoners in Abu Ghraib. It must be a West Virginia station because the commentator seems to take it personally that Specialist England is from that state. He, however, consoles his listeners by reminding them that as far as female soldiers go the state has produced a great heroine and role model in the form of Private Jessica Lynch who was held prisoner by Iraqis and was the first prisoner of war to be rescued by American forces since the Second World War. The state therefore knows the glory and the ignominy of women in the military.

The persecution of poor Lynndie England infuriates Ruth and she wonders aloud why they don't want to let the matter rest. They have been on about the Iraqi prisoners from the time the scandal was exposed seven months ago, as if nothing else of importance has happened in the world since then. "Why they make all that noise about them prisoners in Iraq? The Iraqis would've done the same to American prisoners."

Again it is one of those moments when I'd rather not voice a contrary opinion. But Ruth is very clever. She can sense that I don't quite share her sympathies with Specialist England. "Todoloo!" she says. "Enemy prisoners are enemy prisoners. Even God drowned Pharaoh's soldiers to save Moses and the Israelites."

I shift uncomfortably on my chair. Through the window I can see Mahlon on the porch. He is standing on a chair and is polishing the wind chimes. Ruth yells at Orpah to shut the darn radio off or at least lower the volume. She opts for switching it off. After a brief moment I see her standing next to Mahlon, looking up at him and telling him something that makes him stop his work and climb down from the chair. He embraces Orpah and she breaks out into sobs that visibly shake her body. The two walk together to the swing and sit on it and it begins to sway in a slow rhythm.

Ruth is watching them too. She shakes her head pityingly. Then she tells me as she walks to the kitchen that she is going to make some dandelion salad. Orpah loves dandelion salad. She will forget about her silliness when she tastes the salad.

That's the Ruth I have come to know. Food is her solution to every problem, although I do not know what her problem with

Orpah is. Yes, she is a moody woman, but surely she can't be crying just because her mother demanded that she lower the volume or switch the radio off. And why is Ruth so eager to make amends?

"Ain't you gonna ask where I get dandelions in winter?" she asks.

"I don't know anything about dandelions," I tell her.

"I have my secret ways," she says in her conspiratorial voice.

In spring when the weed is plentiful she uses the leaves for salad. She also harvests the flowers, wraps them in flour mixed with eggs and deep fries them. She has her own way of drying the flowers so that her family can enjoy this delicacy all year round. It will never be as good as fresh dandelions though, but it is better than no dandelion at all. And it is important to use only yellow dandelion flowers, she stresses, as if I threatened to go get some. White dandelions are bitter. So when she talks of dandelion salad in this case, she is really talking of deep-fried dandelion flowers.

"I always tell them kids," she says, "don't kill the dandelion. It's more than just a weed."

As Ruth is busy with her delicacy in the kitchen—taking care to make it just as her Orpah likes it—I wander back to the living room. That's when I see the drawings in the trash can. They are all in pieces. I retrieve them and spread the pieces on Ruth's quilting table. I try to put them together. It is not easy because some pieces are just too small. But I can make out the usual ghost trees. Usual only in that they are ghost trees. They are all different and each one seems to have a life of its own, with symmetric roots poking through the ground for some distance, then re-entering the earth. From the few pieces I am able to put together I notice that there are human figures this time. Two figures, one white in a black background and the other black in a white background sitting like fetuses in the stylized heart of a ghost tree. The same figures in another picture are ice skating on what is obviously a frozen river. The pose is more like that of the figure skaters that I have seen on television, although these are in silhouette.

At this point Obed arrives and I know immediately that he will have the scheme-of-the-day for me since I haven't seen him since last night at dinner time.

"What's up, homey?" he asks. Then he sees the jigsaw puzzle on the table and warns me in a very serious tone: "You don't wanna mess with those."

"She's very talented . . . Orpah is," I say.

"Yeah," says Obed. "And she's got issues too. It's because of the mark of the Irishman."

"What on earth is the mark of the Irishman?"

Obed is suddenly quiet and when I look up I know why. Orpah is standing a few feet away, glaring at us.

"You little shit," she says to Obed. "You gonna announce to the whole world about the fuckin' mark of the fuckin' Irishman?"

This is the first time I hear her voice. She sounds like a younger Ruth. Except for the cussing, of course. I have never heard Ruth use this kind of language.

I break into a friendly smile and look into Orpah's eyes. Even though the content of her voice is so crude, its texture is gentle. And tired. I am ashamed to tell you that her profanity gives me a hard-on; not, of course, in the way that her sitar did. But every *shit* and *fuckin'* she utters makes my body tingle. I wish I knew more about the mark of the Irishman.

"I was telling your brother that these are wonderful works of art," I say. "What I don't understand is why you would want to destroy them like this."

"I didn't," she says. "Ruth did."

So Ruth is Ruth to her while she is mama to Obed.

"Why would Ruth do such a thing?"

"She hates anything beautiful."

"But this is wonderful art. Only the Taliban destroys works of art."

She almost smiles. Her face becomes gentler.

"She is the Taliban in the house," she says.

Obed laughs. "That's a good one," he says, and then in rap style: "Mama is da Taliban in da house!"

That accounts for the drawings in the ghost tree. She was not throwing them away. She was hiding them from Ruth. That's what she has to do every time Ruth is spring-cleaning. And when Ruth is spring-cleaning she leaves no room unscathed. She cleans mine too, although I am always there, pleading with her to leave it alone since I do clean it on a regular basis. So every time Ruth is in her cleaning mood Orpah must hide her artworks. But sometimes Ruth decides on the spur of the moment to storm through the house cleaning everything in sight because her nostrils have detected an odor that no one else's nostrils can. Then of course Orpah is caught off guard and has no opportunity to hide her work. Ruth pounces on it and destroys it. Orpah cries because she says she will never be able to repeat those particular designs.

"She should be encouraging this work instead of destroying it," I say.

I have been careful not to tread on Ruth's toes. But I think I must take this matter up at the dinner table. Taking advantage of the vulnerability that I have seen in Orpah, and hoping that she now sees me as an ally and not the enemy she must have taken me for, I invite her to join the family for dinner. I think it is important that the matter is discussed openly in her presence. The irony is not lost on me that I, a visitor, am inviting her to dinner in her own home. She turns the invitation down because she will not sit at the same table with her mother until she learns to respect both her art and her privacy.

I am beginning to understand Orpah. I remember how my own father used to despise my artistic attempts as a little boy, and what that used to do to me. He was a blacksmith and used to create metal figurines from dreams. He mocked my creations because they did not come from dreams. He was not impressed even when my painting won a prize and was made into a calendar. Perhaps now I would have been a successful artist if I had not received such early discouragement.

At dinner time I share this memory with the table. But no one responds to it. Mahlon just keeps on smiling and chomping on the deep-fried dandelions. Obed looks at me with a don't-you-start-now expression and pays close attention to his grits and pork. Ruth looks at me inquiringly for a while, and then urges me to try the dandelions since she can't wait to hear what I think of them. I try them and like them. I say so. I commend her for her culinary skills, but still I am not prepared to let the matter of Orpah's works rest.

"Orpah was crying this afternoon," I say.

"She's got issues, that's why," says Ruth.

"It's that darn mark of the Irishman on her," says Obed. "It's giving her the temper of our Irish ancestor, the first Quigley."

"You shut up about that, boy," says Ruth. "You don't know nothing about it. Orpah just got issues, that's all."

"Her main issue is that you destroy her artwork," I say.

"You think it's normal for a woman of forty-plus to sit in her room all day scribbling meaningless children's drawings?"

"I saw some of her work," I say. "I think it is charming. It would make wonderful quilts."

I shouldn't have placed Orpah's work and quilts in the same sentence. There is a flash of anger in Ruth's eyes. But soon she controls herself, I suspect because she figures she is dealing with an ignoramus here. Her face now displays the patience of a saint as she explains to me that in the same way that her mother taught her how to quilt, she took the trouble of teaching Orpah as well. But she gave up in disgust when Orpah haphazardly appliquéd bits of cloth on top of the revered ancestral patterns and embroidered what she claimed were sycamores on some of the pieces, and even went so far as to attach beads and sew collages of found objects on the quilts. The whole thing was hideous to behold and disrespectful of the wonderful culture of quiltmaking passed from one generation to the next. Ruth remembers an instance when the "girl" actually sewed feedsack batting at the back of the quilt, *on the outside*! Every fool knows that batting belongs inside a quilt in order to make it into a comforter. That was the day she vowed that Orpah would never touch her sewing machine again until she learned some manners. That is why now she resorts to drawing the patterns on paper and colors them with crayons like a little child. And that is why Ruth will continue to destroy them. If it were not for these drawings that have captured her soul like the demons that Jesus expelled from a certain guy named Legion into the very swine we are eating today, the "girl" would have made something of her life. But of course there is the sitar as well, a new demon that has taken over her life and sunk her deeper into a world of her own.

So, the problem did not really begin with the sitar as I was led to believe. It did not begin with the Gothic stories and Native American tales either. The stories don't seem to be much of a factor because ever since Ruth mentioned them as "ghost stories" once I haven't heard anyone talk of them again. The fact is it all started with the drawings and their destruction!

"Them newfangled designs are not our tradition," says Ruth. "We're people of tradition. Our patterns have come down from our great-great-grandmothers, and ain't no little squirt's gonna change that."

Yes, that darn sitar, Obed adds with a mischievous twinkle in his eye, it's a sacrilege to play bluegrass—such wonderful hillbilly music—with a strange instrument of "them Indians." Especially that these are not "our" Indians but those that hail from India. I can see that the scoundrel is just trying to get on the good side of Ruth. Orpah's sitar and its origins have never bothered him before.

Of course Ruth is too smart to buy into this false alliance. She slaps his shoulder gently and says: "You ain't no better yourself. You ain't done nothing with your life."

"You screw up everything I try to do with my life, Mama. Like my hand trembling business."

"Look at Nathan," says Ruth. "He's got a real job; not some hand trembling scam."

"It ain't no scam, Mama. It's tradition. You want Orpah to do tradition but you don't want me to do no tradition."

"It ain't the same thing, boy. Now she draws people too. Like she's God or something. My folks never did them people on their quilts. Only the Monkey Wrench and the Drunkard's Path and meaningful things like that."

She vows she will continue to destroy Orpah's work even though it hurts her no end to do so. That's what tough love is all about. She will do it for the next hundred years if it comes to that. She has the stamina for it. This has been going on for years, from Orpah's high school years or even earlier. And we better believe that she will go on until the "girl" learns to behave like the adult she should have been by now. And when she says this she looks at Obed and then at me, as if challenging us to dare oppose her. I notice that she does not challenge Mahlon.

This is not an empty threat. Ruth is relentless in the destruction of the designs whenever and wherever she finds them, burying Orpah deeper into solitude. She destroys them with religious fervor because she believes they are the work of the demon that inhabits her daughter, making her sluggish and ambitionless.

"The Monster with the White Eyes," says Mahlon with a distant look in his eyes. Everyone looks at him expectantly but he does not proceed. He just looks at each one of us and smiles.

"We all know that one, Mr. Quigley," says Ruth. "The warning of the Cherokee elders and all." Then to me: "Mr. Quigley likes the old stories. He told them to the kids when they was little. Maybe if he told them Bible stories instead they wouldn't be the way they are."

"A prophecy," says Mahlon as if to himself. "It says them folks were the walking dead 'cause they didn't have no connection to the memories of their ancestors."

"Ain't no true prophecy but the one in the Bible, Mr. Quigley," says Ruth respectfully.

"Our roots are Shawnee," says Obed. "He should tell Shawnee stories, not Cherokee. He should talk about Our Grandmother."

"You don't know nothing about it, boy. We ain't no Shawnees. And them Shawnees were crazy anyways. How can God be a woman?"

Obed is about to defend his Shawneeness when I butt in: "Please . . . let's talk about Orpah."

"She's gotta settle down with Nathan and stop being silly," says Ruth.

I doubt if Nathan would be the remedy in this case, I say quite boldly. Her creative spirit should be set free to go wherever it wants to go. She is a grown woman after all, and I don't understand why she should let herself be captive to a situation she feels does not allow her the freedom to create. Ruth is taken aback because I have never attempted to state views that contradict hers before.

I love tradition too, I continue, but sometimes people want to create their own traditions. Just as I did with professional mourning. It is not part of the culture of any of the people in my country. I even thought that I had invented it. I only discovered later that some faraway lands elsewhere do or did have this tradition. That's what set me on the road in search of the tradition of professional mourning. And in search of mourning itself. Let Orpah be the founder of her own tradition. Or participate in other traditions that have been founded by others. People out there are already doing wonderful things with quilts. People out there have long transformed the quilt from being a mere bedcovering with geometric patterns that, granted, have cultural significance, into works of modern art that make statements about their world today. Orpah has something to say to the world, let her work give her an unhampered voice.

Ruth is stunned. She glares at me. It is the glare that usually makes everyone freeze or jump into action, depending on the situation, and has been christened "the evil eye" by her children. But I do not flinch. Mahlon looks at me and at Ruth. And then back at me. His smile has faded a bit and his eyes show some vague traces of anxiety. Obed looks at me and at Ruth. And then back at me. He shakes his head and says under his breath: "She ain't gonna like you after this, man. She ain't gonna like you no more."

"This ain't Africa, Mr. Professional Mourner," Ruth finally says, trying to muster as much sarcasm in her tone as she can. "We got our way of doing things here."

This shuts me up. She orders Obed to clear the dishes, but while he tries to do so she stands up and clears the table herself. She always does that. Gives her children chores to do, but ends up doing them herself, not because they have shirked but because she thinks they are not doing a proper job of it.

I have heard her ask Obed to do the laundry. But even before he gets to do it Ruth takes over and does it herself with her rickety washing machine in the small room adjacent to the kitchen. She then wakes up early in the morning to hang it on the line. The clothes, especially the sheets, become rock solid even before she has properly hung them. She dips her hands in a bucket of hot water and then hangs another garment, while complaining that her children are lazy and want her to do all the work. The winter sun dries the clothes by the end of the day and they acquire a beautiful fresh winter scent.

With these dishes for instance, she takes over because she says Obed is doing the job half-heartedly. I also stand up to assist her, and in the kitchen we decide that we might as well wash the dishes rather than leave them there for another time. I wash, she dries. Not a word passes between us, which makes me very nervous. I miss the Ruth who is always ready with a smile and the stories of how her "race of people" came into being, and how they are the future of the world, and of the greatness of her favorite politician of all times, who is the chosen one since he gets his messages from God. This smarting Ruth is not the Ruth whose company I would like to keep. As soon as I finish washing the last plate I dash out to the living room to join Obed and Mahlon.

They are staring at the blank screen of the television, a ritual they have been following since the set broke down a few days ago. We have been waiting for Nathan to come and fix it—another feather in his cap since he is handy at fixing gadgets and Obed is not. Ruth returns from the kitchen and we all silently watch the television. For the past few days it has been painful to watch the withdrawal symptoms of the family, especially Ruth and Obed. Orpah, of course, could not have cared less since she has her drawings and her sitar in her room. I don't know if Mahlon was bothered at all since his expression never changes. But Ruth and Obed! They became irritable and cantankerous. But now they are getting used to the absence of television and are waiting patiently for Nathan's return from construction sites in neighboring counties.

Television is the family's lifeblood. The family interacts with the rest of America through television. They partake of the American dream through the lives of the celebrities whose wealth, love affairs, divorces and pregnancies are followed faithfully. When they comment on them it is as though they know them personally. In this way they are no different from third world people who have never set foot on American soil yet live on a daily diet of these programs and American food aid. The Quigleys depend for their survival on food rations from the Kilvert Community Center. They "shop" for all their clothes at the Center. Since my arrival I contribute toward the groceries. And I pay for room and board. Which all goes a long way toward giving our dinner table some variety.

But of course I am digressing now. We are watching the blank screen. Silent. Smiling smileless smiles. Moping. Smarting. Even Orpah's sitar is silent. Perhaps she is creating replacements for the designs that have been destroyed today.

The absence of television doesn't really bother me because even when it is blaring above any meaningful conversation it rarely ever gives me a picture of what is happening in the world. America is kept ignorant of the world; except of course of the places where the homeland's troops are actively involved. Even in that case they only know what it is in the national interest to know, for their free and independent media are patriotic and will therefore not give all sides of the story. This last observation may appear commonplace to most American readers. They may even think it lowers the tone of my story. But it will certainly amaze those who are following my story from South Africa; they think that the media here are the freest ever and that journalists can report on anything without fear of being labeled unpatriotic.

Anyway, Americans can afford to be ignorant about the world because they don't need the world. They are, after all, as their Commander-in-Chief once put it, God's gift to humanity. Even Obed, who otherwise does not share Ruth's faith in the Commander-in-Chief, believes that he is God's gift to humanity. He has said as much whenever we disagree on something. He always resorts to invoking his Americanness as a way of convincing me of the rightness of his position.

After an uneasy silence on my part I break it. I apologize to Ruth for my indiscretions. I admit that her family matters are none of my business. Encouraged by the slight smile on her face I tell her how much I have admired her and her love of tradition. Her tradition of making food, for instance. Her face brightens and her smile broadens. I knew I would get her there. Food. I have become a scoundrel like Obed.

"Lots of us have not lost that tradition," she tells me.

Then she goes on about the great tradition of making food that must last for the whole year. Preserving corn, beans and vegetables. Bottling the food that lends itself to bottling. Making her own dressing and ketchup. Hanging the meat and smoking it in the smoke room. Scraping mold from it before cooking it.

I have seen some of this food for it is stored in the cellar where I sleep. Except for the smoked meat, which was moved to the attic some time back, after I could not stomach the smell at night. This tradition, I tell her, is nourishing. We are so much at peace with each other that I do not voice my thoughts that the destruction of Orpah's work is not a nourishing tradition.

"One day Orpah will know I am doing all this for her," says Ruth. "To save her from herself. Why don't she understand that? Why don't she wanna learn nothing?"

She breaks into a sob. For the first time I see an anxious look on Mahlon. He looks at me as if he is blaming me for making his Ruth cry.

"Everything's gonna be all right, Mama," says Obed softly, as he helps her up from the car seat. I hand her the cane from the floor. She is sniveling as she waddles off to her room.

Ruth regains some of her confidence in me, and once more we are friends. But it is no longer like before. I can feel that something now stands between us. Yes, we still do sit on the swing when Mahlon is not hogging it. This afternoon the winter winds are blowing such a chill it would be death to sit outdoors. So we sit in front of the stove enjoying the sleep-tempting sounds of the flames and taking in the waxy smell of the burning wood. She has that beautiful faraway look as she tells me about the first Quigley (Lord have mercy on him); a great Irishman who was a conductor of the Underground Railroad; a friend and ally of the Tablers after whom Tabler Town was named before it became Kilvert. He had pretty black hair. "I suppose that's where I get my pretty black hair," she adds. I look at the mop on her head. It is no longer the pretty black hair she is talking about. It is predominantly silver and brown with only a few streaks of black. I remember Obed telling me about the first Quigley to settle in Tabler Town. That one was blond. I also remember observing within myself that hair was the first feature they mentioned whenever they talked of their forebears.

The beautiful faraway look continues as she relates how her great-great-grandfather crossed a *frozen* Mississippi River, escaping from slavery. I think it is more romantic to make him come from the deepest South and cross a greater river than the mere Ohio. And, of course, she shares with me memories of her childhood: how as a little girl she and her friends went to bathe at the Federal Creek.

"The last thing you did at night was to take a dive in that creek," she says. "Right in the middle of a cold winter!"

Those were beautiful carefree days.

"We was poor," she says. "But we was never hungry. My mama would make something out of nothing."

I think she has taken after her mother. She is the sole breadwinner and her quilts don't sell that well. And yet she is able to conjure up food from her garden and from the food pantry at the Center, and prepare real tasty and wholesome meals. And have something left to preserve for leaner times.

Life was not complicated in those days, she continues.

"We raised our own meat . . . our cellar was full. Our tradition was to go to town every Saturday. Even if you had nothing to buy you went to town for the gossip."

This was where they met racism. Because of their dark skin they were refused seats at restaurants and no barbershop would touch their hair. They were not even allowed to attend the same schools as children of the neighboring villages. The neighboring village of Chesterhill even outlawed people of color altogether. Some of the kids were yellow enough to pass for white and therefore were sent to a white school in Stewart. But soon the people there discovered that they were from Kilvert and all hell broke loose. Others, however, melted into white society and just became white.

"Ain't it surprising now we see people who're obviously Caucasian claiming minority status to benefit from them programs?" she asks. "After kicking us out of their schools too?"

Kilvert had its own one-roomed school, which the darker kids who couldn't go to Stewart because of their complexion attended. Both she and Mahlon attended that school.

"So, that's where you met?" I ask.

No, they knew each other from the time they were toddlers. He is only a year or two older. They were like brother and sister. In fact, they are cousins. They are both descendants of the first Quigley and of Abednego and of Harry Corbett. And of the generations of African Americans, Native Americans and Caucasian Americans who intermarried after that. They are all part of the inbreeding that has happened over the decades in Kilvert.

From what Ruth tells me, it becomes clear that Kilvert's poverty is no accident. It is the legacy of the past isolation. Kilvert was denied services such as electricity until the 1950s and natural gas lines were only made available as late as 1967. Ruth tells me this with pride because it shows how tough her people are, and how they did not need any of these modern amenities that have made everyone lazy. That is why she still keeps her coal stove despite the fact that she has a gas one.

"Oh, man, those were them days," says Ruth with some nostalgia that I fail to understand since from what she is saying "them days" didn't seem like pleasant days at all. "I remember them cross burnings of the 1950s. I was a kid but I remember them like it was yesterday. People from Stewart hated us. Stewart was all white. Even today there's only one black family in Stewart— Barbara Parsons' boy."

You do remember Barbara Parsons: the food bank manager and fund-raiser at the Kilvert Community Center.

"Talking of Barbara Parsons, I was at the quilt auction at the Center the other day," I say. "I saw none of your quilts."

The quilt auction is an occasional event organized by Irene Flowers and Barbara Parsons. I was fortunate to catch one a few weeks after my arrival. Most of the quilts on sale were made by the two women. Obed was the auctioneer. That's where I saw that he could be useful sometimes. He was a very charming auctioneer too, making jokes about the bidders and the inspiring things they could do on those lovely quilts. He had the ladies eating out of his hand. I had expected to see some of Ruth's quilts.

"I don't take my quilts there no more," she says. She does not want to talk about it. Instead she leans over and in her conspiratorial tone asks me to follow her to her bedroom, where she will show me something very important.

Right at the bottom of her quilt box she takes out an old almost threadbare quilt folded neatly in a pillow case. She spreads it on her bed. I do not tell her that I know something about this quilt. I have actually seen it a few times when she airs it. There has been a lot of derisive gossip from Obed about it. It is an Irish Wheel. Ruth points out a faint image on the quilt; rust in color. She says that is the image of the first Quigley—Lord have mercy on him. He died on this quilt. Although she does not make the comparison, it is obvious that to her this quilt is like the shroud of Turin. She does not let it be washed and it is always kept under lock and key in her oak chest. I chuckle to myself at the memory of Obed telling me that he and Orpah often laugh at the quilt behind Ruth's back. They say that the outline on the quilt is that of dry urine rather than an image of a person. But, you know, you can see a person in that image if you look hard enough.

Later I hear from the women at the Center that Ruth does not send her quilts to the auction because she does not talk to them anymore. When she banned Orpah from ever touching her sewing machine Orpah went to learn quilting at the Center. Ruth heard about it and quarreled with the women there. But they continued to teach Orpah even after her mother threatened never to send her quilts to the auction again. It was Orpah who gave up the lessons on her own because she felt her tutors were just as traditionalist as her mother in their approach to quilts, although they were not rabidly opposed to anyone who wanted to dabble in the newfangled art quilts.

✺

If I thought I had regained Ruth's trust I was wrong. She gradually gets disillusioned with me because of the negative influence she claims I have on her children: approving Orpah's wayward behavior; encouraging Obed to follow his heart into Native American shamanistic practices; going to the local church, which I didn't know she was boycotting; arranging to take quiltmaking lessons with the women at the Center; and inventing silly names such as "Ayatollah Ruth" and "A Taliban in the House," which both Obed and Orpah are calling her behind her back. I am ashamed of this last one. I never thought it would reach her ears. But it did, thanks to Obed's loose tongue.

What crowned her disillusionment with me more than anything else was her discovery of Obed's misadventure at the sorority house and his arrest. You see, Beth called to remind me of the painting job that Obed was supposed to do as soon as the winter was over, and to find out about the kind of paint that was needed and the cost since she was working on the budget. I was at the Center at the time, so Ruth received the call and started to probe, excited that Obed had finally got around to doing something useful with his life. She was shocked to discover that in fact he would not be painting the house for a fee, but to pay for his crime.

"They done lock my baby up and you don't tell me nothing about it," Ruth said as soon as I set foot in the kitchen where she was heaving over a steaming pot.

I couldn't lie. I had to confess the whole story. I assured her that there was nothing to worry about anymore because everything was sorted out through mediation. Her baby would therefore not go to jail. But that was not good enough. She felt that I had betrayed her when she thought we had developed a bond between us. It showed that one could never trust people from Africa. They could easily sell one just as they sold the African Americans into slavery.

When Obed returned from wherever he had been she welcomed him with: "Where were you at, boy? Fondling girls' breasts?"

He glared at me accusingly. I shook my head to say it was not me.

"You don't toy with ghosts, boy. Especially them ghosts that died violently like Nicodemus died," said Ruth as she walked out of the kitchen. "God knows what's gonna happen to you, boy," her voice continued from her workstation. "You don't amount to no good with them ghosts and Indian witchcraft."

I told him about Beth's call. His face brightened when I mentioned her name. He lamented that there were three whole months before he could paint the three-story building. I never thought I would see the day when Obed was looking forward to some labor. The very Obed who would not even split firewood for his mama!

"If it's any consolation," I said, "I admire you for trying to explore the culture of your Native American people. But you need to learn about these things . . . consult people who know . . . serve periods of apprenticeship under genuine shamans and hand tremblers and scryers . . . so that you don't turn a great culture into some buffoonery."

"You didn't say none of that to Mama. You didn't tell her it's a good thing."

"From what I have come to know of your mama, no one tells her anything."

"She likes you, man. Thinks you're the best thing since sliced bread."

"Not after my foolish outburst about Orpah's drawings and now the secret that I kept from her about your arrest."

"Still, she likes you. If I didn't know her no better I'd say there's a thing between you two."

I burst out laughing. What a preposterous thought! I remembered touching Ruth on the shoulder one day when she had said something funny and I was laughing. She froze and gave me a stern look. I withdrew my hand quickly. That is the problem: I come from a place where people are physically demonstrative.

I had not been aware that Ruth could hear every word of this conversation from her workstation until she brought it to my attention by hollering that it was exactly as she had suspected: I was leading her children on a path to hell.

That was the second crime I had committed against her in one day.

Both the quiltmaking and the church-going crimes were committed through my gross ignorance of the politics of the village.

Apparently Ruth heard that I had expressed an interest in quiltmaking and the women at the Center had offered to teach me. They were excited about the whole idea. Although quiltmaking was traditionally a woman's occupation, at the Center they had begun to introduce two or three men to the art, and one was proving to be very good at it. So I was quite welcome to learn as well, they told me. It did not bother me that Obed was against the idea, and felt that I—a role model and an ascetic votary of my own sacred order of professional mourners—had betrayed him by reducing myself to a common quiltmaker. Ruth, on the other hand, felt betrayed because I was now in cahoots with her enemies—people who interfered in her family affairs by trying to teach Orpah how to quilt when she, as Orpah's mother, had decided the "girl" must never touch a sewing machine until she learned to respect the heritage of her people. But through it all I could also see some jealousy, that now she would no longer have the monopoly of her own personal African. I was now going to be Barbara Parsons' African and Irene Flowers' African as well.

The church thing was really a result of my curiosity to see what was going on in that little chocolate building by the road. I passed it every time I went to mourn quietly at the graveyard where Kilvert families—the Tablers, the Flowerses, the Mayleses, the Quigleys, the Jenkinses, the Kennedys—sleep in peace under piles of fresh flowers. So, one Sunday I decided to walk into the church.

I was surprised to find only five people, including the pastor, in the church. They must be the owners of the four SUVs parked outside. The pastor was conducting a thirty-minute Sunday school for his flock of four before the service could start. I kept on hoping for his sake that more people would come and fill the five pews on one side and seven pews across the aisle. Even inside, the church was like a dollhouse, with brown wooden panels on the walls. Brown is the color. There was a wall tapestry of Jesus holding a lamb, in shades of brown. Framed pictures of Jesus as a shepherd surrounded by sheep, in shades of brown.

"When will the resurrection come?" the pastor asked his congregation.

"When the trumpet sounds," they responded in unison. They were reading from the pamphlets they were holding.

"And remember, no one knows when that will be," said the pastor.

The service began. Sister Naomi played the piano and the congregation sang "He Hideth My Soul." Another woman stood behind the lectern at the pulpit rolling her eyes to the heavens while she sang above everyone else's voice. Above the piano too. They all sang in unison and I had never heard such atrocious singing in my life. The pastor punctuated the song with Amens.

And then he preached. "God is the spirit," he said, "and you cannot worship him except in spirit and in truth." He preached to the three men and two women as if he was preaching to a multitude of thirty thousand. My only disappointment was that he was not hoofing. I know of hoofing from black television preachers. I find it very entertaining when they dance about and speak and sing at the same time with the organ taking part in that conversation. I remembered the story Obed told me about his own hoofing experience. Ruth prophesied that he would come to no good when she caught him and two of his friends, one of them Nathan, engaged in a hoofing competition—"back in the day," as he put it. He had invented a contest where boys gathered and competed on who was the best hoofer. "You don't take God's name in vain, boy," Ruth had said, "otherwise you won't come to no good." Fortunately she never got to know that it was worse than she thought. The boys were seasoning their preaching with words that were far from Godly—words about women and sex. All this was done to the music of Nathan's harmonica. The more comedic and vulgar the hoofing, the better the chances for the performer to win the contest.

The preacher's booming voice brought me back to the little church. He was attacking the Catholic concept of purgatory, but added: "That's the blessing of being in America, you have the right to be wrong." Then he told us about a judge in Haiti where he worked for many years as a shepherd of the lost sheep. The man went from being a judge to a busboy at a restaurant in Florida when there was a change of government in Haiti. But he kept his faith. So should we, even in times of the worst of adversities.

Then it was time for testimonies. I was asked to introduce myself and testify. I told them my name and that I was from South Africa and I was glad to worship with them. I left out the professional mourner part. But I knew that they already knew I was Ruth's African. The pastor told me he was Brother Michael and welcomed me to the church. He expressed his hope that I would attend the service every Sunday.

An old man testified: "I'm glad to be here since this morning. I'll come back. Thanks for the prayers."

After more singing we shook hands and the service was over.

I thought Ruth would be happy to hear I had been to church. The family was sitting at the table for lunch when I arrived, and surprise! surprise! Orpah was with them. I blurted out that I was at the church service and was amazed that there were only five of us and the pastor.

"Who was the pastor?" asked Ruth sternly. "Was it the Caucasian man?"

"This is America, Mama, it don't matter if the pastor is Caucasian," said Obed.

"Did I say it matter?" asked Ruth.

"It don't matter 'cause of them Caucasian girls from Guysville," said Orpah, outing Obed's shenanigans in a neighboring village. So, brother and sister do talk about things. They do share little confidentialities. And they do betray each other as siblings are wont to do.

"One girl from Guysville," said Obed. "And it don't matter if she's Caucasian or anything."

"I wouldn't go to that church again if I was you," said Ruth. "Especially if that Brother Michael is still the pastor." I thought she would give me the reasons, but she did not. I turned my attention to the grits and beans and mashed potatoes and pork. I felt my heart pumping in a crazy and misguided rhythm at being so close to Orpah that I could actually smell her cheap perfume. Her presence stole my appetite. I just wanted to watch her as she chewed slowly and deliberately, and as her parents treated her like some visiting royalty, trying very hard to see to it that she was comfortable: Mahlon giving her more meat from his plate, Ruth dishing more potatoes on her plate, and Obed looking at it all unimpressed.

But I wasn't about to let the church issue go unanswered. "What's wrong with Brother Michael," I asked.

"'Cause he's a sinner," said Orpah. And then she chuckled sarcastically.

"It ain't no laughing matter," said Ruth. "The Good Book in Genesis 2, verse 24 says: *Therefore shall a man leave his father and mother and shall cleave unto his wife, and they shall become one flesh.* People have ignored God's principles for marriage."

Orpah seemed to be eager to explain Ruth's riddle to me when she noticed my puzzled look. Brother Michael lived happily in Florida and preached the gospel there until he met a woman from Kilvert. Not just a woman, but a divorced woman. They fell in love and Brother Michael left his wife. The couple migrated to Kilvert where Brother Michael took over the church. Ruth led a campaign against him because he was an adulterer. Her biggest tool was the Bible, particularly Exodus 20:14: *Thou shalt not commit adultery,* and of course the Epistle of Paul the Apostle to the Ephesians 5:33: *Husbands, love your wives, wives, respect your husbands.* That was how people came to boycott their little chocolate church.

But people could have just as easily forgotten his origins, and would have ultimately forgiven his sin—after all Christ himself was all about forgiveness—if the man had not made things worse for himself by foolishly preaching a sermon that rubbed Ruth and her followers the wrong way. Sister Naomi, the diehard believer in Brother Michael, told the people at the Center that Brother Michael had enlightened her about the heathen messages of the slave quilts.

According to the pastor the story that quilts had a code that directed runaways to safety was a myth created by black women who sold quilts on the roadside to romanticize them and increase their value. This infuriated Ruth, who felt that her heritage was being demeaned by the man.

"You know how Ruth feels about them quilts," said Orpah. To me what mattered most was that Orpah was at last opening up to me. She was telling me this story and she was looking at me directly. Not at Obed. Not at Mahlon. Ruth was listening quietly, occasionally mumbling an agreement or shock at appropriate places. I did not understand why the pastor would find the code on the quilts hard to swallow. After all in the motherland (which is what the descendants of slaves fondly call Africa) there were many examples of art that spoke. Particularly fabrics and beadwork and even lids of pots. They did not only adorn or cover our nakedness or our food. They transmitted messages in a practical way. They spoke about the status of the wearer or user; about love life, life's journeys, life's transitions, emotional states, aspirations, protest, even pet peeves. Why wouldn't the African carry on with the tradition of talking fabrics in the new world? Even if the codes did not give the fugitives specific directions to safety they functioned very much like the slogans and songs that we chanted and sang during apartheid. They didn't say anything we didn't know. They didn't give us new insights about apartheid and how to overcome it. But they gave us courage and created a spirit of oneness and camaraderie among us. They gave us strength and reinforced our resolve to fight to the bitter end. The quilts did the same for the slaves. As did their spirituals. They contained folk wisdom. They invigorated memory.

But that the matter should cause such a rift between Ruth and her followers on the one hand and the pastor and his congregation of four on the other was beyond me.

"It didn't help that the man once called us Mulengeons," said Ruth as if in answer to my unasked questions. "He wrote that he was spreading the gospel among the Mulengeons. We ain't no Mulengeons. Mulengeons are Roma people. They got Gypsy blood in them. We ain't no Gypsies."

"It don't matter what anyone call us, Mama," said Obed at last. "We know who we are. It makes no never mind what the pastor says. You don't have to be pissed off about it, Mama. Let the man live and do his job at the church."

🐌

Orpah. We talk. She does not flee from me anymore. She does not go out of her way to be in my presence either. If she is not in her room, presumably drawing, she sits with Mahlon on the swing. Both are bundled in heavy coats and wrapped in woolen scarves and are wearing woolen hats. You wonder why they want to punish themselves in the freezing outdoors. She quietly stares into empty space while he smiles at his gnomes, now all covered in snow. I have not seen Orpah and her father exchange a word, except when she was agitated because Ruth had destroyed her work and he was comforting her.

Ruth and I no longer sit on the swing. Not so much because of the cold. We no longer sit together anywhere else either. Except at the table at mealtime or when we are all in the living room either watching television or a blank screen. And this saddens me. She does talk to me, when she has to, but she no longer tells me the stories of her heritage or outlines the political situation of the world for me. She is relentless about destroying Orpah's drawings though. I have offered to hide them for her so she gives them to me. I know Ruth suspects that I am hiding them among my things. But she is too respectful of my personal property to rummage through it and destroy them. In any event I am always there when she cleans my room and I always insist on doing most of the work. All she does is remove the dust from her bottled foodstuff with a feather duster.

Sometimes Orpah and I meet. By chance. Normally in the kitchen where she makes coffee for herself and where I hang out during those times I have noted are her regular coffee hours so that I can accidentally bump into her. And we talk a little bit. Just small talk. Then she passes a new batch of drawings to me. On one occasion I try to convince her to appease Ruth. Draw the traditional patterns and show them to her mother. She will be happy and will once again allow her to use the sewing machine. She can begin by sewing traditional quilts, and then gradually mix them with her own creations. Before Ruth knows it she will be sewing her designs. But Orpah is as much of a hardliner as her mother. She will not compromise. She will not do slave patterns—or African quilts as they call them here—because she does not need to escape to any place. She adds: "Them slaves did all the escaping for me. I want to invent patterns that tell my own story. Like my music. Nobody's gonna tell me not to play bluegrass on a sitar."

She mentions the sitar because she knows people frown upon this innovation. I have heard Nathan make snide remarks about it, suggesting that there were some traces of insanity in the woman even though he was professing his love for her at the same time.

I tell her that she needs to do something that will prove to Ruth that her art quilts would sell. I know for certain that Ruth's don't sell at all. She works so hard and gets little or nothing in return.

Every Saturday morning she loads five quilts on the GMC pickup and takes them to the farmer's market at the University Mall parking lot in Athens. She displays them on railings. People come and look and say "how beautiful" and go to the next stall to buy organic vegetables. They will only talk about them when they are out of her hearing: the quilts are expertly done, but they are like any other traditional quilts. Same stitches and knots. Same Jacob's Ladder, Bow Tie, Drunkard's Path, Shoofly, Monkey Wrench, Wagon Wheel, Flying Geese, Crossroads, North Star, Log Cabin, Bear's Paw that are found on other traditional quilts. Not that all these designs are found in one quilt at the same time. Only one or two of them feature in a quilt—unless it is a sampler. What may be distinctive are the combination of colors she uses and the patterns on the fabric itself. A brazen and heartless customer sometimes says directly to her that one can easily and cheaply find the same kind of quilts at Wal-Mart and they are used as mere bedcovering rather than works of art that can proudly be hung on the wall.

Every Saturday afternoon Ruth loads five quilts on her GMC and drives back to Kilvert. Once in a while she is lucky and a charitable person buys a quilt. Only once in a while. As a result she has to depend on food stamps, on the Center's pantry and now on my contribution for room and board. When things are a bit tight—the family can't live on the sauces and relishes that are stored in the cellar—she has actually said that I am God-sent, although she hates to be dependent on charity. When on occasion I give her more than she charges me, she is loath to take the money.

But Ruth is so steeped in tradition that even poverty will not move her to be innovative in her use of the very traditional designs. After all, many modern quiltmakers create works of art that are inspired by traditional designs but that venture into new directions. Which is what I was encouraging Orpah to do. It is the same approach that I once suggested to the women at the Center. They are steeped in tradition too. At best they make strip quilts. That's as far as they can venture into the world of "art." But fortunately they go beyond the slave designs in their exploration of traditional quilts. They also do quilts from other American traditions such as the Wedding Ring, the Pinwheel, the Irish Wheel, the Schoolhouse, the Diamond-in-the-Square and many others. At least they did not pooh-pooh the idea. They merely said they were going to teach me how to quilt and I could then create those so-called art quilts that I am always on about, so that they may continue in peace to make quilts the way their great-grandmothers made them.

The sitar. It's been days since I heard it. Here it comes again to-night. Midnight. The sounds seep through the walls to my cellar. Muted. Up to now I had thought that a trumpet was able to trans-mit melancholy better than any other instrument. I was wrong. The sitar in the hands of Orpah achieves just as much. Or better. She has managed to make the sitar speak a new language.

I am aroused to a point of madness. I want to hear the sitar in all its glory. I wake up, put on my robe and walk outside. I stand be-hind Mr. Quigley's sole shrub and begin to abuse myself, to the ex-tent that if I was living in an earlier era I would have been committed to the mental asylum at The Ridges. I go with the rhythm of the sitar, but stop immediately when I see a dark figure appear from the corner of the wrap-around porch. It is Mahlon Quigley. He is in a period costume of some kind. He looks like a pirate of the high seas with a tricorne hat and a patch on one eye. He wears a bandolier over his shoulders and as it falls across his chest I can see that it is empty. He holds a gleaming cutlass in one hand and a tray of food in the other. He walks gingerly until he gets to Orpah's door. He taps at the door with his sword. The mu-sic stops and my hard-on unceremoniously dies. The door opens and against the light there is Orpah still holding her sitar. Even though I can only see her outline because of the backlight she is a pirate girl in a short dress and a big hat, which is likely to be a tricorne as well. Mahlon waltzes into the room and shuts the door.

For some time there is silence. Then a lot of giggling. I walk closer to the window. Mumbling. Singing. One voice. Two voices. Male and female. Laughter. Moans. Giggling. My God! I walk away in disgust.

🌿

The next morning Obed wakes me up with a rude knock. I have a call. I grab my robe and rush to the living room. I suspect it is Beth Eddy because she is the only person who has ever called me here. It is Barbara Parsons at the Center. "I'd like for you to come to our Christmas dinner," she says. I thank her. I was going to go in any case. Everyone in Kilvert is going. Everyone but Ruth, who is still nursing resentment against the Center women.

And there is Mahlon sitting on the swing looking as innocent and serene as the wooden Jesus in his garden. I look at him and suddenly my stomach churns.

"What was the call about," Obed asks.

"It was just the women at the Center," I say.

"I thought it was Beth."

"With a voice like that? Why don't you call her?"

He looks at me as if I have asked him the dumbest question ever. But I am interested in Mahlon Quigley. I want to know more about this man.

"Why?" asks Obed.

"I find him intriguing."

"My old man intriguing?"

"Don't you people know what happens under your own roof at night?" I was getting agitated.

"Oh, you mean about him and Orpah? Of course we know. Everyone knows. They have been doing it since she was little. Since I was little too. But I outgrew it. Orpah's still a child at heart."

Then he walks away.

Mahlon Quigley, I learn from the women at the Center later that day as I help arrange the chairs in the hall, is a respected elder in the community despite his silence. On the rare occasions he utters something everyone listens and takes note. They don't remember when and how his silence started; it just crept on them. They do have a memory of a much younger and vibrant Mahlon though. He and Ruth used to live on a small farm when Obed and Orpah were little. They raised all their food, including meat. They slaughtered hogs and chickens. They raised their own eggs too. But, alas, farms were commercialized and the family had to leave the land.

But no one could take the farmer out of Mahlon. Even when he had moved to the village he kept cows. "He got them as calves and then grew them up till they was big and then sold them for beef," said Irene. Sometimes he had up to eight cows at a time. He had two or three pigs and a few chickens as well. "Back in them days you could keep them animals in your backyard without the government whupping your ass," adds a man who had joined us helping set the place up for the party.

A strange disease attacked his animals; many of them died and others had to be put down. This pained him very much and he decided he would never again grow anything that would die. Hence his garden has gnomes and flags and statues. The only living thing is the bush that has survived for generations and is not likely to die in his lifetime. When women talk of him their eyes become moist and their voices drip honey. One senses awe in the men's tones. Everyone is in agreement: there has never been a gentleman like Mahlon Quigley seen in these parts.

And there is this business about his mother, which the people here would rather whisper. She was a white woman from Stewart who fell in love with a colored man from Kilvert. Naturally her parents objected. She fell pregnant with Mahlon and had to run away to Kilvert to be with her man. She was only in her teens at the time. She found that in Kilvert she was not quite welcome either. People resented the fact that she was from Stewart first and foremost, and secondly that she was white. It was in the early 1940s, Irene reminds me, and prejudice was the order of the day. Why, even today you will still find it!

This intolerance by a community founded on the basis of fighting against intolerance is very sad. Something terrible must have happened to the poor woman. I remember Ruth telling me when we were still great buddies that her greatest wish at the moment was to get a proper tombstone on the presently nameless grave of Mr. Quigley's mother.

🐟

Christmas dinner at the Kilvert Community Center. Five days before Christmas day. Everyone laments that it is not going to be a white Christmas. The rainbow people of the village have gathered and the hall is full. Little girls in red and white Christmas dresses. Little boys playing pranks on other little boys. Big and slender teenage girls with lipstick smeared thickly on their lips standing in a group next to a Christmas tree with red and white decorations. They are holding their babies in their arms. They are all in the latest of designer jeans. Grandmothers feeding their grandchildren. It strikes me that the children have become lighter in complexion than their parents down the generations. Some look totally Caucasian.

There is Margaret Tabler standing behind a long table under the picture of Martin Luther King Jr., directing the traffic that has lined up for the food. The table is bedecked with trays of cookies and cakes and pretzels and sandwiches and candy and hot dogs and chips and cans of pop. Irene insists that I must fill my paper plate many times over.

There are Nathan and Orpah sitting on a couch by the door. He waves at me and I wave back. They are laughing at something

Nathan has said. Yes, Orpah is actually laughing. I am happy that she has been persuaded to come out and enjoy herself with other human beings. But also there is a slight pang of jealousy that she is with Nathan. I should have been brave enough to ask her out for this dinner. Who knows? She might have said yes. They look good together though: Orpah and Nathan. I am sure Ruth is happy too. She has been encouraging Orpah to go for Nathan because Nathan is a good man and Nathan is a hard-working man and Nathan is a responsible man who will look after her and Nathan will bring some sanity into her life.

"Nathan's a wild man, Ruth," that's what Orpah said the last time I heard them talk about him.

"She's looking for a tame man. They're hard to come by. She's gotta tame one for herself," said Ruth, not addressing her daughter directly but looking at me for confirmation.

"I am not looking for no man, period," that was Orpah's response as she walked away.

And now here they are, Nathan and Orpah, laughing together under a red and white banner with a gold star of Bethlehem and the three wise men on camels.

There is Santa Claus sitting on a chair next to two big boxes with presents wrapped in colorful paper. The children are lining up for their gifts. A child sits on his lap and they exchange a few words, I don't know about what, and then he selects a present from one or the other box depending on the sex of the child. Older children don't sit on his lap but receive their presents while standing in front of him. Santa spots me and waves at me with a big grin. I can see Obed under that sloppy white beard and red and white hat. The scoundrel can be useful when he wants. It is amazing how he is able to bring out a giggle even from the shy kids.

There is Mahlon Quigley sitting with men who are obviously much older than him. Two men are trying to charm an equally senior citizen whose face and neck are mapped with deep furrows of wisdom. She is giggling like a teenage girl and her blue eyes glisten with tears. I think she has been laughing her dear little heart out. Mahlon for his part is just smiling as always.

Once again I wonder what goes on in that head. Especially after what I saw last night. I cannot understand why even the stormy Ruth holds this man in such awe and reverently refers to him as Mr. Quigley and never Mahlon. Mr. Quigley this, Mr. Quigley that, and Mr. Quigley needs to be well fed. He turns his head and looks at me. Maybe it is my imagination but I think the smile faded a bit. I get the feeling that if I were to compete for Orpah's attention at all it would not be with Nathan but with Mahlon Quigley.

The thought sickens me and I slip out of the room. I walk among the many cars and SUVs parked in the yard to the gate and stand there alone. Why on earth would I think of competing for any woman in Kilvert? I think I am getting too comfortable in Tabler Town. I have forgotten my mission. I came here in search of mourning. Not to fight duels with fathers over their daughters. And how presumptuous of me to imagine that a woman like Orpah would be remotely interested in someone like me!

The sciolist nagged me until he got tired: *Toloki, you are a professional mourner. You have a vocation to fulfill. Do not be seduced by the life in Kilvert. We must see that you are here for a reason. We must see why you are a professional mourner and not just a man from South Africa who finds himself in a southeast Ohio hamlet.* That voice has since gone silent.

Santa Claus walks out of the building and is about to take off his costume behind one of the SUVs when he sees me. I join him.

"Why would you strip naked in this cold?" I ask.

If he strips in the hall he will spoil the illusion for the kids.

"You think those kids are dumb? They know who you are."

It is too cold, so he decides that he will take the costume off at home. The party is not over but his part is done. He would stay only if there was beer.

"I'll walk with you," I tell him.

We walk slowly past the little church. I am suddenly overwhelmed

by an urge to mourn. My whole body cries for mourning. I tell Obed
that I'll find him at home. I need to go to the cemetery. He insists that
he is coming with me. He has seen me mourn a few times and claims
he finds the experience inspiring. But we don't go into the cemetery.
We walk toward the woods instead. We are drawn by the ghost tree
gleaming among the maples and elms and walnuts. We tread lightly
into the woods. Everything is still. Only our boots disturb the silence.
I think Obed is warm enough in his Santa suit since it is stuffed with
old clothes to give him a round figure. I am cold in my Windbreaker,
which I am wearing over a light shirt that was never meant for such a
chilly winter night.

It is dark in the woods but we are able to find our way with the
aid of my penlight. We have no idea where we are going or why.
The urge to mourn has dissipated, perhaps with the realization that
I cannot mourn in civvies. I can only mourn effectively in my sacred costume. Something gleaming on the ground attracts my attention. It is a piece of porcelain. There is a mound covered by
leaves and lots of debris. More broken pottery. We clear the leaves
and discover a lamp chimney and a pot. We rummage some more in
the leaves with our fingers. There is a white ceramic hen. There are
seashells surrounding part of the mound. Clearly this is a grave.

"We must find the gravestone," I tell Obed.

But it is too dark. We mark the spot with a cairn of stones so as
to make it distinguishable in daylight. We walk back home, my
heart pumping from the discovery. This is not just any grave. It is
an African grave.

The next morning Obed and I return to the woods armed with
a small digging spade, hoping that we did not just dream the
grave. Today I am wearing my mourning costume, for I am going
to mourn the African sleeping under that mound. Children titter
along the way and ask Obed why I am wearing a Halloween costume when it is long past Halloween.

"It ain't no Halloween costume, you little asshole," says Obed.
"My man here is an African shaman."

"You don't talk like that to children," I admonish.

But the kids don't seem to mind. They laugh and one of them asks: "What the fuck is an African shaman?"

He is not offended at all but promises to explain to them next time.

Well, the grave is still there. And this time we are able to find the headstone with ease. After scraping the mud from it the crude inscription becomes clear: *Here lies Niall Quigley—Slave Owner, Slave Trader, Slave, Slave Stealer, Professional Witness. Died: 1875.*

"Who was Niall Quigley?" I ask.

"The first Quigley," says Obed.

"I wonder why they buried him like an African."

"What they wrote here is bull, man," says Obed. "My great-grampa was no slave owner. He was no slave trader either. They got it all wrong, man. There were no slaves in Ohio."

"We'll know when we mourn the man," I assure him.

We kneel at the mound and I teach him new mourning wails. They are like the sound of a coyote, he observes. I combine them with groans and moans and sacred chants of my own invention. Obed follows faithfully and together we are able to muster a two-part harmony at one time, and a call-and-response at another. Our mourning transports us to another place; another realm; another time.

6

White Slave

The story is told by the mound and the white chicken and the headstone: Niall Quigley lost everything he owned in the gambling dens of County Tipperary, Ireland. After serving time at the Bridewell for some fraudulent transaction aimed at recouping his losses, he traveled steerage aboard a vessel to the new world where he hoped to start a new life. He endured the rough seas in crammed and filthy conditions. Some of his fellow passengers fell sick and perished, and were thrown overboard. He was determined to survive the voyage, and when his provisions ran out—passengers in steerage provided their own food—he stole from others. Even after a beating that left him all bloodied and tattered for most of the journey, the thought of the great fortunes awaiting him in America sustained him.

When we meet him for the first time in the gaming dens of New York he had not made the fortune, but like any decent white man he had a slave of his own. Ownership of this particular property was a source of great mirth at his haunts, not only because New York was no longer a slaveholding state, and hadn't been one for fourteen or so years, but also for the fact that Quigley was a lowly Irishman. In the eyes of his fellow citizens he was not of a much higher breed than his property.

He won the property in a card game—a toothless scrawny African who would not fetch any price at the slave market in any of the slaveholding states. Even those who had offered to buy the slave before he became Quigley's property had only done so for the good-Samaritan purpose of putting the poor creature out of its misery by shooting it dead at a target practice.

Quigley walked around the dirty streets of Five Points with his slave on a leash around his neck, and used him to beg as a "performing Negro." But the fellow did not have any talent at all and people laughed at his attempts to sing and dance. His venture into some variation of tap dance was pathetic. Five Points citizens had seen better. After all, Five Points invented tap dance, although they didn't call it that in those days. They called it "buck and wing" or the Juba Dance after the great "Master Juba" Lane whose nimble footwork of African rhythms combined so expertly with Irish clogging to create magic.

"What kinda Negro is this who can't sing and dance?" people asked as they walked away, with their fingers trying in vain to stop the atrocious sounds from polluting their ears. The kinder souls put a coin or two in Quigley's hat and fled to the bordellos in the tenements as fast as they could.

The partnership's only bane was the band of ragamuffins who played cruel tricks on the performer and disrupted Quigley's business. One day they set fire to the tattered seat of the slave's pants for better entertainment than his performance was able to provide. He ran up and down the street screaming. At first Quigley enjoyed the sight and laughed. But when he realized that the pants had really caught fire and there were some flames he dived onto the fellow and rolled him on the ground. The ragamuffins ran off laughing.

That night in the church basement they shared with rats— courtesy of a kindly Methodist minister—Quigley took the leash off his slave and broke out laughing as he cleaned his scorched buttocks with cold water and lye soap that was never meant for human skin but for laundry.

"You son of a bitch!" said the slave. "You let them do this to me."

"You saw I didn't let 'em, you ninny!" said Quigley still laughing. "But you must admit it was damn funny."

"I'm gonna do it to you one of them days and you tell me if it's funny."

The fellow was not able to sit for a few days. But the show had to go on. Every day they went out on the streets to perform, and then to the taverns to partake of the good life. Once in a while they went to the bordellos and Quigley treated his slave to more good life with either the Negro or Irish prostitutes; those who were so destitute that they accepted any customer.

It was at the bordellos that Quigley was struck by a brilliant idea. There were many stray white children in the street. Abandoned by women of the town. Some not quite abandoned but neglected by mothers who had to spend days and nights servicing customers. These children had to fend for themselves in the streets or even follow their mothers' profession before the age of ten. At night Quigley discussed the welfare of these children with his slave. There could be good business here.

"All we need is to transport 'em down to Virginia," he said.

"And then set up a house for orphans for them down in Virginia," said the slave with a sarcastic chuckle.

"Sell 'em as slaves, you ninny."

"I ain't gonna kidnap nobody's child," said the slave.

"We lure 'em, man, we don't kidnap 'em. We promise 'em a better life and jobs and the like."

"Who's gonna buy white slaves, you ninny?" asked the slave.

"Oh, they buy 'em all the time! You call 'em mulattos they buy 'em. No questions asked. They know pretty damn well they ain't no mulattos. I hear Irish girls make excellent slaves as if they had nigger blood running in their dear li'l souls."

It was easy to capture stray Irish and German girls in the streets of Five Points and other New York slums. When Quigley could not sell them at the House of Reception on West 13th Street because of the competition of more professional slave traders, he loaded them on a wagon and drove for days to Richmond, Virginia. He invested a lot of resources in treating the children very well, feeding them the kind of meals they would never even have dreamed of in the streets or at their bordello homes, and made sure that their clothes were clean even though most were tattered. The reason for this generosity was that healthy-looking slaves fetched a better price. But also it helped to keep the girls from ever thinking of escaping. If the journey to the South was this comfortable, what of the life that awaited them? Only a foolish girl would even think of escaping from such a prospect.

Quigley and his slave never used the children for any nefarious purposes. They were not unscrupulous at all. When it was necessary to satisfy their manly needs they went to the auction rooms. No, not to auction their children. Those were going to be sold directly to specific customers at the plantations that had placed previous orders. Each child was earmarked for a specific owner even as she was being captured or lured by the two. Quigley and his slave went to the auction rooms to rent women for the night. Slave dealers who were entrusted with girls to sell at the auction earned some extra money by hiring the girls out for the night. Whenever Quigley heard a new batch of female slaves had arrived he whispered in his slave's ear, "Let's go get some fresh pussy from the auction rooms." And they tittered like two naughty schoolboys.

So, the children in their care were never in any danger of being used for the gratification of the two kindly gentlemen who were taking them for wonderful jobs with kind-hearted employers. Through most of the journey they sang happy songs and dreamed beautiful dreams. They were happy to have Quigley's slave at their beck and call, for they did not know that soon they would themselves be slaves and would be used for the pleasure of their new masters.

Sometimes there were women among the children. Irish and German women who had had enough of destitution and were quite willing to walk into servitude and even slavery with their eyes open. Most of these were sold to rich Negroes who kept white slaves. In Virginia and Maryland there were a number of free blacks who were quite wealthy and were slave owners. Some of these were happy to keep white women both as slaves and concubines. It was a better life for the women than the cold and hunger at Five Points, and Quigley was always ready to rescue them from

that life and transport them to the South. Some of the women—
denounced as depraved by white society—ended up marrying
their black masters.

Things were looking up for Quigley and he wondered why he
had wasted so many precious months begging with his performing
Negro instead of engaging in such a lucrative business. At ten dollars cash per slave, and the cost of transporting it, he was making a
killing. Even his slave seemed to be gaining more flesh on his
bones. But alas, Quigley couldn't stay away from the gaming dens.
The wealthier he became the more he stayed for nights on end losing money, and then staying for more hours hoping to recoup his
losses. His slave was always by his side, still on his leash, or sometimes in chains in order to emphasize to the onlookers that the fellow was a slave and he was indeed the master. This enhanced his
status. Or so he thought.

Sometimes he won a few dollars but most times he lost everything he had in his purse that night at the roll of a die. The gambling binges became frequent and he began to neglect the business.
This worried the slave and he tried to talk to his master about it.
But Quigley was too stubborn to listen to a mere slave. He made
the money through his brilliant ideas; he had the right to enjoy it.
The fountain would never run dry as long as indigent women continued to manufacture babies.

They had moved from the church basement to one of the tenements, and sometimes Quigley forgot to pay the rent. The landlord
would come knocking and threatening to evict them without notice. The slave, who had taken to hiding some of the money under
his own mattress, would pay the rent. Quigley would then ransack
the house for more hidden money, which he would promptly take
to the gaming dens.

That was how Niall Quigley and his slave fell on hard times.
Creditors took everything he owned, including his precious wagon
and horses that he used to transport slaves to the South. With only
his clothes wrapped in a bundle Quigley and his slave trekked

down South with the hope of finding new ventures in Virginia, perhaps with the assistance of the rich men he used to provide with fresh supplies of slaves. But none of them wanted to know him. Even the wealthy black landowners who had bought one or two white women from him and were now living with them in holy matrimony or blissful concubinage did not want to have anything to do with him. In cities like Richmond and Norfolk he tried to revive the old act of a "performing Negro" but it just didn't get off the ground. There were no takers, and more often than not property owners drove them away from the sidewalks with whips.

The slave was now sickly and a burden to keep. Quigley tried to sell him. He took him to the auction rooms but the auctioneers would have none of him. Putting a scrawny fellow like that under the hammer would destroy their reputation as auctioneers of quality slaves. In any event no one in his right mind would bid for him. "A scurvied Negro like this ain't good for nothing," they said.

"He's good for breeding," Quigley insisted. "Like all men of his race he's more robust in love than any white man."

At this he displayed his penis, which was quite sizeable.

But the auctioneers and prospective buyers dismissed the whole idea. They didn't think the children sired by the slave would be big and strong.

"Nobody's gonna buy me, you ninny. You're stuck with me," said the slave with much glee.

There were no takers even when he wanted to exchange the impertinent fellow for a mere bottle of rum.

The concerns of the slave owners about breeding good healthy slaves gave Quigley an idea. He was going to invent a potion that would make slaves breed faster; a fertility drug that would ensure multiple births. He would take his example from nature. If dogs and rabbits could give birth to so many young ones at the same time, why not humans? Right there at the auction rooms he shared the brilliant idea with his slave, who merely laughed it off as the most ridiculous thing he had ever heard.

Quigley was not to be discouraged by the slave's lack of faith in human credulity. Thus he became a snake-oil salesman, except he didn't sell any snake-oil but a slave-breeding concoction of his own manufacture. He traveled from plantation to plantation meeting breeders and interesting them in his invention. Its main ingredient was extracted from the most fertile bitches, he told his customers. It was the same chemical substance that made dogs give birth to many puppies at the same time. The white drug was to be mixed with water and given to the females twice a day. In no time they would conceive. Not only would the potion induce multiple births but the period of gestation would be decreased by half. Quigley embellished on the powers of the potion as he went along and as more greedy plantation owners bought it.

Once more signs of health returned to both the man and his slave. Their cheeks began to fill out and their faces gleamed as they walked the countryside, the leashed slave carrying a sack of the powder and following the master. The leash was not to stop the slave from escaping. He had no intention of doing so for it was good enough for him that they shared the spoils. They were male-factors and scallywags of equal standing. The leash, therefore, served a symbolic function. It reminded the slave that he was a slave despite the companionship, and the master that he was the master despite the partnership in crime. The leash also showed the customers that the great inventor of the magic potion was a man of substance and a property owner. The fact that they were walking the countryside instead of riding on steeds was a matter of choice; so he made those who wondered believe.

Alas, the plantation owners discovered to their cost that the Irish-man had duped them. They bayed for his blood, but it was too late because he had moved westward in the direction of Kentucky.

A plantation owner in Putnam County did not give up. The owner's name was David Fairfield of Fairfield Farms. He had re-turned from carousing in Charleston one evening to find his wife excited about a purchase she had made from a wonderful salesman—a potion that would make their breeding business the most profitable ever. She showed him the white powder for which she had paid a lot of money. The Owner was suspicious at once. Unlike those who had discovered the chicanery months after trying the potion, The Owner was smart enough to know that no such mixture existed anywhere in the world, let alone in Virginia. He set out after the salesman with a posse of three of his trusted mulattos.

They caught up with the scallywags on the banks of the Guyandotte where they had set up camp and were barbecuing meat on an open fire. The Owner was very friendly. He joined the pair while his mulattos stayed mounted a short distance away. He introduced himself as The Owner of Fairfield Farms where they had so kindly sold their wonderful potion. Unfortunately he had been away on business, otherwise he would have loved to entertain them for the good service they were providing to the slave breeding industry. As the biggest slave breeder in the region he needed more of their wonderful potion. That was why he had followed them. He wanted to buy all the stock in their possession and order more for future delivery. Quigley was pleased to hear this. Most of his customers only bought small quantities to experiment with the potion first. He was surely going to strike it rich. He invited The Owner to join him at his meal. The slave was ordered to serve the two masters and then stand aside while they ate. He would have the bones afterward. The slave did all that willingly for he knew why the whole charade was necessary.

"Oh, I have lotsa whiskey for you," said The Owner. He stood up and walked to his mulattos, who were still on their horses. He called the slave to come and take the bottles and bring them back to his master.

Quigley did not ask himself why they spent such a long time taking out whiskey from the saddlebags or what The Owner was talking about with the slave so animatedly or why the mulattos broke out laughing and the slave displayed such a big toothless grin. He was preoccupied with counting the tens and even hundreds of dollars he was going to receive for the bag of baking soda mixed with salt and any other white substance he could find on the cheap. He was already planning how he was going to use the money. The first thing he would do would be to celebrate with his trusted slave at the nearest bordello they could locate. Or perhaps the wise thing would be to buy two horses first, and maybe a cart, and then the bordello, and then find the nearest big city where he would buy more baking soda, and then cross the border to Kentucky to find new customers.

He was lost in this beautiful dream of a beautiful future when The Owner returned with the slave and two bottles of imported Irish whiskey. The Owner invited the slave, who had become timid all of a sudden, to join him and his master for a drink to celebrate the great transaction that was about to be made.

Barbecued meat went very well with whiskey and soon Quigley and The Owner were singing Irish and Appalachian songs. The slave was clapping and the mulattos looked on in amusement from their horses. *Over the hills and far away,* the drunken pair sang, and after an out of tune rendition they burst out laughing and shamelessly embraced each other. Then they lunged into the next song. By the time they got to singing *Black, black, black is the color of my true love's hair; her lips are like a rose so fair,* Quigley's eyes were misty. There was a deep longing in them. When the song came to an end the singers broke out laughing again and the slave couldn't help but jump up and perform a stupid jig that nevertheless increased the volume of the masters' laughter.

"Tell you what, mate," said The Owner, "I wanna buy your slave."

"Can't sell him, mate," said Quigley. "He's a great help on the road."

"I am talking to him," said The Owner pointing at the slave. "I am buying you from him. You *are* the slave, ain't you?"

Quigley laughed at the joke.

"It ain't no joke, you ninny," said the slave. And then to The Owner: "What's your offer?"

"For how much are you selling me, you ninny?" asked Quigley, getting into the spirit of the joke. The whole situation was indeed funny and he burst out laughing once more. This new friend was proving to be such a bundle of fun. All of a sudden the friend was no longer laughing. And the mulattos had dismounted and were slowly walking toward the revelers.

"Ten dollars," said The Owner.

"Fifty," said the slave.

"Twenty," said The Owner.

"Thirty," said the slave.

"Sold," said The Owner.

Things were looking serious. The mulattos closed in. They grabbed him. He fought back and kicked and scratched and bit. They pinioned his arms tightly behind him with a rope. He watched as The Owner counted thirty dollars and gave it to the slave. The Owner asked the slave to sign a receipt. Since he could not write he made a cross.

"He ain't no free black," said Quigley. "He's a slave. He won't get far."

"You're the slave," said The Owner. "I've got his manumission papers."

He reached for the papers in the saddlebag.

"What's your name, fella?" asked The Owner. When the slave hesitated he turned to Quigley and asked him the name of his former slave. It was only then that Quigley realized that he never really knew his slave's name. He was just a slave. He should have given him a name. The saying goes that you can never exercise full power over anything until you name it. If he had named him he would not have betrayed him like this. He would have owned him totally. The property would have been in awe of the master.

The slave had no memory of a name that ever belonged to him.

The Owner named him John Tyler after the President of the Union and signed the papers. He also wrote *John Tyler* next to the X the slave made on the receipt.

"You'll never get away with this, you ninny," screamed Quigley. "I am a white man born and bred. I can't be a slave."

"You ain't no white man, you ain't," said The Owner. "You are a mulatto. You are a fugitive from my plantation and now I am taking you back."

When the mulattos got mahogany chips from their saddlebags and boiled them in water on the very fire on which he had roasted his meat and then forcibly washed his face and hands with the concoction until he was brown, it became clear to him that The Owner had planned this whole thing even before he left his plantation. With the same fire The Owner heated an iron rod and the mulattos used it to curl the new slave's hair to imitate the African kink.

The look of his erstwhile master as a brown man with nappy hair brought a burst of toothless laughter to the erstwhile slave. He emptied all the white powder into the Guyandotte, took the bundle of clothes and provisions that previously belonged to the master but were now obviously his and bade everyone goodbye.

"Fare thee well, Mr. President," said The Owner, giving him a mock salute. The mulattos stood to attention and saluted as well. They watched him hobble away until he disappeared in the woods. Then they rode back to Fairfield Farms with their new slave securely tied with ropes.

❧

The Fairfield Farms community marveled at the new lackadaisical slave, a mulatto who kept on insisting that he was a white man. There were stories that he had been purchased from Alabama, though he kept on insisting that he was tricked and sold by his own slave to Mr. Fairfield. How could a slave have a slave? It was obvious to all that he had delusions of grandeur. That was why he had cultivated a white man's accent. And that was why he did not want to mix with other slaves.

From the time he arrived deep in the night and was chained to the wall in the guardroom, black slaves had made overtures of friendship toward him, as they always tried to assist the new arrivals to adapt to life at Fairfield Farms. They attempted to talk to him, but he sneered at them and faced the other way. Even when they brought him something to drink he gulped it grudgingly and did not even say thank you. When he was unchained after three days or so, and was assigned his duties, they continued to try to make him feel at home. They were rebuffed at every turn.

The community thought that as a mulatto he believed he was better than everyone else. Yet unlike other mulattos, who were a privileged lot, he worked with the black men in the fields. The community did not know why he was being treated so harshly. They did not understand why every week the man was forced by the faithful mulatto house slaves to take a secret bath in the guardroom, and why he hollered and cussed to the heavens every time he undertook these ablutions.

How could they believe his reason for smarting? After all, it was a known fact at the plantation that some of the slaves designated mulatto were in fact white. Even as The Owner registered them as his mulatto property after acquiring them, the authorities knew that they were white. Why would The Owner disguise the fact that the new slave was in fact white? Another thing: all the white slaves at Fairfield Farms were women, and were there for breeding mulatto children. What would The Owner be doing with a white male slave? If he was meant to mate with black women why was he never at the mating bays? The man must be delusional. He was clearly a mulatto. He just needed somebody to take him back to mother earth from the clouds on which he seemed to be floating.

Though the slave failed to convince the inhabitants of the plantation of his racial pedigree he knew that deep down under the brown dye of the mahogany chips he was a white man, as pure as The Owner himself. For many days after his capture he sank into a deep depression and stayed unwashed and stinking. Then he took to marching outside the big house singing Irish songs and demanding justice as an Irishman. The community was convinced that the new slave had gone raving mad. House slaves found this entertaining, especially when he took to calling The Owner names and demanded to see the lady of the house. They let him go on with his hollering for a while, especially when both targets of his invective were away. When everyone was tired of the entertainment the burly mulattos seized the slave, gave him a few whacks and then sent him to the guardhouse where they chained him to the walls.

Once the lady of the house came out to see what the commotion was about. Immediately the man saw her he threw himself at her feet and pleaded that she tell the truth. When the burly mulatto guards rushed forward to protect her she asked them to let the man speak. She was enjoying the mortification of the rogue who had exploited her naivety and almost cheated her of a fortune. The brown tone on his skin, the curly hair, the tattered calico pants and shirt, the black shoeless feet and the smudges of filth on his face arms and legs gave the lady of the house much satisfaction.

"You know me, you do," said the slave. "I sold you the potion and I'm sorry about it. You've humiliated me enough with the brown paint. Please ask your man to set me free, madam. I've learned my lesson."

But the lady of the house said she did not know what the lunatic was talking about. She denied ever setting eyes on him. She knew nothing about the potion either and did not understand the gibberish about brown paint. She ordered the guards to take him back to the guardhouse and chain him to the walls until he came to his senses. Only then could he return to the field to work with the other black men.

It was much better to be in the field than to be chained. Soon the slave calmed down and stopped his nonsense.

He seemed to get into the groove of things at the plantation and everyone thought he had accepted his lot like a man, though he kept to himself. Even the guards got careless and sometimes left his pen unlocked.

One day he took a chance and escaped. He told his story to white men he encountered outside the boundaries of Fairfield Farms. They did not believe him. Or they pretended not to believe him. Instead they brought him back to The Owner. He received a few lashes for that. Yet he tried again. But the slave chasers caught him before he could get far. He was, after all, ignorant of the art of flight and since he did not mix with the others, who he felt were naturally inferior, he did not learn anything about the message of the quilts and of the spirituals and about the slave stealers and all the lore surrounding freedom.

For a long time he steadfastly refused to socialize with other slaves. Until it became necessary to do so in order to get the hooch that the blacks covertly brewed or distilled. He realized that he had missed the communion of other men and women. For his survival he gradually developed the habits of Africans. By now he was no longer brown but white. The Owner and his minions had finally got tired of browning him with mahogany chips. They had humiliated him enough. But of course the change of color did not mean his situation had changed. The Owner still insisted that he was a mulatto and he was no different from the other white slaves who had been declared mulattos. To the Africans his white complexion did not matter anymore. What mattered was that he identified with Africans and therefore he was an African.

He became even more African when he was introduced to a mysterious fellow who lived by himself in his own cabin. It was known by now that he was Mrs. Fairfield's toy. Even small children knew that. The Owner himself knew that. The plantation gossip had it that The Owner had no choice but to let his wife have a male concubine because he had lost his potency after indulging himself with all and sundry until his penis shriveled into a small

worm because of disease. Some believed that the disease had af-
fected his head. Otherwise why would he turn a blind eye when
the big black fellow imported from Louisiana some years back ser-
viced the mistress of Fairfield Farms?

Sometimes he was seen walking his tiger on a leash, a gift from
the lady of the house purchased from a circus in Richmond after
it had become too old to perform tricks. The fellow was quite
friendly to the white slave when he first met him on one of his
rounds with his tiger. And the white slave thought the fellow was a
good man. Until he saw him being rude and arrogant to the black
slaves, people the white slave had come to consider his friends. The
big man was too good even to return their greeting. It was in reac-
tion to the behavior of this pitch black fellow who felt superior to
other blacks just because he slept with a white woman that the
white slave resolved to be even more African than ever before.

Although he was now armed with information about the slave
stealers who occasionally visited the region to whisk away slaves
across the Ohio River, he was too impatient to wait. In the second
year of his slavery he tried to escape again. This time he had learned
a few tricks and was gone for a few days. The slave chasers searched
in vain. Yet he was not far from Fairfield Farms all that time. He
had taken refuge in a church in Winfield. It was his good fortune
that the Quaker minister was an abolitionist.

The minister nevertheless respected the law of the land and did
not play an active role in assisting fugitives. When he heard the
slave's story he believed it and chose to take the legal route. He took
the matter to the Supreme Court of Virginia.

The case became a cause célèbre. Mr. David Fairfield engaged
the services of a well-known lawyer from Port Royal, Virginia, Mr.
George Fitzhugh.

Although Mr. Fitzhugh normally practiced as a criminal lawyer
he was particularly suited for this case because of his interest in slavery. He had written extensively in such papers as the *New York Day-
book*, *De Bow's Review* and the *Richmond Examiner* on the subject.

His position was that slavery was a natural and rightful condition of society.

The Owner's position in this case was that the slave in question, a mulatto male of undetermined age, was his rightful property. He brought witnesses, his own happy mulattos who were present when he purchased the said property from a white man on the banks of the Guyandotte. He produced papers and a receipt with a mark made by the former owner, a Mr. John Tyler. There were guffaws, as the name belonged to the President of the United States, a son of Virginia no less, but also a man who had lost favor with all political parties, including his own Whig Party, for exercising the veto indiscriminately. He had lost even more favor with the Democrats for his public declaration that in principle he was opposed to the perpetuation of slavery. This was much further than the Whigs of the South were prepared to go for they were lukewarm on slavery. As far as his fellow Virginians were concerned Tyler had clearly adopted the radical anti-slavery position of the northern Whigs. He had therefore betrayed their trust.

The similarity in names was a mere coincidence, the lawyer assured the judge. Another coincidence, said the lawyer playing to the gallery, was that the John Tyler from whom the slave was purchased was also a Whig. There was further mirth among the counselors and the officials of the august court, who were obviously Democrats. Derisive hisses of "His Accidency" were heard from the gallery.

The Quaker abolitionist knew immediately that among these old boys his man had no chance. As a "Negro" he was not even allowed to give evidence on his own behalf. The abolitionist spoke for him and outlined his whole journey from Tipperary County in Ireland and his misfortunes in the new world. He pleaded that they allow the poor fellow to utter a few words so that they could hear his accent was clearly Irish.

There was absolute silence when Mr. Fitzhugh made his closing remarks. His client had proved that the man in question was his mulatto slave, and the Quaker minister should in fact be charged with theft of an honest man's property. But that was not the end of it, he said. It was important that his countrymen should note carefully what he was about to say, because he was talking on behalf of many property owners of the South whose rights were being gradually eroded by the new order.

"The man is clearly a mulatto, your honor," said Mr. Fitzhugh, "and we know that there are many like him who can easily pass for white. In any event poor whites are better off as slaves. Class rather than race should be the determining factor for slavery."

The gallery of property owners could not help applauding. The bailiff ordered silence in the court. But it took the lawyer a few more seconds to resume his speech.

He went on to outline these ideas to the fascination of The Owner and his fellow owners in the gallery, many of whom already kept white slaves in any case.

His position was not based on the inferiority of the black race, Fitzhugh argued. The principle of only enslaving the descendants of Africans was an antiquated one. The time had now come, as was the case in Greece and Rome, to embrace slavery of every race and variety of complexion. This was to protect the interests of the affluent class of whites in the slaveholding states. There was a sense of helplessness among these privileged classes because the South was breeding slaves that were now indistinguishable from pure whites. "If slavery was to be at all vindicated," he said, "it must not now be on the narrow basis of color but on the broad grounds that there is an inherent right in the stronger and more wealthy classes to reduce the poorer and ignorant orders to a state of perpetual bondage."

The perplexed judge asked if such ideas would not instill the rebelliousness that was already apparent in the Negro. Would the Negro not think that he now ranked on the same scale of humanity as a white man? Would ideas like these not reinforce the arrogant attitude that was already evident in the free Negroes who even owned slaves themselves?

"It is obvious to all, including to the Negro himself, that he should be a slave for he is fit only to labor and not to direct," said Mr. Fitzhugh. "But the principle of slavery is, itself, right and does not depend on difference of complexion."

These views, of course, had by now become commonplace among the literate. Mr. Fitzhugh and others who thought like him had put them on the national agenda through articles in the newspapers. Those who were alive a decade later saw these ideas published in his famous book, *Sociology for the South.*

But in court that day the judge emphasized that whatever decision the court reached would not be on the basis of whether whites should be slaves or not, since that was not yet the law of the Commonwealth of Virginia. It was clear to him from the evidence presented that the complainant was a fraud. He was a mulatto male, rightful property of Mr. David Fairfield. The poor Quaker minister had been duped by the mulatto, and this illustrated that ministers who often did these things from the kindness of their heart in their service to God needed to be careful. He, as the judge of the Commonwealth, therefore, did not blame the poor minister at all. The mulatto slave was obviously a scoundrel. He had mastered an Irish accent from his previous master where he had been a house slave and was now using this to cheat his way into the world of free men. The Honorable Mr. David Fairfield should therefore take his property and go home in peace. The Quaker minister should be grateful for the mercy of the court and of the Honorable David Fairfield. Otherwise he would have been charged with the theft of someone else's property.

The slave screamed and uttered Irish profanities to no avail.

The Owner took his mulatto slave back to Fairfield Farms where he became an African again.

❧

To the slave's surprise, after this episode he was not treated harshly anymore. He resigned himself to his fate. He performed his duties well, and soon he was promoted to a supervisory position at the vegetable gardens. By this time he was free to mingle with other white slaves, including the aristocratic ones who worked in the household. But he always preferred the company of the Africans. He was more at home with the field slaves and shared in their folklore. He found that some of the stories they told in the evenings were very similar to the folk stories he used to hear as a child back in Ireland.

One favorite story told over and over again was about a woman called the Abyssinian Queen and how she herself used to tell stories. She was so beautiful that The Owner ran mad with desire for her. She was powerful too, for the ancestors who lived in her stories protected her and even The Owner was in awe of her. She had two sons, Nicodemus and Abednego. They were as wily as Ananse the Spider of their mother's stories. One day the sons escaped and crossed the River Jordan. She was punished severely for their escape and for weeks or even months she lay sick on her bed, and was nursed by blind matriarchs. One day a big blue fly came and hovered over her. For the first time her pain seemed to go away. She laughed and whispered: "Thank you, Lord. Oh, thank you, my sweet Lord!" The sound of the blue fly seemed to lull her to sleep. She died smiling a broad smile.

The white slave was fascinated by the beautiful death of the Abyssinian Queen. He vowed that one day he would retrace the steps of her two boys. One day he too would cross the River Jordan. The plantation grapevine had brought the news back to Fairfield Farms: the Abyssinian Queen's boys lived in a paradise called Tabler Town, a day's journey from the River Jordan. Both were crowned chiefs of Indian tribes. And both had vowed that one day they would come with their Indian braves to free everyone at the plantation.

The white slave was not prepared to wait for that day though. Even if it took him years he would find his way to Tabler Town. He would bide his time. He would not leave anything to chance next time he escaped. He would study the methods that were used by the boys. He would learn about the quilts and the secret messages they contained. He would study other escapes recorded in folklore. He would take time to work out an elaborate plan. Next time he escaped, he vowed, no one would catch him.

He had been a slave for eight years when slave stealers from Ripley, Ohio, secretly visited the region. As usual the message was relayed through songs, and the white slave, now adept at the ways of the slaves, was one of those who were able to escape.

🪶

The Tablers of Tabler Town welcomed a new resident, a craggy Irishman by the name of Quigley. The family employed the man as a farmhand, and in the evenings listened to his stories of slavery. He told them of his escape from Fairfield Farms assisted by the sons of the Reverend John Rankin of Ripley, Ohio, of the succor he received at the home of the same Rankin overlooking the mighty Ohio River, of the insistence that he wanted to proceed to Athens County and to find two Africans he regarded as his brothers though he had never met them, namely Nicodemus and Abednego, and of his final journey to Tabler Town as a fully fledged white man after he had spent about six months with the Rankins recovering from the scars of slavery.

He was not sure whether he actually experienced the journey to Athens County or whether he dreamed it. He remembered or dreamed an intersection where he had great difficulty turning onto the road that would lead him to Tabler Town. There were many wagons, carts and carriages that moved very slowly, blocking the road. There were also many people selling their wares and blaring bullhorns. Among them he saw his slave dressed like a Native American in a black hat and a Navajo blanket worn poncho-style. The slave looked quite different though, his formerly skeletal figure filled with glistening flesh. The slave walked among the people selling scrolls and cloths that were red and white in color. He dashed from one side of the road to the other showing his wares to people who were hurrying about. The slave approached Quigley and Quigley shouted, "Hey, you ninny, how much are those scrolls?" The slave said they were ten dollars. One year's savings for a working man! Quigley felt there must be something about the scrolls.

"What are they used for?" he asked.

"As a room divider," the slave said, stretching one so that the prospective customer could see its full length and breadth. The slave did not recognize his master, and the master did not reveal his identity.

Although Quigley thought the scrolls were too narrow to use as dividers he still bought one. One day he would have a bedroom of his own. And a wife. He was determined not to go back to his old life of whiskey, whores and gaming. He would use the scroll to demarcate his territory so that his wife would know which side was his and which was hers. He had become very territorial from his experience of sleeping in slave quarters.

When he stretched the scroll he discovered that it was very long. It was made of fluffy feather-like material. On it were symbols and figures. He did not know how he learned to decipher such inscriptions, but he read them and discovered that the scroll contained the story of his life—from his past to the present. He could actually read the very present—reading about himself reading the scroll. There were other symbols that he tried to decipher but with great difficulty. He assumed they contained the story of his future and of the generations that would emerge from his loins. But he could not be sure about this.

After this the only thing he remembered vividly was an early morning after a particularly rainy night. He was waiting for a flood to subside with a group of people who were on their way to Tabler Town and beyond. Even as he stood there he was not sure if he had experienced the crossroads incident or dreamed it. No one

among the people waiting knew anything about any such crossroads anywhere in the region. Yet he still had the scroll with him.

If Quigley happened to be at his house when he told the story he
would take out the scroll and show his listeners. They would mar-
vel at the symbols and the figures and he would tell them what they
meant. Right up to the time he was telling the story.

"One day I'm gonna know what the rest means, and when that
happens I will tell the future," he said with conviction.

The first thing he did when he got to Tabler Town was to seek
out Nicodemus and Abednego. He found Abednego and wept
when he learned of the death of Nicodemus. Quigley suggested to
Abednego that one day they should set out to avenge Nicodemus's
death, in memory of the fellow Africans that they left behind at
Fairfield Farms and of all those who had been captured and sold
and tortured and killed.

At first Abednego thought this was just idle talk. He had never
really entertained any thoughts of vengeance. He was happily married to one of Harry Corbett's beautiful daughters and was im-
mersed in his father-in-law's experiments with growing pawpaw in
his orchards. He spent most of his days sitting there, staring at the
trees as if willing them to grow, sometimes talking to them, egging
them on and promising them the world if only they would show a
peep of flowers. This was beginning to show results. Trees that
had been growing slowly in the five years since the enterprise was
started were almost the height of a man and had bloomed. Later
the leaves would grow compact and dense. The plants looked
healthier than those that grew in the wild. There was reason to celebrate, for the challenge of growing pawpaw as transplants had
been won.

These were the beautiful thoughts that occupied Abednego's
mind, not vengeance. The white man was not making sense, although Abednego suddenly felt ashamed that he had forgotten
about Nicodemus while he established his new life in Tabler
Town. But vengeance was not part of his makeup. He did not see

how it would help his dead brother. Surely it would not bring him back to life. He doubted if his mother would have wanted him to commit such an act. To get rid of Quigley he promised him he was going to think seriously about it, and Quigley said that he was keen to help. He was still angry about what had been done to him and he had to take out that anger on someone.

Abednego heard for the first time from Quigley how the Abyssinian Queen died laughing and praising the Lord after the return of Massa Blue Fly. It was a good thing, thought Abednego, that she never knew that Nicodemus did not quite reach the Promised Land. She must have been surprised on reaching the Otherworld to find Nicodemus there, newly arrived as well. Or did the Abyssinian Queen arrive before Nicodemus? There was no way of knowing how long it took Massa Blue Fly to reach her.

As months went by a strong bond developed between Quigley and Abednego. They went hunting and fishing together. Sometimes they were brave enough to venture to Athens to watch college students play a new version of rounders called baseball. It was always dangerous to go to Athens because lurking behind the friendly face of a college town were the likes of William Tobias who were now resorting to abducting free blacks and taking them across the Ohio into slavery. Men like these were a law unto themselves. Since 1831 there were penalties for kidnapping free blacks, but that did not give any comfort to blacks because slave chasers were not deterred by such laws.

Abednego was the best man when Quigley married one of Harry Corbett's daughters. People talked about the wedding for a long time, but not because it was particularly grand. On the contrary it was meant to be a quiet affair at the Methodist church. What people talked about was not how beautiful the bride looked, but how her uncle, Harry Corbett's hothead brother, caused a commotion outside the church by preaching his own sermon denouncing what was happening in the church.

People generally dismissed the man as a rabid Indian nationalist who felt that the Negro had degraded and destroyed his Indian race by marrying into it, to the degree that it was no longer respected by other races—by which of course he meant by the whites. He also said that the Indian claim of the Tabler Town area as an ancestral land would be rejected by the state of Ohio on the basis of what he called mongrelization. But no one had thought that the man would also denounce a marriage between a daughter of the tribe and a white man. Was it because this particular white man identified more with the black people? Or did the man disburse his hatred equally without fear or favor? He had an audience too. Those citizens of Tabler Town who could not be accommodated in the small church had no choice but to listen to his sermon.

At the same time another sermon was being delivered in the church. Perhaps the minister thought it best to take advantage of the presence of people of color—who didn't normally attend his church, but who had now gathered in great numbers for the wedding of this important community member—and preach a sermon on issues that had been bothering him. He was a liberal man, well-beloved by the colored community. So people gasped when he preached against the Underground Railroad. His grounds were that it worked against the attempt to keep the races separate in America. He emphasized that he was saying all this because he was a friend of the Negroes. It was in the interests of the Negro to keep the races apart. People knew that he supported the move started a decade or so before to send all black folks to Africa. He was active in collecting funds from the wealthier citizens and in staging fund-raising events to pay for their passages. If the Negroes married other races—be they races of European origin or Indian—they would see no need to return to their continent, and the continent would then be deprived of their skills and of the civilizing influence they would have on the hordes of savages still roaming naked in the jungles of that unfortunate continent.

Both the groom and his best man found the sermon disgusting,

although it was not their first time to hear such ideas. They had
read in newspaper articles where liberals—some of whom were
even stationmasters of the Underground Railroad—were roundly
condemning such communities as Tabler Town for promoting
"the amalgamation between white and black races, which was not
desirable and was not in the interests of the Negro." What made
Quigley mad was that the minister chose the occasion of his wedding to preach such garbage. It was obvious to him that the minister had agreed to solemnize a marriage between an Indian woman
and a white man in order to use it as a platform to propagate his
ideas. Or perhaps he approved of the "amalgamation" of whites
and Indians but not of Africans and the other races. And he was
saying all these things because of his brimming love for the black
races of the earth.

Quigley felt that his wedding had been defiled and turned into a
circus both by the uncle outside and the minister inside.

With the encouragement of his best man he went through the
service with stoicism.

❧

They had been inducted by Birdman. And for four years they had
worked tirelessly as conductors of the Underground Railroad. They
had crossed the Ohio River on many occasions to steal slaves on the
other side. Or to assist those who had escaped up to the river to cross
to freedom in skiffs. They had had close shaves with the law: de-
cades-old slave laws stipulated that blacks were not permitted to re-
side in Ohio unless they could prove they were free. Abednego did
not have any such proof. Nor did the countless fugitives they con-
ducted to safety. In the very free state of Ohio it was a criminal of-
fense to harbor blacks or to aid a fugitive. Once, Quigley had been
kidnapped by a party from Stewart for the crime of aiding and
abetting fugitives, and all in Tabler Town had been up in arms as a

result. The Stewart folks had to release him. Slave hunters were fearful of Tabler Town as a result.

And now on this beautiful day here were Quigley and Abednego standing on the banks of the Ohio River at Gallipolis, looking helplessly as the steamboat took Birdman away. He had been captured in the woods in Meigs County. Quigley and Abednego suspected that William Tobias had something to do with it, although admittedly they had not heard of Tobias for some months, or even years. For some reason he was lying low. If it was not Tobias who captured their mentor, destroyed his old manumission papers that he used in Ohio to prove he was a legal black and dragged him to the steamboat in chains, then it was one or other of the slave hunters who were always lurking around, sniffing like bloodhounds and ready to pounce on any black they came across. They had taken to capturing free blacks to sell in Virginia or Kentucky. But most importantly, they were always on the lookout for Underground Railroad conductors, who were lucrative bounty. Everyone knew there was a big price on Birdman's head. Even as Quigley and Abednego stood there, watching the steamboat sail away, shaking in anger, they knew that they were not safe at all for there was a two thousand dollar reward—money raised by plantation owners—for the assassination of the Underground Railroad operators.

The message came too late to them. They were working in their father-in-law's orchard when a young rider came with the news that Birdman had been captured and was held hostage in a house in Athens. Without wasting time they took their guns and rode to Athens. They planned to invade the house and save their mentor. But they were too late. He was already being transported to Gallipolis. There was no time to go back to Tabler Town to warn their families that they would be away, perhaps for a number of days. In any event their wives and young children understood the nature of their work. They rode toward Gallipolis, hoping to catch the wagon transporting the captive even before it got to Pomeroy. They never did.

When they arrived in Gallipolis it was too late. The steamboat was already sailing away. Birdman was going to be sold as a slave in Kentucky. All they could do was to curse the steamboat captain. They knew him very well. They had often bribed him to take runaways to the Ohio side. The scoundrel worked both ways. He was sometimes bribed by slave hunters to take their captives to the Virginia side of the river. The bastard worked for the highest bidder.

Abednego and Quigley had on many occasions recovered abducted blacks in steamboats before they sailed away. It pained them greatly that they failed to recover their mentor.

In the weeks and months that followed the two men went on with their daily lives. Yet deep inside each one of them was a deep pain that could not be healed. Abednego gradually withdrew from the Underground Railroad and focused on the orchards and on experimenting with pawpaw. Quigley built a whiskey still and rode the countryside flogging his moonshine made of corn and wheat; or negotiating for the freedom of human property in exchange for great quantities of his potent whiskey with the Christianized Cherokees across the river who had adopted the European habit of buying and selling Africans. He was relentless in his quest for the freedom of others. He was also relentless in another quest: that of redeeming his soul. He became part of the Great Awakening, attending religious revivals that were sweeping the Appalachians, screaming the name of the Lord at nightlong Methodist and Baptist vigils without discrimination.

His active participation in religious revivals did not stop him from dabbling in the art of predicting the future using his red and white scroll whose inscriptions he continued to struggle to interpret. But he told people whatever they wanted to hear and therefore he spread happiness all around.

When he returned to Athens County from his quests he helped his good wife, who was now running a full-time Underground

Railroad station on the outskirts of the city. Not only did he become an esteemed stationmaster, but he bore witness whenever it was necessary to do so. Black people could not bear witness in cases involving white people. Even free blacks who had been captured by slave hunters could not bear witness on their own behalf against their white captors. They needed a white person to testify on their behalf; otherwise they were denied legal protection. This, of course, emboldened slave hunters who defied the laws against kidnapping free blacks. Quigley always stepped forward to bear witness for the free blacks. He was such a regular at the courts that the judges derisively dubbed him a "professional witness" and placed little or no weight on his testimony.

In the evenings Quigley and Abednego sat on the porch of Harry Corbett's house smoking their pipes. At these moments they did not speak much to each other. Only the smoke rings that floated above their heads spoke of their sorrow. At odd moments one of them would remember something from the very distant world of Fairfield Farms. Then they would ruminate about it. And after some more silence one would provide some piece of wisdom. Like when Quigley related some titbit from the Underground Railroad grapevine: Mrs. Fairfield was rumored to have manumitted her exotic slave and run away with him to Ohio. Since the runaway lovers could not feel safe anywhere in the state, they were en route to Canada. After digesting the news with a few puffs and a number of lazy smoke rings Abednego observed that the hunting season would provide particularly tasty deer that year.

One day, after a particularly long silence, Abednego jumped up and said: "We gotta do something!"

"'Bout what?" asked Quigley.

"Birdman . . . Nicodemus. You was right, Niall. We gotta find Tobias."

"Yeah," agreed Quigley. "None of us gonna be top dollar till we do something about the bastard."

It was not easy to find William Tobias. People had not heard of him for many years, which was rather strange because he had been a flamboyant fellow who was in love with his own booming voice and was fond of riding the paved streets with a throng of body-guards in red and black uniforms that resembled those of some storybook military guard. And then one day, poof, William Tobias was not there!

It took a lot of patience to find him living a frugal life in the town of Ripley, Ohio. Clearly the man was enamored of the Ripley name since his origins were in a town of a similar name in Virginia. The two men could not understand how Tobias had fallen on hard times since slave hunting, even in those dying years of slavery, was still a lucrative business. When they found him in a run-down house he was in conference with another man who soon left on horseback. Quigley knew him immediately as one of the sons of the Reverend Rankin and wondered what a respected abolitionist and slave stealer was doing with a dirty man like Tobias.

Abednego was suddenly seized by a fit of anger, which he tried to control nevertheless. He remembered that face very well, although Tobias was now much grayer and the face had lost its luster and chubbiness. The man extended his hand to greet the visitors but Abednego could not bring himself to touch the hand that had murdered his brother. Quigley quickly withdrew his in solidarity.

Tobias did not know who the men were, but he invited them in and offered them his hospitality despite the obvious meagerness of his means. Even when the men introduced themselves their names did not mean anything to him. He assumed that they had come to join him for evening prayers or had some slave fugitive business to discuss.

"So how come you so poor if you still in that business?" asked Quigley.

Tobias laughed, and then said his guests were misunderstanding him. If they were looking for a slave hunter they had come to the wrong place. He had found the Lord, or the Lord found him, years ago. He was now a Quaker and an abolitionist. He was working in cahoots with the Rankin family and other Underground Railroad operators. That was why he had settled in Ripley by the Ohio River.

"Shite," screamed Quigley, "you wanna make things difficult for us. We came to bloody do you in."

"Why do you want to kill me?" asked Tobias.

"'Cause you killed my brother," said Abednego. He did not say anything about Birdman. It was already obvious to both men that Tobias had nothing to do with Birdman's capture. When it happened he was already a Quaker abolitionist.

"I don't know your brother," said Tobias.

Abednego took this as an indication that William Tobias was a callous liar who was now denying murdering his brother when he saw him do it with his own eyes. He hit him on the head with his Brown Bess, the flintlock musket that he used to carry during his conductor days but that had never fired a shot in anger. Tobias fell on the floor. He pleaded with the men to leave him alone for he had no money to give them. Whatever he owned had been given to the poor years ago. He had had a personal encounter with God. Because God's spirit lived deep in his soul he was a pacifist and did not believe in any form of violence or in the taking of human life.

"Shut up, you son of a bitch," yelled Abednego, blinded by rage. "You killed my brother Nicodemus in cold blood. You captured fugitives and took them back to slavery."

At this time Tobias was on his knees, his shaking hands together as if in prayer.

"That was then; I am a changed man now. I renounced that sinful life years ago. I disavowed all belief in slavery and in the inferiority of any race of God's people. I have the Inner Light. God has forgiven me."

"That ain't gonna bring my brother back," said Abednego raising the musket and taking aim. Quigley was too slow to stop him from blasting the man's head off. Quigley then whipped out his own pistol and shot Tobias's corpse so as to share his friend's guilt and to personally experience any pangs of conscience that were sure to attack Abednego when he regained his sanity.

The two mounted their horses and escaped. They knew that the abolitionists of Ripley would be up in arms searching for the killers, thinking that they were slave hunters. The two former slaves wept uncontrollably as they fled for their lives from the wrath of the abolitionists.

The killing of William Tobias did not heal the two men's deep sorrow. Instead it became worse. They spent the remaining days of their lives sitting on the porch brooding about William Tobias. They had killed a man who did not fight back. A man who was kneeling down in prayer.

*O*rpah. She will never know the things I have done with her in
my dreams. In my sleeping and waking hours. In the day
and in the night. Throughout the winter months right up to this
scented season—the final weeks of spring. Even as I sit on a
mound wailing like the wind for the child who is lying in a small
white coffin my thoughts are racing up and down the contours of
her naked body. It does not help that she is standing across from
me in a black dress and black lampshade hat. I have never seen her
in a dress before. It makes her look more voluptuous than she really is. She is holding a small bouquet of rambling roses. The
serenity on her face is befitting to the occasion.

I try very hard to focus on the business at hand; namely, mourning the child in the coffin. I need to excel myself, for this is the first
opportunity I have had in this community to mourn in public. The
audience are the relatives of the deceased, which is the same as saying every adult in Kilvert. From the depths of my soul I draw deep
and hollow groans, howls, whimpers and moans as rhythmic as
they are harrowing. My lamentations are meant to help the grieving relatives who have been numbed by the pain of death come to
terms with their sorrow. Through my tears I share their anguish
with the rest of the world. For me this is a glorious moment. It's
been a while since I have mourned at a live funeral.

Ruth and Mahlon are here too. He brought a chair for her since
she cannot stand for long periods. He dutifully stands behind her.
She is in a navy blue dress with yellow flowers and a black and
white fur pillbox hat. She has obviously sewn the dress herself and
it hangs like a tent on her. He is in a rumpled gray suit, white shirt

and a colorful tie with an image of Mickey Mouse. Even on this solemn occasion he has a smile, although it is fainter than usual. He holds a Bible with his left hand and Ruth's ample shoulder with his right.

I am determined to save Orpah from him.

Even my favorite scoundrel is here. Instead of his usual khaki or denim shorts today he is formal in a blue dress-shirt, a very English tweed jacket, black pants and black brogues: all courtesy of the Kilvert Community Center, as is the case with everyone's attire here. He would not have missed this funeral for all the beer in Athens. The self-satisfied smile on his face is well earned. He worked very hard to have me as a mourner here today. Sister Naomi, the mother of the deceased, was adamant that she was not going to have a professional mourner at her child's funeral. Obed went twice to the pokey in Athens where she is awaiting trial to plead with her to let me mourn on her behalf and on behalf of the community. She declined the offer. She claimed that she was a good woman of the church and would not have unchristian practices, even if they were African, at her son's funeral. Obed went to the other relatives, who gave differing views on the matter. One of them, a certain Ruth Quigley, pooh-poohed the whole idea out of hand. Professional mourning was not in the Bible, she said.

I was not surprised at Ruth's attitude. She had said as much to me on a few occasions before. It started when she waged a campaign against me for defending and even hiding Orpah's drawings. She had attacked me for performing heathen practices.

Although I am not an expert on the Bible I know that in my country it was used to oppress and to fight against oppression. It was used to justify apartheid on the one hand, and the liberation struggle on the other—by liberation theologists, for instance. When Obed and I were cracking our heads on how to convince Sister Naomi and her relatives I told him about the usefulness of the Bible in justifying anything you want to justify, and he thought that was the most exciting thing he had heard in a long time. The

Bible would come in handy not only for this special occasion of the funeral, but for all his future dealings with his mother. Why, he could even have used the Bible to counter Ruth's biblical attacks on his hand trembling business!

Obed went to Brother Michael and asked him to search the Bible for any mention of professional mourning. I had also told him that in my quest I had not only learned about the Greeks and the Romans, but had also enriched my own mourning from the practice of Old Egypt where funeral processions pulled by oxen were accompanied by professional mourners hired to wail and gnash their teeth. In today's world I had learned how the Taiwanese employed professional mourners such as the Filial Daughters Band to wail, scream and create the kind of anguish the weary bereaved were too numb to generate for themselves. I had also been inspired by the children of Israel who, in biblical times, did not only lament and weep bitterly for their dead but employed professional mourners to add more anguish to their sorrow. Even the poorest of families in Old Israel saw fit to engage the services of at least one professional mourner. It was for this reason then that Obed thought Brother Michael as a preacherman of The Word would be the best person to find a passage in the Bible that would justify my wails at the funeral.

The best Brother Michael could come up with was a few words on the burial of a man called Stephen in the Acts of the Apostles 8:2: *And devout men carried Stephen to his burial, and made great lamentation over him.* This was good enough to take to Sister Naomi, and the fact that it had been Brother Michael who discovered the passage in the Bible convinced her that indeed God did want her to have great lamentation at her son's funeral. And who was best suited to provide that if not a professional mourner? The sundry cousins and aunts and uncles had to follow suit whether they agreed with this or not. Sister Naomi was the mother, after all, even though it was her irresponsible behavior that led to the death of the child.

When Ruth heard that Brother Michael decreed lamentations would be allowed at the funeral, and that they would be led by the African shaman to whom she had given succor under her roof, she felt betrayed once more. Not so much by Brother Michael, from whom no good could be expected in any event since he was a known adulterer, but by the so-called African shaman who used to be her own African only a few months back. At first she thought she would boycott the funeral. But common sense prevailed. That is why she is here today. And that is why she kept on telling her friends just before the service began that she was only here for the child, who could not be blamed for the foolishness of his mother and of those who professed to be messengers of The Word of God.

Obed had to explain the rudiments of my mourning before Brother Michael took over the service, so that the people did not get the shock of their lives when they saw a strange figure in black top hat, cape and tight pants punctuating hymns and scriptural readings with strange noises. He manufactured some origins for me that dated back to the pharaohs of Egypt. That is why everyone is looking at me in awe as I go full throttle with lamentations that even I did not know were possible.

But the scoundrel did not stop there. In his own Kilvert vernacular he explained to the congregation that every one of them was totally inept at handling grief. That was just how human beings were created. Hence the need for a professional mourner. He reached for his mother's Bible resting on her lap. Ruth was caught by surprise and at first instinctively held on to her holy book, but soon released it. Her son paged through the good book frantically while everyone looked expectant. He read a paragraph from a letter that St. Paul wrote to the Romans urging them to rejoice with those who rejoiced and weep with those who wept. Then he paged through again until he got to Jeremiah 9:17—*Thus says the Lord of hosts: Consider the call for the mourning women that they may come; and send for skillful wailing women, that they may come. Let them make haste and take up wailing for us, that our eyes may run with tears, and our eyelids gush with water.*

It was at this reading that I started the mourning sounds that I have sustained at varying volumes to this point.

I could see tears swelling in Ruth's eyes. She was clearly proud of her son. She looked at me and smiled. The Bible had finally convinced her of the legitimacy of my profession. Then she looked at Obed as he went on to clarify to the congregation that skillful wailing women were in fact professional mourners. In those days professional mourning was a female occupation. But they could not begrudge his African brother for being a male professional mourner since these were equal opportunity days. One could not discriminate on the basis of gender.

The attention is still on me even when Brother Michael reads from The Second Book of Samuel 12:21–23—*Then his servants said to him, "What is this that you have done? You fasted and wept for the child while he was alive, but when the child died, you arose and ate food." And he said, "While the child was alive, I fasted and wept: for I said, 'Who can tell whether the Lord will be gracious to me, that the child may live?' But now he is dead; why should I fast? Can I bring him back again? I shall go to him, but he shall not return to me."*

Throughout this reading I am moaning in monotone, which blends so beautifully—even if I say so myself—with his booming voice. I can see that Brother Michael is fighting for his dignity and for his good name. He will not be outdone by Obed, who, as far as the pastor knows, has not set his foot in church since the days before the man of the cloth came to Kilvert and the boy was forced by his parents to attend church. What he must be smarting about most is the fact that Obed found a more relevant passage about professional mourners than he, even with all his Bible School training.

Occasionally I throw a glance at Obed, who is standing next to Nathan. Nathan is not dressed up for the occasion but is in his dirty work clothes. I can see Obed's pride from his gestures and his beaming face. Obviously he is explaining all the intricacies of mourning to his friend, who looks rather bemused.

Unlike the funerals back home, no one takes it upon himself or herself to narrate the death of the child. No one even whispers that the child was killed by his own mother and her boyfriend; that the very pious Sister Naomi of Brother Michael's church was a meth cook on the side; that she used her SUV, one of those I saw parked outside the little chocolate church, as a mobile meth lab; that the fertilizers and chemicals in the concoction exploded one evening, killing the little boy who was playing near the vehicle; that Sister Naomi had sent this little boy and her other children to smurf for her—buying two packets of Sudafed, then moving to the next store to do the same to circumvent the law.

At the funerals back home The Nurse—a person designated by the family of the deceased to narrate the death of the deceased, and that was given that title because in the olden days it would have been the person who had nursed the deceased during the sickness that led to death—would have made meat of this scandalous story. The kind of Nurse who saw himself or herself as a moral guardian of the community would have gone on to give lessons about the dangers of the crystal meth or super-speed that is devastating the rural communities of America, and can be made from the common cold remedies that have ephedrine as an ingredient. He or she would have gone to town blaming the mother and the boyfriend, especially because this was not the first time she had been in trouble with the law. The people of Kilvert do remember, after all, that Sister Naomi was once in the pokey for child endangerment and was released after a strong warning. The Nurse would have uttered all these things in a sad sanctimonious voice under the guise of warning the people against such practices that were destructive to the very soul of the community. But none of these things were even whispered here. To these people a funeral is not a place for recrimination.

After the funeral Sister Naomi's relatives pay me a few banknotes, mostly singles, and coins, since it was impressed upon them that it is absolutely essential to pay the mourner some money for the mourning to have any effect, even if it is a token fee. Professional mourning without a fee is not professional mourning but just downright pedestrian mourning. They shake my hand and some say: "Thank you, Brother African Shaman," while others repeat: "Thank you, Son of Egypt."

❧

I meet Ruth on Monday—the morning after the funeral. She is sitting at her workstation contemplating pieces of fabric, maybe planning where each will go in the grand scheme of cut pieces that are neatly arranged on the table.

"Brother African Shaman, hey?" she says without looking at me. "You know you can't serve God and be a shaman at the same time?"

"I have never called myself a shaman, Ruth," I protest.

I cannot be blamed for the labels that people give me. In fact, her son was to blame for my shaman title, which I don't relish at all. It was of his invention. He is the one who propagated it. Now everyone thinks that I am indeed a shaman. Even the kids hollered when they saw me in my sacred costume after the funeral: "Hey, Brother African Shaman! Give us one of them yells, my man."

"Yeah, that's what they called you yesterday," she says, rubbing it in. "Brother African Shaman. Son of Egypt."

She looks at me and smiles. She seems to have warmed to me a bit. I suspect it is the result of the biblical justification of my profession. Or perhaps my pharaonic connections—again manufactured by her son—have something to do with it. I return her smile uneasily. I need to tread lightly here. She invites me for a cup of sassafras tea.

"Know what sassafras tea is, Son of Egypt?"

Sarcasm does not suit her.

"This ain't the one you buy from Kroger," she says. "That one ain't no good 'cause it's made from shaven bark. Bet you never tasted the one I am gonna give you."

"Never tasted any sassafras tea whatsoever."

It's brewed already on the stove. She asks me to bring it and two coffee mugs. The steaming liquid is dark red and the taste is good, especially with sugar and cream.

"You can take it as iced tea as well," Ruth tells me. "Without cream or sugar . . . or maybe just a li'l sugar."

The tea is made from the roots of a young sassafras tree, I learn. Every year at the end of February Mahlon Quigley digs out the roots in the woods, which are then preserved to last for the whole year. It is important to remember that one can only dig out the roots from the end of February to about March 20. After that date the sap goes up to the bark and to the branches and leaves, and the roots lose their wonderful taste.

"The best tea," says Ruth as she sips with much satisfaction, "is when the sap is still in them roots . . . when they're still red like blood. Then you boil it good. You ain't gonna see none of us buy sassafras tea from stores. Here we dig the root 'cause it gives a much better flavor."

It cleans the blood, she adds. She takes four cups a day to keep her blood pure. It is not like her red slate, which she eats for the joy of it, in memory of her childhood, and of the slaves who were forced to eat mud to ease the pangs of hunger. Sassafras tea is medicinal in addition to its tasty pleasures.

The taste takes her back to the period people here refer to as "back in the day," to the log house in which she was raised. Her mother used to brew the tea on a stove. The fascinating thing about the stove was that it had a water tank on the side to warm water while the food was cooking on the top. "There was no water heaters in them days," she says with satisfaction. "We slept in one room measuring about twenty by twenty." I did not see the connection between the lack of hot water heaters and the sleeping arrangements.

Many things have changed since then. Even the name changed from Tabler Town to Kilvert. The new name came with coal mining.

"Back in the day there was coal mines here," Ruth says. "There was a mine from Irene's place to the cemetery next to the church. Not strip mining. Them miners went down."

There used to be many houses in Kilvert in those days, right across the Federal Creek bridge. Kilvert was a thriving community during its coal mining days. The railroad to Cincinnati went through here near Cutler. You could catch a train to Cincy right here. There was even a post office in the village. Now the nearest post office is in Stewart, a world away if you have to walk. There was a saloon also; though it's a good thing that there is no saloon anymore. Men used to drink themselves silly and everyone forgot about God. There was money to waste, that's why. The coal mine bosses were locals: the Jenkins family, for instance. When the mines went out of coal it was the downfall of Kilvert. People left to get jobs elsewhere. They went as far as Chicago to work in the factories. Those who had coal in their blood left for the coal mines of West Virginia. There are now only about seventy families remaining in Kilvert. But those who left always come back to visit those who remained. Or to get old and die in the bosom of their ancestors. For example, the wealthy Jenkinses moved to Kenton, but the rest of the Jenkins family is still here.

Oh, yes, things have changed in Kilvert. But one thing has remained the same. They listen to weather reports and store food when there are predictions of rain. The floods have always been a constant through the generations.

❧

Ruth accepts my professional mourning with grace, but if the Kilverters thought she would be impressed by my grand Egyptian connections they were soon proven wrong. It turns out she has no regard for the pharaohs because in the Bible they are villains. They oppressed the children of Israel and tried to stop Moses from leading them to freedom. Ruth identifies with the children of Israel. The pharaohs are therefore cast in the same mold as the slaveholders who kept her people in bondage in the South. But she is generous enough to tell me that she does not hold the actions of my ancestors against me. I try to put the record straight that nothing is pharaonic about me and my ancestry is totally South African but she dismisses that as an attempt at denying my roots because of the shame I must be feeling for the pharaohs' repressive actions. She had seen from the day I arrived that my complexion was too "yella" for an African. One only had to take a walk down Court Street in Athens during the Africa Day Street Fair to see that Africans are much darker-skinned. Now, thanks to her Obed, she understands why my complexion is different: I am an Egyptian rather than an African. Once more she generously assures me that she does not hold it against me and therefore I must relax.

"Egyptians are Africans, Ruth," I feebly correct her.

"Ain't no Africans in the Bible," she says, not looking at me but continuing with the sewing that she has been doing even before I woke up. "You should have gone with them men instead of sitting here getting to be so smarty-pants."

The men—Mahlon and Obed—have gone turkey hunting deeper into the Wayne National Forest. They left in the GMC at dawn armed with shotguns and a crossbow. Ruth inspected them with pride, making sure that Mr. Quigley's camo hunter orange jacket sat on him well and that Obed's orange T-shirt with "Got Deer" printed on it was clean. She fussed over the fact that her son was not wearing any jacket. What was the point of wearing a hunter orange camo hat with ear covers if one was not wearing a jacket? But Obed was just as stubborn. It was going to be hot, he said. The only thing he needed was his orange shoulder bag for the packed lunch and water.

Last night Obed invited me to come along but I confessed my

squeamishness. I enjoy meat as well as any man, but I'd rather someone does the killing for me, preferably in my absence. He thought I was being unmanly, but then again remembered that as a shaman I had my own habits that he was not qualified to question. I stood next to Ruth and watched them drive away. I was pleased to see that at least there were things that father and son do together. Ruth had a big smile on her face.

"I'd rather go to the Center and put in some quilting," I tell Ruth. I know she does not like this one bit, but she must get used to the idea that I am my own man. She stops sewing and looks at me closely.

"Men are out in them woods doing man things, and you going quilting?"

"You heard what Obed said the other day. These are equal op- portunity days. Professional mourning used to be a woman thing too, but now I am doing it."

"Since when do you listen to Obed?"

"Since the funeral. There's a brain in that head."

Ruth smiles. Not openly. She dare not show me that she is proud of her son . . . that even she recognizes that he is not a total loss but is good for something.

"I never knew he knows the Bible so well. Maybe one of them days he's gonna be a pastor. God does work miracles."

I am tempted to observe that if Obed were to be a pastor she would surely insist on writing his sermons. But I am smart enough to keep that opinion to myself.

"He gets it from you, Ruth," I say instead, hoping that she won't detect a sarcastic tone in my voice. I told you I have become as much of a scoundrel as Obed. "Where else would he learn so much about the Bible but from his mama?"

Ruth takes the flattery in her stride. She is undoing a stitch that has gone awry when I walk out of the living room for my first quilting lesson.

I find the women at the Center sitting at one of the long tables discussing the state of the nation. This is what I have been telling the sciolist when he was beginning to haunt my dreams complaining that the story of my life in Kilvert was becoming too political instead of focusing on the psychological motivations of my friends and hosts. Politics dominates the conversation of the people here. Even as the five women are sitting at the table, with Barbara cutting the blocks on some brown material, Irene paging through a magazine with patterns of dresses and three other women just relaxing on what is obviously a social call for them, they are talking about Social Security and why George W. Bush wants to change it.

"He says people should gamble with it on the stock market," says one of the women.

"The stock market has been there all along and never did nobody no good," says Irene.

Barbara does not comment. I have noticed on previous visits that she never participates when others attack Mr. Bush. Like Ruth, she must be a lone Republican in a sea of rabid Democrats.

The women are excited that I actually made it for my first quilting class. At first they thought that I was joking when I said I wanted to learn how to quilt. Even after I had given money to Barbara to buy the necessary fabric, some of them still didn't believe I would go on with it. One says she didn't think Ruth would allow me. I tell her that it is not for Ruth to allow me or not, even though the communal wisdom is that I am her African. Yes, she is not enamored of the idea and she blames the Center for stealing her African. First they tried to steal her daughter and failed. But now they have succeeded with the African, who is in fact an Egyptian as has been revealed—"And we all know what the Bible says about them Egyptians."

Barbara has already cut some of the blocks for me. When I express the wish that I would have liked to start there, to learn how to cut the blocks myself, she says she did not want me to have a difficult time on my first day. However, she teaches me how to cut a block on cardboard, and how to use that to draw lines with a pencil on the fabric. Then I cut the fabric, keeping the scissors sliding on the top of the table so as to cut straight. Mine is the four-inch block because, according to Barbara, four-inch blocks are prettier than three-inch ones and are easier to work with. Then she teaches me how to handle the machine and how to thread the bobbin. She issues one instruction after another as I struggle to figure out what she wants me to do exactly: "Put the color face to face when you start sewing. Raise your presser foot—the lever at the back. Pin the seams together. Always put your presser foot down before you sew."

In no time I am sewing together two blocks. My stops and starts are not clean at all, and my first block is a bit messy. But the women cheer and are encouraging. They claim that my first attempt is better than their own first attempts when they were learning to quilt as little girls, even though the blocks have come out uneven because my seams are not equal. Barbara teaches me how to correct this by having a pin between the seams when sewing blocks together.

As I am beginning to enjoy this, a tall graceful middle-aged woman enters and announces in a husky voice that she has come to see how her relatives are doing. She is obviously one of the daughters of Kilvert who have done well and live in a city somewhere. Everyone is excited to see her. Her name is Marge, I am told.

"His name is Toloki," Irene tells Marge. "We're learning him how to sew."

At least now I am not just Ruth's African.

Marge is pleased to see me and wants to know how I discovered Kilvert. But even before I can answer she breaks into a song. She is a happy soul, this Marge. She goes to the piano in the corner, uncovers it with a flourish and starts playing. She sings in a beautifully robust voice: *Why should my heart be lonely?* When she gets to the chorus they all join her and sing in unison: *I sing because I am happy. Oh, yes, I sing because I am free.* There are unshed tears in my eyes. I love these people. I join in the chorus. No one cares that my voice was not made for singing. What matters is that the song moves me. It is very much unlike the music I heard at the chocolate church the other day.

A baritone joins the chorus from the door. It is Nathan and he is in hunter orange. When the song comes to an end, and after exchanging greetings with Marge, he says he is looking for me.

"What are you doing with a sewing machine?" he asks.

"We're learning him how to sew," says Irene.

He's going to join Obed and Mahlon at the turkey hunt and would like me to come with him. He couldn't leave with them at dawn because he had to make an urgent delivery of a septic tank at some construction site. Ruth told him he would find me here. He doesn't have to tell me that she urged him to take me with him to do "man things."

"It's fun," he says. "You won't regret it."

I have been quilting for an hour or so, observes one woman. That is enough for my first day lest I get bored and never come back again. The other women agree that it will do me a world of good to get some fresh air in the woods while shooting wild turkeys, which, if I do not know it yet, are much tastier than domestic ones. But Irene dampens their enthusiasm by noting that since I had not planned to go turkey hunting in the first place I do not have a hunting permit. What is Nathan going to do about that?

This is my chance to wiggle out. Much as I would have loved to join the turkey hunt, I announce grandly, I would not like to break the law. If spring turkey permits are required for turkey hunting, then I will get one at some later date and will join the men for their next hunt. This ruse will hopefully buy me time.

The next turkey hunting season will be next fall, Nathan explains. The hunting season is very short. This one, for instance, started on April 18 and ends on May 15. And since hunters are allowed only two bearded turkeys per hunter per hunting season the Quigleys and Nathan himself will not be going hunting again until next fall. If I thought this was good news for me, I was wrong. Nathan is very persuasive.

"Okay, you won't hunt," he says. "You'll just follow me to see how an experienced hunter works, but you won't shoot nothing."

Perhaps we'll be fortunate enough not to find any turkey to shoot, so I let everyone prevail on me. This may also be an opportunity to learn more about Nathan, and therefore about Orpah. Especially about Orpah and her relationship with her father. This is something that has bothered me ever since I saw the man waltzing into her room that first night. And it had bothered me even more when I saw it happen again. And again. On two more occasions. He was in a period costume on both of them. A knight in armor one night, and a Sultan in flowing robes on another. I do not know if Orpah was in costume too, since she did not appear at the door. Both instances I went to the window to listen but could only hear mumblings and humming and declamations with indistinct dialogue and singing and giggling and laughing. He was in her room for more than an hour before he snuck out and Orpah played her sitar. Although she plucked the strings with a vengeance the music did not arouse me this time, though I could not ignore its melancholy.

I had been determined to save Orpah from Mahlon. But after these two visits I decided that she was too far gone to be saved. Despite myself I began to feel some resentment toward her. Even when she tried to reach out there was some resistance in me. Such as one early morning when we both rushed to the bathroom at the same time. She smiled and said I should go ahead. I did not return the smile. I merely turned and walked away, even though I knew that she was going to spend hours in the bathroom as is her habit. No one knows what she does there all that time. She called after me but I walked on. I went to take a dump in the woods—a practice I found strange and unacceptable at first, until Obed asked me: "What do you think we do when we go hunting in the woods? Take our shitter with us?" So, everyone else does it when Orpah is hogging the bathroom. Except Ruth, who hollers and stamps her feet until Orpah scurries out of the little room.

But later I was ashamed of my open resentment of her, although I still felt that I should stay as far away from her as the circumstances of my living under her parents' roof would allow.

☙

We drive in the woodlands in Nathan's red Chevy Blazer. The dirt road is so narrow that I wonder what he'll do if another vehicle approaches in the opposite direction. He tells me about the trees. I didn't think he cared about them. I seem to remember that he was dismissive of Obed's ghost trees that flood day we rode with him in his truck slightly more than six months ago. But here he talks of them with passion. I guess you can't live in the midst of this wealth and then fail to appreciate it. This forest is not more than seventy years old, he tells me. It was planted as one of the Public Works Department programs during the Depression. Some kind of poverty alleviation. His late grandfather told him that when he first came to settle here (he married into the Kilvert community after being recruited from Wales for his expertise in the smelting of iron) there were only bare hills and poor cornfields. There were no wild animals either. Not a single deer or turkey. Not even a beaver. All the trees that used to grow here hundreds of years ago were destroyed. They had been cut down for wood and lumber, and exported to New York and other states. Some of the timber was used for charcoal to feed the iron furnaces where his grandpa worked. Then of course there were the deep wounds left by strip mining.

"You can't see them no more now 'cause of the new forest," he says.

"After the old forest was gone how did it come back?" I ask. It is such a thick forest with gigantic trees that it is hard to believe that these were once barren hills only a few generations ago.

The farmers were starving to death. They couldn't pay the taxes either. They couldn't even sell the land to anyone because nobody would buy such poor land. Some abandoned it and went to look for work in the cities. So, the federal government bought more than a million acres. The farmers, one of whom was his grandpa, who had by then retired from the iron furnaces and was scraping the land for a meager livelihood, were told they could live free of charge in their houses and could keep only a small vegetable garden. The rest of the land was used for planting trees. Many people got employment planting the millions of trees that have today become the Wayne National Forest.

"So, you see, this is a very young forest," he says.

"Though it looks like it's been here from time immemorial," I say.

"Oh, some of these trees are even much younger," he says. "The elm, for instance. It's thanks to guys like Mahlon Quigley that we have some elms in this forest."

Mahlon organized a community action group to save the elm after the tree had been devastated by the fungus known as the Dutch elm disease, imported to these parts from Holland via Cleveland in the 1930s. When Mahlon grew up as a young man there were no longer any elms in the region. The elm only made its comeback years later when the man organized his community. Many Dutch elm disease–resistant trees were planted. He fought vigorously when those who wanted shortcuts were bent on replacing the American elm with either the Chinese elm or the less elegant but fast growing silver maple. Yes, in some places the Chinese elm and the silver maple were planted, but Mahlon's genuine elms also thrived. Even though the man has now retreated into silence the forests will forever sing his praises. At this point Nathan's voice has become very solemn. It is as though he is talking of a saint.

I am tempted to ask him about the man's nighttime shenanigans, but I decide against it lest I be accused of spreading malicious gossip about my gracious host.

Nathan parks the car near a small lake and we walk deeper into the woodlands for some distance until we get to an area with poor patches of cultivated land and riverbank bluffs. He is armed with a shotgun. He tells me that he was here scouting with Obed two days ago. He was hoping to find him and his father in this part of the woodlands, unless they are done with their hunt. But we would have seen them on their way back. We each hide behind a tree and Nathan takes out a wing bone caller and begins to suck on it. It produces a clucking sound.

I saw this instrument for the first time yesterday. Mahlon's was made the previous year from the wing bone of a wild turkey, while Obed was shaping his from the bones of a hen after boiling them to remove the marrow. Mahlon dismissed Obed's creation. It was not a genuine wing bone caller, he said. Obed proved that his was much better by producing sharp and clear yelping, clucking and kee-kee sounds. Mahlon's wing bone caller could not compete. Even after reshaping it with a sharp knife and rearranging the two smaller bones inserted in the bigger one and resealing the joints with glue, his sound could not beat Obed's. I was impressed not so much by these instruments but by the fact that father and son were involved in some activity together and seemed to be enjoying it. Obed did not seem to need anything more than his father's sparse words to understand him completely.

So here now Nathan is putting the wing bone caller into use. But no turkey appears. He turns to me and says this is not the best time for a hunt. The people who came in good time are Obed and Mahlon, who are likely to have bagged something by now. I tell him that I want to walk back and sit in the car. It is not safe, he says. The blue of my denim and red and white of my shirt are the wrong colors to be wearing on a turkey hunt. Some hunter may mistake me for a turkey and shoot me down. We are just lucky that it is a weekday and there's not much pressure from other hunters as would have been the case on a weekend. I remind him that I had no intention of coming for any hunt, so he would do well not to blame my attire.

"I ain't complaining, man," he says. "I'm just saying."

Then he blows and sucks on the wing bone caller again.

He takes a breath and says: "The gobble call can be dangerous too, you know. It attracts other hunters and the lousy ones can shoot in your direction thinking you're a turkey."

"Then why do you do it?" I ask.

"It's the only way I'll attract a turkey at this time," he says.

While I hide behind my tree, he stands with his back against his tree. He continues his call. Soon two large birds fly up the hill. I didn't see where they came from. They land a short distance from us. I hide my face in my hands as shots blast.

"I got it," shouts an excited Nathan. "I got it."

But now he does not know where it is. Perhaps it took to the air after being shot. It was the right one, he was sure of that. It was a bearded turkey. He has never made a mistake and shot a hen, which, he emphasizes to me—as part of training me as a future hunter—would have been illegal. There is a heavy fine for shooting a hen.

I believe that turkey is gone. Or maybe he missed it. But Nathan is confident that we'll find it somewhere. After walking for a few yards we see feathers and tracks. It flew only a short distance and landed. But there is no trail of blood.

"It ran this way," he says. "There's no point in running after it. No man can run faster than a turkey."

After more than an hour of following what Nathan claims is a trail we find the turkey. It is dead. Nathan yells and performs a funny jig of victory. I know turkey, but this is not the kind of turkey I expected. It is only half the size of a domestic turkey, and from the trouble it has given us it is sleek and fast and is not dim-witted like the turkeys you would find at a farm.

"I didn't know turkeys could fly," I say.

"Wild ones do," he says as he takes an orange tarpaulin bag from the pocket of his orange jacket, unfolds it and places the bird in it. He tags it.

It is a long way back to where we parked our vehicle. As we trudge along I ask Nathan what his chances are with Orpah and why he is so patient with her.

"I am sure a guy like you can get any girl," I say.

"She'll come around one of them days," he says. "If only Ruth stops interfering."

"She's interfering on your side. I thought you'd like that."

Right now Orpah is playing hard to get in order to annoy Ruth, Nathan believes. Her mother has always prevailed over her about everything. For once Orpah has something on which to defy her. Once the mother stops badgering her about him she will know that they will be good together. After all, they were once lovers and were good together. Granted it was puppy love but it could have developed into something serious had Ruth not interfered, that time against him. It was before he had become the success he is to-day, and Ruth wanted her daughter to forget about boys and focus on her studies.

"Another problem is Mahlon," says Nathan.

Now we are beginning to talk.

"So long as Mahlon is there Orpah don't need nobody but Mahlon," he moans. "It ain't no way to raise a daughter."

I wonder to myself how much more raising the woman needs and why all these people keep on talking of her as if she is a little girl. I find it annoying.

Mahlon entertains her whims, complains Nathan. Did I know that for the past week or so Mahlon has been spending days on end in the woods looking for ghost orchids? I did not know this. Come to think of it, I have not been seeing much of Mahlon on his swing on the porch or in the company of the brooding elders at the Center. But what is wrong with looking for ghost orchids in the woods?

Ghost orchids, it turns out, are Orpah's new obsession. It all started at the funeral luncheon at Sister Naomi's house when Brother Michael was paging through the Bible to assure himself that what Obed read was actually contained in there. Orpah, who was sitting next to him, saw a ghost orchid which had been flat-tened between the pages until it dried out. She was fascinated by the shape, which she said was like that of a frog jumping into a pond. Brother Michael told her that he got that one in the South, and gave it to her. When Brother Michael told her that ghost orchids did not grow on their own but were hosted by other trees, she wondered why she had never seen them before even though she had practically grown up in the woods, and she spent the next day looking for them in the wooded area next to the cemetery. When Mahlon learned of her search he took it upon himself and spent days on end looking for the orchids even deeper in the forest. If only he could find just one it would make his daughter happy. The very Mahlon who knew so much about trees and had saved the elm now spends his time walking among the white ash trees, the walnuts, the beech, the birch and of course the sycamore, looking for the ghost orchids he has never seen growing in this region in his lifetime.

I have nothing to say on this until we reach our vehicle and drive to a check station where Nathan's turkey is weighed and recorded. As we leave the station Obed and Mahlon rush in. They were almost late. The station closes at 2 P.M. and the law requires that the tagged carcass with head, feathers and feet be brought to the check station on the day the turkey is shot. They had many mishaps, says Obed breathlessly.

It turns out that one of the mishaps was that Obed shot a hen and had to hide it to escape the wrath of the law. To my surprise Nathan does not take kindly to this.

"Don't tell me you fuckin' shot a hen," yells Nathan.

"How was I to fuckin' know? It had a fuckin' beard," Obed yells back.

Mahlon smiles, transferring his gaze from one man to the other as they exchange their anger.

"Don't fuck with me, man! You know this ain't the fuckin' first time in the world a fuckin' hen has a fuckin' beard."

Apparently there are other things that distinguish a hen from a gobbler, such as the black breast feathers for the latter, whereas a hen's breast is rusty. And the white forehead and blue cheeks and back of neck for the gobbler, whereas with hens it is the whole head that is blue. Even small things such as spurs on the gobbler count. Hens have no spurs. Obviously a good hunter must be sharp-eyed so as not to make the kind of stupid mistake that Obed made. If it was a mistake at all. I wouldn't put it past the scoundrel to shoot a hen intentionally given the opportunity, rather than go home to face Ruth without a kill. Mahlon himself had bagged the right bird, the one they had come to weigh.

For serious hunters like Nathan it is shameful and despicable to kill a hen. Real men don't shoot hens.

"What's the big deal, man?" asks Obed as he jumps into his mother's GMC. "It's just a fuckin' turkey!"

His father jumps into the pickup as well, still smiling. It's hard to tell if he is bothered at all by his son's treacherous act.

"Are you coming or not?" asks Obed glaring at me. Now I am caught in the middle of a turkey war.

"You fuckin' go with them, man," says Nathan, also glaring at me. He gets into his Chevy Blazer and speeds away.

❦

Saturday afternoon. The family is gathered in front of the house, each one treading carefully so as not to disorganize Mahlon's garden. Obed is building a barbecue stand with bricks and places a gridiron on top. His busy day continues from the morning hours when he went to Athens to paint the sorority house in Washington Street. That job is not done and he is looking forward to going back on Monday. And on Tuesday. Perhaps for the whole of next week. It seems he wants to linger on this job for as long as it is possible to do so. I suspect it all has to do with Beth Eddy. There would be no other reason for Obed to be so enthusiastic about manual labor. When I told him two days ago that Beth Eddy called and had arranged that the painting should start on Saturday morning he could not contain himself. When he turned down my offer to go with him and give a hand I knew that it was not just the painting he was hoping to achieve at the sorority house.

He is boasting as he stokes the wood in the fire under the grill that the girls served him milk and cookies (at his request; they were suggesting something stronger) while he sent them into titters with stories of how Nicodemus was a wonderful stud at the slave breeding farm. He regaled them with tales of how he escaped and found his way to Athens where he was brutally murdered. The girls, of course, knew of the existence of Nicodemus since he touched them occasionally, but had never heard the details of his life before he came to cohabit with them at their sorority house. They were most fascinated by the fact that he, Obed, was related to this same Nicodemus. So, he went on to tell them about his great-great-great-grandpas Abednego and the first Quigley, and Harry Corbett, and how during the Civil War Quigley's son married Abednego's daughter even though they were first cousins and how Harry Corbett served in that war and was killed. He was the descendant of all these illustrious people. There were some Germans in the mix. And more African Americans. And more Irish. And more Indians.

"Native Americans," piped up a politically correct girl.

Another girl, most likely Beth Eddy herself, suggested that it was all that mixture that had made him into such a hunk.

One would have thought young women would be bored by such stories, but they were all agog. Maybe it was because it had something to do with their Nicodemus.

Beth Eddy is the sweetest of the women, and he hopes to see more of her. But I must not think that is the reason for his eagerness to return to the house. It is the responsible thing to do. After all, he did make a solemn promise at the mediation that he would paint the house. He will do exactly that and complete the job.

Nathan arrives with his two kids—a boy of about twelve and a girl of eight or so. He has also brought his turkey for the barbecue.

There is a slight tension between him and Obed. They face each other hesitantly. Then they break out laughing while they exchange profanities about how stupid they can sometimes be. The kids run to Orpah, who is sitting on the swing with Mahlon. They are all over her and she is at ease with them and is full of laughter. For some reason there are pangs of jealousy in me.

I offer to take Nathan's turkey to Ruth. She is in the kitchen cutting part of Obed's hen into tiny pieces. (She has deep-frozen Mahlon's bird for the future.) She browns them in a pan with cooking oil. In the meantime she asks me to cut the breast of Nathan's bird into slabs for the barbecue, while she puts the pieces of hen into a pot on the stove and adds chopped celery, chopped onion, garlic, cayenne pepper, marjoram, cumin, chili powder, paprika and salt.

"Them men have no use for a wild turkey chili that ain't hot," she says, perhaps in response to my face that must have shown surprise at the hot spices that were all being used together at the same time. "I would add jalapeño too if I had some."

She then adds a can each of undrained pinto beans, diced tomatoes and tomato juice to the whole mixture and lets it simmer on the stove.

She asks me to dip the turkey breast slabs in lemon pepper and Heinz 57.

"That what they call us, Son of Egypt—Heinz 57," she says, as we both use our hands to thoroughly mix the sauce with the meat.

"I hate that name," I tell her.

"And you know why they call us Heinz 57?" she asks, ignoring my protest. "'Cause there's a little bit of everything in us. Get it? Like Heinz 57. See Mr. Quigley? See the high cheekbones?"

At this point I am carrying the tray with the turkey breast past Mahlon, Orpah and the kids. Ruth is heaving behind me with her walking stick. But I do not stop to examine Mahlon's high cheekbones.

"That's the Indian in him," Ruth continues. "Indians don't age. They just fade away. That's why Mr. Quigley don't age. He's Indian through and through. You wouldn't know his mama was a Caucasian girl from Stewart."

From Heinz 57 to Mahlon's mother. I like Ruth!

"It don't matter no how if Grandma was Caucasian or not, Mama," protests Obed, as he takes the tray from me and places it on a metal frame that used to be a chair next to the barbecue stand.

"Did I say it matters, boy? Don't you get into things you don't know nothing about."

She walks to the back garden to get some green onions for the pickle that she plans to make.

"Ruth . . . she makes a bad pickle," says Nathan, obviously looking forward to the prospect of tasting it.

"She likes to judge people," whines Obed. "Mama does."

"She still makes a bad pickle," says Nathan.

"It ain't nice to say things about my grandma," says Obed.

He is basting the meat on the grill. The young men argue about the best way to barbecue the turkey. They agree on one thing though: Heinz 57 is not the best sauce for wild turkey. Nathan should have come early to boil his secret sauce made of butter, lemon juice, thyme, parsley and broth. They are still arguing on how a dose of beer would or would not redeem the sauce when I decide to join Ruth in the back garden. She is no longer there. I find her in the kitchen chopping the green onions. There are three bowls of chopped cucumber, zucchini and okra ready to be mixed for the pickle. These vegetables are not from her garden but from Kroger since the soil is still too cold for them.

"What happened to Mahlon's mother?" I ask.

"Nothing happened," says Ruth. "She died."

After she ran away with Mahlon's father her parents declared that she was insane. They had her committed at The Ridges where she died, was buried and became just a number. What has bothered Mahlon lately is that when he was doing well raising animals for sale he forgot about her and never honored her memory. This continues to torture his soul to this day. If only her grave could be

222 *e Zakes Mda

found, then erecting a proper tombstone with appropriate words to
the effect that she was fondly remembered by her son, daughter-in-
law and grandchildren, and asking for her forgiveness, would
bring peace and good fortune to the rest of the family.

"I'm gonna show you something," says Ruth in her conspiratorial tone. I follow her to her bedroom where she gets an old Bible
from the top drawer of a dressing table. She takes out an old black-
and-white—actually brownish—photograph from the Bible and
hands it to me with a flourish as if she has performed a magic trick.

"That's Mr. Quigley's mama," she says. "Ain't she pretty?"

I can't see any of the prettiness because the picture is too faint.

"Though I last saw her when I was a little kid I remember her
pretty black hair."

I think pretty black hair is a big thing with Ruth. I remember
on a few occasions when she was telling me of Abednego's descendants she would add with great pride: "They had pretty black hair
and high foreheads like white people." Or when she was telling me
of the fugitive slaves who arrived in Tabler Town: "They didn't
look like Africans when they came here. They had pretty black
hair. My own great-great-grandfather looked almost like a white
man. He had pretty black hair."

With Mahlon's mother, of course, it goes without saying that she
would have pretty hair because she was Caucasian. Even though I
cannot see it so well in the photograph, she adds, I must take her
word for it because she remembers it quite vividly. The dress she is
wearing is made of feed sacks.

"Back in them days they made dresses from feed sacks."

Even when she herself was a little girl she wore dresses made
from feed sacks, though her very special Sunday dresses were made
from muslin or gingham. When her mother sewed the dress she
cut the pattern on a newspaper and measured it against her body.
Then she cut out the neck and the sleeves. After that she would
have the whole pattern and would then use the cut newspaper as a

stencil on the material. As I can see in the photograph, that is how Mr. Quigley's mom's dress was made.

I reckon that feed sacks are like the maize meal or flour sacks we have back home. I have seen Ruth use that kind of material as backing for some of her quilts.

"There was nothing wrong with her," Ruth says after considering the photo for some time. "She just fell in love with a colored man. And for that they sent her to a madhouse."

"All because white folks are dead scared of being bred out, which is bound to happen sooner or later," she adds in her conspiratorial tone.

"I suppose that's the price you pay if you go around colonizing people and enslaving them," I say light-heartedly.

"It ain't no price," she says quite adamantly. "Though they don't know it now, it's good for them. It's good for the world."

Just as it happened to her Indian people, it will happen to the white races of the world and to the black races too until everyone looks like the Kilvert people. Her people are harbingers of a new human race.

I have heard this before. Just as I have heard of her boasts of being a Cherokee princess—even though a vindictive Brother Michael has declared publicly at his chocolate church that there is no such a thing as a Cherokee princess—and her claims that her great-great-great-grandmother was a queen in Africa. This last one I heard a lot last January when the Kilvert Community Center celebrated Martin Luther King Jr. Day. At breakfast she hammered it into her children's heads—who would be going for lunch at the Center that day—that they should always hold their heads high because they were descendants of an African queen. It was the first time I heard her talk of her African strand with so much pride. Most times her African and Native American ancestors are mentioned in generic terms whereas the white ancestors have names and individual histories. Abednego Fairfield and Harry

Corbett were resurrected from the depths of collective imagination by the sciolist to remedy this situation.

I cannot pretend to understand some of the contradictions in the lives of my hosts. The people here claim "we don't belong to nobody," yet they celebrate Black History Month in February and the Center organizes a big dinner on Martin Luther King Jr. Day. I do not see them celebrating any other day honoring their Native American or Caucasian heritages. Not even St. Patrick's Day.

By the time Ruth and I return to the barbecue everyone is feasting on the turkey with bread rolls. Mahlon sits alone on the swing smiling at all he surveys. I look at him and I smile back despite myself. I still resent him. God knows I have tried to convince myself that what happens under his roof is none of my business. But somehow I feel that Orpah should be my business. At the same time I feel sorry for him. For what they did to his mama. I am determined to help him find her grave so that he may pay his due respects to it. Why, I'll even mourn for the poor woman. Maybe after that whatever is wrong with Mahlon will become right again. And Orpah will be free.

She and the children have joined Obed and Nathan at the barbecue stand. The children are still clinging to Orpah, who is obviously having a great time with them. As we walk toward them Ruth says, "See? Nathan's kids love her. She can easily be their mama."

"I don't think she is ready to be anyone's mother," I say. Don't ask me why. I can be so stupid sometimes.

"Todoloo! No woman is never ready to be a mother."

Late in the evening Nathan and his kids leave. Ruth insists that he takes some of the wild turkey chili with him. I am surprised that Nathan accepts the container so enthusiastically even though he knows very well it is the hen whose death he took so personally.

"You bring it back," says Ruth. "That ain't no cheap plastic. That's Tupperware."

One thing I know is that Ruth never gives her Tupperware to anyone. Not even to the two men of the house when they went on the wild turkey hunt. She wrapped their sandwiches in foil paper. Not even to me when once I needed to take my bean soup lunch with me on a hike in the woods. I had to use an ice cream bucket.

Evenings are like daytime in late spring. Since the sun is still shining I decide to take a walk. I thought Orpah would go bury herself in her room and play her confounded sitar, but she follows me. I increase my pace when I see that she is about to catch up with me. She also steps up hers to a trot. I give up because I do not want it to be obvious that I am running away from her. She catches up with me. We walk side by side for some time in silence.

"Where you off to?" she asks finally.

"Just a walk . . . on my own."

"I have more drawings for you to hide," she says.

"I don't think I want to do that anymore," I say.

"Come on, man! You know what'll happen when the tsunami finds them in my room."

"I don't think you should call your mama names. It's disrespectful."

"You gave her that name."

Trust her to remember that. I am ashamed that, yes indeed, I gave her mama that name in a moment of wickedness when she was storming through the house doing her spring cleaning in readiness for the New Year. A real tsunami had hit parts of Asia a few days after Christmas. It became part of the exciting family viewing, with every television network showing live pictures of the devastation and the helpless victims and helicopters flying about rescuing people from the treetops. It also became a source of heated argument at the dinner table, with Ruth complaining: "The people of the world think we Americans are one level below God."

"They are right, Mama," said Obed. "Even George W. Bush told us that as an American you're God's gift to the world."

"They want us to do everything," Ruth continued. "Now we're sending three hundred and fifty million big ones to the tsunami victims."

"It's good to do this, Mama," insisted Obed.

"Who said it ain't good, boy?" asked Ruth. "If they don't send no one to look after that money it's gonna end up with them drug lords and all sorts of other lords."

Obed did not have an answer for this and I thought it was the end of the subject. But after considering the matter for a few more seconds she burst out: "There's many poor counties in Ohio . . . like ours. If they gave some of that money to us . . . even if it's two thousand dollars per county . . . it would make all the difference."

And this from the very Ruth who was critical of the handouts that she claimed had made her people poorer. I suppose when it comes from the government it is not a handout but a "program."

"Don't you mean two million dollars?" asked an increasingly impertinent Obed.

"Whatever! You like to contradict me."

That was the end of that discussion. But it was just the beginning of the spring cleaning that month. And of the continuation of the destruction of Orpah's designs. Hence the name. I told Obed: "Don't provoke the tsunami," when he was bent on picking every minor bone with Ruth. He found that funny and started calling his mother a tsunami behind her back. Orpah picked it up and liked it too.

Now she is waiting for my response and when it's not forthcoming she repeats: "You named her that. And Ayatollah Ruth and a Taliban in da House."

"I am sorry I did. It's no less disrespectful that it was started by me."

"Don't be sorry. She messes up my stuff bad. She *is* a tsunami."

"She wants the best for you," I say.

She is taken aback by this. She stops and looks at me. I walk on. She turns her back and walks away. But she changes her mind and calls after me. I pretend I don't hear and walk on. She comes trotting after me.

"What's your problem, man?" she asks.

"You don't hear me complaining of anything. That means I don't have a problem."

I hate Mahlon for making me treat Orpah this way.

She opts for appeasement. She shows me her dry ghost orchid. Her father, she believes, will find her more ghost orchids in the woods. Didn't I want to see her new work? It is inspired by ghost orchids.

I need an excuse to get rid of her. I tell her that I am going to mourn.

"But you ain't in your getup," she says.

"Sometimes I do some of my shaman things without it," I tell her.

I don't know if she can see through the lies or not. I don't care either. She walks away, obviously very disappointed.

In the dying weeks of spring I spend most of my time at the Center. My quilting improves tremendously, though I find the Drunkard's Path very difficult. Barbara is a patient teacher and shows me how to do it by cutting the shapes out on a newspaper.

"Once you master the nine-patch you can do anything," she assures me.

Sometimes even when I have no plans to go to the Center one of the women phones me to come and assist with one thing or the other. Or to help unload the trucks on food give-away days. "You being from Africa and all, you'll really like it when you see all that food," the woman says. I don't have the heart to destroy her delusion that the sight of food is an orgasmic experience for an African.

There is a lot of food to sort before Barbara phones each family in Kilvert to come for their parcels. The Center serves two hundred and forty people at a time. Like many other food pantries in the region the Center orders the food from the Second Harvest Food Bank in Logan. It costs the Center anything between three and four hundred dollars for the number of cases needed to supply the folks on their list, although almost every time some people have to go without. I assist the women to sort the food and divide it into parcels. A parcel contains two cans each of meatballs in tomato sauce, beans, corn, spaghetti sauce, green beans, and orange juice concentrate. Besides the canned foods each parcel contains boxes of rice, spaghetti, egg noodles, cereal and powdered milk.

Barbara calls each person on the list, including Ruth.

Soon there are many rusty pickups, cars and vans parked in the yard, until they overflow into the street. A long line of mostly middle-aged and elderly Kilverters forms at the door. "They're tickled to death to get whatever they can," says Irene. I can see Orpah in the line. Later Obed also comes for his own food parcel. After receiving the food parcel each person comes to my table where I hand out a leaflet titled *Information You Can Use: Medicare Prescription Drug Coverage.*

Orpah continues to look for opportunities to foist herself on me. She comes along on one of my walks to harvest dandelion leaves near the Federal Creek bridge for Ruth's salad. This is the season for the perfect leaves because once the weather gets hot they become bitter and inedible. Orpah follows me like a lovesick puppy, asking me what it is that she ever did to me since I have become "funny" toward her. I am tempted to ask her about the nighttime shenanigans but think better of it. I do not even know if they still go on or not. I have heard the sound of the sitar in the middle of the night, sometimes after midnight, but I always cover my head with the comforter when it becomes too disturbing. I have long stopped going out to see what was happening because I no longer want to torture myself.

Something has indeed changed about Orpah. She now joins us at the dining room table and makes a point of initiating some form of conversation with me, mostly about her ghost orchids. After dinner she joins us to watch television. She argues with Obed when he complains that these days television is boring because good programs are in hiatus. He says he misses the good old days of bombings and live military action, the last of which was about four months ago when the homeland forces marched into Fallujah. Those were the days television screens lit up with big letters: *Operation Phantom Fury* to the background of suspenseful music. I remember, Obed used to come home early and would flip from one cable channel to another as the superheroes changed the world for the better, in the words of the Commander-in-Chief. This used to be family viewing of the highest order. But what I never really understood about Obed, even though he enjoyed the war and rooted for the forces to smother everything in their path, he vehemently argued against the war with his mother. When, for instance, after a particularly bloody battle Ruth said: "We dying to save them Iraqis against themselves," Obed responded: "We destroyed the darn place, Mama. We destroy it in order to save it?"

And here today Orpah is dismissing his nostalgia for the war he didn't personally fight as stupid and boyish, and that no one in their sane mind would be happy for a situation that produced so much collateral damage. While Ruth shushes Orpah for talking rubbish about people who are fighting for America's freedom, Obed makes an observation along the lines that every truth has its counter truth; one man's collateral damage is another man's slaughter of the innocents.

Oh, yes, Orpah has changed! But nothing else has changed in Kilvert. Obed continues with his quest for the occult. He becomes Shawnee or Cherokee depending on the weather. He dabbles in everything that is remotely connected with his heritages, from the smoke scrying of the Native Americans to something he calls hakata, which he says is used by African witchdoctors. He does not believe me when I tell him that where I come from there is no such thing as a witchdoctor—that it's a contradiction in terms. And as always there is a strong profit motive whenever he engages with mysticism. I never get to know what smoke scrying and hakata entail, although he does make a few bucks from the practices. But soon he gets bored with them and tries something else.

He does not get bored with Beth Eddy though. I suspect something has developed between them, although we never get to see the lady. He does not boast about her as he used to with his previous conquests. Some awe seems to surround Beth Eddy's name. His dream is that one day Kilvert will be declared a Native American reservation and he will have his own casino. And maybe, only maybe, someone *like* Beth Eddy will be with him to share the spoils when that happens. Ruth, of course, pooh-poohs such dreams. She declares: "That's why them Indians don't get nowhere and are always so drunk. They sold their souls to the devil with them casinos."

She continues to poke her nose into everything that happens in Kilvert and accelerates her fundamentalist campaign against Brother Michael, who stubbornly stands his ground on the slave quilts: enslaved Africans could not have been intelligent enough to devise such an elaborate code or any code whatsoever. An adulterer is bound to say such things, Ruth declares.

She continues to sew her ancestral designs and to take her quilts to the farmer's market where no one buys them. People don't see any artistry in them. They see wonderful craftsmanship but no artistic vision. She is like a performer of traditional music who does cover versions of songs long composed by others in that genre, instead of composing new songs in the same traditional genre, or at least giving the old ones a new twist, a new angle, a new life. Yet she continues to destroy Orpah's designs because Orpah's designs are not part of the tradition and have no names since they are of her own origination.

As for me and Orpah: I have given up on her, as I stated earlier. I think for her I am just convenient for defending her designs and hiding them from Ruth. I therefore no longer take it upon myself to hide them. Ruth is aware of this and our relationship has improved as a result.

Orpah, on the other hand, continues with her obsession with ghost orchids. For a long time Mahlon searches for them in vain. I do not know if he is merely playing along or not, but he searches earnestly. Until Orpah begins to despair for him. He feels he has failed his daughter. Orpah does not understand why the ghost or- chids are nowhere to be found. She has never seen them in the wild in all her life growing up in Kilvert, but she believes that the only reason is that the ghost orchids that grow in the wild are reputed to be very elusive. Perhaps it is the wrong season. She must find out when the ghost orchids are usually in bloom and the best source for that kind of information would be Brother Michael since she got her orchid from him. To her consternation she discovers that her father's search is a futile one: ghost orchids do not grow in these parts. Mahlon would have to go to southern Florida to find any ghost orchids in the wild. Or perhaps sail to the Caribbean. The one she now possesses was confiscated from a thief who had stolen it from one of the glorious trees of the Fakahatchee.

Instead of calling off the search, Orpah creates her own ghost orchids from thin plastic material and sticks them on the sycamore trees. Where else should ghost orchids grow but on ghost trees?

I observe all these things silently. At first I don't understand what is happening. But the saga of the ghost orchids becomes clearer as it unfolds.

Orpah continues to bug me. She asks me to accompany her to the Silent Chinese Auction at the Center one Saturday morning.

"Why don't you go with Nathan?" I ask her.

"He didn't ask," she says. "Anyway the auction is from ten this morning . . . to two. Nathan's at work."

"Well, maybe you should go with your father," I suggest.

"I'm sure he'll be there as well. I wanna go with you."

I was going to go to the auction in any event. And so Orpah and I walk silently to the Center. She would be exquisite if it were not for her heavy makeup that almost cakes her face and the loud, mostly plastic, jewelery.

There are cakes, pies, hot dogs and sloppy joes on one of the long tables. I buy Orpah a hot dog and we walk from table to table looking at the wares. All these have been donated to raise funds for the Center so that it may pay its utilities and purchase more food from the food bank. There are children's toys, boxes of cutlery, cookbooks, television sets and the ubiquitous quilt. There are also washing machines, sewing machines, a new bike and a number of other household items. Next to each item there is a sheet of paper where one writes one's bid.

Mahlon is glaring at me, sans the smile. I did not know he was capable of not smiling. I have seen him smile at the worst of times. Why, even when a fight was imminent between Nathan and Obed he was smiling. But here he is, looking at me with a smileless face. He certainly does not approve of my "date" with his daughter. Hard luck; I am with her now. And to emphasize that point I grab her hand, which takes her by surprise. But she does not draw it away. She greets him and he responds with a smile. But his face becomes stern again when his eyes shift to me. Orpah adopts the voice of a little girl when talking to Mahlon. I find this very unsettling.

Orpah is fascinated by a gnome. She tops the last bid on it and I am amazed that people want this gnome so much that they are willing to pay a very high price for it. Orpah explains that this is not just any old gnome. It is a famous George W. Bush gnome invented by one Sam Girton, an Athenian no less, and it sells internationally on eBay and always creates a flurry of bidding. It comes with accessories: If you love Bush then you place an American flag in his hand. If you hate Bush you make him hold a bag of money with a dollar sign on it or a machine gun. The gnome is popular with Bush haters and Bush lovers.

"I didn't know you'd be interested in this sort of thing," I say.

"It's not for me," she says. "I'm buying it for you to give to Daddy as a present."

"Why would I give your father a gift?"

"Because he don't like you and you want him to like you."

"I don't want him to like me."

"You staying at his house."

She says she is not going to move away from the gnome so as to outbid anyone who has the intention of topping her bid. And she does so. I have never seen her this happy before. She whispers to me why it is necessary to appease her father. For some time now he has been trying to sabotage my stay at the house. For instance, he was the one who "lost" the key to the cellar and I had to find a place to sleep in Obed's room. I remember the night but didn't know Mahlon had anything to do with it. She finds this very funny and laughs. Now I hear that he has done other things too, but they were always foiled by none other than Orpah. Obviously she is enjoying what she perceives as rivalry between her father and me.

At the end of the auction I discover to my surprise that she has been writing my name on the bid, instead of hers. I am not amused at having to pay for the gnome but I don't argue about it. Later that evening she gives it to her father in my name. In the morning I see it basking in the sun among other gnomes in Mahlon's garden. The man never thanks me for it.

I do not see Orpah after that for a number of days. But I hear her relentless sitar at odd hours of the day or night. The next time I set my eyes on her we are at the Appalachian Rising Bluegrass Festival at a farm outside Huntington, West Virginia. She is with Nathan, who is holding her sitar in a case. I am here with Obed and had no idea Orpah would be here too. I am not one for music festivals but Obed begged me to come with him. He had bought tickets for himself and Beth Eddy, but at the last minute she told him she couldn't make it because of a family commitment. He also felt that Ruth would be more comfortable parting with her GMC for the better part of the day and night if she knew I'd be wherever the GMC was. Obviously the young man has an exaggerated impression of the esteem in which Ruth may or may not hold me.

Orpah looks like a Gypsy queen in her fuchsia skirt, sequinned silver top and coin hoop earrings that almost touch her shoulders. She is ill at ease.

People are enthralled by a band of five—a sliding guitar, a

banjo, a seventy-string hammer dulcimer, a fiddle and an acoustic guitar—playing Celtic traditional music. When they play bluegrass it is heavily Irish-traditional. This prompts a group of men to mount the makeshift stage and begin clogging. There are yells of excitement when the champion fiddler takes a solo while he joins the clogging.

This is my first bluegrass festival and I am enjoying it.

"Bluegrass is human," says Orpah. "It's about people, that's why."

We get pop and some hot dogs. The two guys are on their best behavior. I would have thought they would be drowning themselves in beer by now. Maybe it's Orpah's influence on Nathan.

We walk to another part of the festival and here a different band is on the stage. In addition to the banjo and three fiddles this one also has a ukulele and a mandolin. A woman vocalist with a gravelly voice is very popular with the crowd. People are clapping their hands and stamping their feet.

There are many other stages, but we return to the first one because there is an open mike at this time.

After much persuasion from the three of us, with Nathan holding her to the promise she made before they left Kilvert that she would play for the public for the first time in her life, Orpah takes the stage with her sitar. Its whines bring everyone to attention.

An old guy with a sliding guitar cannot help but join her. So does a flute, a lap dulcimer, a fiddle and a banjo. And soon the impromptu band is giving bluegrass standards a tone that has never been heard before. I don't know what they call an event like this in the bluegrass culture. I would call it a jam session if it was jazz. And it is Orpah's sitar that breaks from the standards in improvised leaps before it returns to them to find the graybeards just ready to reincorporate it in the song with their varied instruments.

The audience doesn't dance. Doesn't yell. Doesn't clap or sing along. Everybody is transfixed. Including us. I am just open-mouthed. We are all mesmerized by what we hear. When the song comes to an end there is utter silence for some time. Then an outburst of cheers and screams. There are tears in my eyes. Nathan is beaming with pride. Obed's face displays disbelief.

The crowd doesn't want Orpah to leave the stage even after open mike time. Band members crowd around her asking for her contact details because they'd like to invite her to join them for this or that gig. At this point Nathan moves forward and takes charge of the situation. Anyone who wants to contact Orpah with any proposal should do it through him. But she dashes away in a huff, elbowing her way through the crowd. The three of us run after her.

"What's up with you, Orpah?" demands Obed when we catch up with her.

"Where do you get off being my owner?" she asks, glaring at Nathan.

"Someone's gotta look after you, Orpah," says Nathan. "You know how they exploit artists here. 'Specially if they're naive like you."

"I ain't no one's artist," she screams. "And no one made you my agent or manager or whatever else you think you are."

Nathan is taken aback by her vehemence. He was only trying to look after her interests, he says. He accuses her of being ungrateful. After all, she didn't even want to come to this festival and he persuaded her. It was also his idea that she bring the sitar along to play during open mike. And now that she sees fame beckoning she is turning against him. This annoys Orpah even more. She demands to be taken back to Kilvert. Not by Nathan, but by her brother and me. But Obed is reluctant to leave because he is still enjoying the festival.

"There'll be other festivals, Obed," I say. "Please do take your sister home."

"Who asked you?" Nathan screams at me. "This ain't Africa. You don't think I know you're into her? You don't think I don't see the way you've been eyeing her?"

A surprised Orpah looks at me questioningly.

Obed is sulking as we walk to the parking area. No one utters a

word in the two hours it takes us to get to Kilvert. It is about 8 P.M.
when Obed parks the GMC and walks away, perhaps to kill time
with a friend.

"You don't wanna come to my room?" asks Orpah.

I do not show her that I am taken aback.

"Was Nathan right?" she asks. "Was he telling the truth?"

"What if your father finds me there?" I ask, ignoring her
question.

"He don't come at this time," she says. All so innocently. "Anyways, he don't come if we don't plan it that way," she adds, I suppose as a way of assuring me that we'll be safe.

Curiosity gets the better of me.

Orpah's room is a shrine to Marilyn Monroe. There are posters
of Marilyn Monroe on the pink walls. Pursed lips blowing into the
mike. Andy Warhol's Marilyn Monroe. Many posters in different
sizes. Some mounted. Others framed. The wind blowing her skirt.
There is a framed picture of a much younger Orpah—maybe a
high school Orpah—standing on an air vent with air blowing her
dress in a Marilyn Monroe pose. Norma Jean in two larger than
life cardboard cut-outs. There is even a coffee mug with the face of
Marilyn Monroe.

I find the presence of this dead woman in Orpah's room unsettling.

The only chair in the room has piles of pine-scented laundry so
I sit on the bed. For a while we don't know what to do with each
other. Then, as if on cue, we simultaneously reach for each other
and kiss.

"Oh, I am going to smudge your makeup," I say. "But what the
heck, you only live once."

I have not been with a woman in the biblical sense since the
death of Noria almost two years ago. She is still very much in my
mind because I never mourned her. My people have a saying that a
doctor cannot heal himself. When a lawyer is charged with a crime
he needs another lawyer to defend him. Likewise a professional

mourner cannot mourn his own loss. My hope has been that in my wanderings I would find another competent professional mourner who would mourn Noria for me. Until she has been mourned she will continue to be very much part of me. Or so I thought. Until I saw Orpah and heard her sitar. Now my body is raging with desire.

We undress each other in a manner that speaks only of lust. And there in front of me stands the most beautiful thing in the world. But what strikes me about the pubic hair is that it is blonde. Almost golden. And it is gleaming in the light. She notices my astonishment and turns away as if in shame.

"It's the fuckin' mark of the fuckin' Irishman and I've got to live with it," she says vehemently. It's beautiful, I assure her. It is not, she retorts. Her hair is black. Her armpits are black. Why should it be "fuckin' blonde"?

She will never know that I have never looked at a pussy before. Never seen it and its intricacies. Never explored its various corridors. Years back, when I broke my vows of celibacy and gave up my life as a monk of my own order of professional mourners for Noria, I plunged into her without ever looking at it. She used to tease me about that: "What if there's nothing there . . . that I have tricked you with an artificial one made of plastic?" And I would respond: "Guess I will never know. It's fine that way."

But Orpah is now withdrawn. She rolls herself in a fetal position. I hold her in my arms. We cuddle on her pink duvet. Nothing happens beyond that. I just rest my member on her thighs until the fury is over. And we both drift into a deep sleep.

Medium Man

*D*awn is a whisper away and soon the birds will chirp. The medium man treads lightly in the forest looking for ghost orchids. Broken limbs of trees are scattered on the ground. His socks in his shoes are soggy and the lower legs of his pants are wet with dew. Before entering the forest he walked on the grass dotted with yellow dandelions waiting to unfold their petals with the rise of the sun.

The medium man has spent many days and many nights looking very closely at the trunks of trees. He hopes nighttime will bear fruit in the form of a gleaming ghost orchid. Perhaps they come out in the night and sleep during daytime. They are, after all, ghosts. That may be the reason he has failed to find them in the day. He imagines they transform from the shape of a frog that has been flattened by a car to a tiny ball particularly to hide themselves from him. And when they think he is fast asleep or he is performing his memories for the spirit child they unfold themselves and spread out and become the ghost orchids they were meant to be.

The spirit child instructed him to pay particular attention to ghost trees, for they are the likeliest hosts of ghost orchids. The medium man therefore looks into the hollow hearts of those ghost trees that have hollow hearts. It is in the hearts that secrets are hidden.

The moon is full; the ghost trees are ghost trees.

The medium man is not in the forest today as a medium man. He is looking for ghost orchids to make the spirit child happy, and is beginning to be despondent that he has not found any. The ghost trees do not care that his mission is different today. To them a medium man is always a medium man. Therefore they whisper stories to him. As they are wont to do when he walks in the forest. Be it day or be it night. From the branches that touch the sky the leaves breathe out stories of another time and gently blow them down to him. Memories of how an Abyssinian Queen flapped her wings and swooped to the ground and of how the sun was once lonely because it had no one to play with. His body soaks in these memories, so that his mouth may retell them later.

Yet he does not forget his quest. And his persistence later pays. At sunrise when he is walking home he discovers his first ghost orchid. At the edge of the forest. On the first tree he would have encountered when he got there. And yet he had missed it. There it is in all its glorious whiteness. Stuck on the mottled part of the trunk so as to stand out, waiting to be discovered by him. He is jumping with joy as he plucks it. His smile is not only on his lips, but in his eyes as well.

He knows what he'll do that night. He will dress up like . . . he will decide later what character he will assume. But he will be in full costume when he presents it to the spirit child.

🐾

These things had not been revealed to me yet, for the sciolist kept them close to his chest. I did not know about the medium man and the spirit child. That is why I am wondering where Mahlon Quigley comes from so early in the morning and why there is a bounce in his gait. I am standing at the front door when I see him approach. I give way and he enters without giving me a glance. I think he has made up his mind that I don't exist. He goes to his room, perhaps to sleep.

Ruth stands up from her workstation and walks to the kitchen. I follow her. She starts fussing around preparing breakfast of peanut butter and jelly sandwiches and coffee for her Mr. Quigley.

"Where does Mr. Quigley go at night?" I ask.

"Mr. Quigley has his ways," says Ruth.

She sets the food on the table.

"What are his ways?" I persist.

"The question is: what's your ways, mister? You think we don't know you slept in Orpah's room the other night? And Mr. Quigley don't like it one bit. I don't like it neither."

"Who told you that?" I demand, ready to deny the incident if only to protect Orpah's reputation. After our moment of weakness Orpah and I have avoided each other. Our eyes don't meet when I chance upon her. We behave like two guilt-ridden teenagers.

"Mr. Quigley knows everything," says Ruth, glaring at me. "And he's gonna protect his own."

As I make a shamefaced exit I brush against Mr. Quigley, who is coming for his breakfast. He ignores me as before.

It is too early to go to the Center so I loiter in Mahlon's garden, wondering how I'll continue to live under his roof after my scandalous behavior. If only Obed were here he would advise me exactly how to handle this . . . how to control the damage. But he has been scarce lately, thanks to Beth Eddy.

I need to talk to somebody, but there's no one here but the gnomes. And there's one of mine standing on a pedestal squinting at me. The Bush gnome, I mean, which really belongs to Mahlon. It holds a machine gun, which tells me that Obed was here not so long ago. Maybe last night. That's what he does when he is here: places a machine gun in Mr. Bush's hand. After some time Ruth will notice what Obed has done and will yank the weapon out of the President's hand and replace it with an American flag. This has happened many times over—a battle of wills fought over Mahlon's gnome. I don't know why Ruth hasn't thought of breaking the plastic machine gun to pieces and throwing it away where Obed will not find it. Maybe she is just respectful of it because it is Mr. Quigley's property.

Mahlon witnesses this battle without comment, and never interferes with either the machine gun or the American flag.

Orpah walks out of her room toward the swing. She is in a pink robe and her hair is in curlers. She makes for the living room door when she sees me. I call her name and she stops, but does not look at me. I walk toward her.

"Ruth knows," I blurt out. "How the heck did she know?"

"About what?" she asks, looking at me innocently.

"What we did."

"We didn't do nothing," she says, averting her eyes.

"I know. But they don't know that," I say, not looking away this time but staring into her eyes.

"They know we didn't do nothing. I told my daddy."

"You told him I spent the night?"

"Yeah. I tell my daddy everything. He wanna kill you."

She walks away.

"Oh, that's just great," I call after her. "Your father wants to kill me and you just walk away like that?"

She stops and smiles. She can afford to smile at a time like this. She looks cherubic without her garish jewelery and makeup.

"I got new pictures," she says. "Wanna save them from the tsunami?"

Without waiting for my response she rushes to her room and in no time is back with a stack of drawings. She dumps them in my hand and runs back to her room.

She has incorporated the ghost orchid motif in her designs.

❧

I have lost Ruth. I do not know if I will ever regain her. And it hurts me very much. Especially when she starts waging a campaign against me, telling all and sundry that I am up to no good and have brought evil to her family. I will surely go to hell "one of them days," and the unfortunate thing is that I will take her children with me to the eternal fires. Her children used to listen to her until Obed dragged me into the peaceful Quigley home. Her conscience is clear, however, because she has done her Christian duty by all of us, and will continue to show us the path of righteousness by sharing with us relevant biblical passages that will be responsible for our salvation if we follow them.

Of course, Ruth has never said any of these things to me directly. I hear of them at the Center. The women seem to enjoy my distress and every time I am at the Center they give me new titbits about my road to eternal damnation as mapped out by Ruth. Obed has also intimated his mother's displeasure, although he never really goes into as much detail as the women at the Center.

Ever since Obed established his life elsewhere I spend a lot of my time sewing and listening to village gossip at the Center. But this also does not sit well with Ruth. She continues, not to me but to others, with her woeful story of how the Center stole her African. If I wanted to know how to make a quilt why didn't I say so? She would have taught me herself. In any case, making quilts is a woman's job. What kind of a man am I? Why doesn't anyone see how right she is when she says I am up to no good?

I am working on my quilt when one woman offers me unsolicited advice: "You should of left Orpah's problems with her mama alone."

"Yeah, that's where it all starts," another one concurs. "You should of minded your own business."

"It's all Mahlon's fault," says the first woman. "He's gotta pay more attention to Ruth and stop playing his silly games with Orpah like they was little children."

I prick up my ears, but the arrival of a guest disrupts the gossip. She is selling rotary cutters and makes a spirited demonstration on how they make the usually tedious and boring work of cutting blocks easier. They look like pizza cutters to me. She folds the fabric many times over and using a broad flat ruler with grids on it she first cuts a square, which becomes many squares because of the folds, and then cuts the squares into triangles.

"The rotary cutter will change your life," she says, and then points out that my squares wouldn't be so terribly uneven if I had used a rotary cutter.

Barbara comes to the defense of her star pupil and points out that I am new at this. She says a few encouraging words, adding that what I am doing is a new design.

"I've never seen one like that," she says. "Your fingers are becoming finer. Your quilt becomes art . . . like a sculpture."

But the guest doesn't buy it. She insists that a rotary cutter will make things much easier for me.

"And he'll never learn to cut straight on his own with scissors," says one of the women.

"You are cutting on your own when you use a rotary cutter," the guest says. "It doesn't cut by itself. You direct it."

I like the idea of a rotary cutter and I buy two. I also buy two rulers.

"One's for Ruth," I say when I see their puzzled look.

"Yeah, maybe she's gonna change her mind 'bout you," says another woman and everyone laughs. I let them have their fun at my expense and go on with my sewing.

It is late afternoon when I leave the Center. The sun is still shining. I dread going home. Perhaps I should sit and while away time with the brooding elders who are sitting on the porch chewing Kodiak and spitting onto the grass a few feet away, silently competing as to whose black jet will get the farthest. At the risk of losing my appetite by the time I get home for dinner I take one of the car seats, which would have been Mahlon's if he were here. I guess he's gone back to the forest.

The brooding elders don't talk much. They just brood. I am hoping to change that, so I ask after their friend Mahlon.

"You don't wanna cross Mahlon," says an elder. "We know what you've done and he don't like it no ways."

Everybody knows. The whole world knows.

"I didn't do anything," I say.

"That Mahlon," chuckles another elder, "he's gonna whup you ass so bad you gonna wish you never laid your darn eyes on his li'l girl."

I may think I am younger, another elder observes, but their Mahlon is stronger. It is because he never worked in the mines. Every man they know was finished by coal dust, but Mahlon was too smart to go underground. He worked on his farm and kept animals instead. The Quigley family has always been smart, from the very first Quigley—Lord have mercy on him—who was a prophet and used a red scroll to tell the future right up to Mahlon's generation. I am rather disappointed that Obed and Orpah don't seem to feature in the generations that have distinguished themselves with their wisdom.

"Yep," says an elder with a mouthful of Kodiak. "Them Quigleys fought damn hard when coal and timber companies was kicking our grampas' ass off their land."

But another elder decides to burst the Quigley bubble. Not all the Quigleys were good guys, he points out. Doesn't anyone remember that one of them used to be a gunslinger hired to force striking miners from their houses back to work?

"It was back in them days. It was before our time," says one elder dismissively.

"Yeah, but my pap tol' me about them Quigleys that was hired guns for the Baldwin-Felts Detective Agency," says the elder.

"We didn't have nothing like that here," argues another elder.

It was in West Virginia, explains the elder. That was where the Quigleys who were hired guns worked. They took all their thuggery from Kilvert to West Virginia where miners were fighting for the right to unionize. The Quigleys were mine guards and became strike breakers, sometimes fighting pitched battles with the miners.

These events remind another elder of yet another Quigley who was not as good as Mahlon or as the revered first Quigley. This one ran a store owned by the mining company in Kilvert. Oh, yes, there was once a store in Kilvert!

"It left folks in debt by giving them scrip," says the elder. "All their wages went back to the company."

"It ain't Quigley's fault if folks was stupid," says a defender of the Quigley legacy.

The elders have obviously forgotten all about me as they argue about the good old Quigley days. I quietly leave.

🐚

Mahlon is not in the forest after all but is all greasy under the hood of the GMC trying to fix something. In the kitchen Ruth is arguing with Obed. I can hear them from the living room. I dare not go in there lest I be dragged into whatever they are screaming about.

"They're jealous of our democracy, that's why," says Ruth. "They're jealous of our standard of living."

"Why don't they bomb Sweden, Mama? It's a democracy with a higher standard of living. Why ain't no one jealous of Sweden?" says Obed.

"You been reading the *Athens News*. They gonna say anything 'cause they hate America. Ain't no country in the world that's got a better life than the good ol' U. S. of A."

"Lotsa countries, Mama," says Obed. "And no one bombs them."

" 'Cause they appease them terrorists, that's why."

" 'Cause we mind everybody's business, that's why."

Orpah appears from the inside door of her room and shouts: "Will y'all shudap? I'm trying to sleep." She must be feeling good that they obey her order instantly. But it is really that Obed has stormed out of the kitchen and out of the house. He does not notice me sitting on one of the car seats in the living room.

Ruth walks out of the kitchen and sits at her workstation. She sobs softly. I shift uncomfortably and she notices me for the first time. She tries to hide her eyes with her hands while bowing her head. I go to her and give her my gift of a rotary cutter and ruler. She looks at them for some time and then smiles wanly at me.

"Thank you," she says.

"I am sorry Obed annoys you so," I say. "I don't think you two should take politics so personally."

I almost add that I doubt if her hero, the man who runs the whole country, gets as many sleepless nights as she does over international affairs, but think better of it.

"It ain't that," says Ruth between sniffles. It's just that her children don't appreciate her. No one appreciates her for the sacrifices she has made for the family. Then she sobs once more. I never know what to do in such situations. I don't have a tissue to hand her. I stand there for a few seconds looking foolish, and then I quietly make for the door.

Obed is with his father under the hood of the GMC. He sees me and his face lights up. I know immediately that there is a new money-making scheme he wants to share with me.

"Hey, homey, don't see much of you lately," he says, coming to join me on the porch. We sit down on the steps.

"You shouldn't do this to your mother," I say.

He says Ruth started the whole thing. All he was asking for was the GMC for a few days because he has to see his Shawnee brothers in Oklahoma on a matter that will benefit the family. If she had given him the pickup he would have borrowed some money from me since he knows for sure he would be able to pay me back with a hundred percent interest. When he explained his mission to Ruth she pooh-poohed the whole idea, and added insult to injury by claiming that the Quigleys have no Shawnee blood in them. They are Cherokee. It was only then that he decided to hurt Ruth by condemning America's international adventurism. He knows which buttons to press to raise his mother's blood pressure.

He shows me a book he is currently reading—thanks to Beth Eddy—that is opening his eyes to the things that are happening out there in the world. *The Rule of Christian Fundamentalists* is the title.

I congratulate him for reading a book but question the wisdom of driving all the way to Oklahoma in search of his people's mystic secrets.

"I know you want to be a shaman, but you may be chasing a mirage," I add.

"It ain't nothing like that," he assures me.

He wants to attend a tribal convocation where he is going to present a case for Kilvert to the Shawnee chiefs and elders. He takes out a page of the *Athens News* from his book and unfolds it.

"Athens County is among the many Ohio counties that have been named in a recent federal lawsuit by an Oklahoma Indian tribe, which is seeking to reclaim its aboriginal possessory land rights to a large portion of the state," states the paper. "Ohio Attorney General Jim Petro has said that the lawsuit by the Eastern Shawnee Tribe of Oklahoma has no strong legal foundation. He has suggested that the tribe is mainly seeking to force Ohio to accept casino gambling—an assessment that attorneys for the tribe have essentially confirmed. The suit, filed in the U.S. District Court, demands ownership of more than 93,000 acres in northwest Ohio, as well as hunting, fishing and gathering rights in a large chunk of central and southern Ohio."

There is a map that shows the counties that are the subject of this litigation. Basically these are the counties that are enclosed by the Miami River in the west, the Ohio River in the south and the southeast, and the Hocking River in the east and a line north of Columbus. The suit, based on the 1795 Treaty of Greenville, claims that historically the Shawnee hunting grounds stretched from the Hocking River, and Obed wants to ascertain that Kilvert is included there.

"This is the chance for my people," he says. "We gonna have a casino in Kilvert one of them days."

He has been following this issue for quite some time, even before the paper publicized it. He wants this casino very much for his children and will not let Ruth's insistence on a Cherokee heritage deprive him of what is rightfully his. It becomes obvious to me that here we have the present reshaping the past in its image.

"You don't have children," I say.

"I am gonna have them one day," he says matter-of-factly.

"With Beth Eddy?"

He chuckles shyly and says: "It don't matter with who."

"She's a good influence. Now you're shy all of a sudden."

"She don't influence me no how. It don't mean just because she's a college girl she influence me."

"She makes you read."

"I make me read."

"She is beautiful," I say.

"She's put together good," he agrees and laughs.

Ruth walks out of the house. I suspect she is not pleased to see the "boy" who infuriated her only a few minutes ago sitting on the steps with me and laughing in such a carefree manner. She mutters something to herself. It is really meant for our ears. She says that ever since I came here her children think they know everything. And now I think I am going to buy everybody with presents. First I gave Mr. Quigley a gnome. And now I am trying to bribe her with newfangled quilting tools that she will never use since her mother and her grandmother taught her how to quilt the right way.

"That's what the Devil gone and done to Christ . . . with ten pieces of silver."

"They was thirty, Mama," Obed calls after her as she takes the corner. "They was thirty pieces of silver."

We no longer hear what else she has to say. Obed laughs even louder at my befuddled look.

❦

I get another opportunity to mourn at a live funeral. Sister Naomi's funeral. She had continued to keep the sheriff busy with her meth labs, despite the fact that Brother Michael and the congregation spent hours praying for her and on three occasions she testified in the chocolate church that she had finally seen the light and her ways had changed. The Lord had mercy on her, but super-speed was merciless. It made her do things that were frowned upon by good Christians like Ruth. Such as cruising the bars of Athens looking for men and demanding that they should do her in the backseats of their cars. Super-speed made her insatiable. She was indeed uncontrollable and people started questioning why she was set free from the slammer since she did not seem to have learned any lessons from her son's death. Well, she was freed because she denied knowing anything about the meth lab in the van, and her boyfriend was the one who was found guilty and was serving a long prison term in Nelsonville.

Kilverters had to watch helplessly as Sister Naomi wasted away, spending up to twelve hours a day in bed, fast asleep, neglecting everything and everybody, hiding the smile that used to be so brilliant. Her teeth had now fallen out and her gums were black. She was losing so much weight she was but a skeleton. Her skin had lesions. "She looks like she's been bobbing for French fries," the women at the Center whispered. She was too far gone to be saved from the addiction, and when she died there was relief all around. And all this happened so fast, in a matter of weeks.

I am sitting on a mound, as is my custom, wailing softly as Brother Michael reads the scriptures. He testifies on how Sister Naomi used to be the pillar of the church. People should rather remember her beautiful voice when she sang for the Lord rather than the last days of her life when the Devil tempted and won her soul over.

"But who are we to judge?" he asks in his booming voice. "Who are we to cast the first stone?"

I punctuate these words with squeals borrowed and adapted from Sister Naomi's own atrocious singing as I remember it that single occasion I went to the chocolate church—when Sister Naomi was still Sister Naomi. Despite my spirited mourning both

Ruth and Mahlon pretend that I am not here at all. Not even a glance in my direction. They look fixedly at the coffin as it is low-ered in the grave. Mahlon's smile is even more pronounced. Ruth's face is expressionless.

Orpah is here too in her shimmering black dress and lampshade hat. She came with me this time. Early in the morning she came to my RV all dressed up and ready for the funeral. It was in blatant de-fiance of her parents, who decreed after I moved out of their house that the "children" should have nothing to do with me. Orpah has been to my RV almost every day to see if things were all right with me. So has Obed, before he took the Greyhound to Connecticut where he hopes to connect with casino bosses who will give him a few pointers on how to establish one in Kilvert.

He was not very pleased with me when he left yesterday because he felt I was not being helpful in his venture. First of all I had ex-pressed my disapproval when I discovered that his real reason for reclaiming his heritage was that he wanted to have his own casino. He had no qualms about it because he claimed that many other people who had no connection at all to that heritage were reaping millions from it. Why shouldn't he, a true son of the tribes, get his share?

I made things worse when I refused to go to Connecticut with him to look for Sol Kerzner, a South African who had taken ad-vantage of apartheid laws and established casinos in South Africa's own black reservations. When he heard that the South African bil-lionaire had subsequently established casinos at the Native Ameri-can reservations in Connecticut, and these were doing wonderfully both for him and the Native American shareholders, he imagined that if he went to see the man with me things would be much smoother. He argued that I should accompany him to Connecticut because my South African origins would gain us an audience with the man. He brought with him a black striped suit that he found at the Center and suggested that I should spruce myself up and look like a proper businessman.

"I am just a professional mourner, Obed," I told him. "A billionaire like Kerzner would know nothing about me. Nor would he wish to see me."

When he left in the morning to catch a bus to Columbus and then another one to Connecticut he did not come to my RV to say goodbye. He could have left after Sister Naomi's funeral, who was after all some aunt of his, but I supposed he decided to miss my mourning as a way of punishing me. Well, he has missed the new sounds that I have invented especially for this funeral. As the biggest fan of my mourning routine he would have marveled at the way I am able to toss my audience around and then throw them on an emotional roller-coaster depending on the theme of the hymn or on Brother Michael's readings and preachings.

After the funeral I receive payment from those relatives who believe in the concept of a professional mourner, and congratulations seasoned with references to my purported Egyptian origins. The payment is token, but I do not complain. I am not exactly poor although I do not flaunt my wealth. I made a reasonable fortune from mourning the boring deaths in southern Africa. That is why I am able to travel the world in search of mourning. Now I mourn for the joy of it. For fulfillment rather than remuneration. But then for professional mourning to have any meaning some payment should be made, even if it is only token.

I walk back to my RV, which is parked in the grounds of the Center, thanks to the generosity of the women who have given it a temporary home until I decide what to do next. In return I continue to be useful as a handyman—fixing handles on the cupboard, mopping the floor, loading and unloading foodstuffs, and taking old clothes to the incinerator behind the Center. These are clothes that have been lying around the porch for too long without anyone choosing them. We burn them to make room for new arrivals after selecting those that may be useful as batting for quilts.

Orpah did not want me to move. She pleaded with me to stay.

She even cried. Orpah cried for me. Or was she really crying for herself?

She didn't think I was serious when, at the dinner table one night, I first brought up the idea of moving. All five of us were present when I announced my intentions. Obed was not surprised because I had spoken with him about it already. Mahlon maintained his smile. Ruth wanted to know if I was going back to Africa.

"Ultimately, yes," I said. "But not yet. I am still in search of mourning."

Orpah said if there is any search for mourning at all she wants to be part of it. I thought she was not serious. Perhaps it was her way of challenging her parents; of getting back at them; of showing some rebellion. She didn't think I would actually move. She didn't think I would take to the road in search of mourning either.

Obed, on the other hand, encouraged the move. He suggested that I buy an RV, which would make my wanderings more comfortable. The idea was worth exploring, though it seemed far-fetched at the time. After all, my ways were no longer austere and ascetic as they used to be when I was still a votary who adhered strictly to the self-imposed discipline of my own order of professional mourners. A little comfort here and there would not corrupt my soul.

"What do I do with an RV when I can't even drive?" I asked.

"I'll teach you, homey," said Obed. "It's easy."

"I'll teach you too," said Orpah.

I couldn't help thinking that Obed really wanted the RV for himself, to use in some of his scams. Or even to travel to Oklahoma since his mama refused her GMC.

Obed knew exactly who would help us find a good used RV. Nathan.

Nathan was quite open about his motives for helping me find an RV. He hoped I would move out of the house and out of everyone's life. I had caused enough troubles for the family. If I left, Orpah would surely regain her sanity and would appreciate what he was

trying to do for her. He was aiming at the Grand Ole Opry for Orpah. She would surely make it big there because she had added a
new dimension to what used to be disparagingly called hillbilly
music. With his guidance she could easily be at the Grand Ole
Opry. I was misleading Orpah because I was from Africa and did
not know what was at stake here. If I left, my evil hold on Orpah
would leave with me. And everything would be as it was before.
Except for the fact that Orpah would agree to marry him and they
would live happily ever after with him managing her lucrative
career.

The RV that Nathan found for me was a 1982 Ford Shasta. I
went to fetch it from Lancaster with Obed and as we drove back to
Athens he assured me that the engine was still very good. I, on the
other hand, was impressed by the red-carpeted interior, the refrig-
erator, the gas stove, the two couches newly covered with pink corduroy fabric, the dining area, the roominess. It was like owning a
house.

When I took my suitcase and went to say goodbye to Ruth at her
workstation I was surprised when she said she did not want me to
leave. If I was going back to Africa she would understand, or at
least if I was leaving town altogether. But to vacate her house only
to park at the Center was an insult to her.

"I have enjoyed your hospitality for seven months, Ruth," I said.
"It is time to move on. I will always remember your house as my
home."

I was going against her wishes, she said. After one or two sniffles
she added that in any event she would not expect her wishes to
count with me because they don't count even with her own children.

I could hear more sniffles as she gave me some of her bottled
sauces and relish and a glazed clay jar of stewed tomatoes, which
she said I should keep until winter and only eat the contents then.
After that I must return her jar. Did she expect me still to be here
next winter?

Mahlon was quite dispassionate about my leaving, if you discount the smile. He was sitting on his swing when I said goodbye. Obed and Orpah were helping me to my RV with my suitcase, Ruth's bottles and other odds and ends that I had accumulated during my stay in Kilvert. These included manila folders with Orpah's designs saved from the tsunami. All he said as I shook his hand, assuring him that I would see him from time to time at the Center, was: "Don't let the bedbugs bite." And then he went back to gazing at his garden while swinging to the rhythm of the chimes.

"Todoloo! You ain't gonna see nobody at the Center," said Ruth standing at the door. "You'd better come and visit and have a wholesome meal."

I feel like lord of the manor as I open my RV and am welcomed by a whiff of stale cooking oil. I like the way they have refurbished the RV. It is worth every penny of the seven thousand dollars I paid for it.

The interior is enhanced by a dogwood quilt with yellow, brown and green sunflowers on white. The backing is of bleached muslin. It is a gift from Barbara and was made by her grandmother in 1935. I did not think I deserved such a valuable and highly sentimental present but she told me: "It needs to be given to someone who will love it. So, I figure you'd do that." It's been in the family for all the years, and what makes it even more valuable is that it was hand-sewn—nine stitches an inch, which look so fine they can easily be mistaken for machine-sewn stitches. I would have loved to keep this quilt in a box so as to preserve it for posterity, but Barbara insisted that I hang it on the wall.

Mourning can be exhausting, so I kick off my shoes and sprawl myself on the bed that is covered with another quilt: a green and white Irish Chain that I bought from Ruth months before I left her house. At first she had been reluctant to sell it to me, and then later agreed to part with it at a great discount, adding: "I don't sell nothing to my kids. Might as well not sell nothing to you neither."

I reach for one of the manila folders next to my bed and look at Orpah's latest work. The ghost trees are still there. But on them there are collages of ghost orchids made from bits of plastic, paper and fabric. I remember her telling me this morning when she delivered this last batch before we went to the funeral: "I want them pictures to tell a story. Like back in them days if something happened there'd be a song wrote about it."

These collages are a song.

🔊

The women have remarked on how vastly my quilting has improved. It is because I do nothing much but quilt. I sit at the Center and cut blocks—not with the rotary cutter, but the scissors that the women insist I should learn to master. I arrange the blocks on the long table into the pattern I want, and listen to gossip. Often my opinion is sought since the belief that I am some kind of a shaman persists. They believe that because I am from Africa I have knowledge of mysterious cures. Such as the plant they tell me cured Sissy—I think she was one of their relatives—who suffered from diabetes. She had tried some of the best doctors to no avail. Then she went to Africa and learned of a plant from an old shaman. The shaman told Sissy to boil the plant and drink half a cup a day. When she returned to the U.S.A. she discovered that the plant was in fact rhubarb. She boiled the rhubarb every morning and after a few months Sissy's blood sugar became normal. Sissy died at ninety-five from old age—after suffering from diabetes from the time she was a child.

The common wisdom among my quilting partners is that I know more of such cures but am hiding my light under a bushel, which is what Jesus preached against in the Sermon on the Mount. One of them adds: "Because he don't like folks that hide their talent and don't share it with nobody."

Orpah takes to hovering around the Center, doing what they call here "hanging out." Women, and an odd man now and then, usually hang out at the Center for the conversation. I have heard some

of the hottest political debates in these hanging out sessions. But
Orpah never participates in the conversation. She just sits there and
watches me quilt, with a deep longing in her eyes. I take it that she
wishes she could be doing what I am doing at that time, although I
suspect she despises it for it is not as adventurous as her own would
be. Mine are blocks and triangles that any traditional quiltmaker
can do. Now and then she giggles or chuckles when someone says
something funny.

When Mahlon is tending his garden of gnomes Orpah is at the
Center. When Mahlon is brooding with the other elders at the Center Orpah goes home and locks herself in her room, I suppose drawing or playing the sitar or reading what her mother once referred to
as ghost stories.

Her first visit to my RV was unannounced. She just knocked at
the door, and when I opened she dumped new drawings in my
hands and left. Not a single word. Then the visits became more
frequent even when there were no new drawings to keep. I love
these visits, although I fear what Mahlon will do one of these days
because she defiantly walks into my RV even when she can see that
her father is looking on from the porch at the Center. The women
have jokingly said that one day he'll burn my RV. Obviously they
find the whole thing entertaining. My life has become the village's
soap opera.

When Orpah visits we just sit and talk. Nothing else happens.
She is usually here at lunchtime and she opens a can of Spam or
takes out a frozen pizza from the fridge and tosses it into the mi-
crowave. Then she tells me about her troubles with Ruth. Her eyes
light up when she talks of her works that have escaped her spring
cleaning, which has become more frequent. One day when I am
better skilled, I promise her, I will translate some of her designs into
quilts.

Sometimes Obed visits as well and the siblings talk about their
own things that I know nothing about, or about Nathan. From

what I gather things have soured between Nathan and Orpah since the festival. Now she makes cruel jokes about him.

"I look at that guy and I don't like his haircut," she says. "He looks like a Muppet and I find that disturbing."

"Which of the Muppets?" Obed asks.

"The mad scientist . . . I forget his name."

"He can't be no scientist . . . not even a mad one. He's just a dumb-ass prick."

And then they laugh.

He is saying all these mean things about Nathan because he has had a falling-out with him, for a different reason. To raise money for his trip to Connecticut Obed disposed of a trophy that he, Nathan and two other guys won at a tractor pulling contest at the County Fair last August. They had agreed that the trophy would be with each one of them for three months at a time. After it had graced the two guys' mantelpieces they had handed it over to Obed in February and at the end of May he was supposed to give it to Nathan. Nathan discovered that Obed had pawned the trophy. He is now so pissed off with him that they almost came to blows at a bar in Athens. Obed tells me: "He threatened to whup my ass and I told him, 'Bring it on, bitch.'" The denizens of the bar stopped the fight before it could become bloody and messy.

I am happy that things are back to normal between me and Obed. For a number of days after his return from Connecticut he sulked a bit and didn't want to have anything to do with me because he blamed me for his failure to meet Mr. Kerzner—the man who developed and operated the casinos on behalf of the Native American tribes. He discovered that the man was basking in the sun somewhere in the Caribbean and rarely visited any of the casinos. If I were there, Obed reckoned, some dialogue would have happened between me and the Native Americans who own the casinos, and they would have listened to me because I am Mr. Kerzner's countryman.

He came back without making any headway with the casino owners because they didn't take him seriously. If Kilvert was not a reservation, how could he even dream of opening a casino there? they asked. When he told them about the Shawnee claim that was already in the courts they said he should come back to them when the Shawnee had won their case and Kilvert had been declared an Indian reservation. Only then would they consider going into business with him on his new casino venture.

Although he was not impressed by the way he was treated by the casino operators, who even denied him an audience with the chiefs of either the Mohegan or the Mashantucket Pequot tribes, he was encouraged by what he discovered there. The Mashantucket Pequots, for instance, own what they claim is the world's largest casino. Yet only thirty-five years ago they were not a tribe at all but were down to one person—one Elizabeth George. The descendants regrouped from other parts of the country and now they are the richest tribe ever. What can stop his Kilvert people from rising like the Mashantucket Pequots?

His people deserved a chance. They have never had a fair deal.

A few days later Obed brings me a yellowing article from the *Athens Magazine,* Winter 1984, to show me just what he means when he says his people have never been treated well. He got the magazine from the Center.

Wanted: a few good jobs for Indians, says the headline. I read on:

The leaders of a growing minority movement centered in the tiny hamlet of Kilvert have developed a combative style. Are they terrorists or squeaky wheels? "I believe in confrontation and violence if necessary. I believe in tearing things apart if necessary. We want jobs, we don't want more rhetoric," said Melton Fletcher, an American Indian activist. Spoken last fall at an Athens County Minority Association press conference, Fletcher's words express the sentiments many area minorities share—bitterness, disappointment, frustration and anger—at what they believe are long-standing discriminatory hiring practices in Athens.

The article goes on to name Fletcher as a Choctaw Indian and a co-chairman of the ACMA who has been fighting for the rights of the American Indians in southeast Ohio.

Most of Athens County's Indian population is clustered around the tiny Rome Township hamlet of Kilvert, 20 miles from Athens. Only within recent years have the racially-mixed black, white and Indian people there begun to gain a collective historical, cultural and political self-awareness.

Since the coal mines closed in the 1930s, says the article, the employment situation has been bleak for the Native Americans in southeast Ohio. Eighty percent are unemployed.

"So what happened to Fletcher?" I ask.

"I don't know. Maybe he gave up and packed and gone to better places," says Obed. "Or maybe he died."

Obed sees himself as the new Fletcher, although his methods will not be Fletcher's. Times have changed. Instead of advocating the use of violence to empower his people he will open a casino. Do I now see why Kilvert should be declared a reservation? After all, the Kilvert Community Center used to be the southeast Ohio headquarters of the North American Indian Council. Do I also see why he is so pissed off with Ruth when she keeps on insisting on a Cherokee heritage and other Kilverters who keep on claiming a Powhatan heritage? How will they get a reservation if they don't even know which tribe they belong to? Can't they see the advantages of being Shawnee once and for all?

They are no longer sure what their tribe is because they hankered for and lionized whiteness to the suppression of their Indianness and Africanness during the days of oppression. Many of them could only sing genealogies of their white ancestors. Today they are keen to reclaim all three heritages since they are a source of pride and make them a unique people. But they no longer remember who they were, on the African and Native American side. It does not help that in this area three different tribes lived side-by-side—the Cherokee, the Powhatan and the Shawnee.

"You can only be one tribe to get a reservation," says Obed sadly. "And Shawnee is the way to go."

Orpah never spends the night. In the evening, just before sunset, she goes home. I would like her to spend the night, though I have never outrightly asked her. I have hinted at it. She does not get it. Or pretends not to get it. I don't pursue the matter though my desire for her has returned with a vengeance, especially when I am alone at night and can imagine her sitar whining the night away. Until Mahlon comes in his strange costumes. And all desire suddenly dies.

Sometimes Orpah and I go for a walk in the woods. And she shows me where her father has found the latest ghost orchid. I do not ask her how she knows the exact spot where the ghost orchid was found as she was not there. It is better that she does not know that I know that she plants the ghost orchids herself for her father to find.

We walk to the Federal Creek and she shows me where Ruth used to swim as a little girl. She surmises that her dad used to peek at the girls swimming in the buff from the bluffs. But no one can swim in the creek now because it is polluted.

"There's septic tanks and all that crap," she laments.

On sunny days—and there are many of them—we go mushroom hunting in the woods. She has her favorite spot where the sponge-like morels grow. She teaches me how to pick them out. I must not confuse them with the false morels, which are poisonous,

she warns me. There'll be other kinds as well late in the summer:
the chanterelles and the chicken-of-the-woods. But if I come on my
own I should stick to the morels because they are easier to identify,
she warns. Unless I want to die from mushroom poisoning, even before her daddy kills me. She adds this last one with a naughty twinkle in her eye.

Fresh mushrooms must wait for Obed because he is the only one
who knows how to cook them properly. When he comes, if he is
not spending that evening with Beth Eddy, he returns to the wild
to dig from the ground wild garlic and shallots. Wild mushrooms
taste like the most heavenly meat when they are sautéed with wild
garlic and shallots. And Obed is the master.

As we sit eating his creation with rice he confides in me that
things have not been good at home lately. There is no food in the
house, except for the bottled sauces and relishes. For a long time
now no money has come from the quilts. No rent from me since I
left. The food from the Center is not enough and is intermittent.
The family no longer gets Orpah's share because she spends a lot
of time at my RV. Obed spends a lot of time with Beth Eddy at her
apartment in Athens since she moved from the sorority house.
Mahlon broods even more.

"Why tell him all this?" asks Orpah. "It ain't none of his business."

"It ain't none of his business 'cause you eat here all the time,"
says Obed.

This embarrasses me.

"You mooch here and at Beth Eddy's too," she says.

I wonder why Beth Eddy became Beth Eddy to us and not just
Beth.

"Ruth, she don't do nothing 'cause she's thinking about a bunch
of religious crap all the time," Orpah adds.

"We'll see if it's crap when you go to hell," says Obed.

"Ain't no hell but Kilvert," says Orpah.

"That's a lot of bull and you know it," says Obed. "Ain't no better place than Kilvert. Kilvert's gonna be heaven when I'm done with my casino."

❧

I have got to help Ruth. Next morning I do not go quilting but take the short walk to her house. The chimes and Orpah's sitar take me back to my stay here. I was happy here. I have missed this house. I have missed Ruth.

My body tingles at the sitar. The sitar has a way of playing these random games with me. Sometimes it is just pleasant music and does nothing more. Like when she played at the bluegrass festival. At other times it arouses me to madness. Perhaps it is the particular song that she plays at the time. The particular mood she is in when she plays it.

Ruth is at her workstation but she is not doing any work. She is just sitting staring at a pile of fabric. The first thing she utters when I walk in is: "Where them kids at?"

I don't know where Obed is, I tell her. But Orpah must be in her room for I can hear her sitar. Surely she can hear it too? She starts complaining about how I have been a negative influence on her children since they no longer spend their time at home. Before I came here they used to listen to her. Can I believe that even Mr. Quigley is doing naughty things he would never dream of doing before I came here? For instance, she found dandelion moonshine in Obed's bedroom. She only learned later to her utter shock that Mr. Quigley was involved in the manufacture of this potent beverage from the dandelion flowers.

"Mr. Quigley shouldn't do such stuff with them kids," she says. Between sobs she says that the first Quigley, Lord have mercy on him, must be turning in his grave when his descendants are behaving in this manner. The first Quigley was a man of God and a prophet. It is unfortunate that none of the men who came after him followed his path of righteousness.

"Mr. Quigley will go to hell one of them days," she says.

"I hope this will make you feel better," I say, giving her five twenty-dollar notes.

She looks at me for a while, and then smiles. She shakes her head and withdraws both her hands to her ample chest.

"Better you give it to them starving kids in Ethiopia," she says.

"Okay," I say, "I am buying a quilt with it . . . from you."

"Ain't got no quilt to sell," she says. And then adds with emphasis: "To you."

She insists I can't leave without drinking her sassafras tea. She says she also has corn bread for me; despite the lies that Orpah must have told me that there is no food in her house. I stay with her for a while, eating her corn bread with the tea and listening to her latest political hobbyhorse. This time it has to do with crime that is creeping into such peaceful places as Kilvert. They should hang the criminals and they will learn a good lesson. Folks need guns to protect themselves. She announces grandly that she is pro-gun and pro-death penalty. Yet she is pro-life!

I tell her that I am pro-death. How else do I mourn without death?

"The best thing you can do for me," she says when I am about to leave, "is to get me some gingham from Africa. They must still have it there. Old-timers used gingham for their quilts. You can't buy it in the U.S. of A. no more. I wanna make my quilts with gingham and you'll see how folks gonna buy them like they was hot cakes."

🖝

It must be after midnight. I can hear the sitar. Maybe it is just whining in my head, for the house is too far to actually hear it from here. But I can hear it as clear as if it was just outside the RV. And it does to me what it did that first night. The night I had to flee from my own erection. This time I will not flee. I will challenge it. I wake up and put on my jeans, plaid shirt and sneakers. I practically run to the house.

I hide behind Mahlon's bush and abuse myself. If the asylum at The Ridges were still in operation I would abuse myself all the way to Athens and get myself committed. That is what this sitar is doing to my head and my body. Just as the rhythm gets faster I stop abruptly. Mahlon is walking to Orpah's room. He must have come out through the kitchen door. He must have dressed up in his own bedroom, which confirms my suspicion that Ruth knows all about his nighttime shenanigans.

Tonight he is in a dark double-breasted frock coat of a Union Army major general, white gloves, gold epaulettes, dark pants and Nike sneakers. His black Confederate officer's slouch hat is too big for his head. He walks stylishly swinging a sword.

The music stops as he floats into Orpah's room. And then the laughter and the mumblings and the screeching. I want to hear what they are saying. A little devil in me tells me to kick the door and barge in. Instead I walk closer to the window. I almost place my ear against the pane, making sure that I don't touch it lest they discover me before I discover what they are up to, in which case my mission to save Orpah from the man and from herself will flop.

Through the slits between the worn blinds I can see Mahlon pacing the floor as he recites something about a long journey that Massa Blue Fly undertakes over snowy hills and through forests devoid of leaves. He buzzes like a fly and Orpah laughs like a little girl. I can't see her though. She must be somewhere on or near the bed. Mahlon "flies" around the room, his arms outstretched like the wings of a plane. The more he flies with the buzzing sound the harder Orpah laughs. And then he stops the flying and resumes tracing the long journey across frozen rivers and down slippery slopes. Until Massa Blue Fly arrives at his destination and gives some good news to the Abyssinian Queen. Somehow ghost orchids find their way into the celebrations that follow Massa Blue Fly's good news. Ghost orchids float in the sky and fall on the ground and on the flowing robes of the dancers. The Abyssinian Queen swoops down from the topmost branch of a ghost tree and floats with the ghost orchids.

I can hear Orpah and Mahlon clapping their hands and singing "The Song of Massa Blue Fly." The singing is far from being wonderful. Neither singer seems to take their singing seriously. It is obvious that the song is being improvised on the spot and the singers mix it with laughter. I am hoping she will play the sitar but she never does.

Mahlon says, "Shhhhh," and they are both silent.

He is very close to the window.

The blinds are suddenly yanked open and the light splashes all over me. Mahlon is smiling at me menacingly. Surely he is going to kill me this time. He opens the door and says, "Why not come in if you wanna hear right?"

I walk into Orpah's mother-in-law room. The Marilyn Monroe cut-outs are stacked on one side to create more room. Orpah is sitting in a Buddha-like pose on the bed and is in the pirate's costume she was wearing that first night, although tonight she is wearing a maroon Victorian bonnet. She does not look amused at all.

"He can't come in," she says. "He ain't got no costume."

"It don't matter," says Mahlon. "Let him stay. Let him see what he wanna see."

"I promise I'll be quiet," I say. "I won't utter a word."

She does not address me. She's not even looking at me but at her father when she says, still in a little girl's voice: "Without costume he's like naked. You don't do them memories when you're naked."

She is surrounded by crayons on the comforter. She holds a sheet of paper on which there is a work-in-progress: stylized ghost orchids floating among stylized branches of ghost trees.

So this is how she creates her work.

"I knew the motherfucker was out there all the time," says Mahlon as he ushers me to sit on the bed next to Orpah.

"He can't take no part in our memories," says Orpah.

"He won't take no part," says Mahlon. "But it don't matter if he see them memories, little girl. He can't change them no ways."

"They're not for seeing by nobody."

"He's seen some already."

"He's a fuckin' spy," she says. "He's the one who's gonna tell on the Abyssinian Queen."

She still does not look at me. It is as if I am not there at all.

"I am not going to tell anything," I protest.

"We'll kill him if he tells on her," says Mahlon.

He is a medium man. He gets his stories from the ghost trees. He transmits them to Orpah who then re-creates them.

Mother of All Mourning

Now I know why it is always winter in Orpah's pictures; why her ghost trees are devoid of foliage: Mahlon's midnight stories are set in wintry landscapes. His memory begins and ends with winter frolics, winter journeys and winter crossings. When Orpah's obsessions force into the performances ghost orchids, which by nature bloom only in summer, they adapt to the season of Mahlon's visions and float like snow flakes among the naked branches of ghost trees. They fall on the flowing garments of dancing celebrants where they gleam like misshapen stars on undulating skies.

Mahlon's performances date back to the time when the children were children. And when Mahlon was still Mahlon. When his face was not marred by a permanent smile. When his hogs and cows were thriving. When his garden was blooming with flowers. He read bedtime stories to the children before they slept. They all shared the same bedroom at the time. Mahlon sat on the children's bed and read them stories about little mermaids, mermaids that were headless, princesses and peas, Ali Baba and the Forty Thieves and many others. Stories set in faraway lands and written in bold letters and illustrated in colorful pictures in books that Mahlon brought from the Center and from used-book stores in Athens.

When he could not get more books he read the same stories over and over again. Until the children could complete the sentences. Until they were bored with them. Then he took to creating his own tall tales. These were not confined to bedtime. He told them after dinner at the kitchen table. Or on the porch during balmy summer evenings. He did not only tell them. He performed them.

Later he went to the forest to get more stories from the ghost trees. And from all sorts of other trees. Those that could bear witness to how things used to be. Those that sprouted from the seed that fell from those that saw and remembered. That is how stories became memories. That is how he became the medium man.

At first Ruth did not mind these stories. But the more she read the Bible and The Word was revealed to her, the more she felt uncomfortable with them. Stories about the sun that was lonely because nothing else had been created yet and about a black woman who flapped her wings and swooped down from ghost trees that were so high they touched the clouds were unchristian. She banned them from the house.

Her Mr. Quigley did not want to upset her. But he was too addicted to the performances to give them up. And so were the children. By this time Mahlon had sold his small farm and the family had moved to the present house. Mahlon took to performing his stories for Obed and Orpah in Orpah's room. Soon the costumes were introduced. At about the same time Obed was gradually withdrawing from the performances because he had outgrown them. Orpah never outgrew them. Instead she became a co-creator of the stories. Mahlon would come up with only the beginning of a new tale, and between father and daughter a tandem story would develop. Or Orpah would complete the stories by painting them.

Ruth knew what was happening in Orpah's room, but gave up on her Mr. Quigley. "One day God is gonna make him stop," she said. God hasn't made him stop yet. She never got to know that the pictures she relentlessly destroyed were inspired by the storytelling sessions. She still thinks Orpah draws them when she locks herself in her room all day long.

After piecing all this together from Obed and also from Orpah—who is reluctant to talk about it or even to acknowledge that I was present at one such session the other night—I decide I must make it up to Mahlon for having thought evil thoughts about him. Whether he knows or not that I hated him is not important. I know. And it gnaws at me. I think it is only proper that I assuage my guilt by doing something for him. Perhaps make an offering of a whole bunch of gnomes. Or better still, find his mother's grave. That will have greater impact, I think. Ruth once told me that there will be peace in him only if he finds his mother's grave and does what is right by her. She said even his fortunes would change. I had marveled at the time that these people's beliefs about appeasing the dead were very much similar to ours. Yes, I am going to help Mahlon find that grave. I do not know yet how I will go about it. But I certainly will.

When I was at The Ridges on the night of the parade of creatures about ten months ago I noted that three or four of the graves had tombstones with inscriptions on them. Some of the relatives were able to locate and identify the exact graves where their loved ones were sleeping. I must find out how that was done and proceed to locate the grave. It may take a lot of detective work, but it is the least I can do for Mahlon, and for Ruth. It may not mean anything to Orpah and Obed. Especially to Obed, who seemed to find the discussion embarrassing at that first dinner with the family.

I pay Ruth a surprise visit to suggest the idea of searching for the grave. She is at the clothesline near her vegetable patch airing her pre–Civil War quilts. I can see the Turin-like image of the first Quigley on one of them. The one the "kids" claim is nothing but a urine stain.

"We don't see you no more," she says by way of returning my greeting.

She is right. Throughout the summer months I have only had a few glimpses of her from a distance—one of the dark figures on the luxuriant green of Kilvert.

"But I hear you come like a thief at night for Mr. Quigley's silly memories," she adds.

This is not quite accurate, but I don't say that to her. I did come, yes, but only that one time Mahlon caught me eavesdropping at the window. The night he invited me in despite Orpah's protestations.

That was weeks ago. And that performance had bombed as soon as I got seated on her bed. It was no longer carefree and smooth-flowing as before. It lacked the abandon I had seen through the window. Mahlon seemed to be self-conscious. He tried to glide as I saw him do, but his movements were wooden. He kept giving me a sideways glance. When he introduced a song to the story of how the sun shed one big tear that rolled downhill and broke into many tears that in turn became children, his voice was hesitant. When he came to the part where the sun farted out a giraffe and a character called Divided, Orpah's response to Mahlon's chants tried to be as spirited as before, but soon she gave up in exasperation because Mahlon's calls had gone limp. Her hand did not move with ease on the page. She was not happy with the result and tore the pictures in frustration. Then she glared at me accusingly. Mahlon ushered me out mumbling: "You son of a bitch, you messed up our memories." I stood outside for a moment and listened while Orpah accused her father of allowing me into their secret world of memories. Then Mahlon made an unceremonious exit. Though he saw me standing there he ignored me and marched like a defeated soldier—sword sheathed—into the house using the kitchen door.

Orpah came to my RV the next morning and behaved as if nothing had happened. Instead she gave me a new picture, pre-sumably created the previous night before I spoiled the perfor-mances. It was truly an inspired piece and in my view would be even more beautiful if reinterpreted into a quilt. To my surprise Orpah did not object to the idea. If there was anyone who could make this into a quilt it would be me since I was the only one, to her knowledge, who had ever expressed an appreciation of her work. Ruth destroyed it and Obed ignored it. Mahlon did sympa-thize with her but never came out openly to challenge Ruth. Even though he was part of its creation since it was inspired by the memories he performed, he thought that the destruction did not matter that much because Orpah would always produce new work as long as the stories continued. For him the destruction meant the

continuation of the performances. I was the only one who had de-
fended this work publicly and had even challenged her mother
about its destruction. Now that I have learned how to quilt she
would allow me to render her work in fabric and found objects,
provided I thought I had acquired enough skill to do so.

"Maybe now you won't mind if I attend more of Mahlon's performances," I said. "That may help me understand the inspiration
of your work."

"No," she screamed, as if I had suggested we engage in some
abominable act. Her face was mapped with disgust. "They're our
memories . . . me and Daddy's."

"They must be shared, Orpah," I pleaded. "They are too beautiful not to be shared."

"They are our memories. They belong to me and Daddy . . . and
to Obed when he still loved them. They don't belong to no stranger."

As far as she was concerned that was the end of it. But I continued to raise the matter occasionally. She was adamant that she did
not want me to "mess with" their memories. I gave up, and after
every few days I accepted new works from her. At least now I
know where they come from and what inspires their creation.

Ruth, however, thinks I am a regular at the storytelling sessions.

"You've been washing the quilts?" I ask.

"I don't wash them no more," she says. "I just air them."

She tells me that she used to wash the quilts using buttermilk as
bleach. But now the fabrics have become too delicate. It is best to
hang them on the clothesline occasionally to cut down moisture so
as to preserve them for her grandchildren, which she doubts she
will ever have since her children don't seem to be prepared to settle
down and be responsible family people. The children will surely
be the death of her, she adds.

She stands back to admire the quilts.

"Them old-timers knew what they was doing," she says.

Unlike the quilts that Orpah tried to make from her silly sketches,
these have profound meaning. They speak a secret language. I do

not want to upset her by defending Orpah's work. I do not tell her
that though I may not understand what Orpah is trying to tell the
world her work is powerful enough to invoke in me strong emotions. For me that is enough.

Of course the quilts on the clothesline move me too. In a different way. Whether or not one believes that the geography of freedom is mapped on the quilts, one cannot but be moved by them,
especially when they are spread out like this in the sun. Even if the
Drunkard's Path did not—according to skeptics—map out a specific zigzag path, there is no reason it would not serve as a general
reminder to the escapees of the wisdom of indirect and circuitous
routes. It does not matter if the codes did or did not contain specific instructions to be followed to the letter for specific escapes,
and if they did not conceal actual signposts marking actual routes.
It should be enough even for people like Brother Michael that these
wonderful patterns, designs, stitches and knots were at one time
used as celebration of escapes, or even as records of stories of escape. They were a source of inspiration for future escapes. After
all, memory is what you make of it. If Ruth believes this is how it
happened, then it is how it happened. Whether there is historical
evidence or not that the likes of Abdenego and Nicodemus used
the quilts to escape from slavery is not important. What matters is
that their descendants believe that they did, and therefore they did.
We all construct our past as we go along.

As for the image of the first Quigley, Lord have mercy on him,
it remained intact even when she used buttermilk to wash the
quilt. Even when the "old-timers" used lye soap the first Quigley
stubbornly stayed where he belonged. Doesn't that convince me
that the first Quigley, Lord have mercy on him, was a man of
God? He was a great prophet who used to read the future from a
red scroll. He was able to decipher figures and symbols that revealed the lives of future generations. The life of the family as it
unfolded was all written in the Quigley scroll. Unfortunately the
scroll was buried with him.

"And no one knew a darn thing about nothing since then," she says.

"But since we discovered his grave surely we can dig the scroll out," I say. Of course, I am just bullshitting the dear heart.

She is greatly alarmed by my suggested sacrilege. It is unheard of to disturb the dead from their rest or to rob their graves. Her people do not behave like what she refers to as my people, the Egyptians, who have allowed wholesale robberies of the dead pharaohs. Digging out the scroll would enrage the first Quigley. He is not totally happy with the family, as it is.

"Like now he ain't too pleased I don't go to church no more," she adds ruefully. "But he understands. The first Quigley, Lord have mercy on him, understands."

"Maybe you should forgive Brother Michael and go to church," I say. "You're not going there for him, after all. He doesn't own the church."

She says she is determined to stand her ground. Brother Michael would think he has won if she went to that church. In the meantime her soul is nourished by televangelists. There are so many wonderful programs screened these days no soul needs to starve. Her favorite is one Pat Robertson. She has followed his sermons for years, even when she was still a regular at the chocolate church. What she likes most about the holy man is that he looks after the good people of America. A few days ago the holy man spoke of the wrath of God against a man called Hugo Chávez of Venezuela. She is not quite sure what this Chávez has done but Mr. Robertson has declared that he must be killed.

"He done something," says Ruth. "Pat Robertson is a man of God. He don't wanna kill you if you don't do nothing bad."

I chuckle a bit, but stop myself when Ruth looks at me disapprovingly. I don't want her to think I am beyond redemption, but her story reminds me of a fatwa that was once issued by a powerful ayatollah for the death of a writer whose novel he did not like. Ruth's land is the land of powerful Christian ayatollahs. Old Testament fundamentalists who serve a wrathful and vengeful God. And like all ayatollahs of the world they get their instructions directly from Him. I do not know though if anyone will carry out Mr. Robertson's fatwa since he can't dangle seventy-two virgins in front of the eyes of prospective executioners. His religion lacks such juicy incentives. But at a secular level oil is juicy enough.

Ruth contemplates Quigley's image on the quilt and says, "Oh, yeah, he was a man of God. Them children are full-blooded Quigleys 'cause both me and Mr. Quigley are descendants of the first Quigley, Lord have mercy on him. But God only knows why they don't have none of his strength, his faith, his goodness. And they don't have none of the strength and goodness of me and Mr. Quigley neither."

This is my opportunity to tell her of my plan to look for Mahlon's mother's grave. What did she think of the idea? Would she give me her blessing?

"What for?" she asks, looking at me with suspicion.

I follow her back to the porch.

"Because I won't do it if you don't think it's a good idea."

"Why you wanna look for the grave?"

She sits on the swing but does not invite me to sit next to her as she used to.

"I like you and Mahlon and your son and daughter. I want to help. You once told me it would make all the difference in Mahlon's life if the grave was located and a tombstone was erected on it."

"Mr. Quigley don't have no time for you . . . you know that. He's gonna kill you one of them days."

I laugh and say, "Mahlon Quigley can't kill anybody."

"He's a good man," she says, looking at me pityingly, "but if you piss him off too much you never know what he's gonna do."

It is an empty threat and she knows I know it. I can see it in her expression that even as she makes it she is aware that I don't believe her. The nighttime performances have shown me how much of a gentle soul Mahlon Quigley is.

"No one who tells such wonderful stories can kill anybody," I say.

"How you gonna find the grave? You come all the way from Africa and you think you can find graves here in the good ol' U. S. of A.?"

"I have a grave-radar," I say jokingly. "Remember, I found Niall Quigley's African grave under a tree in the woods."

Of course she remembers. Was she not the one who decreed that it must not be disturbed but must be left as it was? Didn't she over-rule Obed, who wanted to turn it into a shrine for his heathen practices or even a tourist attraction to be advertised in the *Athens News* so that people could come and pay money to see it? How would the first Quigley, Lord have mercy on him, rest in peace with all those crude eyes ogling his resting place?

"You stealing my kids away and now you say you wanna help find their grandma's grave?"

I don't see the connection, but Ruth will always be Ruth.

"They're not children, Ruth. They're adults. You don't steal adults away."

"I hear Orpah is always in your RV. God knows what you do there. And Obed, we don't see him no more 'cause your meddling got him together with that Beth Eddy or whatever. He says she's gotten him a job or something. And now they shack together, which is a sin against the Bible."

Throughout my stay here Ruth has been complaining that Obed doesn't want to make anything of his life. Yet she wants to maintain a strong hold on him and doesn't want to let him go. The specter of his independence scares her.

Mahlon arrives with tackle and a lunch box. His boots and jeans are muddy. I think he has come from an unsuccessful fishing expedition at a nearby pond.

"Hi, Mahlon," I say displaying a broad smile to emphasize the fact that I am desperate to be friends with him. "They didn't bite today, did they?"

He merely looks at me with his smile. I can detect contempt in it. Somehow one is able to read different moods in the unchanging smile when one gets to know the man enough. He pretends that I don't exist and walks into the house.

"I told you he hates you," says Ruth gleefully. "He thinks you taking Orpah away from him."

"You think so too, don't you? You just said I am stealing your children away."

"I think so too. But I'm a Christian woman; I don't hate nobody."

"I don't understand this, Ruth. You always complained that Orpah did not get out enough . . . that she was not independent enough . . . that she sat in her room all day long playing the sitar and drawing pictures."

She takes out bits of red slate from one of the pockets of her sweats and chews furiously. In no time her teeth are red like blood.

"She ain't independent when she's with you," she says.

"You want her to be with Nathan?"

" 'Cause he's gonna make her a good husband."

"And he won't take her away?"

"Damn right he won't. Orpah's ours. No one must take her away."

❧

In August the different shades of green that dominate the Kilvert summer now sport patches of yellow. The leaves become smaller; you can see further into the woods. And Orpah and Mahlon don't talk anymore. Although Ruth thinks it is my fault, I learn from Orpah after pleading with her to tell me what the problem is that I have nothing to do with it.

Mahlon discovered her deception about ghost orchids. He learned that she was creating them from found objects and sticking them on the sycamores for him to discover. And he was presenting them to her as gifts from the memories. They ended up in her collages. I don't know what devil got into Orpah to confess that she was the creator of the ghost orchids in the first place. She expected Mahlon to take the whole thing as the big joke it was meant to be and was astonished when he exploded and accused her of betrayal. Not only had she betrayed him she had also pissed on the sanctity of the memories. He added that she would never have betrayed him if it were not for my evil presence in their lives.

I must admit that I am a bit skeptical about Mahlon's anger here. How could a man who knows so much about trees not have known in the first place that ghost orchids don't grow around these parts and the ones he discovered were artificial? Was he play-acting or did his memories close his eyes and his mind to the fact?

But his anger has lasted for a few days. At first Orpah did not take it seriously and thought that her father would come around and they would have their midnight memories again. On the third day she began to worry. She missed Mahlon. She missed the memories. She begged for his forgiveness but he ignored her. He goes about his life without even looking at her when they chance upon each other in the house.

I know how it is when Mahlon decides you don't exist.

Orpah spends even more time in my RV than ever before. But she never brings the sitar with her even when I beg her to. I am just wondering what that sitar would do to my body if she played it in my RV. Would it have the same effect that it had on me when the sound leaked from her room or would it just be beautiful music as it was at the bluegrass festival in Huntington, West Virginia? It did not have any adverse physical effect on me that night. I guess I have no way of knowing as long as she won't play it here.

But what has happened over the days, even without the aid of the sitar, is that we have eased each other into intimacy. The first night she spent at the RV was difficult. She was all bravado, claiming great experience, and I was a whimpering fool. But soon she

became the whimpering one. I have a tongue that knows its way
around the strategic parts of bodies, thanks to Noria's lessons. And
her memory did intrude just at that time. Noria. She won't rest until she is mourned.

It was different with Noria. She had been experienced by many
men before me and that made her even more desirable. Orpah, on
the other hand, was not only an emotional virgin. She was a virgin
virgin. And this discovery did not make our first real night together particularly memorable.

I remember Obed telling me once: "Orpah, she never messed
with nobody. Whenever some teenager had gotten knocked up my
mama fear it was gonna happen to Orpah. She took her to the doc
for a diaphragm. To Orpah that was an insult 'cause she didn't
plan to be doing nothing with boys."

Tonight is the fourth night and our bodies are beginning to find
each other. Me and Orpah are screaming like there is no tomorrow.

❧

Whenever Obed honors us with a visit he has that idiotic facial
expression of a lovestruck man. He thanks me all the time because
he credits me for the mediation that brought him together with
Beth Eddy. He thinks I am a great seer who has changed his path
in life. I tell him that he should thank the ghost of Nicodemus instead.

I don't know how many times I have suggested to him to invite
Beth Eddy for dinner at his home so that she may meet his parents.
He always says it is a good idea, but for later. Things are a bit awk-
ward at the moment. He does not want Ruth to embarrass him in
front of the love of his life. All in good time he will gather enough
courage to introduce the lady to Ruth and Mahlon. And of course
to Orpah.

The foolish expression is even more pronounced today when he
finds me sewing at the Center. I tease him that he is a real lover

man now; tender, unguarded and vulnerable. He doesn't get my meaning; or pretends not to. Instead he laughs at the "ugly" quilt I am stitching together. I am trying to translate three of Orpah's designs into a single quilt. The ghost trees are made with materials from old burlap sacks. I am attaching on the quilt strings and all sorts of found objects such as baby sneakers, an old plastic wallet and some glistening trinkets from the junk on the porch with the donated clothes.

Irene smiles and nods in agreement. She too despises string art quilts, as she calls them. But of course she is not as rabid as Ruth in opposing them. She does not mind if I create them at the Center using her machine, although she thinks it is a pity that I am spending so much valuable time doing this sort of hideous work when I have not yet mastered the traditional quilt.

"Oh, yeah," she says to Obed, "anything goes with them string art quilts."

Obed says he wants to discuss some private matter with me, so I pack my stuff and store it away in a chest. We go out. He says he heard from Ruth that she has given me permission to locate his grandmother's grave. I didn't know she had given me her blessing because the day I was there we didn't come to any conclusion.

"Why you wanna do that, man? Why you guys don't wanna let sleeping dogs sleep?" he asks.

"Your grandmother is not a dog, Obed. She died a lonely death at a mental home. She was never mourned. Your folks want to build an engraved tombstone or maybe have a plaque. I want to mourn your grandmother. I believe that will restore her dignity."

We are slowly walking toward my RV. I can see Nathan's Chevy Blazer parked at Ruth's.

"You came with Nathan?" I ask Obed.

"Yep. He bring me from Athens."

Obed says although he thinks the whole idea is stupid he can tell me exactly how to find his grandmother's grave.

"If you knew all along why didn't you find it?" I ask.

He didn't think it was that important. It was mentioned at his home once or twice, but no one ever took it seriously enough to actually do something about it. He says there is a man called Terry Gilkey who works for the City of Athens Division of Water and Sewer. He is the keeper of records of the city cemeteries. He is well known as an expert on the mental asylum cemeteries at The Ridges. Mr. Gilkey will advise me how to go about locating his grandmother's grave.

"I'm going to phone Mr. Gilkey sometime soon," I say.

"Sure, he's in the book," says Obed.

By this time we have reached the back of the RV. I can hear Orpah arguing with Nathan at the front. We stop to listen, Obed shushing me not to spoil his fun by revealing our presence.

"I just want us back together, Orpah."

"We was never together, Nathan."

"We was, we was."

"When we was kids, yes. You gone and married someone else."

" 'Cause you wouldn't marry me."

"I ain't gonna marry you still."

I really don't want to be listening to this. Obed tries to pull me back as I walk to the front of the RV. Immediately Nathan sees me he spits out the words: "He's from Africa, Orpah. You don't wanna live in Africa with them lions."

"Good afternoon to you too, Nathan," I say with a broad smile.

"You don't wanna take a dump in the jungle with them snakes looking at you," says Nathan as he walks away back to Ruth's.

"It looks like nobody likes you in this town, homey," says Obed. He is obviously enjoying this, although he regrets that there was no real showdown.

I chuckle: "The women at the Center do."

"Hey, Nate, you don't wanna leave me here, man," says Obed running after him.

Orpah gets into the RV and plunks herself on the Irish Wheel covering my bed. I do likewise. She does not say anything about Nathan; about what has just happened. I don't say anything either.

"We better move on," she says after a long silence. "Ain't no reason for us to be here no more."

This comes out of the blue. Move on where? What amazes me—pleasantly so—is that she is including herself in that moving on.

"Didn't you say you was going in search of mourning?" she asks. "Don't you want me to come along?"

"Yes, I do. I do, Orpah."

"And you can do your mourning thing or whatever and I'm gonna play my sitar."

"I once heard of Virginia mourners. That will be our starting point—Virginia. We'll search for the Virginia mourners. But you can't drive alone. You promised you'd teach me to drive."

"We'll do that on the road. I am gonna pack right away. We gonna leave today."

"It can't be today, Orpah. It can't be tomorrow either. We've got to take our time. Plus I've got to find your grandma's grave. I've got to mourn for her."

She is disappointed. No. She is crushed. She glowers at me, her eyes flaming flames. Then she stands up and stamps her feet and yells at me. She throws a tantrum that would be the envy of any spoiled brat. Why should we stay to mourn people who died decades ago? Why should it matter to me if I find the grave or not? Why should I expect her to stay in Kilvert when her daddy won't even talk to her?

She takes one of her pictures lying on the pillow and tears it to pieces.

"Now you're doing Ruth's work for her?" I ask. I have never seen her like this. This thing with Mahlon must really be getting to her.

She jets out of the RV and runs all the way to her house.

✒

I don't see Orpah for many days after this. Since she won't come to the RV anymore I go to her house. I can hear her playing her sitar furiously. It is *the* sitar. The one that makes my blood rage all over the place. Ruth tells me gleefully: "She don't wanna see you."

She lets me use her phone and I call a cab from Athens. I need to get as far away from the damnable sitar as possible. I also need to locate the grave, mourn the dead and leave Kilvert and southeast Ohio once and for all. I will go the way I came. I will not take the RV with me. I can't drive the damn thing in any case. They can do what they want with it. Maybe Obed will sell it to finance one of his shaky ventures. Although he has been quiet for quite some time now about them. Since the Beth Eddy thing got more serious. He has been quiet even about the casino, although he continues to await the outcome of the Shawnee claim with eagerness.

It's high time I bought my own cellphone and that's the first thing I do when I get to the East State Street stores. I get a phone book and call Terry Gilkey. He is prepared to talk to me even at such short notice. He gives me directions to his place of employment, and I ask the cabdriver to take me to the city's Division of Water and Sewer on the west side of town.

Gilkey tells me he is the keeper of the records of the city cemeteries. He was assigned that role by the mayor around 1988 because no one was interested in it. It has been his hobby over the years and it results from his interest in genealogy. His forebears lived in these parts even before the city was established slightly more than two hundred years ago. For the city it is a public relations exercise to let Gilkey help people locate the graves of their loved ones for no fee. He is regarded as an expert in the field. Even the historical society directs people to him.

The process of locating graves is a painless one. Gilkey has records. He got some of these from the State Department of Mental Health and from the psychiatric hospital on West Union Street.

After giving him the name and estimated year of death of old Mrs. Quigley he pages through an old book titled *Athens Mental Health Center Grave Record #1 Female 1880–1945*. I think the woman will be in this book. Mahlon is about sixty-five years old. The woman was committed while she was pregnant with him. He was actually born at the mental home at The Ridges. He was handed back to the Quigleys when he was about six months old. I think being separated from her baby broke the poor woman's heart even more and she died a year later.

"Lots of these folks were not crazy at all," says Gilkey. "Some of them had Alzheimer's or something that we understand today."

"I know," I say. "This one's madness was that she was Caucasian and fell in love with a colored man from a neighboring village."

"That was madness all right. Back in the day they were dead scared of intermarriages."

"It was fine . . . at least it was tolerated . . . for guys like the first Tabler and the first Quigley to have colored wives, but for a colored man to have a white wife was a crime. I just wonder what reasons were documented for her committal."

Gilkey suggests that we can find the committal papers of these patients in the archives at the university. They have an index of all the committal papers on microfiche. From these papers we can see where the patient came from, who committed her and what reasons were given for the committal. I thank him for the offer but tell him that that kind of information is not important for my purposes. All I need is to locate the grave.

Gilkey pages through the book. The names are listed alphabetically with grave numbers next to each name. But there is no Quigley here. I call Ruth.

"I didn't think you was gonna do it," she says. "Of course there ain't no Quigley there. It ain't the Quigleys who committed her. It's her own family. They wouldn't have used no Quigley 'cause they didn't recognize the marriage. She was of the Tobias family. Margaret Tobias."

And there is her name with a grave number. She died and was buried in 1943.

"Her grave's gonna be at Cemetery Number 2," says Gilkey.

We drive to The Ridges. As the van makes its way on a steep hill I recognize the cemetery I visited that night of the pagans. It is Cemetery Number 1, says Gilkey. Everybody here was buried much earlier than '43. The graves date from 1880 to 1901. This is the cemetery where people were buried with only numbers on their gravestones. Most families cannot pay respects to their relatives who died condemned as lunatics because there is no information on the graves. They are not aware how easy it is to locate these graves if only they can consult Terry Gilkey.

There is a third cemetery across the lane from the Dairy Barn. All the graves in that one have names and it goes up to 1949 or perhaps 1950—Gilkey can't quite remember.

At Cemetery Number 2 the grounds are as well kept as in the others—thanks to The Ridges Restoration Project. Half of the graves only have numbers and the rest have names and numbers. Men were buried on one side and women on a separate side. The decorum of the age: no mixing and no hanky-panky even in death.

Margaret Tobias's grave has no name, but it is not difficult to locate it because of Gilkey's meticulous records.

"So now that you found it what're you gonna do with it?" asks Gilkey.

"The relatives will construct a tombstone when they can afford it," I tell him. "In the meantime I will mourn her death."

"Hey, she died decades ago," he says. He thinks I am joking.

"I mourn deaths. Even if they happened centuries ago," I explain. "I am a professional mourner."

He still thinks I am joking.

"Like the Aztecs? They used to have this funny guy who stood at the entrance of the pyramids and made a hell of a noise every time somebody died. Until the bereaved came and paid him money."

"I am that guy."

✒

Sunday morning. September leaves are falling. Golden. Yellow. Red. The sun is shining starkly through the branches once hidden. The wind playfully picks up the leaves and lets them float in the air before dropping them on the grass. We stand around Margaret Tobias's grave. There is Ruth in her blue sweats despite the hot weather, Obed in his khaki shorts and red plaid shirt, Orpah and Mahlon, both in denim jeans and T-shirts. I am, of course, in my professional mourner costume of black top hat, black cape and black pants.

The gravestone with the number is under a pile of assorted flowers bought from Kroger. There is a pile of pawpaws with their rough green skins next to the flowers. They are some kind of offering since one of the Native American ancestors used to grow the fruit. This one, however, is from the wild and was brought by Obed a few days ago.

"We should of invited Brother Michael to do them prayers," says Obed.

"We ain't gonna taint your grandma with no Brother Michael," says Ruth. "We all know how to pray."

Then she goes on to tell us about biracial kids. She is obviously referring to Mahlon because she is looking at him. It is good that her visitor found the grave. Biracial kids need to know their history because biracial kids pick up all sorts of diseases. Blacks give them black diseases such as diabetes and whites give them their own white diseases.

I don't know why she says Mahlon is biracial. Maybe tri-racial is not in her vocabulary. No one questions her about how locating this grave will help Mahlon escape white diseases. She reminds her small congregation that her people come in all colors of the rainbow, and therefore they are the race of the future. Unfortunately during the days of the very same Margaret Tobias we are honoring today, those who had pale faces and blond hair changed their names and did not want to associate with those of color anymore. They tried to live like Caucasians among Caucasians. But guess what? Many are now coming back to claim their heritage. It is now fashionable to be a person of color.

"And you know why?" she asks looking at each one of us expectantly. But no one wants to provide the answer.

"Because of them programs," says Ruth.

"It is more like they are drawn back by the ancestors, not some darn programs," says Obed, getting fed up with his mother's digressions.

I thought the young man had learned not to contradict Ruth unnecessarily. Otherwise he'll get her started. Before she can lash out I appeal for calm in both of them. We have come here to return Margaret Tobias's dignity. The discussion is important, but there will be time for it later.

"Today I am going to mourn for you like I've never mourned before," I tell the small congregation. "Your culture frowns upon excessive display of crying at a funeral. You were taught to be embarrassed to show grief in public. I am therefore going to do it on your behalf. I am hoping that your genes still understand public wailing. After all, some of your ancestors came from Ireland and the Irish have mastered public mourning at wakes. They know how to keen and lament for all the world to witness. When the Irish bereaved can't do it themselves they hire professional mourners to do it for them. Surely your genes have memory of this? Surely Mahlon's stories have memory of this?"

"My memories ain't got no memory of their own," says Mahlon quietly. "I can only tell what the ghost trees tell me."

He is defensive, but I was not trying to blame him for anything. I don't want to agitate him. It was not easy to convince him to come here. He is still unhappy with Orpah and did not want to involve himself in anything that has to do with me. It was only after Obed sat out on the porch with him and showed him that he would not be coming here for me or for Orpah or for anybody else but his own mother. Ruth also helped to persuade him. When he got into the GMC this morning he kept on repeating that he was only doing this for his wife.

Ruth asks Obed to lead us in prayer. It is at this stage that I begin my mourning routine. I do not sit on the mound as I usually do. There is no mound to sit on. But also I want to perform the mourning. For the first time in my mourning career I want to perform. I want to dance to my wails. And I wail my laments so loud that the trees begin to shake and shed more leaves. I howl and growl and cry like the wind. Tears run from my eyes like the waters of the Hocking River. I incorporate some of the movements I saw Mahlon perform through the window. My whole performance routine, except for the sounds, is informed by his routine.

Mahlon recognizes himself in my movements and breaks out laughing. Everybody looks at him in astonishment. Mahlon has not laughed for ages.

I screech like an animal in pain. I am drenched in sweat and tears. I perform variations that draw from his movements. I can see that he is mesmerized. Orpah is open-mouthed. Obed is wide-eyed. Ruth is befuddled. This is the crowning glory of my mourning since I arrived in this country. I continue furiously for about an hour. Then I fall down in utter exhaustion.

Mahlon breaks out into applause. The others join him and they applaud for a long time. Even Ruth applauds, albeit briefly.

Mahlon helps me up. There is a glint in his eyes. He says, very softly as if he does not want the others to hear: "We must die so the earth should continue." I whisper back: "The earth is a cannibal. It feeds on our corpses. That's how it continues."

Obed gives me a quarter.

"A professional mourner must be paid," he says. The man has learned fast.

Orpah is jumping about in excitement.

"We should of brought our costumes, Daddy," she screams. "I wanna be a mourner. I wanna mourn with you. We gonna mourn up a storm!"

Mahlon embraces her. The ice is melting.

"That was silly," says Ruth laughing aloud. "Good, but silly."

"Thank you, Son of Egypt," says Mahlon.

It sounds like a term of endearment when it comes from Mahlon.

Once More the Pagans—
Without the Saints

October 31. The seasons have come full cycle and the creatures have returned to Court Street. The madness is mild for the night is still young. As it ages the pagans will rage on the paved street. Many of them are still in the process of transforming themselves, stealing identities from American cultural and fictional icons. Fueling their bodies with the spirits that will give them pluck to be as free-spirited as the occasion warrants.

Quite a few of the pagans are here already. Grown men in diapers are strutting about. They mingle with cowgirls and pirate wenches in miniskirts. Giant spoons dance with giant forks. The uninspired superheroes are obviously the staple of the parade. They were here in great numbers last year—Superman, Spiderman, the Incredible Hulk, Batman and the rest. They are here again this year—the last resort for a lazy pagan who can't think of original ideas for the night.

This is a day of saints, although the pagans don't recognize the fact. None of the saints with whom I aspired to socialize at the Durham Cathedral will be seen here tonight. No Venerable Bede. No St. Cuthbert. This is also the day of the disembodied spirits of those who died last year. They come back in search of living bodies to possess for the next year. That is their only chance of an afterlife. The Court Street creatures, of course, do not have in their minds the Celtic roots of the feast as they prance around, even though their ghoulishness is reminiscent of the original Celts. It was a look that was meant to frighten the disembodied spirits away so that they fail to take possession of any living man, woman or child.

I follow Orpah. We elbow our way through the crowds. She

looks sensual in a nun's habit—black flowing gown, white collar, black veil with white headpiece, rubber sandals, a rosary for a belt. She bought it especially for the occasion at an East State Street mall. I, on the other hand, am in my regular mourning costume.

We stop to watch a man frying on the street. His whole body is made of rashers of bacon. He is squirming as a girl made of deep yellow yolk and white albumen is dancing around him. She has red horns on her head; she is deviled egg. Orpah is enjoying this bacon and egg show and she is laughing like there is no tomorrow. I have never seen Orpah so carefree.

As we move on I am struck by the absence of politicians this year. No Dick Cheney. No Donald Rumsfeld. No George W. Bush. No Jimmy Carter. Unless they will invade the parade later in the night. But the usual enemies in Arab garb are here. And an odd renegade with an unpalatable statement about Guantánamo Bay: *Charge or Release Detainees*. The slogan sounds very familiar. It takes me back to years ago. Protesters used to chant it during the apartheid years of detention-without-trial in South Africa. During those sad times in the history of that country politicians said their normal laws of due process could not deal with terrorism. It was therefore necessary to do away with the niceties of habeas corpus. Exactly as they are saying here. The state was under threat, the apartheid government said, the country was at war. Civil liberties were undermined, and white citizens accepted that it was for their protection. Until they woke up one day and found that they had been living a lie. Even their own liberties as citizens had been eroded. Not only the enemy's. I have gone back in time. Things have come full cycle. Lessons have been learned well.

Besides the Guantánamo Bay man I do not see as many political statements as I saw at the last parade, which was in an election year—except for the bejeweled Billionaires for Bush whose messages on their placards are *Bring the Troops Back Home* and *No Billionaire Left Behind*.

Instead of hard-core politics we are entertained by a fight between a white cock and a yellow chicken, Milli Vanilli dancing down the street, Dorothy from the Wizard of Oz cuddling with Raggedy Ann and a bluegrass band at the corner of Court and Washington Streets.

We stop here for a while. I wish Orpah had brought her sitar with her. She would liven up things with this very dull band. She doesn't seem to think it is dull though. She is giggling and softly singing along. She has been giggling a lot today. Since we left Kilvert this morning. She is excited like a little girl. The journey we are about to undertake fills her with joy. It fills me with joy too. Especially because she is part of the journey.

Days of blissful mourning await us.

✌

We spent the better part of September perfecting our lamentations—our plan was to leave early in October in search of the Virginia mourners. I did not know who they were, nor where in Virginia they were located. The sciolist didn't know either. All he had were rumors of their existence. Orpah and I talked about them. We imagined what they did and romanticized them. We were rehearsing for Virginia. After that we would go where the mourning wind blew us.

On a typical day we woke up at dawn and Orpah went back to her house for her ablutions. I took a shower in our RV. I call it "our RV" because Orpah had practically moved in with me. But she preferred a bath so she went to her house for that. After about two hours or so she came back all spruced up, bejeweled in her colorful plastic and smelling of some cheap perfume. After a quick breakfast of cereal we set off to Niall Quigley's grave for our daily dose of mourning.

Orpah took charge and choreographed our routine. She decreed that we should have tattoos of teardrops on our cheeks. One drop for me would suffice, but for her she needed two drops on each cheek since she had not mastered the art of shedding floods of tears at will. We went to a tattoo parlor in Athens especially for this.

Orpah saw herself as the manager and artistic director of this whole enterprise. She went through the opening sequences of our mourning many times over. As part of the opening routine she appropriated Obed's speech—the one he made at the funeral of Sister Naomi's boy about the ineptness of human beings in handling grief and the necessity of professional mourning in bringing back aplomb and dignity to the art of grieving.

I was well aware that in our itinerant mourning people would resist at first. But soon they would be taken in by the novelty of it all, and by the swooping performances that Orpah was choreographing. After all, I was able to mourn professionally in South Africa where the philosophy of *ubuntu,* which espoused the universal bond of sharing that connected all humanity, would have looked askance at anyone who was demanding payment for mourning. I made a good living from the bountiful deaths of South Africa because of that novelty factor. None of the ethnic groups there ever had professional mourners in their culture, for that would have been against the very notions of *ubuntu,* where in its practice you hoe your neighbor's field for no pay because next time the neighbor will hoe your field for no pay. It is like that in death as well: I mourn for my neighbor because when I die my neighbor will mourn for me. Yet when I came and introduced professional mourning some people took it up with gusto. My presence at a funeral became a status symbol. Of course there were those who saw me as a nuisance and drove me away from their funerals and pelted me out of the cemeteries with dead wreaths from neighboring graves. This happened a lot with funerals of the wealthy. The poor often welcomed me, shared their mourning and their food and paid me generously at the end.

It will be the same when we tour the country with Orpah mourning the deaths of Americans.

Although Orpah was eager to test our routine at live funerals right away, I thought it was important for us to search for other mourners and learn a few tricks that we could incorporate into our own mourning. Hooking up with other mourners would also give us legitimacy in the communities.

"Where you gonna find other mourners?" Orpah asked. "There ain't no professional mourners in America."

After nagging him about the location of Virginia mourners the sciolist came to my rescue and gave me a starting point. I found on my bed one day when I returned from the Center a letter that the sciolist received from a professor who had read *Ways of Dying,* which, as I believe you know by now, is the story of my life as conceived and recorded by the same sciolist. The professor, William Edwards, wrote:

Regarding the information on mourners I can say that all of it is anecdotal (much in the oral tradition). My cousin, from NY, has been visiting over the holidays and she recalls in New York City knowing of mourners. A colleague of mine from Louisiana also recalls mourners there. The same is true for close friends who are from South Carolina. I can convey that mourners were exclusively female. They were most likely to appear at funerals of those in the lower (economic) and working classes. It was highly unlikely that they would appear for funerals of the middle class. In Louisiana mourners could be found at Catholic funerals. Most commonly they were phenomena of the Protestant churches, especially those that were given over to more emotional worship. Mourners may or may not have been friends of the family. The women mourners' role was to ensure that the deceased received a due amount of respect through the expression of outward and vocal grief. The expression of grief would most commonly be crying with an occasional uttering of some quality about the deceased ("He was a good man/ woman").

As a sociologist I would interpret mourning as ceremonial rituals performed to anoint the deceased with respect which he/she may not

*have received in their lifetime. This is similar to Sunday worship
where blacks would have special clothing to wear which would
symbolize dignity and worthiness in God's eyes. Duke Ellington
captured some of this in his famous song "Come Sunday." Given
this interpretation you can surmise why mourning was more likely
to occur in the lower class ranks than among the middle class.
Mourning was a kind of legitimation, as noted earlier. It signified
the fact that an individual had a worth which may not have been
acknowledged in the ordinary patterns of social relations. In the
South it was common for people to think of dying as "passing over"
into the promised land. This can be seen in many of the "Negro
Spirituals." Mourning served as a transitional act whereby the deceased would be given a "proper" send-off.*

*There are some aspects of mourning that I am not sure about. Did
mourners receive any pay? Were they invited by the family of the deceased? Could anyone be a mourner? I can understand why most
were women since they, traditionally, have been more expressive than
men. Their crying at a funeral would seem most appropriate.*

The points that the professor raised in this last paragraph were the
most important for me. I did not think we could just gatecrash a
funeral and start mourning. We might need to scour obituaries,
meet the bereaved and convince them that they needed us. Payment plays an important part in the practice of professional
mourning. It is what elevates professional mourning from downright pedestrian mourning. We would have to convince the bereaved of this. Plus, my reserve of funds would not last forever.

As for the observation that women were more expressive, in our
case I was the most expressive. After all, I perfected the art of
mourning over the years. Orpah's expressiveness came through her
sitar and the quilts that we hung on rails next to Niall Quigley's
grave.

Although the quilts were sewn by me they were an interpretation of her designs. Sometimes we worked on them together at the

Center. I sewed bits of discarded cloths together and she decided where the found objects—such as shells and beads and mirrors—should be placed in the collage. Those objects that could not be sewn were glued on. The shape of the ghost orchid was the theme that ran through the quilts.

"You are truly a fabric poet, Orpah," I told her once.

The quilts, the sitar and my wails and moans gave color to our mourning. The fabrics were bright and dazzling and the mirrors and gleaming metals captured our souls and reflected them back to us. Her sitar also had a wide range of tone colors. Despite the fact that she changed her tunes in line with the sounds of my own invention, her strumming did not lose its sense of wonder and mystery.

As our joint creations developed I resuscitated the skill I thought I had lost as a child—that of drawing pictures. I remembered vaguely winning an art prize at elementary school. I also remembered the discouragement I received from my father, who ironically had extended his blacksmithing into fashioning metal figurines of creatures who visited his dreams. Here, with the influence of Orpah's sitar, I was steadily contributing stylized human figures to her designs. And our work was an expression of joy. Joy that was not dressed with anything to make it valid. Naked joy.

And the nakedness extended into the nights at our RV. The tinge of guilt continued with our romps; as if I was betraying the memory of Noria. Things used to be different with Noria. The connection was more of a spiritual nature. I do not recall any memorable orgasms. With Orpah, on the other hand, every night brought with it earth tremors and sounds that could only be unworldly. She was no longer afraid of the mark of the Irishman. She was no longer ashamed of it. She danced in front of me naked and said: "Admit it; this is the most beautiful pussy you've ever seen."

"It looks like an angel's," I said.

And that, of course, gave rise to more numinous sounds.

It was these sounds that we tried to reproduce as we went through our routine at the first Quigley's grave. Here at the hands

296 Zakes Mda

of Orpah I was developing from mere professional mourner to performer. After all, the roots of tragedy lie in mourning. I am talking here of tragedy on the stage. For the ancient Greeks dramatic tragedy was a ritual that took the songs of professional mourners at funerals to the levels of performance. It gave the dead a voice since the corpses could not utter a sound anymore. Like actors who steal the voices of those who cannot speak for themselves, professional mourners are hypocrites who weep for those who never belonged to them in the first place. Through Orpah's direction the hypocrisy of the actor and of the professional mourner converged. And the movements that resulted from that union were intense and stirring.

All this mourning heightened our appreciation for each other. Sometimes in the middle of a movement we were so possessed by the demons of the flesh that we had to repair to the RV to relieve the tensions. We could only hope that the visitors to the Center did not wonder about the strange movements of the vehicle.

Throughout this period of our perfecting our act and of reveling in each other's bodies we did not see Obed. I think we forgot about him altogether.

One day a man came to the Center while I was putting together one of Orpah's collages. The women knew him at once, and one told me he was one of the greatest dulcimer players in southeast Ohio. After having a good laugh at what he considered pieces of ugly rags that I was sewing together he said that he had come to invite Orpah to play with his bluegrass band at a fund-raising event for the victims of Katrina—the hurricane that had destroyed New Orleans at the end of August.

"I don't wanna play no gig," said Orpah even before the man finished his story.

"Where's this going to be held?" I asked.

"At the Stuart's Opera House in Nelsonville," said the man.

"We got our own gig on the road, baby," said Orpah.

"It's for a good cause, Orpah," said the man looking at me for support. But I have no intention of involving myself in this. I saw what happened to Nathan when he tried to be Orpah's "manager." The women thought it would be a good idea if Orpah took part in the concert—it would be the American thing to do. She said she would think about it and contact the man later.

That evening Orpah decided she would participate at the fund-raiser provided the bluegrass guys picked her up from Kilvert and returned her after the show. This would only be her second time playing for the public and she would be more comfortable if Obed was there as well. She needed his moral support, especially after I told her I would not attend the event myself since I had to catch up with a lot of sewing before we hit the road. Many of Orpah's drawings demanded to be translated into quilts. There were those I felt were so essential in our lamentations that I just had to re-create them before we left.

The next morning after our mourning rehearsal we went to Ruth's. The first thing that struck me was Mahlon's garden. There was something different about it. For a while I couldn't put my finger on it until Orpah pointed out that her daddy had gone back to having living things in his garden. And there I could see rose bushes among the gnomes. Some of the mini flags were still there, planted on the grass, but most were now decorating the bushes. The Bush gnome stood on its pedestal. But this time it held neither gun nor flag.

Orpah went to her mother-in-law room while I knocked at the living room door. I knew that her Marilyn Monroes missed her. That was how she usually put it, rather than the other way round. I worried a lot about those Marilyn Monroes. I dreaded her taking them with us on the road.

Ruth sat at her station cutting some glittering fabric. Not with the scissors, but with the rotary cutter I gave her as a present months before. She tried to hide it under the fabric when she saw it was me, but it was too late.

"It does a nice job, doesn't it," I said.

"You shacking with Orpah full time now and you ain't even ashamed of it," she said. "You living in sin and the Bible don't like it no ways. Mr. Quigley too."

"Orpah has all her stuff here, Ruth," I said, hoping it would be some comfort. "She only goes to the RV to visit. We're on to big things with Orpah. We're going to conquer the world."

"That's what you think, mister," she said. "Mr. Quigley won't let you mess our girl's life no ways."

"I haven't seen Mahlon for a while," I said. "How is he? And Obed? Actually I've come to find out about Obed. Do you know how I can get in touch with him?"

"She's gonna be sorry, you know? Orpah is gonna be very sorry. She ain't like Obed. Obed has turned out so good. He's now a man of God."

Obed a man of God?

Ruth gushes on about her Obed: he came here with Beth Eddy the other day. Beth Eddy was a nice girl and no one could hold it against her that she was Caucasian. In any event she was going to lighten her long-awaited grandchildren. But that was not the most important thing. The most important thing was that Obed was going to Bible School to be a pastor. He was going to take over Brother Michael's church. It was high time the church was in the hands of a son of Kilvert, a son who had not been soiled by adultery, a son who would respect the culture of his people and would not dismiss the heritage they held dear as false and meaningless.

"So the hoofing he used to do as a kid has paid off," I said laughing. I couldn't quite believe what I was hearing.

"It ain't no laughing matter 'cause if you laugh you laughing at God."

That, of course, stopped my foolish chuckles immediately. I don't want to laugh at God.

Obed's conversion did not end there. In August he went gleaning with a Bible study group to which he and Beth Eddy belonged. They joined the Appalachia Harvest gleaning group for a successful harvest of corn. They handpicked thousands of ears of sweet corn that were left on the field after harvest and would have otherwise gone to waste. The corn was then transported to local food pantries, including the Kilvert Community Center, for distribution to the poor and for community dinners. Late in August they gleaned tomatoes which the group processed into pasta sauce and salsa, also for distribution to food pantries. When he came here with Beth Eddy they brought some of the sauce and salsa with them.

To prove her point Ruth stood up and waddled to the kitchen. She brought back a bottle of pasta sauce which she said I could take to my sinful RV and taste what the hand of the Lord had brought. I was just happy to hear that my favorite scoundrel had changed so much. But how come I didn't know anything about it?

"What about his casino? What about the Shawnee claim? Has he given up on his casino?" I asked.

"What part of he's-a-man-of-God don't you understand?"

"Do you have his number, Ruth?" I asked.

"What you want it for? So that you can take him away from the Lord?"

I told her about the Katrina concert. She became very agitated. Not about the concert. About Hurricane Katrina.

"We are Americans," she said. "How can this happen to us?"

It was because of homosexuals, she declared. Pat Robertson said as much. According to this ayatollah—the same one who issued a fatwa for the death of the Venezuelan—the country had brought the catastrophe upon itself by being tolerant of homosexuals and lesbians to the extent that in some states they can even marry, which was against all the laws of nature and of God.

On returning to the RV I found Orpah lying naked on the Irish Wheel. We spent all our lives in the RV naked even when we had no intention of doing any naughty things. When I told her about Obed's conversion she was not surprised at all. Obviously she knew all about it. She even knew that he had been in Kilvert with Beth Eddy. They came to the Center to see us, but we were not

there. Nor was our RV. It was the day Orpah drove in our un-
wieldy vehicle to a parlor on Stimson Avenue to tattoo the tears on
our cheeks.

"You knew and you didn't tell me?"

"It's all crazy stuff, baby, and it got nothing to do with us."

I didn't go to the Katrina concert. But I was told that Orpah was
a resounding success. I cursed that concert. Not for the assistance it
gave the victims of Katrina. Not for her success. But for the fact
that after the bluegrass people dropped her at Ruth's, she did not
come to the RV that night. She did not come the following day either. On the third day I braved Ruth and went looking for her. I
could hear the sitar. No, not the deadly one that left me confused
and horny. Not the one we played at Niall Quigley's grave either.
But some fast-paced and dancey bluegrass number.

I knocked softly but she could not hear me. I banged at the door
and it flung open.

"What's up with you?" she asked. She seemed quite irritated.

"The question is, what's up with *you*?"

"I won't go with you no more," she said. "I don't wanna be no
mourner. Not when Daddy and me are talking again. I can't leave
my daddy. He needs me for the memories."

🐚

My eyes are searching for a monk in a brown robe. A wannabe
saint with a hanging belly. But I can't see the sciolist in the milling
crowds. Perhaps this year he does not think the parade is worth his
while. I would not be here either if Orpah had not insisted we attend the Halloween block party, as she calls it, before crossing the
Ohio River.

"I think we have seen enough," I say, as I follow her pushing her
way through a bunch of Christian fundamentalists in civvies who
are trying very hard to disrupt the very pagan circus of which they

have become part, their leader hollering the Lord's name above the din. "We have a long way to go."

"Come on, baby," she says. "Still early. You don't have to worry about driving anyways."

I want to go to the bathroom very badly. Orpah stops to talk to two women—one a fat witch in black and the other an overgrown fairy in pink and white. They went to the same high school at Amesville, she tells me. They giggle about our tattooed tears, which they think are part of the occasion. They ask me how I like Kilvert and what I think of the block party. Small talk is what makes the world go round. But for now I can't contribute my share to either its rotation or revolution. I excuse myself and walk into a nearby restaurant to use the men's room. It is filthy with feces and puddles of piss on the floor. I am not surprised. I have gotten used to dirty toilets in the fast food restaurants of this city. Of the state even. It is not just the result of the crowds. On a normal day I have been greeted by the filthiest of toilets ever at McDonalds, Burger King and even at the original Wendy's in Columbus.

When I return to the sidewalk Orpah and the women are no longer there. I wait a bit hoping she will show up, but have to move when the area is overrun by the Christian zealots. They are proclaiming The Word and condemning everyone present to the eternal fires of hell. The ghosts and the nurses and the bleeding souls with broken limbs ignore The Word and go about their business of strolling, gamboling or prancing up and down.

"Hey, homey, I thought you was in Virginia by now." The voice of Obed comes from a tall Darth Vader made of glowing orange plastic. He is with another action figure—a fluorescent yellow Young Anakin who asks me in the voice of Beth Eddy what I did with Orpah. I am happy to hear these familiar voices.

"According to Ruth's wishes you should be thumping the Bible with those people," I say to Darth Vader, pointing at the zealots.

"Those folks are loonies, my man," says Darth Vader.

I tell them I was beginning to panic because Orpah got lost in the crowd.

"Uh-ah! You don't think she changed her mind again?" asks Darth Vader.

I hope not. When she changed her mind about going with me I was crushed. I was prepared to abandon the RV at the Center and hit the road on my own. After she told me she couldn't leave her daddy I didn't see her for days. I supposed that time she was doing the memories with him. And she was painting the pictures. She didn't bring them to me to translate into quilts or just to keep. I took it that our mourning relationship had come to a sad end. It was another loss in a life of losses.

"Somehow I don't think so," I tell Darth Vader. "I think she just got carried away meeting old friends. She's somewhere in the crowds."

Young Anakin says she hopes we find Orpah since this is her last opportunity to meet her.

"It can't be the last," I say. "Orpah is not leaving forever. She'll be back one day."

"Only she?" asks Young Anakin. "What about you? Surely you're not deserting us forever."

She has always been such a sweet person.

"I'll come back too," I tell her. "Kilvert was my home for one year. I'll come back to see Ruth. And of course her Mr. Quigley. And you, Beth. And my favorite scoundrel here. I am glad to see that today he has adopted a much safer identity than that of a ghost partial to girls' breasts."

She laughs. And then says that she is always grateful to the ghost of Nicodemus. And to the mediation that I suggested. Darth Vader says that he hopes the ghost of Nicodemus is resting in peace tonight.

"It was avenged," I say. "Why can't it sleep in peace like all decent ghosts that have been avenged?"

Darth Vader and Young Anakin walk me to the RV, which is

parked on the parking lot of a closed down supermarket on Stimson Avenue. I realize that I do not have the keys. They are with Orpah, wherever she is. Young Anakin says they will keep me company until Orpah arrives.

"If she'll arrive at all," says a skeptical Darth Vader.

"She will arrive," I say confidently. "But you don't have to keep me company out here. I insist you go your way. Go back to the parade of creatures and have a good time, kids. I'll be all right here."

They laugh at my characterization of their Halloween block party as a parade of creatures.

"I'll come check in the morning," Darth Vader offers. "If Orpah's gone back home I'll help you drive the darn thing back to Kilvert."

As they leave I call after Darth Vader: "Ruth tells me you've given up on your dream for a casino!"

"I don't need no casino," he calls back. "I've got Beth now. And I've got the church too."

My wait is only an hour, although it seems like half the night because of anxiety and the chill. Orpah arrives and says she was looking for me all over the place. We can't drive at this hour. I agree. We need some sleep. I take off my cape and top hat. We get under the Irish Wheel, fully clothed. She is a nun today. She is divine. And this makes her more appetizing. But I long ago learned the art of self-control and self-denial. No carnal pleasures tonight.

Her teardrops make her face look like that of a clown. I burst out laughing.

"What're you laughing at?" she asks.

"Your tears are beautiful," I say.

"Your tears are beautiful too," she says.

We cuddle into each other's arms and sleep. I pray that no one comes in the night and tows the RV away since I suspect it is illegally parked. My thoughts float back to Kilvert; to Ruth and Mahlon.

By the end of October Mahlon's garden of gnomes had become smaller. Half of it was taken by flowers. Mahlon was becoming a flower man again. He just woke up one day and decided to plant something Ruth called "live-forever." It would dry with the winter chill in a few weeks' time, but would come back to life in spring. It would repeat that cycle over and over again till, according to Ruth, the end of time.

I saw this garden when I went looking for Orpah after I had not seen her for days since the Katrina concert. And when I went again the next day to plead with her.

"She's come to her senses," said Ruth as she fussed over Mahlon's flowers.

Instead of talking about Orpah and what she meant exactly by her coming to her senses she was more excited about the flowers. They were daffodils, she said. Besides the bushes of roses. Her Mr. Quigley secretly planted the bulbs a month before, which was a wise time because daffodils liked to establish their roots before the ground froze. They needed the cold weather to form flower buds. I would see them in full bloom early in spring, perhaps in March, because as far as she knew I would still be here at that time since Orpah was not going anywhere.

"I want to hear that from her," I said to Ruth.

But she would not see me. I decided at that time that she was a lost cause. I would stop chasing after her, pack my things and leave Kilvert once and for all. I would leave her the RV because it was useless to me without her.

The next time I went to Ruth's the garden was still thriving, despite the drought that was devastating southeast Ohio. The summer had been dry and farmers were fearful that in winter their animals would have no feed. Some had started to use winter feed as early as August. The county was declared a disaster area by the U.S. Department of Agriculture, although the drought conditions were rather spotty. The bottom of the hills had some water while the hills were dry.

It did not seem like the drought was having any effect on Mahlon's garden. It was getting greener by the day. Ruth's garden of Swiss chard, parsley and cabbages was luxuriant too.

On the driveway Mahlon was feeding a cow with his hand. Orpah was holding a basin of cow feed. She was sobbing in convulsions. None of them paid any attention to me. I could see though that Mahlon was trying to comfort Orpah. I could hear something along the lines of "don't worry, little girl, everything will be all right." I decided not to stop.

There were changes at the porch as well. Ferns were hanging among the wind chimes. There was fuchsia hanging in a basket.

In the living room Ruth was at her workstation cutting some fabric with the rotary cutter. She did not try to hide it this time. Asian beetles were giving her a hard time though. It was the season once more. I remembered how I helped her stamp them out a year ago. Now they were getting into her coffee, and some had died in the mug while she was still enjoying her drink. Others were biting her arms since she was in a short-sleeved blouse. One was impertinent enough to fly into her cleavage, obviously attracted by warmth. She just froze there since she could not take it out in my presence.

She was all smiles, despite the pests. Her eyes were bloodshot.

"Something very bad has happened in my life," she said softly. "But I don't wanna talk about it. God says we forgive and forget. It's hard to forget though."

At this the smile disappeared and tears ran down her cheeks.

"What is it, Ruth? What happened?"

"I don't wanna talk about it," she said. And then forced a smile on her face again.

Instead she wanted to talk about her new fuchsia. Did I see it? It was going to bloom for the whole summer, she boasted. And did I see Mr. Quigley's cow? Wasn't it wonderful that Mr. Quigley was going back to keeping animals? The farmers on the hills were forced to sell some of their cattle cheaply because the pastures were parched. Mr. Quigley raised some money to buy himself a cow.

The farmer was kind enough to accept a deposit. Mr. Quigley would pay the balance later. And did I know where the money for the deposit came from? From Obed. Her own Obed who had become a man at last.

"I want you to get me a book on Bible quilts," she said. "I wanna learn me how to make them Bible quilts."

Orpah entered and sat on one of the car seats. She was sniffling.

Ruth explained that with Bible quilts you appliqué figures from Bible stories on the quilt. She had already cut some of these figures. She pointed at one which she referred to as Moses and showed me on a quilt where the Red Sea would run and where the Moses figure would see a burning bush. With a rotary cutter, she said, she could cut human figures that were as accurate as if they walked out of the Bible itself. I observed that it was wonderful that she had now learned that she could preserve the ongoing tradition while expressing her own ideas.

"Ruth, I have come to say goodbye," I said. "I am leaving tomorrow morning."

"How you gonna drive that ugly thing of yours?" she asked.

"I'm coming too," said Orpah, jumping up and charging to the workstation. "I'm leaving too, Ruth."

"No, you're not," I said firmly.

"Oh yeah, she must go," said Ruth. "She caused enough trouble already."

Orpah burst out bawling.

Between Orpah's snivels and Ruth's fulminations I learned that Ruth was on a mission to spring-clean and kill the Asian bugs when she came across Orpah's new drawings in her room. Old habits die hard. She regretted it after she had already ripped them in two. She had not seen Orpah's drawings for many months and would not have destroyed them if she'd thought about it first.

When Orpah found her precious work in pieces like that she ran out wailing as if someone was dead. At the clothesline she found one of the pre–Civil War quilts—yes, the one with the first Quigley's image, Lord have mercy on him—and she ripped it with her bare hands. The material had almost pulverized and was going to fall apart on its own in any case, Orpah cried in her defense.

Recounting these events brought more tears to both of them. I was caught in the middle of a storm. I embraced Ruth with my left arm and Orpah with my right. I let them cry as much as they wanted, holding them very close to me.

I could not leave the next day. Not when things were like this. Instead I went to the Center for a dose of sanity. I helped the women package food for distribution. The drought did not help the hunger situation in the Appalachians. Food pantries and soup kitchens were busier than usual. Some soup kitchens in the county were closing down because they could not raise enough donations for food. Yet despite the decrease in donations, lines were becoming longer at soup kitchens. Families in places like Chauncey were uncertain where the next meal would come from. It was the same in Kilvert. Children were suffering from poverty-induced obesity.

"You can't close your eyes when your neighbor is living in poverty," said Irene.

"It is the American way to help," said Barbara.

"It ain't just the drought," said another volunteer. "It's always like this. It's the story of our lives. We've been hungry for generations. From the time the mines closed."

In other ways the droughts had made things better. It left a lot of the crops unmarketable and therefore the gleaners got more than in previous years. They got enough tomatoes, for instance, to make enough bottles of the fire-roasted pasta sauce that the food pantry at the Center was able to give each family at least one bottle.

Orpah came to the RV two days later and said that she really wanted to go with me.

"Oh, no," I said. "I don't want to be let down again, Orpah. You use me like a tissue. When your tears are dry you will discard me like before."

She was not running away from anything this time, she said.

She had made peace with her mother and both her parents had come to terms with her leaving. Not that she needed their blessings. She was going to leave with me even if they objected. As it was they were giving their blessings reluctantly. But that did not matter to her, because she was her own person. This last one surprised me some because all this time I didn't know she saw herself as her own person.

The good news that had made Ruth happy was the discovery of Abednego's quilt—which, for those who knew the story, was really Nicodemus's sampler—used as batting in the quilt Orpah tore. A professor at Ohio University had evaluated it. He said if it was auctioned at Christie's or some such place it would fetch not less than $12,000. It might even fetch ten times more. It would take the family out of poverty. But Ruth was adamant that she would not sell it. When Obed heard of her stubbornness he said his mama got fulfillment from poverty. She got solace from the Bible, which promised the last would be first and the meek would inherit the earth. But to Ruth the fact that the quilt was made by the Abyssinian Queen—for if indeed it was Abednego's or Nicodemus's it must have been made by her—was more important than any money in the world.

I could not resist Orpah. She knew I would not say no forever.

A few days later we parked our RV on Ruth's driveway and Orpah packed her stuff in it. Thankfully she didn't bring any of the larger than life cut-outs. She said Marilyn Monroe was going to look after her room while she was gone.

Obed was here to wish us well too. Beth Eddy couldn't come because she was at work. Obed came in her car, which he also used to deliver pizza to earn his keep.

Ruth and Mahlon were sitting together on the swing and it was swaying gently.

"Don't worry too much for Orpah, Mama," said Obed, as Ruth sniffled. "She's gonna come back. Our people always come back. It's the pull of the ancestors."

Ruth said she knew that her daughter would come back even if she were to go as far as Africa. At least she took comfort in the fact that Obed would return to take over the church in Kilvert when he finished his Bible studies and was ordained. Obed said he already belonged to a church, but not the one in Kilvert. He and Beth Eddy had joined the Church of the Healing Path, which taught its members how to experience shamanistic journeys and how to access the circle of ancestors for personal healing.

"What mumbo-jumbo is this?" asked Ruth. "And you had to choose a time like this to tell me?"

"It ain't no mumbo-jumbo, Mama," said Obed. "It's serious stuff. We'll invite you to our church one day. Me and Beth. It's got plenty members. Very nice folks."

"I ain't going to no shaman church," said Ruth vehemently. "What'd Pat Robertson say?"

We didn't want any explosive situation so early in the morning to delay our departure. Orpah went to the swing and hugged both parents.

"I'll come back, Daddy," she said. "We gonna do them memories again."

"It don't matter, child," said Mahlon. "You take your time. Memories are always there. They don't go nowhere."

"We ain't no rootless people," said Ruth. "It matters to us where we are buried. You know where you gonna be buried? Our people know where they gonna be buried. Here in Kilvert."

"Barn owls driving spotted owls out of the forest," said Mahlon softly, in a rhythm that told me he was reciting words learned by heart, "stealing their homes and their tongues, reducing them to a deathly silence."

We all looked at him for some time, trying to understand what he was talking about. After a few beats we gave up and I reached for Ruth's hand and shook it while giving her a peck on the cheek. I also shook Mahlon's hand. After giving me a firm grip he held his hands up and looked at me sternly.

"Don't you hurt my baby now," he said. "These hands have killed hogs. They can kill you just the same."

I assured him he had nothing to worry about.

"What route are you gonna take?" asked Ruth.

"We gonna cross at Pomeroy, Ruth. Route 33. Then we gonna drive through West Virginia to Virginia."

"Oh, shoot!" said Ruth. "I thought you was gonna take Route 50. I've always wanted to take Route 50. You know at Mount Zion and the Armory in Athens? That used to be called 'The Cross-roads of America.' That's where Route 33 and Route 50 met. And Route 50 ran right up to Washington, D.C., in the east and to the end of America in the west. They don't call it that no more."

"Well, we ain't gonna take Route 50 no ways, Ruth," said Orpah.

"I was just saying," said a deflated Ruth.

We were walking down the steps to our RV when Ruth called us back. She went into the house. While we waited Obed told us that the Church of the Healing Path had opened his eyes to many things he did not see before. He had discovered animal and plant energies that were linked to lineages. And the services were so much fun. The people chanted and played drums and other percussive instruments.

Ruth came back with two canning jars and gave one each to Orpah and me. It was the sweetest coleslaw we would ever taste, she said. Autumn cabbage was very sweet and tender, much better than the stuff picked in the summer. She added grated carrots, also from her garden. When we ate that coleslaw we would remember her.

"Todoloo! It's time to get your picture took," she said.

Mahlon whipped out a disposable camera—obviously purchased for this occasion—from the pocket of his shirt, and clicked as Orpah and I posed with the coleslaw.

When we were walking away to the RV Obed tried to steal away to Beth Eddy's car.

"I ain't finished with you, mister," said Ruth.

He went back to his mama. There was more upbraiding to be

done. The three of them waved at us as we drove away. Mahlon was sporting his regular smile. Ruth's teeth were like blood from the red slate.

The swing swayed gently and Obed waited uneasily.

We had left early because we wanted to reach Virginia the same day. But when we got to Athens Orpah wanted to attend the Halloween parade.

"But that's only in the evening," I said. "And from what I saw last year there is nothing exciting about it. Just walking up and down the street."

"We'll get to Virginia, baby," she said. "We ain't in no hurry for nothing. We gotta lifetime of mourning."

"Let's go back to Kilvert then and leave tomorrow."

She was horrified at the suggestion.

"There's no going back," she said. "You dare not change your mind about leaving."

As if I would.

She assured me that she would be able to drive at night.

We killed time walking among the stalls at the farmer's market. When some of the stallholders saw Orpah they asked where Ruth was. They had not seen her peddling her quilts for quite some time. Was she well?

"Nothing wrong with her so far as I know," said Orpah.

We transformed Orpah into a nun at the Halloween costume store at the East State Street Mall. Later I got into my own professional mourning costume after we had found a spot to park our RV.

❧

We cross the Ohio River at Pomeroy. Exactly where Nicodemus and Abednego crossed, according to Orpah.

"Look down there," she says. "You can see them gliding on ice in the opposite direction."

I can only see the long barges laden with coal, sailing on the river so early in the morning. Orpah cannot contain her excitement. She almost hits a deer as soon as we cross the bridge. It is breeding season and the deer become blinded with lust. Although I am pretending to be calm I am excited too. I am looking forward to our search for mourning, and to the performances and exhibitions with which we'll dazzle the bereaved. I know already that skeptics will dismiss us as New Age hustlers. To the true believers, however, we are enlightenment personified.

Before I came to Kilvert I lived only in the past and in the future. I therefore found the present a very lonely place to be. A very boring place. Orpah is a kindred spirit in this respect. Hopefully together we'll discover how to live in the present. And we'll do so without the aid of the sciolist. We have left him and his rambling narratives in Athens.

The sciolist is in the God business. And like all Gods he lives his life vicariously through his creations. Like all Gods he demands love from his creations. That's why he creates them in the first place . . . so that they can shower him with love . . . so that they can worship him and praise him . . . so that they can bribe him with offerings. Creation is therefore a self-centered act.

I need my independence from him.